Praise for THE BURIED GIANT

"Powerful . . . vivid, tense, thoughtful and moving—and entirely worthy of Ishiguro's formidable oeuvre."

The Globe and Mail

"A deeply affecting portrait of marital love."   *The Guardian*

"A wondrous tale set in the sixth century . . . [that] transcends its genre to ask larger questions that deal with the frailty of human-kind, and the strength of emotional bonds that tie us."

National Post

"A literary tour de force so unassuming that you don't realize until the last page that you're reading a masterpiece." *USA Today*

"A profound meditation on trauma, memory and the collective lies nations and groups create to expiate their guilt. . . . Ishiguro steers the tone of *The Buried Giant* masterfully between the shock of the fantastical and the texture of the real."

The Boston Globe

"Extraordinarily atmospheric and compulsively readable. . . . A beautiful, heartbreaking book about the duty to remember and the urge to forget."   *The Observer*

"It's as emotionally ruinous an ending as any I've read in a very long time, and it made me circle back to the opening pages, to re-enter the strange mist of this sad and remarkable book." *Slate*

KAZUO ISHIGURO

THE BURIED GIANT

Vintage Canada

VINTAGE CANADA EDITION, 2016

Published in Canada by Vintage Canada, a division of Penguin Random House
Canada Limited, in 2016. Originally published in hardcover in Canada by Knopf
Canada, a division of Penguin Random House Canada Limited, in 2015, and
simultaneously in the United States by Alfred A. Knopf, a division of Penguin
Random House LLC; and in the United Kingdom by Faber & Faber Limited,
Bloomsbury House, London. Distributed in Canada by Penguin Random House
Canada Limited, Toronto.

Vintage Canada with colophon is a registered trademark.

www.penguinrandomhouse.ca

Library and Archives Canada Cataloguing in Publication

Ishiguro, Kazuo, 1954–, author
     The buried giant / Kazuo Ishiguro.

ISBN 978-0-345-80941-4
eBook ISBN 978-0-345-80942-1

     I. Title.

PR6059.S5B87 2016   823'.914   C2014-906368-7

Cover design by Alceu Chiesorin Nunes/Companhia das Letras
Cover illustration by Pedro de Kastro

Printed and bound in the United States of America

2 4 6 8 9 7 5 3 1

Penguin
Random
House

VINTAGE CANADA

DEBORAH ROGERS

1938–2014

PART I

Chapter One

You would have searched a long time for the sort of winding lane or tranquil meadow for which England later became celebrated. There were instead miles of desolate, uncultivated land; here and there rough-hewn paths over craggy hills or bleak moorland. Most of the roads left by the Romans would by then have become broken or overgrown, often fading into wilderness. Icy fogs hung over rivers and marshes, serving all too well the ogres that were then still native to this land. The people who lived nearby – one wonders what desperation led them to settle in such gloomy spots – might well have feared these creatures, whose panting breaths could be heard long before their deformed figures emerged from the mist. But such monsters were not cause for astonishment. People then would have regarded them as everyday hazards, and in those days there was so much else to worry about. How to get food out of the hard ground; how not to run out of firewood; how to stop the sickness that could kill a dozen pigs in a single day and produce green rashes on the cheeks of children.

In any case, ogres were not so bad provided one did not provoke them. One had to accept that every so often, perhaps following some obscure dispute in their ranks, a creature would come blundering into a village in a terrible rage, and despite shouts and brandishings of weapons, rampage about injuring anyone slow to move out of its path. Or that every so often, an ogre might carry off a child into the mist. The people of the day had to be philo-sophical about such outrages.

In one such area on the edge of a vast bog, in the shadow of some jagged hills, lived an elderly couple, Axl and Beatrice. Perhaps these were not their exact or full names, but for ease, this is how we will refer to them. I would say this couple lived an isolated life, but in those days few were 'isolated' in any sense we would understand. For warmth and protection, the villagers lived in shelters, many of them dug deep into the hillside, connecting one to the other by underground passages and covered corridors. Our elderly couple lived within one such sprawling warren – 'build-ing' would be too grand a word – with roughly sixty other vil-lagers. If you came out of their warren and walked for twenty minutes around the hill, you would have reached the next set-tlement, and to your eyes, this one would have seemed identical to the first. But to the inhabitants themselves, there would have been many distinguishing details of which they would have been proud or ashamed.

I have no wish to give the impression that this was all there was to the Britain of those days; that at a time when magnifi-cent civilisations flourished elsewhere in the world, we were here not much beyond the Iron Age. Had you been able to roam the countryside at will, you might well have discovered castles con-taining music, fine food, athletic excellence; or monasteries with inhabitants steeped in learning. But there is no getting around it. Even on a strong horse, in good weather, you could have ridden for days without spotting any castle or monastery looming out of the greenery. Mostly you would have found communities like the one I have just described, and unless you had with you gifts of food or clothing, or were ferociously armed, you would not have been sure of a welcome. I am sorry to paint such a picture of our country at that time, but there you are.

To return to Axl and Beatrice. As I said, this elderly couple lived on the outer fringes of the warren, where their shelter was less protected from the elements and hardly benefited from the fire in the Great Chamber where everyone congregated at night. Perhaps there had been a time when they had lived closer to the fire; a time when they had lived with their children. In fact, it was just such an idea that would drift into Axl's mind as he lay in his bed during the empty hours before dawn, his wife soundly asleep beside him, and then a sense of some unnamed loss would gnaw at his heart, preventing him from returning to sleep.

Perhaps that was why, on this particular morning, Axl had abandoned his bed altogether and slipped quietly outside to sit on the old warped bench beside the entrance to the warren in wait for the first signs of daylight. It was spring, but the air still felt bitter, even with Beatrice's cloak, which he had taken on his way out and wrapped around himself. Yet he had become so absorbed in his thoughts that by the time he realised how cold he was, the stars had all but gone, a glow was spreading on the horizon, and the first notes of birdsong were emerging from the dimness.

He rose slowly to his feet, regretting having stayed out so long. He was in good health, but it had taken a while to shake off his last fever and he did not wish it to return. Now he could feel the damp in his legs, but as he turned to go back inside, he was well satisfied: for he had this morning succeeded in remembering a number of things that had eluded him for some time. Moreover, he now sensed he was about to come to some momentous decision – one that had been put off far too long – and felt an excitement within him which he was eager to share with his wife.

Inside, the passageways of the warren were still in complete darkness, and he was obliged to feel his way the short distance back to the door of his chamber. Many of the 'doorways' within the warren were simple archways to mark the threshold to a chamber. The open nature of this arrangement would not have struck the villagers as compromising their privacy, but allowed rooms to benefit from any warmth coming down the corridors from the great fire or the smaller fires permitted within the warren. Axl and Beatrice's room, however, being too far from any fire had something we might recognise as an actual door; a large wooden frame criss-crossed with small branches, vines and thistles which someone going in and out would each time have to lift to one side, but which shut out the chilly draughts. Axl would happily have done without this door, but it had over time become an object of considerable pride to Beatrice. He had often returned to find his wife pulling off withered pieces from the construct and replacing them with fresh cuttings she had gathered during the day.

This morning, Axl moved the barrier just enough to let himself in, taking care to make as little noise as possible. Here, the early dawn light was leaking into the room through the small chinks of their outer wall. He could see his hand dimly before him, and on the turf bed, Beatrice's form still sound asleep under the thick blankets.

He was tempted to wake his wife. For a part of him felt sure that if, at this moment, she were awake and talking to him, whatever last barriers remained between him and his decision would finally crumble. But it was some time yet until the community roused itself and the day's work began, so he settled himself on the low stool in the corner of the chamber, his wife's cloak still tight around him.

He wondered how thick the mist would be that morning, and if, as the dark faded, he would see it had seeped through the cracks right into their chamber. But then his thoughts drifted away from such matters, back to what had been preoccupying him. Had they always lived like this, just the two of them, at the periphery of the community? Or had things once been quite different? Earlier, outside, some fragments of a remembrance had come back to him: a small moment when he was walking down the long central corridor of the warren, his arm around one of his own children, his gait a little crouched not on account of age as it might be now, but simply because he wished to avoid hitting his head on the beams in the murky light. Possibly the child had just been speaking to him, saying something amusing, and they were both of them laughing. But now, as earlier outside, nothing would quite settle in his mind, and the more he concentrated, the fainter the fragments seemed to grow. Perhaps these were just an elderly fool's imaginings. Perhaps it was that God had never given them children.

You may wonder why Axl did not turn to his fellow villagers for assistance in recalling the past, but this was not as easy as you might suppose. For in this community the past was rarely discussed. I do not mean that it was taboo. I mean that it had somehow faded into a mist as dense as that which hung over the marshes. It simply did not occur to these villagers to think about the past – even the recent one.

To take an instance, one that had bothered Axl for some time: He was sure that not so long ago, there had been in their midst a woman with long red hair – a woman regarded as crucial to their village. Whenever anyone injured themselves or fell sick, it had been this red-haired woman, so skilled at healing, who was immediately sent for. Yet now this same woman was no longer to be found anywhere, and no one seemed to wonder what had occurred, or even to express regret at her absence. When one morning Axl had mentioned the matter to three neighbours while working with them to break up the frosted field, their response told him that they genuinely had no idea what he was talking about. One of them had even paused in his work in an effort to remember, but had ended by shaking his head. 'Must have been a long time ago,' he had said.

'Neither have I any memory of such a woman,' Beatrice had said to him when he had brought up the matter with her one night. 'Perhaps you dreamt her up for your own needs, Axl, even though you've a wife here beside you and with a back straighter than yours.'

This had been some time the previous autumn, and they had been lying side by side on their bed in the pitch black, listening to the rain beating against their shelter.

'It's true you've hardly aged at all down the years, princess,' Axl had said. 'But the woman was no dream, and you'd remember her yourself if you spared a moment to think about it. There she was at our door only a month ago, a kindly soul asking if there was anything she might bring us. Surely you remember.'

'But why was she wishing to bring us anything at all? Was she a kin to us?'

'I don't believe she was, princess. She was just being kind. Surely you remember. She was often at the door asking if we weren't cold or hungry.'

'What I'm asking, Axl, is what business was it of hers to single us out for her kindness?'

'I wondered myself at the time, princess. I remember thinking here's a woman given to tending the sick, and yet here's the two of us both as healthy as any in the village. Is there perhaps talk of a plague on the way and she's here to look us over? But it turns out there's no plague and she's just being kind. Now we're talking about her there's even more comes back to me. She was standing there telling us not to mind the children calling us names. That was it. Then we never saw her again.'

'Not only is this red-haired woman a dream from your mind, Axl, she's a fool to be worrying herself about a few children and their games.'

'Just what I thought at the time, princess. What harm can children do us and they just passing the time of day when the weather's too dreary outside. I told her how we hadn't given it a second thought, but she meant kindly all the same. And then I remember her saying it was a pity we had to spend our nights without a candle.'

'If this creature pitied us our lack of a candle,' Beatrice had said, 'she had one thing right at least. It's an insult, forbidding us a candle through nights like these and our hands as steady as any of them. While there's others with candles in their chamber, sense-less each night from cider, or else with children running wild. Yet it's our candle they've taken, and now I can hardly see your outline, Axl, though you're right beside me.'

'There's no insult intended, princess. It's just the way things have always been done and that's all there is to it.'

'Well it's not just your dream woman thinks it strange we should have our candle taken from us. Yesterday or was it the day before, I was at the river and walking past the women and I'm sure I heard them saying, when they supposed I'd gone out of hearing, how it was a disgrace an upright couple like us having to sit in the dark each night. So your dream woman's not alone in thinking what she does.'

'She's no dream woman I keep telling you, princess. Everyone here knew her a month ago and had a good word for her. What can it be makes everyone, yourself included, forget she ever lived?'

Recalling the conversation now on this spring's morning, Axl felt almost ready to admit he had been mistaken about the red-haired woman. He was after all an ageing man and prone to occasional confusion. And yet, this instance of the red-haired woman had been merely one of a steady run of such puzzling episodes. Frustratingly, he could not at this moment think of so many examples, but they had been numerous, of that there was no doubt. There had been, for instance, the incident concerning Marta.

This was a little girl of nine or ten who had always had a reputation for fearlessness. All the hair-raising tales of what could happen to wandering children seemed not to dampen her sense of adventure. So the evening when, with less than an hour of daylight remaining, the mist coming in and the wolves audible on the hillside, the word went around that Marta was missing, everyone had stopped what they were doing in alarm. For the next little while, voices called her name all around the warren and footsteps rushed up and down its corridors as villagers searched every sleeping chamber, the storage burrows, the cavities beneath the rafters, any hiding place a child might go to amuse herself.

Then in the midst of this panic, two shepherds returning from their shift on the hills came into the Great Chamber and began warming themselves by the fire. As they did so, one of them announced how the day before they had watched a wren-eagle circle above their heads, once, twice, then a third time. There was no mistake, he said, it had been a wren-eagle. Word quickly went around the warren and soon a crowd had gathered around the fire to listen to the shepherds. Even Axl had hurried to join them, for the appearance of a wren-eagle in their country was news indeed. Among the many powers attributed to the wren-eagle was the ability to frighten away wolves, and elsewhere in the land, it was said, wolves had vanished altogether on account of these birds.

At first the shepherds were questioned eagerly and made to repeat their story over and over. Then steadily a scepticism began to spread among the listeners. There had been many similar claims, someone pointed out, and each time they had proved unfounded. Someone else stated that these same two shepherds had only the previous spring brought back an identical story, and yet no further sightings had followed. The shepherds angrily denied bringing any such previous report, and soon the crowd was dividing between those taking the shepherds' side and those claiming some memory of the alleged episode the previous year.

As the quarrel grew heated, Axl found coming over him that familiar nagging sense that something was not right, and removing himself from the shouting and jostling, went outside to stare at the darkening sky and the mist rolling over the ground. And after a while, fragments began to piece themselves together in his mind, of the missing Marta, of the danger, of how not long ago everyone had been searching for her. But already these recollections were growing confused, in much the way a dream does in the seconds after waking, and it was only with a supreme act of concentration that Axl held onto the thought of little Marta at all while voices behind him continued to argue about the wren-eagle. Then, as he was standing there like that, he heard the sound of a girl singing to herself and saw Marta emerge before him out of the mist.

'You're a strange one, child,' Axl said as she came skipping up to him. 'Aren't you afraid of the dark? Of the wolves or the ogres?'

'Oh, I'm afraid of them, sir,' she said with a smile. 'But I know how to hide from them. I hope my parents haven't been asking for me. I got such a hiding last week.'

'Asking for you? Of course they've been asking for you. Isn't the whole village searching for you? Listen to that uproar inside. That's all for you, child.'

Marta laughed and said: 'Oh stop it, sir! I know they've not missed me. And I can hear, that's not me they're shouting about.'

When she said this, it occurred to Axl that sure enough the girl was right: the voices inside were not arguing about her at all, but about some other matter altogether. He leaned towards the doorway to hear better, and as he caught the odd phrase amidst the raised voices, it began to come back to him, about the shepherds and the wren-eagle. He was wondering if he should explain something of this to Marta when she suddenly skipped past him and went inside.

He followed her in, anticipating the relief and joy her appearance would cause. And to be frank, it had occurred to him that by coming in with her, he would get a little of the credit for her safe return. But as they entered the Great Chamber the villagers were still so engrossed in their quarrel over the shepherds only a few of them even bothered to look their way. Marta's mother did come away from the crowd long enough to say to the child: 'So here you are! Don't you be wandering off that way! How often must I tell you?' before turning her attention back to the arguments raging around the fire. At this, Marta gave Axl a grin as though to say: 'See what I told you?' and vanished into the shadows in search of her companions.

The room had grown significantly lighter. Their chamber, being on the outer fringe, had a small window to the outside, though it was too high to gaze out of without standing on a stool. It was at this moment covered with a cloth, but now an early ray of sun was penetrating from one corner, casting a beam over where Beatrice was sleeping. Axl could see, caught in this ray, what looked like an insect hovering in the air just above his wife's head. He then realised it was a spider, suspended by its invisible vertical thread, and even as he watched, it started on its smooth descent. Rising noiselessly, Axl crossed the small room and swept his hand through the space above his sleeping wife, catching the spider within his palm. Then he stood there a moment looking down at her. There was a peacefulness on her sleeping face he rarely saw now when she was awake, and the sudden rush of happiness the sight brought him took him by surprise. He knew then he had made up his mind, and he wanted again to awaken her, just so he might break to her his news. But he saw the selfishness of such an action – and besides, how could he be so sure of her response? In the end he went back quietly to his stool, and as he seated himself again, remembered the spider and opened his hand gently.

When earlier he had been sitting on the bench outside waiting for the first light, he had tried to recall how he and Beatrice had first come to discuss the idea of their journey. He had thought then he had located a particular conversation they had had one night in this same chamber, but now, as he watched the spider run round the edge of his hand and onto the earthen floor, it struck him with certainty that the first mention of the subject had come that day the stranger in dark rags had passed through the village.

It had been a grey morning – was it as long ago now as last November? – and Axl had been striding beside the river along a footpath overhung with willows. He was hurrying back to the warren from the fields, perhaps to fetch a tool or receive new instructions from a foreman. In any case, he was stopped by a burst of raised voices from beyond the bushes to his right. His first thought was of ogres, and he searched quickly around for a rock or stick. Then he realised the voices – all of women – though angry and excited, lacked the panic that accompanied ogre attacks. He nevertheless pushed his way determinedly through a hedge of juniper shrubs and stumbled into a clearing, where he saw five women – not in their first youth, but still of child-bearing age – standing closely together. Their backs were turned to him and they went on shouting at something in the distance. He was almost up to them before one of the women noticed him with a start, but then the others turned and regarded him almost with insolence.

'Well, well,' said one. 'Perhaps it's chance or something more. But here's the husband and hopefully he'll drive sense into her.'

The woman who had seen him first said: 'We told your wife not to go but she wouldn't listen. She's insisting she'll take food to the stranger though she's most likely a demon or else some elf disguised.'

'Is my wife in danger? Ladies, please explain yourselves.'

'There's a strange woman been wandering around us all morning,' another said. 'Hair down her back and a cloak of black rags. She claimed to be a Saxon but she's not dressed like any Saxon we ever met. She tried to creep up behind us on the riverbank when we were attending to the laundry, but we saw her in good time and chased her away. But she kept returning, acting like she was heart-broken for something, other times asking us for food. We reckon she was all the while aiming her spell straight towards your wife, sir, for twice this morning already we had to hold Beatrice back by the arms, so intent was she on going to the demon. And now she's fought us all off and gone up to the old thorn where even now the demon's sitting waiting for her. We held her all we could, sir, but it must be the demon's powers already moving through her because her strength was unnatural for a woman so thin-boned and aged as your wife.'

'The old thorn . . .'

'She set off only a moment ago, sir. But that's a demon to be sure, and if you're off after her you'll watch you're not stumbling or cutting yourself on a poisoned thistle the way it will never heal.'

Axl did his best to hide his irritation with these women, saying politely: 'I'm grateful, ladies. I'll go and see what my wife is up to. Excuse me.'

To our villagers, 'the old thorn' denoted a local beauty spot as much as the actual hawthorn tree that grew seemingly right out of the rock at the edge of the promontory a short walk from the warren. On a sunny day, provided the wind was not strong, it was a pleasant place to pass the time. You had a good view of the land down to the water, of the river's curve and the marshes beyond. On Sundays children often played around the gnarled roots, sometimes daring to jump off the end of the promontory, which in fact had only a gentle drop that would cause a child no injury, but simply to roll like a barrel down the grassy slope. But on a morning like this one, when adults and children alike were busy with tasks, the spot would have been deserted, and Axl, coming through the mist up the incline, was not surprised to see the two women were alone, their figures almost silhouettes against the white sky. Sure enough, the stranger, seated with her back against the rock, was dressed curiously. From a distance, at least, her cloak appeared to be made of many separate pieces of cloth stitched together, and it was now flapping in the wind, giving its owner the appearance of a great bird about to take flight. Beside her, Beatrice – still on her feet, though with head lowered towards her companion – appeared slight and vulnerable. They were in earnest conversation, but spotting Axl's approach below, stopped and watched him. Then Beatrice came to the edge of the promontory and called down:

'Just stop there, husband, no further! I'll come to you. But don't climb up here and be disturbing this poor lady's peace now she's at last able to rest her feet and eat a little of yesterday's bread.'

Axl waited as instructed and before long saw his wife coming down the long field-path to where he was standing. She came right up to him, and concerned no doubt that the wind would carry their words up to the stranger, said in a low voice:

'Have those foolish women sent you after me, husband? When I was their age, I'm sure it was the old ones were full of fear and foolish beliefs, reckoning every stone cursed and each stray cat an evil spirit. But now I'm grown old myself, what do I find but it's the young are riddled with beliefs like they never heard the Lord's promise to walk beside us at all times. Look at that poor stranger, see her yourself, exhausted and solitary, and she's wandered the forest and fields for four days, village after village commanding her to travel on. And it's Christian country she's walked across, but taken for a demon or maybe a leper though her skin bears no mark of it. Now, husband, I hope you're not here to tell me I'm not to give this poor woman comfort and what sorry food I have with me.'

'I wouldn't tell you any such thing, princess, for I see for myself what you're saying is true. I was thinking before I even came here how it's a shameful thing we can't receive a stranger with kindness any more.'

'Then go on with your business, husband, for I'm sure they'll be complaining again how slow you are at your work, and before you know they'll have the children chanting at us again.'

'No one's ever said I'm slow in my work, princess. Where did you hear such a thing? I've never heard a word of such complaint and I'm able to take the same burden as any man twenty years younger.'

'I'm only teasing, husband. Right enough, there's no one complaining about your work.'

'If there's children calling us names, it's not to do with my work being fast or slow but parents too foolish or more likely drunk to teach them manners or respect.'

'Calm yourself, husband. I told you I was just teasing and I won't do so again. The stranger was telling me something that greatly interests me and may some time interest you too. But she needs to finish the telling of it, so let me ask you again to hurry on with whatever task you have to do and leave me to listen to her and give what comfort I can.'

'I'm sorry, princess, if I spoke harshly to you just then.'

But Beatrice had already turned and was climbing the path back to the thorn tree and the figure in the flapping cloak.

A little later, having completed his errand, Axl was returning to the fields, and at the risk of testing the patience of his colleagues, deviated from his route to go past the old thorn again. For the truth was that while he had fully shared his wife's scorn for the suspicious instincts of the women, he had not been able to free himself from the thought that the stranger did pose some sort of threat, and he had been uneasy since leaving Beatrice with her. He was relieved then to see his wife's figure, alone on the promontory in front of the rock, looking out at the sky. She seemed lost in thought, and failed to notice him until he called up to her. As he watched her descending the path, more slowly than before, it occurred to him not for the first time that there was something different lately in her gait. She was not limping exactly, but it was as though she were nursing some secret pain somewhere. When he asked her, as she approached, what had become of her odd companion, Beatrice said simply: 'She went on her way.'

'She would have been grateful for your kindness, princess. Did you speak long with her?'

'I did and she had a deal to say.'

'I can see she said something to trouble you, princess. Perhaps those women were right and she was one best avoided.'

'She's not upset me, Axl. She has me thinking though.'

'You're in a strange mood. Are you sure she hasn't put some spell on you before vanishing into the air?'

'Walk up there to the thorn, husband, and you'll see her on the path and only recently departed. She's hoping for better charity from those around the hill.'

'Well then I'll leave you, princess, since I see you've come to no harm. God will be pleased for the kindness you've shown as is always your way.'

But this time his wife seemed reluctant to let him go. She grasped his arm, as though momentarily to steady herself, then let her head rest on his chest. As though by its own instinct, his hand rose to caress her hair, grown tangled in the wind, and when he glanced down at her he was surprised to see her eyes still wide open.

'You're in a strange mood, right enough,' he said. 'What did that stranger say to you?'

She kept her head on his chest for a moment longer. Then she straightened and let go of him. 'Now I think of it, Axl, there may be something in what you're always saying. It's queer the way the world's forgetting people and things from only yesterday and the day before that. Like a sickness come over us all.'

'Just what I was saying, princess. Take that red-haired woman . . .'

'Never mind the red-haired woman, Axl. It's what else we're not remembering.' She had said this while looking away into the mist-layered distance, but now she looked straight at him and he could see her eyes were filled with sadness and yearning. And it was then – he was sure – that she said to him: 'You've long set your heart against it, Axl, I know. But it's time now to think on it anew. There's a journey we must go on, and no more delay.'

'A journey, princess? What sort of journey?'

'A journey to our son's village. It's not far, husband, we know that. Even with our slow steps, it's a few days' walk at most, a little way east beyond the Great Plain. And the spring will soon be upon us.'

'We might go on such a trip, certainly, princess. Was there something that stranger said just now got you thinking of it?'

'It's been a thing in my thoughts a long time, Axl, though it's what that poor woman said just now makes me wish to delay no further. Our son awaits us in his village. How much longer must we keep him waiting?'

'When the spring's here, princess, we'll certainly think about just such a journey. But why do you say it's my wishes always stood in the way of it?'

'I don't remember now all that's passed between us on it, Axl. Only that you always set your heart against it, even as I longed for it.'

'Well, princess, let's talk about it more when there's no work waiting and neighbours ready to call us slow. Let me go on my way just now. We'll talk more on it soon.'

But in the days that followed, even if they alluded to the idea of this journey, they never talked properly about it. For they found they became oddly uncomfortable whenever the topic was broached, and before long an understanding had grown between them, in the silent way understandings do between a husband and wife of many years, to avoid the subject as much as possible. I say 'as much as possible', for there appeared at times to be a need – a compulsion, you might say – to which one or the other would have to yield. But whatever discussions they had in such circumstances inevitably ended quickly in evasiveness or bad temper. And on the one occasion Axl had asked his wife straight out what the strange woman had said to her that day up at the old thorn, Beatrice's expression had clouded, and she had seemed for a moment on the verge of tears. After this, Axl had taken care to avoid any reference to the stranger.

After a while Axl could no longer remember how talk of this journey had started, or what it had ever meant to them. But then this morning, sitting outside in the cold hour before dawn, his memory seemed partially at least to clear, and many things had come back to him: the red-haired woman; Marta; the stranger in dark rags; other memories with which we need not concern ourselves here. And he had remembered, quite vividly, what had happened only a few Sundays ago, when they had taken Beatrice's candle from her.

Sundays were a day of rest for these villagers, at least to the extent that they did not work in the fields. But the livestock had still to be cared for, and with so many other tasks waiting to be done, the pastor had accepted the impracticality of forbidding everything that might be construed as labour. So it was that when Axl emerged into the spring sunshine that particular Sunday after a morning of mending boots, the sight that greeted him was of his neighbours spread all around the terrain in front of the warren, some sitting in the patchy grass, others on small stools or logs, talking, laughing and working. Children were playing everywhere, and one group had gathered around two men constructing on the grass the wheel for a wagon. It was the first Sunday of the year the weather had permitted such outdoor activity, and there was an almost festive atmosphere. Nevertheless, as he stood there at the warren entrance and gazed beyond the villagers to where the land sloped down towards the marshes, Axl could see the mist rising again, and supposed that by the afternoon they would be submerged once more in grey drizzle.

He had been standing there a while when he became aware of a commotion going on over down by the fencing to the grazing fields. It did not greatly interest him at first, but then something in the breeze caught his ear and made him straighten. For though his eyesight had grown annoyingly blurred with the years, Axl's hearing had remained reliable, and he had discerned, in the muddle of shouting emerging from the crowd by the fence, Beatrice's voice raised in distress.

Others too were stopping what they were doing to turn and stare. But now Axl hurried through their midst, narrowly avoiding wandering children and objects left on the grass. Before he could reach the small jostling knot of people, however, it suddenly dispersed, and Beatrice emerged from its centre, clutching something with both hands to her breast. The faces around her mostly showed amusement, but the woman who quickly appeared at his wife's shoulder – the widow of a blacksmith who had died of fever the previous year – had features twisted with fury. Beatrice shook off her tormentor, her own face all the time a stern, near-blank mask, but when she saw Axl coming towards her, it broke into emotion.

Thinking about this now, it seemed to Axl the look on his wife's face then had been, more than anything else, one of overwhelming relief. It was not that Beatrice had believed all would be well once he had arrived; but his presence had made all the difference to her. She had gazed at him not just with relief, but also something like pleading, and held out to him the object she had been jealously guarding.

'This is ours, Axl! We'll not sit in darkness any longer. Take it quickly, husband, it's ours!'

She was holding towards him a squat, somewhat misshapen candle. The blacksmith's widow tried again to snatch it from her, but Beatrice struck away the invading hand.

'Take it, husband! That child there, little Nora, she brought it to me this morning after making it with her own hands, thinking we'd grown tired of spending our nights as we do.'

This set off another round of shouting and also some laughter. But Beatrice went on gazing at Axl, her expression full of trust and entreaty, and it was a picture of her face at that moment which had first come back to him this morning on the bench outside the warren as he had sat waiting for the dawn to break. How was it he had forgotten this episode when it could have occurred no more than three weeks ago? How could it be he had not thought about it again until today?

Although he had stretched out his arm, he had not been able

to take the candle – the crowd had kept him just out of reach – and he had said, loudly and with some conviction: 'Don't worry, princess. Don't you worry.' He was conscious of the emptiness of what he was saying even as he spoke, so he was surprised when the crowd quietened, and even the blacksmith's widow took a step back. Only then did he realise the reaction had not been to his words, but to the approach behind him of the pastor.

'What manners are these for the Lord's day?' The pastor strode past Axl and glared at the now silent gathering. 'Well?'

'It's Mistress Beatrice, sir,' the blacksmith's widow said. 'She's got herself a candle.'

Beatrice's face was a tight mask again, but she did not avoid the pastor's gaze when it settled on her.

'I can see for myself it's true, Mistress Beatrice,' the pastor said. 'Now you'll not have forgotten the council's edict that you and your husband will not be permitted candles in your chamber.'

'We've neither of us ever tumbled a candle in our lives, sir. We will not sit night after night in darkness.'

'The decision has been made and you're to abide by it until the council decides otherwise.'

Axl saw the anger blaze in her eyes. 'It's nothing but unkindness. That's all it is.' She said this quietly, almost under her breath, but looking straight at the pastor.

'Remove the candle from her,' the pastor said. 'Do as I say. Take it from her.'

As several hands reached towards her, it seemed to Axl she had not fully understood what the pastor had said. For she stood in the middle of the jostling with a puzzled look, continuing to grip the candle as if only by some forgotten instinct. Then panic seemed to seize her and she held the candle out towards Axl again, even as she was knocked off balance. She did not fall on account of those pressing in on her, and recovering, held out the candle for him yet again. He tried to take it, but another hand snatched it away, and then the pastor's voice boomed out:

'Enough! Leave Mistress Beatrice in peace and none of you speak unkindly to her. She's an old woman who doesn't understand all she does. Enough I say! This is no fit behaviour for the Lord's day.'

Axl, finally reaching her, took her in his arms, and the crowd melted away. When he recalled this moment, it seemed to him they stayed like that for a long time, standing close together, she with her head resting on his chest, just the way she had done the day of the strange woman's visit, as though she were merely weary and wishing to catch her breath. He continued to hold her as the pastor called again for the people to disperse. When finally they separated and looked around themselves, they found they were alone beside the cow field and its barred wooden gate.

'What does it matter, princess?' he said. 'What do we need with a candle? We're well used to moving around our room without one. And don't we keep ourselves entertained well enough with our talk, candle or no candle?'

He observed her carefully. She appeared dreamy, and not particularly upset.

'I'm sorry, Axl,' she said. 'The candle's gone. I should have kept it a secret for the two of us. But I was overjoyed when the young girl brought it to me and she'd crafted it herself just for us. Now it's gone. No matter.'

'No matter at all, princess.'

'They think us a foolish pair, Axl.'

She took a step forward and placed her head on his chest again.

And it was then that she said, her voice muffled so he at first thought he had misheard:

'Our son, Axl. Do you remember our son? When they were pushing me just now, it was our son I remembered. A fine, strong, upright man. Why must we stay in this place? Let's go to our son's village. He'll protect us and see no one treats us ill. Will your heart not change on it, Axl, and all these years now passed? Do you still say we can't go to him?'

As she said this, softly into his chest, many fragments of memory tugged at Axl's mind, so much so that he felt almost faint. He loosened his hold on her and stepped back, fearing he might sway and cause her to lose her own balance.

'What's this you're saying, princess? Was I ever the one to stop us journeying to our son's village?'

'But surely you were, Axl. Surely you were.'

'When did I speak against such a journey, princess?'

'I always thought you did, husband. But oh, Axl, I don't remember clearly now you question it. And why do we stand out here, fine day though it is?'

Beatrice appeared confused again. She looked into his face, then all around her, at the pleasant sunshine, their neighbours once more giving attention to their activities.

'Let's go and sit in our chamber,' she said after a while. 'Let it be just the two of us for a while. A fine day, right enough, but I'm all tired out. Let's go inside.'

'That's right, princess. Sit down and rest a while, out of this sun. You'll soon feel better.'

There were others awake now all around the warren. The shepherds must have gone out some time ago though he had been so lost in thought he had not even heard them. At the other end of the room Beatrice made a murmuring sound, as though she were preparing to sing, then turned over under the blankets. Recognising these signals, Axl made his way across to the bed in silence, sat carefully on its edge and waited.

Beatrice shifted onto her back, opened her eyes partially and gazed at Axl.

'Good morning, husband,' she said eventually. 'I'm glad to see the spirits chose not to take you away as I slept.'

'Princess, there's something I want to talk about.'

Beatrice went on gazing up at him, her eyes still only half open. Then she brought herself up to a sitting posture, her face crossing the beam of light that earlier had illuminated the spider. Her grey mane, untied and matted, hung stiffly down past her shoulders, but Axl still felt happiness stir within him at this sight of her in the morning light.

'What is it you have to say, Axl, and before I've had time to rub the sleep from my eyes?'

'We talked before, princess, about a journey we might make. Well, here's the spring upon us, and perhaps it's time we set off.'

'Set off, Axl? Set off when?'

'As soon as we're able. We need only be gone a few days. The village can spare us. We'll talk to the pastor.'

'And will we go to see our son, Axl?'

'That's where we'll go. To see our son.'

Outside the birds were now in chorus. Beatrice turned her gaze towards the window and the sun leaking past the cloth hung over it.

'Some days I remember him clear enough,' she said. 'Then the next day it's as if a veil's fallen over his memory. But our son's a fine and good man, I know that for sure.'

'Why is he not with us here now, princess?'

'I don't know, Axl. It could be he quarrelled with the elders and had to leave. I've asked around and there's no one here remembers him. But he wouldn't have done anything to bring shame on himself, I know for sure. Can you remember nothing of it yourself, Axl?'

'When I was outside just now, doing my best to remember all I could in the stillness, many things came back to me. But I can't remember our son, neither his face nor his voice, though sometimes I think I can see him when he was a small boy, and I'm leading him by the hand beside the riverbank, or when he was weeping one time and I was reaching out to comfort him. But what he looks like today, where he's living, if he has a son of his own, I don't remember at all. I was hoping you'd remember more, princess.'

'He's our son,' Beatrice said. 'So I can feel things about him, even if I don't remember clearly. And I know he longs for us to leave this place and be living with him under his protection.'

'He's our flesh and blood, so why would he not want us to join him?'

'Even so, I'll miss this place, Axl. This small chamber of ours and this village. No light thing to leave a place you've known all your life.'

'No one's asking us to do it without thought, princess. While I was waiting for the sun to rise just now, I was thinking we'll need to make this journey to our son's village and talk with him. For even if we're his mother and father, it's not for us to arrive one fine day and demand to live as part of his village.'

'You're right, husband.'

'There's another thing troubles me, princess. This village may only be a few days away as you say. But how will we know where to find it?'

Beatrice fell silent, gazing into the space before her, her shoulders swaying gently with her breathing. 'I believe we'll know our way well enough, Axl,' she said eventually. 'Even if we don't yet know his exact village, I'll have travelled to ones nearby often enough with the other women when trading our honey and tin. I'll know my way blindfolded to the Great Plain, and the Saxon village beyond where we've often rested. Our son's village can only be a little way further, so we'll find it with little trouble. Axl, are we really to go soon?'

'Yes, princess. We'll start preparing today.'

Chapter Two

There were, however, plenty of things to attend to before they could set off. In a village like this, many items necessary for their journey – blankets, water flasks, tinder – were communally owned and securing their use required much bargaining with neighbours. Moreover, Axl and Beatrice, advanced though they were in years, had their burden of daily duties and could not simply go away without the consent of the community. And even when they were finally ready to leave, a turn in the weather delayed them further. For what was the point of risking the hazards of fog, rain and cold when sunshine was surely just around the corner?

But they did eventually set off, with walking sticks and bundles on their backs, on a bright morning of wispy white clouds and a strong breeze. Axl had wished to start at first light – it was clear to him the day would be fine – but Beatrice had insisted on waiting till the sun was higher. The Saxon village where they would shelter the first night, she argued, was easily within a day's walk, and surely their priority was to cross the corner of the Great Plain as close to noon as possible, when the dark forces of that place were most likely to be dormant.

It had been a while since they had walked any distance together, and Axl had been anxious about his wife's stamina. But after an hour he found himself reassured: though her pace was slow – he noticed again something lop-sided about her gait, as if she were cushioning some pain – Beatrice kept moving on steadily, head down into the wind in open land, undaunted when confronted by thistles and undergrowth. On uphills, or ground so muddy it was an effort to pull one foot out after the other, she would slow right down, but keep pushing on.

In the days before their journey's start, Beatrice had grown increasingly confident of remembering their route, at least as far as the Saxon village which she had regularly visited with the other women over the years. But once they lost sight of the craggy hills above their settlement, and had crossed the valley beyond the marshland, she became less certain. At a fork in a path, or facing a windswept field, she would pause and stand for a long time, panic creeping into her gaze as she surveyed the land.

'Don't worry, princess,' Axl would say on such occasions. 'Don't worry and take all the time you need.'

'But Axl,' she would say, turning to him, 'we don't have time. We must cross the Great Plain at noon if we're to do so in safety.'

'We'll be there in good time, princess. You take all the time you need.'

I might point out here that navigation in open country was something much more difficult in those days, and not just because of the lack of reliable compasses and maps. We did not yet have the hedgerows that so pleasantly divide the countryside today into field, lane and meadow. A traveller of that time would, often as not, find himself in featureless landscape, the view almost identical whichever way he turned. A row of standing stones on the far horizon, a turn of a stream, the particular rise and fall of a valley: such clues were the only means of charting a course. And the consequences of a wrong turn could often prove fatal. Never mind the possibilities of perishing in bad weather: straying off course meant exposing oneself more than ever to the risk of assailants – human, animal or supernatural – lurking away from the established roads.

You might have been surprised by how little they conversed as they walked, this couple usually so full of things to tell each other. But at a time when a broken ankle or an infected graze could be life-threatening, there was a recognition that concentration was desirable at each and every step. You might also have noted that whenever the path grew too narrow to walk side by side, it was always Beatrice, not Axl, who went in front. This too might surprise you, it seeming more natural for the man to go first into potentially hazardous terrain, and sure enough, in woodland or where there was the possibility of wolves or bears, they would switch positions without discussion. But for the most part, Axl would make sure his wife went first, for the reason that practically every fiend or evil spirit they were likely to encounter was known to target its prey at the rear of a party – in much the way, I suppose, a big cat will stalk an antelope at the back of the herd. There were numerous instances of a traveller glancing back to the companion walking behind, only to find the latter vanished without trace. It was the fear of such an occurrence that compelled Beatrice intermittently to ask as they walked: 'Are you still there, Axl?' To which he would answer routinely: 'Still here, princess.'

They reached the edge of the Great Plain by late morning. Axl suggested they push on and put the hazard behind them, but Beatrice was adamant they should wait till noon. They sat down on a rock at the top of the hillslope leading down to the plain, and watched carefully the shortening shadows of their sticks, held upright before them in the earth.

'It may be a good sky, Axl,' she said. 'And I've not heard of any wickedness befalling a person in this corner of the plain. All the same, better wait for noon, when surely no demon will care even to peek out to see us pass.'

'We'll wait, just as you say, princess. And you're right, this is the Great Plain after all, even if it's a benevolent corner of it.'

They sat there like that for a little while, looking down at the land before them, hardly speaking. At one point Beatrice said:

'When we see our son, Axl, he's sure to insist we live at his village. Won't it be strange to leave our neighbours after these years, even if they're sometimes teasing our grey hairs?'

'Nothing's decided yet, princess. We'll talk everything over with our son when we see him.' Axl went on gazing out at the Great Plain. Then he shook his head and said quietly: 'It's odd, the way I can't recall him at all just now.'

'I thought I dreamt about him last night,' Beatrice said. 'Standing by a well, and turning, just a little to one side, and calling to someone. What came before or after's gone now.'

'At least you saw him, princess, even if in a dream. What did he look like?'

'A strong, handsome face, that much I remember. But the colour of his eyes, the turn of his cheek, I've no memory of them.'

'I don't recall his face now at all,' Axl said. 'It must all be the work of this mist. Many things I'll happily let go to it, but it's cruel when we can't remember a precious thing like that.'

She moved closer to him, letting her head fall on his shoulder. The wind was now beating hard at them and part of her cloak had come loose. Putting an arm around her, Axl trapped the cloak and held it tightly to her.

'Well, I dare say one or the other of us will remember soon enough,' he said.

'Let's try, Axl. Let's both of us try. It's as if we've mislaid a precious stone. But surely we'll find it again if we both try.'

'Surely we will, princess. But look, the shadows are almost gone. It's time for us to go down.'

Beatrice straightened and began rummaging in her bundle. 'Here, we'll carry these.'

She handed to him what looked like two smooth pebbles, but when he studied them he saw complex patterns cut into the face of each one.

'Put them in your belt, Axl, and take care to keep the markings facing out. It will help the Lord Christ keep us safe. I'll carry these others.'

'One will be enough for me, princess.'

'No, Axl, we'll share them equally. Now what I remember is there's a path to follow down there and unless rain's washed it away the walking will be easier than most of what we've had. But there's one place we need to be cautious. Axl, are you listening to me? It's when the path goes over where the giant is buried. To one who doesn't know it, it's an ordinary hill, but I'll signal to you and when you see me you're to follow off the path and round the edge of the hill till we meet the same path on its way down. It'll do us no good treading over such a grave, high noon or not. Are you fully understanding me, Axl?'

'Don't worry, princess, I understand you very well.'

'And I don't need to remind you. If we see a stranger on our path, or calling us from nearby, or any poor animal caught in a trap or injured in a ditch, or any such thing might catch your attention, you don't speak a word or slow your step for it.'

'I'm no fool, princess.'

'Well, then, Axl, it's time we went.'

As Beatrice had promised, they were required to walk on the Great Plain for only a short distance. Their path, though muddy at times, remained defined and never took them out of sunlight. After an initial descent it climbed steadily, till they found themselves walking along a high ridge, moorland on either side of them. The wind was fierce, but if anything a welcome antidote to the noon sun. The ground everywhere was covered in heather and gorse, never more than knee high, and only occasionally did a tree come into view – some solitary, crone-like specimen, bowed by endless gales. Then a valley appeared to their right, reminding them of the power and mystery of the Great Plain, and that they were now trespassing on but a small corner of it.

They walked close together, Axl almost at his wife's heels. Even so, throughout the crossing, Beatrice continued every five or six steps to chant, in the manner of a litany, the question: 'Are you still there, Axl?' to which he would respond: 'Still here, princess.' Aside from this ritualistic exchange, they said nothing. Even when they reached the giant's burial mound, and Beatrice made urgent signs for them to move from the path into the heather, they kept up this call and response in level tones, as though wishing to deceive any listening demons about their intentions. All the while Axl watched for fast-moving mist or sudden darkenings in the sky, but there came no hint of either, and then they had put the Great Plain behind them. As they climbed through a small wood full of songbirds, Beatrice made no comment, but he could see her whole posture relax, and her refrain came to an end.

They rested beside a brook, where they bathed their feet, ate bread and refilled their flasks. From this point their route followed a long sunken lane from Roman days, lined by oaks and elms, which was much easier walking, but required vigilance on account of the other wayfarers they were bound to meet. And sure enough, during the first hour, they encountered coming the other way a woman with her two children, a boy driving donkeys, and a pair of travelling players hurrying to rejoin their troupe. On each occasion they stopped to exchange pleasantries, but another time, hearing the clatter of approaching wheels and hooves, they hid themselves in the ditch. This too proved harmless – a Saxon farmer with a horse and cart piled high with firewood.

Toward mid-afternoon the sky began to cloud as though for a storm. They had been resting beneath a large oak, their backs to the road and hidden from the passing traffic. A clean sweep of land lay visible before them, so they had noticed immediately the coming change.

'Don't worry, princess,' Axl said. 'We'll stay dry beneath this tree until the sun returns.'

But Beatrice was on her feet, leaning forward, a hand raised to shield her eyes. 'I can see the road ahead curving into the distance, Axl. And I see it's not far to the old villa. I took shelter there once before when I came with the women. A ruin, but the roof was still good then.'

'Can we reach it before the storm breaks, princess?'

'We'll reach it if we go now.'

'Then let's hurry. There's no reason to catch our deaths from a drenching. And this tree, now I'm looking at it, is full of holes the way I can see most of the sky above me.'

* * *

The ruined villa was further from the road than Beatrice remembered. With the first drops of rain and the sky darkening above them, they found themselves struggling down a long narrow path waist high with nettles through which they had to beat their way with their sticks. Though it had been clearly visible from the road, the ruin was obscured for much of this approach by trees and foliage, so that it was with a start, as well as relief, that the travellers suddenly found themselves before it.

The villa must have been splendid enough in Roman days, but now only a small section was standing. Once magnificent floors lay exposed to the elements, disfigured by stagnant puddles, weeds and grass sprouting through the faded tiles. The remains of walls, in places barely ankle high, revealed the old layout of the rooms. A stone arch led into the surviving part of the building, and Axl and Beatrice now moved cautiously towards it, pausing at the threshold to listen. Eventually Axl called out: 'Is anyone within?' And when there was no reply: 'We're two elderly Britons seeking shelter from the storm. We come in peace.'

Still there was silence and they went in under the arch into the shade of what must once have been a corridor. They emerged into the grey light of a spacious room, though here too, an entire wall had fallen away. The adjoining room had disappeared altogether, and evergreens were pressing in oppressively right up to the edge of the floor. The three standing walls, however, provided a sheltered area, with a good ceiling. Here, against the grimy masonry of what once had been whitewashed walls, were two dark figures, one standing, the other sitting, some distance apart.

Seated on a piece of fallen masonry was a small, bird-like old woman – older than Axl and Beatrice – in a dark cloak, the hood pushed back enough to reveal her leathery features. Her eyes were sunk deep so that you could hardly see them. The curve of her back was not quite touching the wall behind her. Something stirred on her lap and Axl saw it was a rabbit, held tightly in her bony hands.

At the furthest point along the same wall, as though he had moved as far from the old woman as possible while keeping under cover, was a thin, unusually tall man. He wore a thick long coat of the sort a shepherd might wear during a cold night's watch, but where it ended, the exposed lower parts of his legs were bare. On his feet were the kind of shoes Axl had seen on fishermen. Though he was probably still young, the top of his head was smoothly bald, while dark tufts sprouted around his ears. The man was standing rigidly, his back to the room, one hand on the wall before him as though listening intently to something occurring on the other side. He glanced over his shoulder as Axl and Beatrice came in, but said nothing. The old woman too was staring at them in silence and only when Axl said: 'Peace be with you,' did they unfreeze a little. The tall man said: 'Come in further, friends, or you will not stay dry.'

Sure enough, the sky had truly opened now and rainwater was running down some section of broken roof and splashing on the floor near where the visitors were standing. Thanking him, Axl led his wife to the wall, choosing a spot midway between their hosts. He helped Beatrice take off her bundle, then put his own down onto the ground.

Then the four of them remained like that for some time while the storm grew ever more fierce, and a flash of lightning illuminated the shelter. The oddly frozen stances of the tall man and the old woman seemed to cast a spell on Axl and Beatrice, for now they too remained as still and silent. It was almost as if, coming across a picture and stepping inside it, they had been compelled to become painted figures in their turn.

Then as the downpour settled to a steady fall, the bird-like old woman finally broke the silence. Stroking her rabbit with one hand while clutching it tightly in the other, she said:

'God be with you, cousins. You'll forgive me not greeting you earlier, but I was surprised to see you here. You'll know you're welcome nonetheless. A fine day for travelling until this storm came. But it's the kind that vanishes as suddenly as it appears. Your journey won't be long delayed and all the better for your taking a rest. Which way do you go, cousins?'

'We're on our way to our son's village,' Axl said, 'where he waits anxiously to welcome us. But tonight we'll seek shelter at a Saxon village we hope to reach by nightfall.'

'Saxons have their wild ways,' the old woman said. 'But they'll welcome a traveller more readily than do our own kind. Be seated, cousins. That log behind you is dry and I've often sat contentedly on it.'

Axl and Beatrice did as suggested, and then there was silence for a few further moments while the rain continued to beat down. Eventually a movement from the old woman made Axl glance towards her. She was pulling back the rabbit's ears, and as the animal struggled to free itself, her claw-like hand kept it firmly in its grasp. Then, as Axl watched, the old woman produced in her other hand a large rusted knife and placed it against the creature's throat. As Beatrice beside him started, Axl realised that the dark patches beneath their feet, and elsewhere all over the ruined floor, were old bloodstains, and that mingled with the smell of ivy and damp mouldering stone was another faint but lingering one of slaughter.

Having placed her knife to the rabbit's throat, the old woman became quite still again. Her sunken eyes, Axl realised, were fixed on the tall man at the far end of the wall, as though she were waiting for a signal from him. But the man remained in the same rigid posture as before, his forehead almost touching the wall. He either had not noticed the old woman or else was determined to ignore her.

'Good mistress,' Axl said, 'kill the rabbit if you must. But break its neck cleanly. Or else take a stone and give it a good blow.'

'Had I the strength, sir, but I'm too weak. I have a knife with a sharp edge and that is all.'

'Then I'll gladly assist you. There's no need for your knife.' Axl rose to his feet, holding out his hand, but the old woman made no move to give up the rabbit. She remained exactly as before, the knife on the animal's throat, her gaze fixed on the man across the room.

At last the tall man turned to face them. 'Friends,' he said, 'I was surprised to see you enter earlier, but now I'm glad. For I see you're good people, and I beg you, while you wait for this storm to pass, listen to my plight. I'm a humble boatman who ferries travellers across choppy waters. I don't mind the work though the hours are long and when there are many waiting to cross there's little sleep and my limbs ache with each thrust of the oar. I work through rain and wind and under the parching sun. But I keep my spirits up looking forward to my rest days. For I'm but one of several boatmen and we're each able to take our turn to rest, if only after long weeks of labour. On our rest days, we each have a special place to go, and this, friends, is mine. This house where I was once a carefree child. It's not as it once was, but for me it's filled with precious memories, and I come here asking only the quiet to enjoy them. Now consider this. Whenever I come here, within an hour of my arrival, this old woman will enter through that arch. She'll sit herself down and taunt me hour by hour, night and day. She'll make cruel and unjust accusations. Under cover of dark, she'll curse me with the most horrible curses. She will not give me a moment's respite. Sometimes, as you see, she'll bring with her a rabbit, or some such small creature, so she can slay it and pollute this precious place with its blood. I've done all I can to persuade her to leave me, but what pity God placed in her soul, she has learnt to ignore. She will not go, nor will she cease to taunt. Even now it's only your unexpected entrance that has caused her to pause in her persecution. And before long it will be time to begin my journey back, to more long weeks of toil on the water. Friends, I beg you, do what you can to make her leave. Persuade her that her behaviour is ungodly. You may have influence on her, being as you are from the outside.'

There was a silence after the boatman stopped talking. Axl remembered later feeling a vague compulsion to reply, but at the same time a sense that the man had spoken to him in a dream and that there was no real obligation to do so. Beatrice too seemed to feel no urge to respond, for her eyes remained on the old woman, who had now taken the knife away from the rabbit's throat, and was stroking its fur, almost affectionately, with the edge of the blade. Eventually Beatrice said:

'Mistress, I beg you, allow my husband to assist with your rabbit. There's no call to spill blood in a place such as this, and no basin to catch it. You'll bring bad luck not only to this honest boatman but to yourself and all other travellers who stray in here seeking shelter. Put that knife away and slaughter the creature gently elsewhere. And what good can come of taunting this man as you do, a hard-working boatman?'

'Let's not be hasty to speak harshly to this lady, princess,' Axl said gently. 'We don't know what has occurred between these people. This boatman seems honest, but then again, this lady may have just cause to come here and spend her time as she does.'

'You couldn't have spoken more aptly, sir,' the old woman said. 'Do I think this a charming way to spend my fading days? I'd rather be far from here, in the company of my own husband, and it's because of this boatman I'm now parted from him. My husband was a wise and careful man, sir, and we planned our journey for a long time, talked of it and dreamt of it over many years. And when finally we were ready, and had all we needed, we set off on the road and after several days found the cove from where we could cross to the island. We waited for the ferryman, and in time, saw his boat coming towards us. But as luck would have it, it was this very man here who came to us. See how tall he is. Standing on his boat on the water, against the sky with his long oar, he looked as tall and thin as those players do when they hobble on their stilts. He came to where my husband and I were standing on the rocks and tied his boat. And to this day I don't know how he did it, but somehow he tricked us. We were too trusting. With the island so near, this boatman took away my husband and left me waiting on the shore, after forty years and more of our being husband and wife and hardly a day apart. I can't think how he did it. His voice must have put us in a dream, because before I knew it he was rowing off with my husband and I was still on land. Even then, I didn't believe it. For who could suspect such cruelty from a boatman? So I waited. I said to myself, it's simply that the boat cannot take more than one passenger at a time, for the water was unsettled that day, and the sky almost as dark as it is now. I stood there on the rock and watched the boat getting smaller and then a speck. And still I waited, and in time the speck grew larger and it was the boatman coming back to me. I could soon see his head as smooth as a pebble, now with no passenger left in his boat. And I imagined it was my turn and I would soon be with my beloved again. But when he came to where I was waiting, and tied his rope to the pole, he shook his head and refused to take me across. I argued and wept and called to him, but he would not listen. Instead he offered me – such cruelty! – he offered a rabbit he said had been caught in a trap on the island's shore. He'd brought it to me thinking it a fitting supper for my first evening of solitude. Then seeing there was no one else waiting to be ferried, he pushed away, leaving me weeping on the shore, holding his wretched rabbit. I let it run off into the heather a moment later, for I tell you I had little appetite that evening or for many evenings after. That's why it is I bring him my own little gift each time I come here. A rabbit for his stew in return for his kindness that day.'

'The rabbit was intended for my own supper that evening,' the boatman's voice broke in from across the room. 'Feeling pity, I gave it to her. It was simple kindness.'

'We know nothing of your affairs, sir,' Beatrice said. 'But it does seem a cruel deception to leave this lady alone on the shore that way. What was it made you do such a thing?'

'Good lady, the island this old woman speaks of is no ordinary one. We boatmen have ferried many there over the years, and by now there will be hundreds inhabiting its fields and woods. But it's a place of strange qualities, and one who arrives there will walk among its greenery and trees in solitude, never seeing another soul. Occasionally on a moonlit night or when a storm's ready to break, he may sense the presence of his fellow inhabitants. But most days, for each traveller, it's as though he's the island's only resident. I'd happily have ferried this woman, but when she understood she wouldn't be with her husband, she declared she didn't care for such solitude and refused to go. I bowed to her decision, as I'm obliged to do, and let her go her own way. The rabbit, as I say, I gave her out of simple kindness. You see how she thanks me for it.'

'This boatman is a sly one,' the old woman said. 'He'll dare to deceive you, even though you're from the outside. He'll have you believe every soul roams that island in solitude, but it isn't true. Would my husband and I have dreamt long years to go to a place like that? The truth is there's many permitted to cross the water as wedded man and wife to dwell together on the island. Many who roam those same forests and quiet beaches arm in arm. My husband and I knew this. We knew it as children. Good cousins, if you search through your own memories, you'll remember it to be true even as I speak of it now. We had little inkling as we waited in that cove how cruel a boatman would come over the water to us.'

'There's truth in just one part of what she says,' the boatman said. 'Occasionally a couple may be permitted to cross to the island together, but this is rare. It requires an unusually strong bond of love between them. It does sometimes occur, I don't deny, and that's why when we find a man and wife, or even unmarried lovers, waiting to be carried over, it's our duty to question them carefully. For it falls to us to perceive if their bond is strong enough to cross together. This lady is reluctant to accept it, but her bond with her husband was simply too weak. Let her look into her heart, then dare say my judgement that day was in error.'

'Mistress,' Beatrice said. 'What do you say?'

The old woman remained silent. She kept her eyes lowered, and went on running the blade sulkily over the rabbit's fur.

'Mistress,' Axl said, 'once the rain stops, we'll be returning to the road. Why not leave this place with us? We'll gladly walk with you some of your way. We could talk at leisure about whatever pleases you. Leave this good boatman in peace to enjoy what remains of this house while it stands. What's to be gained sitting here like this? And if you wish it, I'll kill the rabbit cleanly before our paths part. What do you say?'

The old woman gave no reply, nor any indication of having heard Axl's words. After some time, she rose slowly to her feet, the rabbit held closely to her chest. The woman was tiny in stature and her cloak dragged along the floor as she made her way to the broken side of the room. Some water splashed onto her from a section of the ceiling, but she seemed not to care. When she had reached the far end of the floor, she looked out at the rain and the encroaching greenery. Then bending slowly, she set the rabbit down near her feet. The animal, perhaps stiff with fear, did not move at first. Then it vanished into the grass.

The old woman straightened herself carefully. When she turned she appeared to be looking at the boatman – her strangely sunken eyes made it hard to be certain – then said: 'These strangers have taken away my appetite. But it will return, I've no doubt.'

With that she lifted the hem of her cloak and stepped slowly down into the grass like one easing herself into a pool. The rain fell on her steadily, and she pulled her hood further over her head before taking her next steps into the tall nettles.

'Wait a few moments and we'll walk with you,' Axl called after her. But he felt Beatrice's hand on his arm and heard her whisper: 'Best not meddle with her, Axl. Let her go.'

When Axl walked over to where the old woman had stepped down, he half expected to see her somewhere, impeded by the foliage and unable to go on. But there was now no sign of her.

'Thank you, friends,' the boatman said behind him. 'Perhaps for this day at least, I shall be allowed peace to remember my childhood.'

'We too will be out of your way, boatman,' said Axl. 'Just as soon as this lets up.'

'No hurry, friends. You spoke judiciously and I thank you for it.'

Axl went on staring at the rain. He heard his wife say behind him: 'This must once have been a splendid house, sir.'

'Oh, it was, good lady. When I was a boy, I didn't know just how splendid, for it was all I knew. There were fine pictures and treasures, kind and wise servants. Just through there was the banqueting hall.'

'It must sadden you to see it like this, sir.'

'I'm simply grateful, good lady, it still stands as it does. For this house has witnessed days of war, when many others like it were burnt to the ground and are no more now than a mound or two beneath grass and heather.'

Then Axl heard Beatrice's footsteps coming towards him and felt her hand on his shoulder. 'What is it, Axl?' she asked, her voice lowered. 'You're troubled, I can see it.'

'It's nothing, princess. It's just this ruin here. For a moment it was as if I were the one remembering things here.'

'What manner of things, Axl?'

'I don't know, princess. When the man speaks of wars and burning houses, it's almost as if something comes back to me. From the days before I knew you, it must be.'

'Was there ever a time before we knew one another, Axl?

Sometimes I feel we must have been together since we were babes.'

'It seems that way to me too, princess. It's just some foolishness coming over me in this strange place.'

She was looking at him thoughtfully. Then she squeezed his hand and said quietly: 'This is a queer place indeed and may bring us more harm than the rain ever could. I'm anxious to leave it, Axl. Before that woman returns or something worse.'

Axl nodded. Then turning, he called across the room: 'Well, boatman, the sky looks to be clearing so we'll be on our way. Many thanks for allowing us shelter.'

The boatman said nothing to this, but as they were putting on their bundles, he came to assist them, handing them their walking sticks. 'A safe journey, friends,' he said. 'May you find your son in good health.'

They thanked him again, and were proceeding through the arch when Beatrice suddenly stopped and looked back.

'Since we're leaving you, sir,' she said, 'and may not meet with you again, I wonder if you'll allow me a small question.'

The boatman, standing at his spot by the wall, was watching her carefully.

'You spoke earlier, sir,' Beatrice went on, 'of your duty to question a couple waiting to cross the water. You spoke of the need to discover if their bond of love is such as to allow them to dwell together on the island. Well, sir, I was wondering this. How do you question them to discover what you must?'

For a moment the boatman seemed uncertain. Then he said: 'Frankly, good lady, it's not for me to talk of such matters. Indeed, we shouldn't by rights have met today, but some curious chance brought us together and I'm not sorry for it. You were both kind and took my part and for that I'm grateful. So I will answer you as best I can. It is, as you say, my duty to question all who wish to cross to the island. If it's a couple such as you speak of, who claim their bond is so strong, then I must ask them to put their most cherished memories before me. I'll ask one, then the other to do this. Each must speak separately. In this way the real nature of their bond is soon revealed.'

'But isn't it hard, sir,' Beatrice asked, 'to see what truly lies in people's hearts? Appearances deceive so easily.'

'That's true, good lady, but then we boatmen have seen so many over the years it doesn't take us long to see beyond deceptions. Besides, when travellers speak of their most cherished memories, it's impossible for them to disguise the truth. A couple may claim to be bonded by love, but we boatmen may see instead resentment, anger, even hatred. Or a great barrenness. Sometimes a fear of loneliness and nothing more. Abiding love that has endured the years – that we see only rarely. When we do, we're only too glad to ferry the couple together. Good lady, I've already said more than I should.'

'I thank you for it, boatman. It's just to satisfy an old woman's curiosity. Now we'll leave you in peace.'

'May you have a safe journey.'

* * *

They retraced their steps along the path they had beaten earlier through the ferns and nettles. The storm had made the ground underneath treacherous, so for all their anxiety to put the villa behind them, they proceeded at a careful pace. When they finally reached the sunken lane, the rain still had not ceased, and they took shelter under the first large tree they could find.

'Are you soaked through, princess?'

'Don't worry, Axl. This coat did its work. How is it with you?'

'Nothing the sun won't soon dry when it returns.'

They put down their bundles and leant against the trunk, recovering their breaths. After a while, Beatrice said quietly:

'Axl, I feel afraid.'

'Why, what is it, princess? No harm can come to you now.'

'Do you remember the strange woman in dark rags you watched me talking to up by the old thorn that day? She may have looked a mad wanderer, but the story she told had much in common with the old woman's just now. Her husband too had been taken by a boatman and she left behind on the shore. And when she was coming back from the cove, weeping for loneliness, she found herself crossing the edge of a high valley, and she could see the path a long way before and a long way behind, and all along it people weeping just like her. When I heard this I was only partly afraid, saying to myself it was nothing to do with us, Axl. But she went on speaking, about how this land had become cursed with a mist of forgetfulness, a thing we've remarked on often enough ourselves. And then she asked me: "How will you and your husband prove your love for each other when you can't remember the past you've shared?" And I've been thinking about it ever since. Sometimes I think of it and it makes me so afraid.'

'But what's to fear, princess? We've no plans to go to any such island or any desire to do so.'

'Even so, Axl. What if our love withers before we've a chance even to think of going to such a place?'

'What are you saying, princess? How can our love wither? Isn't it stronger now than when we were foolish young lovers?'

'But Axl, we can't even remember those days. Or any of the years between. We don't remember our fierce quarrels or the small moments we enjoyed and treasured. We don't remember our son or why he's away from us.'

'We can make all those memories come back, princess. Besides, the feeling in my heart for you will be there just the same, no matter what I remember or forget. Don't you feel the same, princess?'

'I do, Axl. But then again I wonder if what we feel in our hearts today isn't like these raindrops still falling on us from the soaked leaves above, even though the sky itself long stopped raining. I'm wondering if without our memories, there's nothing for it but for our love to fade and die.'

'God wouldn't allow such a thing, princess.' Axl said this quietly, almost under his breath, for he had himself felt an unnamed fear welling up within him.

'The day I spoke with her by the old thorn,' Beatrice continued, 'the strange woman warned me to waste no more time. She said we had to do all we could to remember what we've shared, the good and the bad. And now that boatman, when we were leaving, gives the very answer I expected and feared. What chance do we have, Axl, the way we are now? If someone like that asked of us our most treasured memories? Axl, I'm so afraid.'

'There, princess, there's nothing to fear. Our memories aren't gone for ever, just mislaid somewhere on account of this wretched mist. We'll find them again, one by one if we have to. Isn't that why we're on this journey? Once our son's standing before us, many things are sure to start coming back.'

'I hope so. That boatman's words have made me all the more afraid.'

'Forget him, princess. What do we want with his boat, or his island come to that? And you're right, the rain's stopped out there and we'll be drier stepping out from under this tree. Let's be on our way, and no more of these worries.'

Chapter Three

The Saxon village, viewed from a distance and a certain height, would have been something more familiar to you as a 'village' than Axl and Beatrice's warren. For one thing – perhaps because the Saxons had a keener sense of claustrophobia – there was none of this digging into the hillside. If you were coming down the steep valley slope, as Axl and Beatrice were that evening, you would have seen below you some forty or more individual houses, laid out on the valley floor in two rough circles, one within the other. You might have been too far away to notice the variations in size and splendour, but you would have made out the thatched roofs, and the fact that many were 'roundhouses' not so far removed from the kind in which some of you, or perhaps your parents, were brought up. And if the Saxons were happy to sacrifice a little security for the benefits of open air, they were careful to compensate: a tall fence of tethered timber poles, their points sharpened like giant pencils, completely encircled the village. At any given point, the fence was at least twice a man's height, and to make the prospect of scaling it even less enticing, a deep trench followed it all the way around the outside.

That would have been the picture Axl and Beatrice saw below them as they paused to catch their breaths during their descent down the hill. The sun was setting over the valley now, and Beatrice, who had the better sight, was once more leaning forward, a step or two in front of Axl, the grass and dandelions around her as tall as her waist.

'I can see four, no five men guarding the gate,' she was saying. 'And I think they're holding spears. When I was last here with the women, it was nothing more than one gate-keeper with a pair of dogs.'

'Are you sure there'll be a welcome here for us, princess?'

'Don't worry, Axl, they know me well enough by now. Besides, one of their elders here is a Briton, regarded by all as a wise leader even if he's not of their blood. He'll see to it we have a safe roof tonight. Even so, Axl, I think something's happened and I'm uneasy. Now here's another man with a spear arrived, and that's a pack of fierce dogs with him.'

'Who knows what goes on with Saxons,' said Axl. 'We may be better seeking shelter elsewhere tonight.'

'The dark will be soon on us, Axl, and those spears are not intended for us. Besides, there's a woman in this village I was wanting to visit, one who knows her medicines beyond anyone in our own.'

Axl waited for her to say something further, and when she went on peering into the distance, he asked: 'And why would you be after medicines, princess?'

'A small discomfort I feel from time to time. This woman might know of something to soothe it.'

'What sort of discomfort, princess? Where does it trouble you?'

'It's nothing. It's only because we're needing to shelter here I'm thinking of it at all.'

'But where does it lie, princess? This pain?'

'Oh . . .' Without turning to him, she pressed a hand to her side, just below the ribcage, then laughed. 'It's nothing to speak of.

You can see, it hasn't slowed me walking here today.'

'It hasn't slowed you one bit, princess, and I've been the one having to beg we stop and rest.'

'That's what I'm saying, Axl. So it's nothing to worry about.'

'It hasn't slowed you down at all. In fact, princess, you must be as strong as any woman half your age. Still, if there's someone here to help with your pain, what's the harm in going to her?'

'That's all I was saying, Axl. I've brought a little tin to trade for medicines.'

'Who wants these little pains? We all have them, and we'd all be rid of them if we could. By all means, let's go to this woman if she's here, and those guards let us pass.'

It was nearly dark by the time they crossed the bridge over the trench, and torches had been lit on either side of the gate. The guards were large and burly but looked panicked by their approach.

'Wait a moment, Axl,' Beatrice said quietly. 'I'll go alone to speak with them.'

'Don't go near their spears, princess. The dogs look calm but those Saxons look foolish with fear.'

'If it's you they fear, Axl, old man that you are, I'll soon show them their great error.'

She walked towards them boldly. The men gathered around her and as she addressed them they threw suspicious glances towards Axl. Then one of them called to him, in the Saxon language, to step closer to the torches, presumably so they could see he was not a younger man in disguise. Then after a few more exchanges with Beatrice the men allowed them through.

Axl was puzzled that a village which from a distance looked to be two orderly rings of houses could turn out to be such a chaotic labyrinth now they were walking through its narrow lanes.

Admittedly the light was fading, but as he followed Beatrice, he could discern no logic or pattern to the place. Buildings would loom unexpectedly in front of them, blocking their way and forcing them down baffling side alleys. They were obliged, moreover, to walk with even more caution than out on the roads: not only was the ground pitted and full of puddles from the earlier storm, the Saxons seemed to find it acceptable to leave random objects, even pieces of rubble, lying in the middle of the path. But what troubled Axl most was the odour that grew stronger and fainter as they walked, but never went away. Like anyone of his time, he was well reconciled to the smell of excrement, human or animal, but this was something altogether more offensive. Before long he had determined its source: all over the village people had left out, on the fronts of houses or on the side of the street, piles of putrefying meat as offerings to their various gods. At one point, startled by a particularly strong assault, Axl had turned to see, suspended from the eaves of a hut, a dark object whose shape changed before his eyes as the colony of flies perched on it dispersed. A moment later they encountered a pig being dragged by its ears by a group of children; dogs, cows and donkeys under no one's supervision. The few people they met stared silently at them, or else quickly vanished behind a door or shutter.

'There's something strange here tonight,' Beatrice whispered as they walked. 'Usually they'd be sitting in front of their houses or perhaps gathered in circles laughing and talking. And the children would be following us by now asking a hundred questions and wondering if to call us names or be our friends. Everything's eerily still and it makes me uneasy.'

'Are we lost, princess, or are we still going toward the place they'll be sheltering us?'

'I'd been thinking we'd visit first the woman about the medicines. But with things the way they are, we may be better going straight to the old longhouse and keeping out of harm's way.'

'Are we far from the medicine lady's house?'

'As I remember it, not far at all now.'

'Then let's see if she's there. Even if your pain's a trivial thing, as we know it to be, there's no sense in feeling it at all if it can be taken away.'

'It can wait till the morning, Axl. It's not even a pain I notice till we're speaking of it.'

'Even so, princess, now we're here, why not go and see the wise woman?'

'We'll do so if you particularly wish it, Axl. Though I'd have happily left it for the morning or maybe the next time I'm passing through this place.'

Even as they were talking, they turned a corner into what appeared to be the village square. There was a bonfire blazing at its centre, and all around it, illuminated by its light, a large crowd. There were Saxons of all ages, even tiny children in their parents' arms, and Axl's first thought was that they had stumbled upon a pagan ceremony. But as they stopped to consider the scene before them, he saw there was no focus to the crowd's attention. The faces he could see were solemn, perhaps frightened. Voices were lowered, and collectively came through the air as a worried murmur. A dog barked at Axl and Beatrice and was promptly chased away by shadowy figures. Those among the crowd who noticed the visitors stared their way blankly before losing interest.

'Who knows what concerns them here, Axl,' Beatrice said. 'I'd walk away except the medicine woman's house is somewhere near. Let me see if I can still find my way to it.'

As they moved towards a row of huts to their right, they became aware of many more people in the shadows, silently watching the crowd around the fire. Beatrice stopped to talk to one of them, a woman standing in front of her own door, and after a while Axl realised this was the medicine woman herself. He could not see her well in the near-darkness, but made out the straight-backed figure of a tall woman, probably in her middle years, clutching a shawl around her arms and shoulders. She and Beatrice went on conferring in low voices, sometimes glancing towards the crowd, sometimes at Axl. Eventually the woman gestured for them to enter her hut, but Beatrice, coming up to him, said softly:

'Let me speak with her alone, Axl. Help me take off this bundle and wait out here for me.'

'Can't I be with you, princess, even if I hardly understand this Saxon tongue?'

'These are women's matters, husband. Let me talk with her alone, and she's saying she'll examine my old body carefully.'

'I'm sorry, princess, I wasn't thinking clearly. Let me take your bundle from you and I'll be waiting here as long as you wish.'

After the two women had gone inside, Axl felt a great weariness, especially in his shoulders and legs. Removing his own burden, he leaned against the turf wall behind him and gazed over at the crowd. There was now a growing restlessness: people would stride from the darkness around him to join the crowd while others hurried away from the fire, only to return a moment later. The blaze illuminated some faces sharply, while leaving others in shadow, but after a time, Axl came to the conclusion these people were all waiting, in a state of some anxiety, for someone or something to emerge from the timber hall to the left of the fire. This building, probably some meeting place for the Saxons, must have had a fire of its own burning inside, for its windows flickered between blackness and light.

He was on the verge of nodding off, his back to the wall, the muffled voices of Beatrice and the medicine woman somewhere behind him, when the crowd surged and shifted, letting out a soft collective growl. Several men had emerged from the timber hall and were walking towards the fire. The crowd parted and quietened for them, as though in expectation of an announcement, but none came, and soon people were pressing around the newcomers, their voices building again. Axl noticed that attention was focused almost entirely on the man who had come out last from the hall. He was probably no more than thirty but had about him a natural authority. Although he was dressed simply, as a farmer might be, he did not look like anyone else in the village. It was not just the way he had swept his cloak over one shoulder, revealing his belt and the handle of his sword. Nor was it simply that his hair was longer than any of the villagers' – it hung almost down to his shoulders and he had tied some of it with a thong to prevent it swaying over his eyes. In fact the actual thought that crossed Axl's mind was that this man had tied his hair to stop it falling across his vision *during combat*. This thought had come to Axl quite naturally, and only on reflection did it startle him, for it had carried with it an element of recognition. Moreover, when the stranger, striding into the midst of the crowd, allowed his hand to fall and rest on the sword handle, Axl had felt, almost tangibly, the peculiar mix of comfort, excitement and fear such a movement could bring. Telling himself he would return to these curious sensations at some later point, he shut them out of his mind and concentrated on the scene unfolding before him.

It was the bearing of the man, the way he moved and held himself, that so set him apart from those around him. 'No matter that he tries to pass himself off as an ordinary Saxon,' Axl thought, 'this man is a *warrior*. And perhaps one capable of wreaking great devastation when he wishes it.'

Two of the other men who had emerged from the hall were hovering nervously behind him, and whenever the warrior drifted further into the crowd, both men tried their best to stay near him, like children anxious not to be left behind by a parent. The two men, who were both young, also wore swords, and in addition, each was clutching a spear, but it was evident they were quite unaccustomed to such weapons. They were, moreover, stiff with fear and seemed unable to respond to the words of encouragement their fellow villagers were giving them. Their gazes darted about in panic even as hands patted their backs or squeezed their shoulders.

'The long-haired fellow is a stranger arrived only an hour or two before us,' Beatrice's voice said close to his ear. 'A Saxon, but one from a distant country. The fenlands in the east, so he says, where he's lately been fighting sea raiders.'

Axl had been aware for some time that the voices of the women had grown more distinct, and turning, saw that Beatrice and her hostess had come out of the house and were standing at the door just behind him. The medicine woman now spoke softly, for some time, in Saxon, after which Beatrice said into his ear:

'It seems earlier today one of the village men came back out of breath and his shoulder wounded, and when prevailed upon to calm himself told of how he and his brother, together with his nephew, a boy of twelve, were fishing at their usual spot by the river and were set upon by two ogres. Except according to this wounded man these were no ordinary ogres. Monstrous and able to move faster and with greater cunning than any ogre he'd ever seen. The fiends – for it's by that name these villagers are talking of them – the fiends killed his brother outright and carried off the boy, who was alive and struggling. The wounded man himself got away only after a long chase along the river path, the foul grunts coming closer behind him all the while, but he outran them in the end. That would be him there now, Axl, with the splint on his arm, talking to the stranger. Wounded though he was, he was anxious enough for his nephew to lead a party of this village's strongest men back to the spot, and they saw smoke from a campfire near the bank, and as they were creeping up to it, their weapons at the ready, the bushes opened and it seems these same two fiends had set a trap. The medicine woman says three men were killed even before the others thought to run for their lives, and though they returned unhurt, most of them are now shivering and muttering to themselves in their beds, too shaken to come out and wish well these brave men willing to go out now, even with the darkness coming and the mist setting in, to do what couldn't be done by twelve strong men in broad daylight.'

'Do they know the boy is still alive?'

'They know nothing, but they'll go out to the river even so. After the first party returned in terror, for all the urging of the elders, there was not a single man brave enough to join a further expedition. Then as fortune would have it, here's this stranger come into the village seeking a night's shelter after his horse has hurt a foot. And though he knows nothing of this boy or his family before today, he's declared himself willing to come to the village's aid. Those others going out with him are two more of the boy's uncles, and by the look of them, I'd say they're more likely to hinder that warrior than be of help. Look, Axl, they're sick with fear.'

'I see that right enough, princess. But they're brave men all the same, to go out when they're so afraid. We chose a bad night to ask this village's hospitality. There's weeping somewhere even now, and there may be a great deal more before the night's passed.'

The medicine woman seemed to understand something of what Axl had said, for she spoke again, in her own language, then Beatrice said: 'She says to go straight to the old longhouse now and not show ourselves again till morning. If we choose to wander the village, she says there's no telling how we may be greeted on a night like this.'

'My own thoughts exactly, princess. Then let's be taking the good lady's advice, if you can still remember the way.'

But just at that moment the crowd made a sudden noise, then the noise became cheering, and the crowd shifted again, as if struggling to change shape. Then it began to move, the warrior and his two companions near its centre. A low chanting started up, and soon the spectators in the shadows – the medicine woman included – joined in. The procession came towards them, and though the brightness of the fire had been left behind, several torches were moving within it, so that Axl could catch glimpses of faces, some frightened, some excited. Whenever a torch illuminated the warrior, his expression was calm, gazing to left and right to acknowledge words of encouragement, his hand once more on the handle of his sword. They went past Axl and Beatrice, continued between a row of huts and out of view, though the muted chanting remained audible for some time.

Perhaps daunted by the atmosphere, neither Axl nor Beatrice moved for a while. Then Beatrice began to question the medicine woman on the best way to reach the longhouse, and it seemed to Axl the two women were soon discussing directions to some other destination altogether, for they pointed and gestured into the distance towards the hills above the village.

They finally set off for their lodgings only when quiet had descended over the village. It was harder than ever to find one's way in the darkness, and the occasional torches burning on corners seemed only to increase the confusion with their shadows. They were proceeding in the opposite direction to that in which the crowd had gone, and the houses they passed were dark with no obvious signs of life.

'Walk slowly, princess,' Axl said softly. 'If either of us takes a bad tumble on this ground, I'm not certain there'll be a soul coming out to help us.'

'Axl, I think we've lost our way again. Let's go back to the last corner and this time I'll be sure to find it.'

In time the path straightened and they found themselves walking beside the perimeter fence they had seen from the hill. Its sharpened poles loomed above them a shade darker than the night sky, and as they went on, Axl could hear murmured voices somewhere above them. Then he saw they were no longer alone: high up along the ramparts, at regular intervals, were shapes he realised were people gazing out over the fence into the dark wilderness beyond. He had barely time to share this observation with Beatrice before they heard footsteps gathering behind them. They quickened their pace, but now a torch was moving nearby and shadows swung rapidly before them. At first Axl thought they had stumbled upon a group of villagers coming in the other direction, but then saw that he and Beatrice were entirely surrounded. Saxon men of varying ages and builds, some with spears, others wielding hoes, scythes and other tools, were jostling around them. Several voices addressed them at once, and ever more people seemed to be arriving. Axl felt the heat of the torches thrust at their faces, and holding Beatrice close to him, tried to locate with his gaze the leader of this group, but could find no such figure. Every face, moreover, was filled with panic, and he realised any careless move could bring disaster. He pulled Beatrice out of the reach of a particularly wild-eyed young man who had raised a trembling knife in the air, and searched his memory for some Saxon phrases. When nothing came to him, he made do with a few soothing noises, such as he might have made to an unruly horse.

'Stop that, Axl,' Beatrice whispered. 'They won't thank you for singing lullabies to them.' She addressed one, then another of the men in Saxon, but the mood did not improve. Shouted arguments were breaking out, and a dog, tugging on a rope, broke through the ranks to snarl at them.

Then the tense figures around them seemed all at once to sag. Their voices quietened till there was only the one, shouting angrily, somewhere still a little way off. The voice came closer and the crowd parted to let through a squat, misshapen man who shuffled into the pool of light leaning on a thick staff.

He was quite elderly, and though his back was relatively straight, his neck and head protruded from his shoulders at a grotesque angle. Nonetheless all present appeared to yield to his authority – the dog too ceased barking and vanished into the shadows. Even with his limited Saxon, Axl could tell the misshapen man's fury had only partly to do with the villagers' treatment of strangers: they were being reprimanded for abandoning their sentry posts, and the faces caught in the torchlight became crestfallen, though filled with confusion. Then as the elder's voice rose to a new level of anger, the men seemed slowly to remember something, and one by one slipped back into the night. But even when the last of them had gone, and there were sounds of feet clambering up ladders, the misshapen man went on hurling insults after them.

Finally he turned to Axl and Beatrice, and switching to their language, said with no trace of an accent: 'How can it be they forget even this, and so soon after watching the warrior leave with two of their own cousins to do what none of them had the courage for? Is it shame makes their memories so weak or simply fear?'

'They're fearful right enough, Ivor,' Beatrice said. 'Just now a spider falling beside them could set them tearing at one another. A sorry crew you sent out to greet us.'

'My apologies, Mistress Beatrice. And to you too, sir. It's not the welcome you would usually get here, but as you see, you've arrived on a night filled with dread.'

'We've lost our way to the old longhouse, Ivor,' Beatrice said. 'If you'd point us to it we'd be much beholden to you. Especially after that greeting, my husband and I are eager to be indoors and resting.'

'I'd like to promise you a kind welcome at the longhouse, friends, but on this night there's no telling what my neighbours may see fit to do. I'd be easier if you and your good husband agreed to spend the night under my own roof, where I know you'll remain undisturbed.'

'We accept your kindness gladly, sir,' Axl broke in. 'My wife and I are much in need of rest.'

'Then follow me, friends. Stay close behind me and keep your voices low till we arrive.'

They followed Ivor through the dark until they reached a house which, though in structure much like the others, was larger and stood apart by itself. When they entered under the low arch, the air was thick with woodsmoke, which, even as it made Axl's chest tighten, felt warm and welcoming. The fire was smouldering in the centre of the room, surrounded by woven rugs, animal skins and furniture crafted from oak and ash. As Axl went about extricating blankets from their bundles, Beatrice sank gratefully into a rocking seat. Ivor, though, remained standing by the doorway, a preoccupied look on his face.

'The treatment you received just now,' he said, 'I shudder with shame to think of it.'

'Please let's think no more of it, sir,' Axl said. 'You've shown us more kindness than we could deserve. And we arrived this evening in time to see the brave men set off on their dangerous mission. So we understand all too well the dread that hangs in the air, and it's no wonder some should behave foolishly.'

'If you strangers remember our troubles well enough, how is it those fools are forgetting them already? They were told in terms a child would understand to hold their positions on the fence at all costs, the safety of the whole community depending on it, to say nothing of the need to aid our heroes should they appear at the gates pursued by monsters. So what do they do? Two strangers go by, and remembering nothing of their orders or even the reasons for them, they set on you like crazed wolves. I'd be doubting my own senses if such strange forgetfulness didn't occur so often in this place.'

'It's the same in our own country, sir,' Axl said. 'My wife and I have witnessed many incidents of such forgetfulness among our own neighbours.'

'Interesting to hear that, sir. And I was fearing this a kind of plague spreading through our country only. And is it because I'm old, or that I'm a Briton living here among Saxons, that I'm often left alone holding some memory when all around me have let it slip?'

'We've found it just the same, sir. Though we suffer enough from the mist – for that's how my wife and I have come to call it – we seem to do so less than the younger ones. Can you see an explanation for it, sir?'

'I've heard many things spoken about it, friend, and mostly Saxon superstition. But last winter a stranger came this way who had something to say on this matter to which I find myself giving more credence the more I think on it. Now what's this?' Ivor, who had remained by the door, his staff in his hand, turned with surprising agility for one so twisted. 'Excuse your host, friends. This may be our brave men already returned. It's best for now you remain in here and not show yourselves.'

Once he had left, Axl and Beatrice remained silent for some time, their eyes closed, grateful, in their respective chairs, for the chance to rest. Then Beatrice said quietly:

'What do you suppose Ivor was going to say then, Axl?'

'About what, princess?'

'He was talking of the mist and the reason for it.'

'Just a rumour he heard once. By all means let's ask him to speak more on it. An admirable man. Has he always lived among Saxons?'

'Ever since he married a Saxon woman a long time ago, so I'm told. What became of her I never heard. Axl, wouldn't it be a fine thing to know the cause of the mist?'

'A fine thing indeed, but what good it will do, I don't know.'

'How can you say so, Axl? How can you say such a heartless thing?'

'What is it, princess? What's the matter?' Axl sat up in his chair and looked over to his wife. 'I only meant knowing its cause wouldn't make it go away, here or in our own country.'

'If there's even a chance of understanding the mist, it could make such a difference to us. How can you speak so lightly of it, Axl?'

'I'm sorry, princess, I didn't mean to do so. My mind was on other things.'

'How can you be thinking of other things, and we only today heard what we did from that boatman?'

'Other things, princess, such as if those brave men have come back and with the child unharmed. Or if this village with its frightened guards and flimsy gate is to be invaded this night by monstrous fiends wishing revenge for the rude attention paid them. There's plenty for a mind to dwell on, never mind the mist or the superstitious talk of strange boatmen.'

'No need for harsh words, Axl. I never wished a quarrel.'

'Forgive me, princess. It must be this mood here is affecting me.'

But Beatrice had become tearful. 'No need to talk so harshly,' she muttered almost to herself.

Rising, Axl made his way to her rocking chair and crouching slightly, held her closely to his chest. 'I'm sorry, princess,' he said. 'We'll be sure to talk to Ivor about the mist before we leave this place.' Then after a moment, during which they continued to hold each other, he said: 'To be frank, princess, there was a particular thing on my mind just now.'

'What was that, Axl?'

'I was wondering what the medicine woman said to you about your pain.'

'She said it was nothing but what's to be expected with the years.'

'Just what I always said, princess. Didn't I tell you there was no need for worry?'

'I wasn't the one worrying, husband. It was you insisting we go see the woman tonight.'

'It's as well we did, for now we needn't worry about your pain, if ever we did before.'

She gently freed herself from his embrace and allowed her chair to rock back. 'Axl,' she said. 'The medicine woman mentioned an old monk she says is even wiser than her. He's helped many from this village, a monk called Jonus. His monastery's a day from here, up on the mountain road east.'

'The mountain road east.' Axl wandered towards the door, which Ivor had left ajar, and looked out into the darkness. 'I'm thinking, princess, we could as easily take the higher road tomorrow as the low one through the woods.'

'That's a hard road, Axl. A lot of climbing. It will add at least a day to our journey and there's our own son anxious for our arrival.'

'That's all true. But it seems a pity, having come this far, not to visit this wise monk.'

'It was only something the medicine woman said, thinking we were travelling that way. I told her our son's village was more easily reached by the low road, and she agreed herself then it was hardly worth our while, there being nothing troubling me but the usual aches that come with the years.'

Axl went on gazing through the doorway into the dark. 'Even so, princess, we might think about it yet. But here's Ivor returning, and not looking happy.'

Ivor came striding in, breathing heavily, and sitting down in a wide chair piled with skins, allowed his staff to fall with a clatter at his feet. 'A young fool swears he sees a fiend scaled the outside of our fence and now peeking at us over the top of it. A mighty commotion, I needn't tell you, and it's all I can do to raise a party to go and see if it's true. Of course, there's nothing where he points but the night sky, but he goes on saying the fiend's there looking at us, and the rest of them cowering behind me like children with their hoes and spears. Then the fool confesses he fell asleep on his watch and saw the fiend in his dream, and even then do they hasten back to their posts? They're so terrified, I have to swear to beat them till their own kin mistake them for mutton.' He looked around him, still taking heavy breaths. 'Excuse your host, friends. I'll be sleeping in that inner room if I'm to sleep at all tonight, so do what you can to find comfort here, though there's little on offer.'

'On the contrary, sir,' Axl said, 'you've offered us wondrously comfortable lodgings and we're grateful for it. I'm sorry it wasn't better news called you out just now.'

'We must wait, perhaps well into the night and the morning too. To where do you travel, friends?'

'We'll set off east tomorrow, sir, to our son's village, where he anxiously awaits us. But on this matter you may be of help, for my wife and I were just arguing the best road to take. We hear of a wise monk by the name of Jonus at a monastery up on the mountain road whom we might consult on a small matter.'

'Jonus certainly has a revered name, though I've never met the man face to face. Go to him by all means, but be warned, the journey to the monastery's no easy one. The path will climb steeply for much of your day. And when at last it levels you must take care not to lose your way, for you'll be in Querig country.'

'Querig, the she-dragon? I've not heard talk of her in a long time. Is she still feared in this country?'

'She rarely leaves the mountains now,' Ivor said. 'Though she may on a whim attack a passing traveller, it's likely she's often blamed for the work of wild animals or bandits. In my view Querig's menace comes less from her own actions than from the fact of her continuing presence. So long as she's left at liberty, all manner of evil can't help but breed across our land like a pestilence. Take these fiends which curse us tonight. Where did they come from? They're no mere ogres. No one here has seen their like before. Why did they journey here, to make camp on our river-bank? Querig may rarely show herself, but many a dark force stems from her and it's a disgrace she remains unslain all these years.'

'But Ivor,' Beatrice said, 'who'd wish to challenge such a beast? By all accounts Querig's a dragon of great fierceness, and hidden in difficult terrain.'

'You're right, Mistress Beatrice, it's a daunting task. It happens there's an aged knight left from Arthur's days, charged by that great king many years ago to slay Querig. You may come across him should you take the mountain road. He's not easily missed, dressed in rusted chainmail and mounted on a weary steed, always eager to proclaim his sacred mission, though I'd guess the old fool has never given that she-dragon a single moment of anxiety. We'll reach a great age waiting for the day he fulfils his duty. By all means, friends, travel to the monastery, but go with caution and be sure to reach safe shelter by nightfall.'

Ivor began to move to the inner room, but Beatrice quickly sat up and said:

'You were talking earlier, Ivor, about the mist. How you heard something of the cause for it, but then were called away before you could say more. We're anxious now to hear you speak on this matter.'

'Ah, the mist. A good name for it. Who knows how much truth there is in what we hear, Mistress Beatrice? I suppose I was speaking of the stranger riding through our country last year and sheltered here. He was from the fens, much like our brave visitor tonight, though speaking a dialect often hard to understand. I offered him use of this poor house, as I've done you, and we talked on many matters through the evening, among them this mist, as you so aptly call it. Our strange affliction interested him greatly, and he questioned me again and again on the matter. And then he ventured something I dismissed at the time, but have since much pondered. The stranger thought it might be God himself had forgotten much from our pasts, events far distant, events of the same day. And if a thing is not in God's mind, then what chance of it remaining in those of mortal men?'

Beatrice stared at him. 'Can such a thing be possible, Ivor? We're each of us his dear child. Would God really forget what we have done and what's happened to us?'

'My question exactly, Mistress Beatrice, and the stranger could offer no answer. But since that time, I've found myself thinking more and more of his words. Perhaps it's as good an explanation as any for what you name the mist. Now forgive me, friends, I must take some rest while I can.'

* * *

Axl became aware that Beatrice was shaking his shoulder. He had no idea how long they had slept: it was still dark, but there were noises outside, and he heard Ivor say somewhere above him: 'Let's pray it's good news and not our end.' When Axl sat up, however, their host had already gone, and Beatrice said: 'Hurry, Axl, and we'll see which it is.'

Bleary with sleep, he slipped his arm through his wife's and together they stumbled out into the night. There were many more torches lit now, some blazing from the ramparts, making it much easier than before to see one's way. People were moving everywhere, dogs barking and children crying. Then some order seemed to impose itself, and Axl and Beatrice found themselves in a procession hurrying in a single direction. They came to an abrupt halt, and Axl was surprised to see they were already at the central square – there was obviously a more direct route from Ivor's house than the one they had taken earlier. The bonfire was blazing more fiercely than ever, so much so that Axl thought for an instant it was its heat that had caused the villagers to stop. But looking past the rows of heads, he saw the warrior had returned. He was standing there quite calmly, to the left of the fire, one side of his figure illuminated, the other in shadow. The visible part of his face was covered in what Axl recognised as tiny spots of blood, as if he had just come walking through a fine mist of the stuff. His long hair, though still tied, had come loose and looked wet. His clothes were covered in mud and perhaps blood, and the cloak he had nonchalantly flung over his shoulder at his departure was now torn in several places. But the man himself appeared uninjured, and he was now talking quietly to three of the village elders, Ivor among them. Axl could see too that the warrior was holding some object in the crook of his arm.

Meanwhile, chanting had started, softly at first, then gathering momentum, till eventually the warrior turned to acknowledge it. His manner was devoid of any crude swagger. And when he began to address the crowd, his voice, though loud enough for all to hear, somehow gave the impression he was speaking in a low, intimate tone appropriate to solemn subject matter.

His listeners hushed to catch each word, and soon he was drawing from them gasps of approval or of horror. At one point he gestured to a spot behind him and Axl noticed for the first time, sitting on the ground just within the circle of light, the two men who had gone out with the warrior. They looked as if they had fallen there from a height and were too dazed to get up. The crowd started up a chant for them, but the pair seemed not to notice, continuing instead to stare at the air before them.

The warrior then turned back to the crowd and said something which caused the chanting to fade. He stepped closer to the fire, and grasping in one hand the object he had been carrying, raised it into the air.

Axl saw what appeared to be the head of a thick-necked creature severed just below the throat. Dark curls of hair hung down from the crown to frame an eerily featureless face: where the eyes, nose and mouth should have been there was only pimpled flesh, like that of a goose, with a few tufts of down-like hair on the cheeks. A growl escaped the crowd and Axl felt it cower back. Only then did he realise that what they were looking at was not a head at all, but a section of the shoulder and upper arm of some abnormally large, human-like creature. The warrior was, in fact, holding up his trophy by the stump close to the bicep with the shoulder end uppermost, and in that moment Axl saw that what he had taken for strands of hair were tendons dangling out of the cut by which the segment had been separated from the body.

After only a short time, the warrior lowered his trophy and

let it fall at his feet, as though he could now barely work up sufficient contempt for the creature's remains. For a second time, the crowd recoiled, before edging forward again, and then the chanting started up once more. But this time it died almost instantly for the warrior was speaking again, and though Axl could understand none of it, he could sense palpably the nervous excitement around him. Beatrice said in his ear:

'Our hero has killed both monsters. One took its mortal wound into the forest, and will not live through the night. The other stood and fought and for its sins the warrior has brought of it what you see on the ground there. The rest of the fiend crawled to the lake to numb its pain and sank there beneath the black waters. The child, Axl, you see there the child?'

Almost beyond the light of the fire a small group of women had huddled around a thin, dark-haired youth seated on a stone. He was already close to a man's height, but one sensed that beneath the blanket now wrapped around him, he still had the gangly frame of a boy. One woman had brought out a bucket and was washing off the grime from his face and neck, but he seemed oblivious. His eyes were fixed on the warrior's back just in front of him, though intermittently he would angle his head to one side, as though trying to peer around the warrior's legs at the thing on the ground.

Axl was surprised that the sight of the rescued child, alive and evidently without serious injury, provoked in him neither relief nor joy, but a vague unease. He supposed at first this was to do with the odd manner of the boy himself, but then it occurred to him what was really wrong: there was something amiss in the way this boy, whose safety had until so recently been at the centre of the community's concerns, was now being received. There was a reserve, almost a coldness, that reminded Axl of that incident involving the girl Marta in his own village, and he wondered if this boy, like her, was in the process of being forgotten. But surely this could not be the case here. People were even now pointing at the boy, and the women attending him were staring back defensively.

'I can't catch what they're saying, Axl,' Beatrice said in his ear. 'Some quarrel about the child, though a great mercy he's been brought back safe and he himself showing surprising calm after what his young eyes have beheld.'

The warrior was still addressing the crowd, and a tone of entreaty had entered his voice. It was almost as if he was making an accusation, and Axl could feel the mood of the crowd changing. The sense of awe and gratitude was giving way to some other emotion, and there was confusion, even fear in the rumble of voices swelling around him. The warrior spoke again, his voice stern, gesturing behind him towards the boy. Then Ivor came within the light of the fire and standing beside the warrior said something which drew a less inhibited growl of protest from parts of his audience. A voice behind Axl shouted something, then arguments were breaking out on all sides. Ivor raised his voice and for a small moment there was quiet, but almost straight away the shouting resumed, and now there was jostling in the shadows.

'Oh, Axl, please, let's hurry away!' Beatrice cried into his ear. 'This is no place for us.'

Axl put his arm around her shoulders and began to push their way through, but something made him glance back one more time. The boy had not changed his position, and was still staring at the warrior's back, apparently unaware of the commotion before him. But the woman who had been tending to him had stepped away, and was glancing uncertainly from the boy to the crowd. Beatrice tugged his arm. 'Axl, please, take us away from here. I'm afraid we'll be hurt.'

The entire village must have been at the square, for they encountered no one on their way back to Ivor's house. Only as it came into view did Axl ask: 'What was being said just now, princess?'

'I'm not at all sure, Axl. There was too much of it at once for my weak understanding. A quarrel about the boy who was saved, and tempers being lost. It's well we're away and we'll find out in time what's occurred.'

* * *

When Axl awoke the next morning there were shafts of sunlight crossing the room. He was on the floor, but he had been sleeping on a bed of soft rugs beneath warm blankets – an arrangement more luxurious than he was accustomed to – and his limbs felt well rested. He was in good spirits, moreover, because he had awoken with a pleasant memory drifting through his head.

Beatrice stirred beside him but her eyes remained closed and her breathing unbroken. Axl watched her, as he often did at such moments, waiting for a sense of tender joy to fill his breast. It soon did so, just as he expected, but today was mingled with a trace of sadness. The feeling surprised him, and he ran his hand lightly along his wife's shoulder, as though such an action would chase away the shadow.

He could hear noises outside, but unlike those that had woken them in the night, these were of people going about their business of an ordinary morning. It occurred to him he and Beatrice had slept unwisely late, but he still refrained from waking Beatrice and went on gazing at her. Eventually he rose carefully, stepped over to the timber door and pushed it open a little way. This door – it would have been a 'proper' door on wooden hinges – made a creaking noise and the sun entered powerfully through the gap, but still Beatrice slept on. Now somewhat concerned, Axl returned to where she lay and crouched down beside her, feeling the stiffness in his knees as he did so. At last his wife opened her eyes and looked up at him.

'Time we were rising, princess,' he said, hiding his relief. 'The village is alive and our host long gone.'

'Then you should have roused me earlier, Axl.'

'You looked so peaceful, and after that long day I imagined sleep would be welcome to you. And I was right for now you're looking as fresh as a young maid.'

'Talking your nonsense already and we don't even know what happened in the night. From the sound of things out there, they haven't beaten each other to bloody pulp. That's children I hear and the dogs sound fed and happy. Axl, is there water to wash with here?'

A little later, having made themselves presentable as best they could – and with Ivor still not returned – they wandered out into the crisp, bright air in search of something to eat. The village now appeared to Axl a far more benevolent place. The round huts which in the dark had seemed so haphazardly positioned now stood before them in neat rows, their matching shadows forming an orderly avenue through the village. There was a bustle of men and women moving about with tools or washing tubs, groups of children following in their wake. The dogs, though numerous as ever, seemed docile. Only a donkey contentedly defecating in the sun right in front of a well reminded Axl of the unruly place he had entered the night before. There were even nods and subdued greetings from villagers as they passed, though no one went so far as to speak to them.

They had not gone far when they spotted the contrasting figures of Ivor and the warrior standing ahead of them in the street, heads close together in discussion. As Axl and Beatrice approached, Ivor took a step back and smiled self-consciously.

'I wished not to wake you prematurely,' he said to them. 'But I'm a poor host and you both must be famished. Follow me to the old longhouse and I'll see you're given your fill. But first, friends, greet our hero of last night. You'll find Master Wistan understands our tongue with ease.'

Axl turned to the warrior and bowed his head. 'My wife and I are honoured to meet a man of such courage, generosity and skill. Your deeds last night were remarkable.'

'My deeds were nothing extraordinary, sir, no more my skills.' The warrior's voice, as before, was gentle and a smile hovered about his eyes. 'I had good fortune last night, and besides, was ably helped by brave comrades.'

'The comrades he speaks of', Ivor said, 'were too busy soiling themselves to join the battle. It's this man alone destroyed the fiends.'

'Really, sir, no more on this matter.' The warrior had addressed Ivor, but was now gazing intently at Axl, as though some mark on the latter's face greatly fascinated him.

'You speak our language well, sir,' Axl said, taken aback by the scrutiny.

The warrior went on studying Axl, then caught himself and laughed. 'Forgive me, sir. I thought for a moment . . . But forgive me. My blood is Saxon through and through, but I was brought up in a country not far from here and was often among Britons. So I learnt to speak your tongue alongside my own. These days I'm less accustomed to it, living as I do far away in the fenlands, where one hears many strange tongues but not yours. So you must excuse my errors.'

'Far from it, sir,' Axl said. 'One can hardly tell you aren't a native speaker. In fact, I couldn't help notice last night your way of wearing your sword, closer and higher on the waist than Saxons are accustomed to do, your hand falling easily on the handle as you walk. I hope you won't be offended when I say it's a manner much like a Briton's.'

Again Wistan laughed. 'My Saxon comrades ceaselessly jest not only on my wearing of the sword, but my wielding of it. But you see, my skills were taught to me by Britons, and I've never wished for better teaching. It has preserved me well through many dangers, and did so again last night. Excuse my impertinence, sir, but I see you're not from these parts yourself. Can it be your native country is to the west?'

'We're from the neighbouring country, sir. A day's walk away, no more.'

'Yet perhaps in distant days you lived further west?'

'As I say, sir, I'm from the neighbouring country.'

'Forgive my poor manners. Travelling this far west, I find myself nostalgic for the country of my childhood, though I know it's some distance yet. I find myself seeing everywhere shadows of half-remembered faces. Are you and your good wife returning home this morning?'

'No, sir, we go east to our son's village, which we hope to reach within two days.'

'Ah. The road through the forest then.'

'Actually, sir, we mean to take the high road through the mountains, there being a wise man in the monastery there we hope will grant us an audience.'

'Is that so?' Wistan nodded thoughtfully, and once more looked carefully at Axl. 'I'm told that's a steep climb.'

'My guests have not yet breakfasted,' Ivor said, breaking in. 'Excuse us, Master Wistan, while I walk them to the longhouse. Then if we may, sir, I'd like to resume our discussion of just now.' He lowered his voice and continued in Saxon, to which Wistan replied with a nod. Then turning to Axl and Beatrice, Ivor shook his head and said gravely: 'Despite this man's great efforts last night, our problems are far from over. But follow me, friends, you must be famished.'

Ivor marched off with his lurching gait, prodding the earth at each step with his staff. He seemed too distracted to notice his guests falling behind in the crowded alleys. At one point, when Ivor was several paces ahead, Axl said to Beatrice: 'That warrior's an admirable fellow, didn't you think so, princess?'

'No doubt,' she replied quietly. 'But that was a strange way he had of staring at you, Axl.'

There was no time to say more, for Ivor, at last noticing he was in danger of losing them, had stopped at a corner.

Before long they came to a sunny courtyard. There were roaming geese, and the yard itself was bisected by an artificial stream – a shallow channel cut into the earth – along which the water trickled with urgency. At its broadest point the stream was forded by a simple little bridge of two flat rocks, and at that moment an older child was squatting on one of them, washing clothes. It was a scene that struck Axl as almost idyllic, and he would have paused to take it in further had Ivor not kept striding firmly on towards the low, heavily thatched building whose length ran the entire far edge of the yard.

Once inside it, you would not have thought this longhouse so different from the sort of rustic canteen many of you will have experienced in one institution or another. There were rows of long tables and benches, and towards one end, a kitchen and serving area. Its main difference from a modern facility would have been the dominating presence of hay: there was hay above one's head, and beneath one's feet, and though not by design, all over the surface of the tables, blown around by the gusts that regularly swept through the place. On a morning such as this, as our travellers sat down to breakfast, the sun breaking in through the porthole-like windows would have revealed the air itself to be filled with drifting specks of hay.

The old longhouse was deserted when they arrived, but Ivor went into the kitchen area, and a moment later two elderly women appeared with bread, honey, biscuits and jugs of milk and water. Then Ivor himself came back with a tray of poultry cuts which Axl and Beatrice proceeded to devour gratefully.

At first they ate without speaking, only now conscious of how hungry they had been. Ivor, facing them across the table, continued to brood, his eyes far away in thought, and it was only after some time that Beatrice said:

'These Saxons are a great burden to you, Ivor. Perhaps you're wishing to be back with your own kind, even with the boy returned safe and the ogres slain.'

'Those were no ogres, mistress, nor any creatures seen before in these parts. It's a great fear removed they no longer roam outside our gates. The boy though is another matter. Returned he may be, but far from safe.' Ivor leaned across the table towards them and lowered his voice, even though they were once more alone. 'You're right, Mistress Beatrice, I wonder at myself to live among such savages. Better dwell in a pit of rats. What can that brave stranger think of us, and after all he did last night?'

'Why, sir, what has occurred?' Axl asked. 'We were there at the fire last night, but sensing a fierce quarrel, took our leave and remain ignorant of what went on.'

'You did well to hide yourselves, friends. These pagans were sufficiently aroused last night to tear out each other's eyes. How they might have treated a pair of strange Britons found in their midst I dread to think. The boy Edwin was safely returned, but even as the village began to rejoice, the women found on him a small wound. I inspected it myself as did the other elders. A mark just below his chest, no worse than what a child receives after a tumble. But the women, his own kin at that, declared it a bite, and that's what the village is calling it this morning. I've had to have the boy locked in a shed for his safety, and even so, his companions, his very family members, throwing stones at the door and calling for him to be brought out and slaughtered.'

'But how can this be, Ivor?' Beatrice asked. 'Is it the mist's work again that they've lost all memory of the horrors the child so lately suffered?'

'If only it were, mistress. But this time they appear to remember all too well. The pagans will not look beyond their superstitions. It's their conviction that once bitten by a fiend, the boy will before long turn fiend himself and wreak horror here within our walls. They fear him and should he remain here, he'll suffer a fate as terrible as any from which Master Wistan saved him last night.'

'Surely, sir,' Axl said, 'there are those here wise enough to argue better sense.'

'If there are, we're outnumbered, and even if we may command restraint for a day or two, it won't be long before the ignorant have their way.'

'Then what's to be done, sir?'

'The warrior's as horrified as you are, and we two have been in discussion all morning. I've proposed he take the boy with him when he rides out, imposition though this is, and leave him at some village sufficiently distant where he may have a chance of a new life. I felt shame to the depths of my heart to ask such a thing of a man so soon after he has risked his life for us, but I could see little else to do. Wistan is now considering my proposal, though he has an errand for his king and already delayed on account of his horse and last night's troubles. In fact, I must check the boy's still safe now, then go see if the warrior has made his decision.' Ivor rose and picked up his staff. 'Come and say farewell before you leave, friends. Though after what you've heard I'll understand your wish to hurry from here without a backward glance.'

* * *

Axl watched Ivor's figure through the doorway striding off across the sunny courtyard. 'Dismal news, princess,' he said.

'It is, Axl, but it's not to do with us. Let's not dally further in this place. Our path today's a steep one.'

The food and milk were very fresh, and they ate on for a while in silence. Then Beatrice said:

'Do you suppose there's any truth in it, Axl? What Ivor was

saying last night about the mist, that it was God himself making us forget.'

'I didn't know what to think of it, princess.'

'Axl, a thought came to me about it this morning, just as I was waking.'

'What thought was that, princess?'

'It was just a thought. That perhaps God is angry about something we've done. Or maybe he's not angry, but ashamed.'

'A curious thought, princess. But if it's as you say, why doesn't he punish us? Why make us forget like fools even things that happened the hour before?'

'Perhaps God's so deeply ashamed of us, of something we did, that he's wishing himself to forget. And as the stranger told Ivor, when God won't remember, it's no wonder we're unable to do so.'

'What on this earth could we have done to make God so ashamed?'

'I don't know, Axl. But it's surely not anything you and I ever did, for he's always loved us well. If we were to pray to him, pray and ask for him to remember at least a few of the things most precious to us, who knows, he may hear and grant us our wish.'

There was a burst of laughter outside. Tilting his head a little, Axl was able to see out in the yard a group of children balancing on the flat rocks over the little stream. As he watched, one of them fell into the water with a squeal.

'Who's to say, princess,' he said. 'Perhaps the wise monk in the mountains will explain it to us. But now we're speaking of waking this morning, there's something came to me also, perhaps the same moment you were having these thoughts. It was a memory, a simple one, but I was pleased enough with it.'

'Oh, Axl! What memory was that?'

'I was remembering a time we were walking through a market or a festival. We were in a village, but not our own, and you were wearing that light green cloak with the hood.'

'This must be a dream or else a long time ago, husband. I have no green cloak.'

'I'm talking of long ago, right enough, princess. A summer's day, but there was a chill wind in this place where we were, and you'd placed the green cloak around you, though you kept the hood from your head. A market or perhaps some festival. It was a village on a slope with goats in a pen where you first set foot in it.'

'And what was it we were doing there, Axl?'

'We were just walking arm in arm, and then there was a stranger, a man from the village, suddenly in our path. And taking one glance at you, he stared like he was beholding a goddess. Do you remember it, princess? A young man, though I suppose we too were young then. And he was exclaiming he'd never set eyes on a woman so beautiful. Then he reached forward and touched your arm. Do you have a memory of it, princess?'

'There's something comes back to me, but not clearly. I'm thinking this was a drunken man you're talking of.'

'A little drunk perhaps, I don't know, princess. It was a day of festivities, as I say. All the same, he saw you and was amazed. Said you were the most beautiful sight he'd ever seen.'

'Then this must be a long time ago right enough! Isn't this the day you grew jealous and quarrelled with the man, the way we were almost run out of the village?'

'I recall nothing like that, princess. The time I'm thinking of, you had on the green cloak, and it was some festival day, and this same stranger, seeing I was your protector, turned to me and said, she's the loveliest vision I've seen so you be sure to take very good care of her my friend. That's what he said.'

'It comes back to me somewhat, but I'm sure you then had a jealous quarrel with him.'

'How could I have done such a thing when even now I feel the pride rising through me at the stranger's words? The most beautiful vision he'd seen. And he was telling me to take the very best care of you.'

'If you felt proud, Axl, you were jealous also. Didn't you stand up to the man even though he was drunk?'

'It's not how I remember it, princess. Perhaps I just made a show of being jealous as a sort of jest. But I would have known the fellow meant no harm. It's what I woke with this morning, though it's been many years.'

'If that's how you've remembered it, Axl, let it be the way it was. With this mist upon us, any memory's a precious thing and we'd best hold tight to it.'

'I wonder what became of that cloak. You always took good care of it.'

'It was a cloak, Axl, and like any cloak it must have worn thin with the years.'

'Didn't we lose it somewhere? Left on a sunny rock perhaps?'

'Now that comes back to me. And I blamed you bitterly for its loss.'

'I believe you did, princess, though I can't think now what justice there was in that.'

'Oh, Axl, it's a relief we can remember a few things still, mist or no mist. It could be God's already heard us and is hastening to help us remember.'

'And we'll remember plenty more, princess, when we set our

minds to it. There'll be no sly boatman able to trick us then, even if there ever comes a day we care at all for his foolish chatter. But let's eat up now. The sun's high and we're late for that steep path.'

* * *

They were walking back to Ivor's house, and had just passed the spot where they were nearly assaulted the previous night, when they heard a voice calling from above. Glancing around, they spotted Wistan high up on the rampart, perched on a lookout's platform.

'Glad to see you still here, friends,' the warrior called down.

'Still here,' Axl called in reply, taking a few paces towards the fence. 'But hastening on our way. And you, sir? Will you rest here for the day?'

'I too must leave shortly. But if I may impose on you, sir, for a short conversation, I'd be most thankful. I promise not to detain you long.'

Axl and Beatrice exchanged looks, and she said quietly: 'Speak with him if you will, Axl. I'll return to Ivor's and prepare provisions for our journey.'

Axl nodded, then turning to Wistan, called: 'Very well, sir. Do you wish me to come up?'

'As you will, sir. I'll happily come down, but it's a splendid morning and the view is such as to lift the spirits. If the ladder's no trouble to you, I urge you to join me up here.'

'Go see what he wants, Axl,' Beatrice said quietly. 'But be careful, and it's not just the ladder I'm speaking of.'

He took each rung with care until he reached the warrior, waiting with an extended hand. Axl steadied himself on the narrow platform, then looked down to see Beatrice watching from below. Only after he had waved cheerfully did she move off somewhat reluctantly towards Ivor's house – now clearly visible from his high vantage point. He kept watching her for a further moment, then turned and gazed out over the top of the fence.

'You see I didn't lie, sir,' Wistan said, as they stood there side by side, the wind on their faces. 'It's quite splendid as far as the eye will reach.'

The view before them that morning may not have differed so greatly from one to be had from the high windows of an English country house today. The two men would have seen, to their right, the valleyside coming down in regular green ridges, while far to their left, the opposite slope, covered with pine trees, would have appeared hazier, because more distant, as it merged with the outlines of the mountains on the horizon. Directly before them was a clear view along the valley floor; of the river curving gently as it followed the corridor out of view; of the expanses of marsh-land broken by patches of pond and lake further in the distance. There would have been elms and willows near the water, as well as dense woodland, which in those days would have stirred a sense of foreboding. And just where the sunlight went into shadow on the left bank of the river could be seen some remnants of a long-abandoned village.

'Yesterday I rode down that hillside,' Wistan said, 'and my mare with hardly any prompting set into a gallop as though for sheer joy. We raced across fields, past lake and river, and my spirit soared. A strange thing, as if I were returning to scenes from an early life, though to my knowledge I've never before visited this country. Can it be I passed this way as a small boy too young to know my whereabouts, yet old enough to retain these sights? The trees and moorland here, the sky itself seem to tug at some lost memory.'

'It's possible', Axl said, 'this country and the one further west where you were born share many likenesses.'

'That must be it, sir. In the fenlands we have no hills to speak of, and the trees and grass lack the colour before us now. But it was on that joyful gallop my mare broke her shoe, and though this morning the good people here have given her another, I will have to ride gently for one hoof is bruised. The truth is, sir, I brought you up here not simply to admire the country, but to be away from unwelcome ears. I take it you've by now heard what's occurred to the boy Edwin?'

'Master Ivor told us of it, and we thought it poor news to succeed your brave intervention.'

'You may know also how the elders, despairing of what would happen to the boy here, begged I take him away today. They ask I leave the boy in some distant village, telling some story of how I found him lost and hungry on the road. This I'd do gladly enough, except I fear such a plan can hardly save him. Word will easily travel across the country and next month, next year, the boy could find himself in the very plight he is in today, yet all the worse for being lately arrived and his people unknown. You see how it is, sir?'

'You're wise to fear such an outcome, Master Wistan.'

The warrior, who had been speaking while gazing out at the scenery, pushed back a tangled lock of hair the wind had blown across his face. As he did so, he seemed suddenly to see something in Axl's own features and, for a small moment, to forget what he had been saying. He gazed intently at Axl, angling his head. Then he gave a small laugh, saying:

'Forgive me, sir. I was just now reminded of something. But to return to my point. I knew nothing of this boy before last night, but I've been impressed by the steady way he has faced each new terror set before him. My comrades last night, brave though they were when setting out, were overcome with fear as we approached the fiends' camp. The boy, however, even though left at the fiends' mercy for many hours, held himself with a calm I could only wonder at. It would pain me greatly to think his fate's now all but sealed. So I've been thinking of a way out, and if you and your good wife were to consent to lend a hand, all may yet be well.'

'We're keen to do what we can, sir. Let me hear what you propose.'

'When the elders asked me to take the boy to a distant village, they meant no doubt a *Saxon* village. But it's precisely in a Saxon village the boy will never be safe, for it is Saxons who share this superstition about the bite he carries. If he were to be left with Britons, however, who see such nonsense for what it is, there can be no danger, even if the story were to pursue him. He's strong, and as I've said, has remarkable courage, even if he speaks little. He'll be a useful pair of hands for any community from the day he arrives. Now, sir, you said earlier you're on your way east to your son's village. I take it this will be just such a Christian village as we seek. If you and your wife were to plead for him, with perhaps the support of your son, that would surely secure a good outcome. Of course, it may be the same good people would accept the boy from me, but then I'll be a stranger to them, and one to arouse fear and suspicion. What's more, the errand which has brought me to this country will prevent my travelling so far east.'

'You're suggesting then,' Axl said, 'that my wife and I be the ones to take the boy from here.'

'That is indeed my suggestion, sir. However, my errand will permit me to travel at least part of the same road. You said you would take the path through the mountains. I'd happily accompany you and the boy, at least to the other side. My company will be a tedious imposition, but then the mountains are known to contain dangers, and my sword may yet prove of service to you. And your bags too could be carried by the horse, for even if her foot's tender, she'll not complain of it. What do you say, sir?'

'I think it an excellent plan. My wife and I were distressed to hear of the boy's plight, and we'll be happy if we can aid some resolution. And what you say is wise, sir. It's among Britons, surely, he's safest now. I've no doubt he'll be received with kindness at my son's village, for my son himself is a respected figure there, practically an elder in all but his years. He'll speak for the boy, I know, and ensure his welcome.'

'I'm much relieved. I'll let Master Ivor know our plan and seek a way to remove the boy quietly from the barn. Are you and your wife ready to leave shortly?'

'My wife is even now packing provisions for the journey.'

'Then please wait by the south gate. I'll come by presently with the mare and the boy Edwin. I'm grateful to you, sir, for the sharing of this trouble. And glad we're to be companions for a day or two.'

Chapter Four

Never in his life had he seen his village from such a height and distance, and it amazed him. It was like an object he could pick up in his hand, and he flexed his fingers experimentally over the view in the afternoon haze. The old woman, who had watched his ascent with anxiety, was still at the foot of the tree, calling up to him to climb no further. But Edwin ignored her, for he knew trees better than anyone. When the warrior had ordered him to keep watch, he had selected the elm with care, knowing that for all its sickly appearance, it would possess its own subtle strength and welcome him. It commanded, moreover, the best view of the bridge, and of the mountain road leading up to it, and he could see clearly the three soldiers talking to the rider. The latter had now dismounted, and holding his restless horse by the bridle, was arguing fiercely with the soldiers.

He knew his trees – and this elm was just like Steffa. 'Let him be carried off and left to rot in the forest.' That was what the older boys always said about Steffa. 'Isn't that what happens to old cripples unable to work?' But Edwin had seen Steffa for what he was: an ancient warrior, still secretly strong, and with an understanding that went beyond even that of the elders. Steffa, alone in the village, had once known battlefields – it was the battlefields that had taken his legs – and that was why, in turn, Steffa had been able to recognise Edwin for what he was. There were other boys stronger, who might amuse themselves pinning Edwin to the ground and beating him. But it was Edwin, not any of them, who possessed a warrior's soul.

'I've watched you, boy,' old Steffa had once said to him. 'Under a storm of fists, your eyes still calm, as if memorising each blow. Eyes I've seen only on the finest warriors moving coldly through the rage of battle. Some day soon you'll become one to fear.'

And now it was starting. It was coming true, just as Steffa had predicted.

As a strong breeze swayed the tree, Edwin moved his grip to a different branch and tried again to recall the events of the morning. His aunt's face had become distorted out of all recognition. She had been shrieking a curse at him, but Elder Ivor had not let her finish, pushing her away from the doorway of the barn, blocking Edwin's view of her as he did so. His aunt had always been good to him, but if she now wanted to curse him, Edwin did not care. Not long ago she had tried to get Edwin to address her as 'mother', but he had never done so. For he knew his real mother was travelling. His real mother would not shriek at him like that, and have to be dragged away by Elder Ivor. And this morning, in the barn, he had heard his real mother's voice.

Elder Ivor had pushed him inside, into the darkness, and the door had closed, taking away his aunt's twisted face – and all those other faces. At first the wagon had appeared only as a looming black shape in the middle of the barn. Then gradually he had distinguished its outline, and when he had reached towards it, the wood had felt moist and rotten. Outside, the voices were shouting again, and then the cracking noises had come. They had started sporadically, then several had come at once, accompanied by a splintering sound, after which the barn had seemed slightly less dark.

He knew the noises were stones striking the rickety walls, but he ignored them to concentrate on the wagon before him. How long ago had it last been used? Why did it stand so crookedly? If it was now of no use, why was it kept like this in the barn?

It was then he had heard her voice: difficult to distinguish at first, on account of the din outside and the sound of the stones, but it had grown steadily more clear. 'It's nothing, Edwin,' she was saying. 'Nothing at all. You can bear it easily.'

'But the elders may not be able to hold them back for ever,' he had said into the dark, though under his breath, even as his hand had stroked the side of the wagon.

'It's nothing, Edwin. Nothing at all.'

'The stones may break these thin walls.'

'Don't worry, Edwin. Didn't you know? Those stones are under your control. Look, what's that before you?'

'An old and broken wagon.'

'Well, there you are. Go round and round the wagon, Edwin. Go round and round the wagon, because you're the mule tethered to the big wheel. Round and round, Edwin. The big wheel can only turn if you turn it, and only if you turn it can the stones keep coming. Round and round the wagon, Edwin. Go round and round and round the wagon.'

'Why must I turn the wheel, mother?' Even as he had spoken, his feet had started circling the wagon.

'Because you're the mule, Edwin. Round and round. Those sharp cracking noises you hear. They can't continue unless you turn the wheel. Turn it, Edwin, round and round. Round and round the wagon.'

So he had followed her commands, keeping his hands on the upper edges of the wagon's boards, passing one hand over the other to maintain his momentum. How many times had he gone round like that? A hundred? Two hundred? He would keep seeing, in one corner, a mysterious mound of earth; in another corner, where a narrow line of sun fell across the floor of the barn, a dead crow on its side, feathers still intact. In the half-dark, these two sights – the mound of earth and the dead crow – had come around again and again. Once he had asked out loud, 'Did my aunt really curse me?' but no reply had come, and he had wondered if his mother had gone away. But then her voice had returned, saying, 'Do your duty, Edwin. You're the mule. Don't stop just yet. You control everything. If you stop, so will those noises. So why fear them?'

Sometimes he went three or even four times around the wagon without hearing a single sharp crack. But then as though to compensate, several cracks would come at once, and the shouting outside would rise to a new pitch.

'Where are you, mother?' he had asked once. 'Are you still travelling?'

No reply had come, but then several turns later, she had said, 'I'd have given you brothers and sisters, Edwin, many of them. But you're on your own. So find the strength for me. You're twelve years old, almost grown now. You must be by yourself four, five strong sons. Find the strength and come rescue me.'

As another breeze rocked the elm, Edwin wondered if the barn he had been in was the same one in which the people had hidden the day the wolves had come to the village. Old Steffa had told him the story often enough.

'You were very young then, boy, perhaps too young to remember. Wolves, in broad daylight, three of them, walking calmly right into the village.' Then Steffa's voice would fill with contempt.

'And the village hid in fear. Some men were away in the fields, it's true. But there were plenty still here. They hid themselves in the threshing barn. Not just the women and the children but the men too. The wolves had strange eyes, they said. Best not to challenge them. So the wolves took all they wished. They slaughtered the hens. Feasted on the goats. And all the while, the village hid. Some in their houses. Most in the threshing barn. Cripple that I am, they left me where I was, sitting in the barrow, these broken legs poking out, beside the ditch outside Mistress Mindred's. The wolves trotted towards me. Come and eat me, I said, I'll not hide in a barn for a wolf. But they cared not for me and I watched them go right past, their fur as good as brushing these useless feet. They took all they wished, and only after they'd long departed did those brave men creep out of their hiding places. Three wolves in daylight, and not a man here to stand up to them.'

He had thought about Steffa's story as he had circled the wagon. 'Are you still travelling, mother?' he had asked once more, and again had received no reply. His legs were growing weary, and he had grown heartily sick of seeing the mound of earth and the dead crow, when at last she had said:

'Enough, Edwin. You've worked hard. Call your warrior now if you wish. Bring an end to it.'

Edwin had heard this with relief, but had carried on circling the wagon. To summon Wistan, he knew, would require immense effort. As he had the night before, he would have to will his coming from the very depths of his heart.

But somehow he had found the strength, and once he was confident the warrior was on his way, Edwin had slowed his pace – for even mules were driven more slowly towards the end of a day – and noted with satisfaction the cracking noises were growing more sparse. But only when silence had continued for a long time did he finally stop, and leaning against the side of the wagon, begin to recover his breath. Then the barn door had opened and the warrior had been standing there against the dazzling sunshine.

Wistan had come in leaving the door wide open behind him as though to show his contempt for whatever hostile forces had lately been gathered outside. This had brought a large rectangle of sun into the barn, and when Edwin had glanced about himself, the wagon, so dominant in the dark, had looked pathetically dilapidated. Had Wistan called him 'young comrade' straight away? Edwin was unsure, but he did remember the warrior leading him into that patch of light, lifting his shirt and scrutinising the wound. Wistan had then straightened, glanced carefully over his shoulder, and said in a low voice:

'So, my young friend, have you kept your promise of last night? About this wound of yours?'

'Yes, sir. I've done just as you said.'

'You've told no one, not even your good aunt?'

'I've told no one, sir. Even though they believe it an ogre's bite and hate me for it.'

'Let them go on believing it, young comrade. Ten times worse if they learn the truth of how you received it.'

'But what of my two uncles who came with you, sir? Don't they know the truth?'

'Your uncles, brave as they were, became too sick to enter the camp. So it's just the two of us who must keep the secret, and once the wound's healed there's no need for anyone to wonder about it. Keep it as clean as you can, and never scratch it, by night or day. Do you understand?'

'I understand, sir.'

Earlier, when they had been climbing the valleyside, and he had stopped to wait for the two elderly Britons, Edwin had tried to remember the circumstances around the wound. On that occasion, standing amidst the stubbled heather, tugging the reins of Wistan's mare, nothing had formed clearly in his mind. But now, in the branches of the elm, gazing at the tiny figures down on the bridge, Edwin found coming back to him the dank air and blackness; the high smell of the bearskin covering the little wooden cage; the feel of the tiny beetles falling onto his head and shoulders when the cage was jolted. He recalled adjusting his posture and gripping the shaky grid before him to avoid being tossed about as the cage dragged along the ground. Then everything had become still again, and he had waited for the bearskin to be removed, for the cold air to rush in around him, and to glimpse the night by the glow of the nearby fire. For this was what had happened twice already that night, and the repetition had removed the edge from his fear. He remembered more: the stink of the ogres, and the vicious little creature hurling itself at the rickety poles of the cage, obliging Edwin to push as far back as he could.

The creature had moved so quickly it had been hard to get a clear view of it. He had had the impression of something the size and shape of a cockerel, though with no beak or feathers. It attacked with teeth and claws, all the time letting out a shrill squawking. Edwin trusted the wooden poles against the teeth and the claws, but now and then, the little creature's tail would whip by accident against the cage and then everything seemed much more vulnerable. Thankfully the creature – still in its infancy, Edwin supposed – seemed oblivious of the power in its tail.

Although at the time these attacks seemed to go on forever,

Edwin now supposed they had not lasted so long before the creature had been pulled back by its leash. Then the bearskin would thump over him, all would be blackness again, and he would have to grip the poles as the cage was dragged to another spot.

How often had he had to endure this sequence? Had it been just two or three times? Or as often as ten, or even twelve? Perhaps after the first time he had fallen asleep, even in those conditions, and dreamt the rest of the attacks.

Then on that final occasion, the bearskin had not come off for a long time. He had waited, listening to the creature's squawks, sometimes far away, sometimes much closer, and the grumbling sounds the ogres made when talking to each other, and he had known that something different was about to happen. And it had been during those moments of dreadful anticipation that he had asked for a rescuer. He had made the request from the depths of his being, so it had been something almost like a prayer, and as soon as it had taken shape in his mind, he had felt certain it would be granted.

At that very moment the cage had begun to tremble, and Edwin had realised the entire front section, with its protective grid, was being drawn aside. Even as this realisation made him shrink back, the bearskin was pulled off and the ferocious creature flew at him. In his sitting position, his instinct was to raise his feet and kick out, but the creature was agile, and Edwin found himself beating it off with fists and arms. Once he thought the creature had got the better of him, and had for an instant closed his eyes, but then opened them again to see his opponent clawing the air as the leash dragged it back. It was one of the few times he had been permitted a good glimpse of the creature, and he saw that his earlier impression had not been inaccurate: it looked like a plucked chicken, though with the head of a serpent. It came for him again, and Edwin was once more beating it off the best he could. Then quite suddenly, the cage front was restored before him, and the bearskin plunged him back in blackness. And it had only been in the moments afterwards, contorted inside the little cage, that he had felt the tingling on his left side just beneath the ribs, and had felt the wet stickiness there.

Edwin adjusted again his foothold within the elm, and bringing down his right hand, touched gently his wound. There was no longer any depth to the pain. During the climb up the valleyside, the coarseness of his shirt had at times made him grimace, but when he was still, as he was now, he could hardly feel a thing. Even that morning in the barn, when the warrior had examined it in the doorway, it had seemed little more than a cluster of tiny punctures. The wound was superficial – not as bad as many he had had before. And yet, because people believed it to be an ogre's bite, it had caused all this trouble. Had he faced the creature with even more determination, perhaps he could have avoided receiving any wound at all.

But he knew there was no shame in how he had faced his ordeal. He had never cried out in terror, or pleaded to the ogres for mercy. After the little creature's first lunges – which had taken him by surprise – Edwin had met it with head held up. In fact he had had the presence of mind to realise the creature was an infant, and that one could in all probability create fear in it, just as one might in an unruly dog. And so he had kept his eyes open and tried to stare it down. His real mother, he knew, would be particularly proud of him for this. Indeed, now that he thought about it, the venom had gone out of the creature's attacks soon after its opening forays, and it had been Edwin who had gained more and more control of the combat. He recalled again the creature clawing the air, and it seemed to him now likely it had not been displaying an eagerness to continue the fight, but simply panic at the choking leash. It was quite possible, in fact, the ogres had judged Edwin the victor of the encounter, and that was why proceedings had been brought to an end.

'I've watched you, boy,' old Steffa had said. 'You have something rare. One day you'll find someone to teach you the skills to match your warrior's soul. Then you'll be one to fear indeed. You'll not be one to hide in a barn while mere wolves stroll unhindered about the village.'

Now it was all coming to pass. The warrior had chosen him, and they were to go together to fulfil an errand. But what was their task? Wistan had not made it clear, saying only that his king, far away in the fenland, was even now waiting to hear of its conclusion. And why travel with these two elderly Britons who required rest at each turn of the road?

Edwin gazed down at them. They were now discussing something earnestly with the warrior. The old woman had given up trying to talk him down, and all three were now watching the soldiers on the bridge from behind the cover of two giant pines. From his own vantage point, Edwin could see the rider had remounted and was gesticulating into the air. Then the three soldiers appeared to move away from him, and the rider turned his horse and set off at a gallop away from the bridge, back down the mountain.

Edwin had wondered earlier why the warrior had been so reluctant to stay on the main mountain road, insisting on the steep cut up the valleyside; now it was obvious he had wished to avoid riders such as the one they had just seen. But there now seemed no way to proceed with their journey without going down onto the road and crossing the bridge past the waterfall, and the soldiers were still there. Had Wistan been able to see from down where he was that the rider had departed? Edwin wanted to alert him to this development, but felt he should not shout from the tree in case the soldiers somehow caught the sound. He would have to climb down and tell Wistan. Perhaps, while there had been four potential opponents, the warrior had been hesitant about a confrontation, but now with only three at the bridge, he would consider the odds in his favour. Had it just been Edwin and the warrior, they would surely have gone down to face the soldiers long ago, but the presence of the elderly couple must have made Wistan cautious. No doubt Wistan had brought them along for a good reason, and they had so far been kind to Edwin, but they were frustrating companions all the same.

He remembered again his aunt's contorted features. She had started to shriek a curse at him, but none of that mattered any more. For he was with the warrior now, and he was travelling, just like his real mother. Who was to say they might not come across her? She would be so proud to see him standing there, side by side with the warrior. And the men with her would tremble.

Chapter Five

After a punishing climb for much of the morning, the party had found its way obstructed by a fast-flowing river. So they had made a partial descent through shrouded woodlands in search of the main mountain road, along which, they reasoned, there would surely be a bridge across the water.

They had been right about the bridge, but on spotting the soldiers there, had decided to rest amidst the pine trees until the men had gone. For at first the soldiers had not appeared to be stationed there, but merely refreshing themselves and their horses at the waterfall. But time had passed and the soldiers had shown no signs of moving on. They would take turns getting onto their bellies, reaching down from the bridge and splashing themselves; or sit with their backs against the timber rails, playing dice. Then a fourth man had arrived on horseback, bringing the men to their feet, and had issued instructions to them.

Though they did not have as good a view as Edwin's high in his tree, Axl, Beatrice and the warrior had observed well enough all that had passed from behind their cover of greenery, and once the horseman had ridden off again, exchanged questioning looks.

'They may remain a long time yet,' Wistan said. 'And you're both anxious to reach the monastery.'

'It's desirable we do so by nightfall, sir,' said Axl. 'We hear the she-dragon Querig roams that country, and only fools would be abroad there in the dark. What manner of soldiers do you suppose them to be?'

'Not easy at this distance, sir, and I've little knowledge of local dress. But I'd suppose them Britons, and ones loyal to Lord Brennus. Perhaps Mistress Beatrice will correct me.'

'It's far for my old eyes,' Beatrice said, 'but I'd suppose you right, Master Wistan. They have the dark uniforms I've often seen on Lord Brennus's men.'

'We've nothing to hide from them,' Axl said. 'If we explain ourselves, they'll let us go by in peace.'

'I'm sure that's so,' the warrior said, then fell silent for a moment, gazing down at the bridge. The soldiers had seated themselves again and seemed to be resuming their game. 'Even so,' he went on, 'if we're to cross the bridge under their gazes, let me propose this much. Master Axl, you and Mistress Beatrice will lead the way and talk wisely to the men. The boy can bring the mare behind you, and I'll walk beside him, my jaw slack like a fool's, my eyes wandering loosely. You must tell the soldiers I'm a mute and a half-wit, and the boy and I are brothers lent you in place of debts owed you. I'll hide this sword and belt deep in the horse's pack. Should they find it, you must claim it as your own.'

'Is such a play really necessary, Master Wistan?' Beatrice asked. 'These soldiers may often show coarse manners, but we've met many before without incident.'

'No doubt, mistress. But men with arms, far from their commanders, aren't easy to trust. And here I am, a stranger who they may think good sport to mock and challenge. So let's call the boy down off the tree and do as I propose.'

* * *

They emerged from the woods still some way from the bridge, but the soldiers saw them immediately and rose to their feet.

'Master Wistan,' Beatrice said quietly, 'I fear this will not go well. There remains something about you that proclaims you a warrior, no matter what foolish look you wear.'

'I'm no skilled player, mistress. If you can help improve my disguise, I'd hear it gladly.'

'It's your stride, sir,' Beatrice said. 'You have a warrior's way of walking. Take instead small steps followed by a large one, the way you might stumble any moment.'

'That's good advice, thank you, mistress. Now I should say no more, or they may see I'm no mute. Master Axl, talk us wisely past these fellows.'

As they came closer to the bridge, the noise of the water rushing down the rocks and under the feet of the three awaiting soldiers grew more intense, and to Axl had something ominous about it. He led the way, listening to the horse's steps behind him on the mossy ground, and brought them to a halt when they were within hailing distance of the men.

They wore no chainmail or helmets, but their identical dark tunics, with straps crossing from right shoulder to left hip, declared clearly their trade. Their swords were for now sheathed, though two of them were waiting with hands on the hilts. One was small, stocky and muscular; the other, a youth not much older than Edwin, was also short in stature. Both had closely cropped hair. In contrast, the third soldier was tall, with long grey hair, carefully groomed, that touched his shoulders and was held back by a dark string encircling his skull. Not only his appearance, but his manner differed noticeably from that of his companions; for while the latter were standing stiffly to bar the way across the bridge, he had remained several paces behind, leaning languidly against one of the bridge posts, arms folded before him as though listening to a tale beside a night fire.

The stocky soldier took a step towards them, so it was to him Axl addressed his words. 'Good day, sirs. We mean no harm and wish only to proceed in peace.'

The stocky soldier gave no reply. Uncertainty was crossing his face, and he glared at Axl with a mixture of panic and contempt. He cast a glance back to the young soldier behind him, then finding nothing to enlighten him, returned his gaze to Axl.

It occurred to Axl there had been some confusion: that the soldiers had been expecting another party altogether, and had yet to realise their mistake. So he said: 'We're just simple farmers, sir, on our way to our son's village.'

The stocky soldier, now collecting himself, replied to Axl in an unnecessarily loud voice. 'Who are these you travel with, farmer? Saxons by the look of them.'

'Two brothers just come under our care who we must do our best to train. Though as you see, one's still a child, and the other a slow-witted mute, so the relief they bring us may be slender.'

As Axl said this, the tall grey-haired soldier, as though suddenly reminded of something, took his weight from the bridge post, his head tilting in concentration. Meanwhile, the stocky soldier was staring angrily beyond both Axl and Beatrice. Then, his hand still on the hilt of his sword, he strode past to scrutinise the others. Edwin was holding the mare, and watched the oncoming soldier with expressionless eyes. Wistan, though, was giggling loudly to himself, his eyes roving, mouth wide open.

The stocky soldier looked from one to the other as though for a clue. Then his frustration seemed to get the better of him.

Grabbing Wistan's hair, he tugged it in a rage. 'No one cut your hair, Saxon?' he shouted into the warrior's ear, then tugged again as though to bring Wistan to his knees. Wistan stumbled, but managed to stay on his feet, letting out pitiful whimpers.

'He doesn't speak, sir,' Beatrice said. 'As you see, he's simple. He doesn't mind rough treatment, but he's known for a temper we've yet to tame.'

As his wife spoke, a small movement made Axl turn back to the soldiers still on the bridge. He saw then that the tall grey-haired man had raised an arm; his fingers all but formed a pointing shape before softening and collapsing in an aimless gesture. Finally he let his arm fall altogether, though his eyes went on watching with disapproval. Observing this, Axl suddenly had the feeling he understood, even recognised, what the grey-haired soldier had just gone through: an angry reprimand had all but shaped itself on his lips, but he had remembered in time that he lacked any formal authority over his stocky colleague. Axl was sure he had once had an almost identical experience himself somewhere, but he forced away the thought, and said in a conciliatory tone:

'You must be busy with your duties, gentlemen, and we're sorry to distract you. If you'd let us pass, we'll soon be out of your way.'

But the stocky soldier was still tormenting Wistan. 'He'd be unwise to lose his temper with *me*!' he bellowed. 'Let him do so and taste his price!'

Then finally he let go of Wistan and strode back to take up his position again on the bridge. He said nothing, looking like an angry man who had completely forgotten why he was angry.

The noise of the rushing water seemed only to add to the tense mood, and Axl wondered how the soldiers would react were he to turn and lead the party back towards the woods. But just at that moment, the grey-haired soldier came forward until he was level with the other two and spoke for the first time.

'This bridge has a few planks broken, uncle. Maybe that's why we're standing here, to warn good people like yourselves to cross with care or be down the mountainside tumbling with the tide.'

'That's kind of you, sir. We'll go then with caution.'

'Your horse there, uncle. I thought I saw it limping coming towards us.'

'She has a hurt foot, sir, but we hope it's no serious thing, though we don't mount her, as you see.'

'Those boards are rotted with the spray, and that's why we're here, though my comrades think there was some further errand must have brought us. So I'll ask you, uncle, if you and your good wife have seen any strangers on your travels.'

'We're strangers here ourselves, sir,' Beatrice said, 'so wouldn't quickly know another. Though on two days' journey we've seen nothing out of the ordinary.'

Noticing Beatrice, the grey-haired soldier's eyes seemed to soften and smile. 'A long walk for a woman of your years to make to a son's village, mistress. Wouldn't you rather be living there with him where he can see to your comforts each day, instead of having you walk like this, unsheltered from the road's dangers?'

'I wish it right enough, sir, and when we see him, my husband and I will talk to him of it. But then it's a long time since we saw him and we can't help wonder how he'll receive us.'

The grey-haired soldier went on regarding her gently. 'It may be, mistress,' he said, 'you've not a thing to worry about. I'm myself far from my mother and father, and not seen them in a long while. Perhaps harsh words were said once, who knows?

But if they came to find me tomorrow, having walked hard distances as you're doing now, do you doubt I'd receive them with my heart breaking with joy? I don't know the kind of man your son is, mistress, but I'd wager he's not so different to me, and there'll be happy tears no sooner than he first sees you.'

'You're kind to say so, sir,' said Beatrice. 'I suppose you're right, and my husband and I have often said as much, but it's a comfort to hear it said, and from a son far from home at that.'

'Go on your journey in peace, mistress. And if by chance you come upon my own mother and father on the road, coming the other way, speak gently to them and tell them to press on, for their journey won't be a wasted one.' The grey-haired soldier stood aside to let them pass. 'And please remember the unsteady boards. Uncle, you'd best lead that mare over yourself. It's no task for children or God's fools.'

The stocky soldier, who had been watching with a disgruntled air, seemed nevertheless to yield to the natural authority of his colleague. Turning his back to them all, he leaned sulkily over the rail to look at the water. The young soldier hesitated, then came to stand beside the grey-haired man, and they both nodded politely as Axl, thanking them a last time, led the mare over the bridge, shielding her eyes from the drop.

* * *

Once the soldiers and the bridge were no longer in sight, Wistan stopped and suggested they leave the main road to follow a narrow path rising up into the woods.

'I've always had an instinct for my way through a forest,' he said. 'And I feel sure this path will allow us to cut a large corner.

Besides, we'll be much safer away from a road such as this, well travelled by soldiers and bandits.'

For a while after that, it was the warrior who led the party, beating back brambles and bushes with a stick he had found. Edwin, holding the mare by her muzzle, often whispering to her, followed closely behind, so that by the time Axl and Beatrice came in their wake, the path had been made much easier. Even so, the short cut – if short cut it was – became increasingly arduous: the trees deepened around them, tangled roots and thistles obliging them to attend to each step. As was the custom, they conversed little as they went, but at one point, when Axl and Beatrice had fallen some way behind, Beatrice called back: 'Are you still there, Axl?'

'Still here, princess.' Indeed, Axl was just a few paces behind. 'Don't worry, these woods aren't known for special dangers, and a good way from the Great Plain.'

'I was just thinking, Axl. Our warrior's not a bad player at that. His disguise might have had me fooled, and never letting up with it, even with that brute tugging his hair.'

'He performed it well, right enough.'

'I was thinking, Axl. It'll be a long time we're away from our own village. Don't you think it a wonder they let us go when there's still a lot of planting to do, and fences and gates to be mended? Do you suppose they'll be complaining of our absence when we're needed?'

'They'll be missing us, no doubt, princess. But we're not away long, and the pastor understands our wishing to see our own son.'

'I hope that's right, Axl. I wouldn't want them saying we're gone just when they have most need of us.'

'There'll always be some to say so, but the better of them will understand our need, and would want the same in our place.'

For a while they continued without talking. Then Beatrice said again: 'Are you still there, Axl?'

'Still here, princess.'

'It wasn't right of them. To take away our candle.'

'Who cares about that now, princess? And the summer coming.'

'I was remembering about it, Axl. And I was thinking maybe it's because of our lack of a candle I first took this pain I now have.'

'What's that you're saying, princess? How can that be?'

'I'm thinking it was maybe the darkness did it.'

'Go carefully through that blackthorn there. It's not a spot to take a fall.'

'I'll be careful, Axl, and you do the same.'

'How can it be the darkness gave you the pain, princess?'

'Do you remember, Axl, there was talk last winter of a sprite seen near our village? We never saw it ourselves, but they said it was one fond of the dark. In all those hours we had of darkness, I'm thinking it might sometimes have been with us without our knowing, in our very chamber, and brought me this trouble.'

'We would have known had it been with us, princess, dark or not. Even in thick blackness, we would have heard it move or give a sigh.'

'Now I think of it, Axl, I think there were times last winter I woke in the night, you fast asleep beside me, and I was sure it was a strange noise in the room roused me.'

'Likely a mouse or some creature, princess.'

'It wasn't that kind of sound, and it was more than once I thought I heard it. And now I'm thinking of it, it was around the same time the pain first came.'

'Well, if it was the sprite, what of it, princess? Your pain's nothing more than a tiny trouble, the work of a creature more playful than evil, the same way some wicked child once left that rat's head in Mistress Enid's weaving basket just to see her run about in fright.'

'You're right what you say there, Axl. More playful than evil. I suppose you're right. Even so, husband . . .' She fell silent while she negotiated her way between two ancient trunks pressing against each other. Then she said: 'Even so, when we go back, I want a candle for our nights. I don't want that sprite or any other bringing us something worse.'

'We'll see to it, don't worry, princess. We'll talk to the pastor as soon as we return. But the monks at the monastery will give you wise advice about your pain, and there'll be no lasting mischief done.'

'I know it, Axl. It's not a thing to worry me greatly.'

* * *

It was hard to say if Wistan had been right about his path cutting off a corner, but in any case, shortly after midday, they emerged out of the woods back onto the main road. Here it was wheel-rutted and boggy in parts, but now they could walk more freely, and in time the path grew drier and more level. With a pleasant sun falling through the overhanging branches, they travelled in good spirits.

Then Wistan brought them to a halt again and indicated the ground before them. 'There's a solitary rider not far before us,' he said. And they did not go much further before they saw ahead of them a clearing to the side of their road, and fresh tracks turning into it. Exchanging glances, they stepped forwards cautiously.

As the clearing came more into view, they saw it was of a fair size: perhaps once, in more prosperous times, someone had hoped to build a house here with a surrounding orchard. The path leading off from the main road, though overgrown, had been dug with care, ending in a large circular area, open to the sky except for one huge spreading oak at its centre. From where they now stood, they could see a figure seated in the shadows of the tree, his back against the trunk. He was for the moment in profile to them, and appeared to be in armour: two metal legs stuck out stiffly onto the grass in a child-like way. The face itself was obscured by foliage sprouting from the bark, though they could see he wore no helmet. A saddled horse was grazing contentedly nearby.

'Declare who you are!' the man called out from under the tree. 'All bandits and thieves I'll rise to meet sword in hand!'

'Answer him, Master Axl,' Wistan whispered. 'Let's discover what he's about.'

'We're simple wayfarers, sir,' Axl called back. 'We wish only to go by in peace.'

'How many are you? And is that a horse I hear?'

'A limping one, sir. Otherwise we are four. My wife and I being elderly Britons, and with us a beardless boy and a half-wit mute lately given us by their Saxon kin.'

'Then come over to me, friends! I have bread here to share, and you must long for rest, as I do for your company.'

'Shall we go to him, Axl?' Beatrice asked.

'I say we do,' Wistan said, before Axl could respond. 'He's no danger to us and sounds a man of decent years. All the same, let's perform our drama as before. I'll once more affect a slack jaw and foolish eyes.'

'But this man is armoured and armed, sir,' Beatrice said. 'Are you certain your own weapon is ready enough, packed on a horse amidst blankets and honey pots?'

'It's well my sword's hidden from suspicious eyes, mistress. And I'll find it soon enough when I need it. Young Edwin will hold the rein and see the mare doesn't stray too far from me.'

'Come forth, friends!' the stranger shouted, not adjusting his rigid posture. 'No harm will come to you! I'm a knight and a Briton too. Armed, it's true, but come closer and you'll see I'm just a whiskery old fool. This sword and armour I carry only out of duty to my king, the great and beloved Arthur, now many years in heaven, and it's almost as long surely since I drew in anger. My old battlehorse, Horace, you see him there. He's had to suffer the burden of all this metal. Look at him, his legs bowed, back sunk. Oh, I know how much he suffers each time I mount. But he has a great heart, my Horace, and I know he'd have it no other way. We'll travel like this, in full armour, in the name of our great king, and will do so till neither of us can take another step. Come friends, don't fear me!'

They turned into the clearing, and as they approached the oak, Axl saw that indeed, the knight was no threatening figure. He appeared to be very tall, but beneath his armour Axl supposed him thin, if wiry. His armour was frayed and rusted, though no doubt he had done all he could to preserve it. His tunic, once white, showed repeated mending. The face protruding from the armour was kindly and creased; above it, several long strands of snowy hair fluttered from an otherwise bald head. He might have been a sorry sight, fixed to the ground, legs splayed before him, except that the sun falling through the branches above was now dappling him in patterns of light and shade that made him look almost like one enthroned.

'Poor Horace missed his breakfast this morning, for we were on rocky ground when we awoke. Then I was so keen to press on all morning, and I admit it, in an ill temper. I wouldn't let him stop. His steps grew slower, but I know his tricks well enough by now, and would have none of it. I know you're not weary! I told him, and gave him a little spur. These tricks he plays on me, friends, I won't stand for them! But slower and slower he goes, and soft-hearted fool I am, even knowing full well he's laughing to himself, I relent and say, very well, Horace, stop and feed yourself. So here you find me, taken for a fool again. Come, join me, friends.' He reached forward, his armour complaining, and removed a loaf from a sack in the grass before him. 'This is fresh baked, given to me passing a mill not an hour ago. Come, friends, sit beside me and share it.'

Axl held Beatrice's arm as she lowered herself down onto the gnarled roots of the oak, then he sat down himself between his wife and the old knight. He felt immediately grateful for the mossy bark behind him, the songbirds jostling above, and when the bread was passed, it was soft and fresh. Beatrice leant her head against his shoulder, and her chest rose and fell for a while before she too began to eat with relish.

But Wistan had not sat down. After giggling, and otherwise amply displaying his idiocy to the old knight, he had wandered away to where Edwin was standing in the tall grass, holding his mare. Then Beatrice, finishing her bread, sat forward to address the stranger.

'You must forgive my not greeting you sooner, sir,' she said.

'But it's not often we see a knight and I was awe-struck by the thought. I hope you weren't offended.'

'Not offended at all, mistress, and glad of your company. Is your journey still a long one?'

'Our son's village is another day away now we're come by the mountain road, wishing to visit a wise monk at the monastery in these hills.'

'Ah, the holy fathers. I'm sure they'll receive you kindly. They were a great help to Horace last spring when he had a poisoned hoof and I feared he wouldn't be spared. And I myself, recovering some years ago from a fall, found much comfort in their balms. But if you seek a cure for your mute, I fear it's only God himself can bring speech to his lips.'

The knight had said this glancing towards Wistan, only to find the latter walking towards him, the foolish look vanished from his features.

'Allow me then to surprise you, sir,' he said. 'Speech is restored to me.'

The old knight started, then, armour creaking, twisted round to glare enquiringly at Axl.

'Don't blame my friends, sir knight,' Wistan said. 'They were only doing as I begged them. But now there's no cause to fear you, I would cast off my disguise. Please forgive me.'

'I don't mind, sir,' the old knight said, 'for it's as well in this world to be cautious. But tell me now what sort you are that I in turn have no cause to fear you.'

'The name is Wistan, sir, from the fenlands in the east, travelling these parts on my king's errand.'

'Ah. Far from home indeed.'

'Far from home, sir, and these roads should be strange to me.

Yet at each turn it's as if another distant memory stirs.'

'It must be then, sir, you came this way before.'

'It must be so, and I heard I was born not in the fens but in a country further west of here. All the more fortunate then to chance upon you, sir, supposing you might be Sir Gawain, from those same western lands, well known to ride in these parts.'

'I'm Gawain, right enough, nephew of the great Arthur who once ruled these lands with such wisdom and justice. I was settled many years in the west, but these days Horace and I travel where we may.'

'If my hours were my own, I'd ride west this very day and breathe the air of that country. But I'm obliged to complete my errand and hurry back with news of it. Yet it's an honour indeed to meet a knight of the great Arthur, and a nephew at that. Saxon though I am, his name is one I hold in esteem.'

'I take pleasure in hearing you say so, sir.'

'Sir Gawain, with my speech so miraculously restored, I would ask a small question of you.'

'Ask freely.'

'This gentleman now sits beside you, he's the good Master Axl, a farmer from a Christian village two days away. A man of familiar years to yourself. Sir Gawain, I ask you now, turn and look carefully at him. Is his face one you've seen before, though a long time ago?'

'Good heavens, Master Wistan!' Beatrice, who Axl thought had fallen asleep, was leaning forward again. 'What is this you ask?'

'I mean no harm, mistress. Sir Gawain being from the west country, I fancy he might have glimpsed your husband in days past. What harm's in it?'

'Master Wistan,' Axl said, 'I've seen you look strangely at me from time to time since our first meeting, and waited for some account of it. What is it you believe me to be?'

Wistan, who had been standing over where they were sitting three abreast beneath the great oak, now crouched down onto his heels. Perhaps he had done so to appear less challenging, but to Axl it was almost as if the warrior was wishing to scrutinise their faces more closely.

'Let's for now have Sir Gawain do as I ask,' Wistan said, 'and it's only a small turn of his head needed. See it as a childish game if you will. I beg you, sir, look at this man beside you and say if you've ever seen him in days past.'

Sir Gawain gave a chuckle, and moved his torso forward. He seemed eager for amusement, as though indeed he had just been invited to participate in a game. But as he gazed into Axl's face, his expression changed to one of surprise – even of shock. Instinctively, Axl turned away, just as the old knight appeared almost to push himself backwards into the tree trunk.

'Well, sir?' Wistan asked, watching with interest.

'I don't believe this gentleman and I met till today,' said Sir Gawain.

'Are you sure? The years can be a rich disguise.'

'Master Wistan,' Beatrice interrupted, 'what is it you search for in my husband's face? Why ask such a thing of this kind knight, until this moment a stranger to us all?'

'Forgive me, mistress. This country awakens so many memories, though each seems like some restless sparrow I know will flee any moment into the breeze. Your husband's face has all day promised me an important remembrance, and if truth be told, that was a reason for my proposing to travel with you, though I sincerely wish to see you both safely through these wild roads.'

'But why would you know my husband from the west when he's always lived in country nearby?'

'Never mind it, princess. Master Wistan has confused me for someone he once knew.'

'That's what it must be, friends!' said Sir Gawain. 'Horace and I often mistake a face for one from the past. See there, Horace, I say. That's our old friend Tudur before us on the road, and we thought he fell at Mount Badon. Then we ride closer and Horace will give a snort, as if to say, what a fool you are, Gawain, this fellow's young enough to be his grandson, and with not even a passing likeness!'

'Master Wistan,' Beatrice said, 'tell me this much. Does my husband remind you of one you loved as a child? Or is it one you dreaded?'

'Best leave it now, princess.'

But Wistan, rocking gently on his heels, was gazing steadily at Axl. 'I believe it must be one I loved, mistress. For when we met this morning, my heart leapt for joy. And yet before long . . .' He went on looking at Axl silently, his eyes almost dreamlike. Then his face darkened, and rising to his feet again, the warrior turned away. 'I can't answer you, Mistress Beatrice, for I know not myself. I supposed by travelling beside you the memories would awaken, but they've not yet done so. Sir Gawain, are you well?'

Indeed, Gawain had slumped forward. He now straightened and breathed a sigh. 'Well enough, thank you for asking. Yet Horace and I have gone many nights without a soft bed or decent shelter, and we're both weary. That's all there is to it.' He raised his hand and caressed a spot on his forehead, though his real purpose, it occurred to Axl, might have been to obscure his view of the face beside him.

'Master Wistan,' Axl said, 'since we're now speaking frankly, perhaps I may in turn ask something of you. You say you're in this country on your king's errand. But why so anxious to adopt your disguise travelling through a country long settled in peace? If my wife and that poor boy are to travel beside you, we'd wish to know the full nature of our companion, and who his friends and enemies might be.'

'You speak fairly, sir. This country, as you say, is well settled and at peace. Yet here I am a Saxon crossing lands ruled by Britons, and in these parts by the Lord Brennus, whose guards roam boldly to gather their taxes of corn and livestock. I wish no quarrel of the sort may come from a misunderstanding. Hence my disguise, sir, and we'll all of us move more safely for it.'

'You may be right, Master Wistan,' Axl said. 'Yet I saw on the bridge Lord Brennus's guards seemed not to be passing their time idly, but stationed there for a purpose, and if not for the mist clouding their minds, they might have tested you more closely. Can it be, sir, you're some enemy to Lord Brennus?'

For a moment Wistan appeared lost in thought, following with his eyes one of the gnarled roots stretching from the oak's trunk and past where he stood, before burrowing itself into the earth. Eventually he came nearer again, and this time sat down on the stubbled grass.

'Very well, sir,' he said, 'I'll speak fully. I don't mind doing so before you and this fine knight. We've heard rumours in the east of our fellow Saxons across this land ill used by Britons. My king, worrying for his kin, sent me on this mission to observe the real state of affairs. That's all I am, sir, and was going about my errand peaceably when my horse hurt her foot.'

'I understand well your position, sir,' said Gawain. 'Horace and

I often find ourselves on Saxon-governed land and feel the same need for caution. Then I wish to be rid of this armour and taken for a humble farmer. But if we left this metal somewhere, how would we ever find it again? And even though it's years since Arthur fell, isn't it our duty still to wear his crest with pride for all to see? So we go on boldly and when men see I'm a knight of Arthur, I'm happy to report they look on us gently.'

'It's no surprise you're welcomed in these parts, Sir Gawain,' Wistan said. 'But can it really be the same in those countries where Arthur was once such a dreaded enemy?'

'Horace and I find our king's name well received everywhere, sir, even in those countries you mention. For Arthur was one so generous to those he defeated they soon grew to love him as their own.'

For some time – in fact, ever since Arthur's name had first been mentioned – a nagging, uneasy feeling had been troubling Axl. Now at last, as he listened to Wistan and the old knight talk, a fragment of memory came to him. It was not much, but it nevertheless brought him relief to have something to hold and examine. He remembered standing inside a tent, a large one of the sort an army will erect near a battlefield. It was night, and there was a heavy candle flickering, and the wind outside making the tent's walls suck and billow. There were others in the tent with him. Several others, perhaps, but he could not remember their faces. He, Axl, was angry about something, but he had understood the importance of hiding his anger at least for the time being.

'Master Wistan,' Beatrice was saying beside him, 'let me tell you in our own village there are several Saxon families among the most respected. And you saw yourself the Saxon village from which we came today. Those people prosper, and though they sometimes suffer at the hands of fiends such as those you so bravely put down, it's not by any Briton.'

'The good mistress speaks truly,' Sir Gawain said. 'Our beloved Arthur brought lasting peace here between Briton and Saxon, and though we still hear of wars in distant places, here we've long been friends and kin.'

'All I've seen agree with your words,' Wistan said, 'and I'm eager to carry back a happy report, though I've yet to see the lands beyond these hills. Sir Gawain, I don't know if ever again I'll be free to ask this of one so wise, so let me do so now. By what strange skill did your great king heal the scars of war in these lands that a traveller can see barely a mark or shadow left of them today?'

'The question does you credit, sir. My reply is that my uncle was a ruler never thought himself greater than God, and always prayed for guidance. So it was that the conquered, no less than those who fought at his side, saw his fairness and wished him as their king.'

'Even so, sir, isn't it a strange thing when a man calls another brother who only yesterday slaughtered his children? And yet this is the very thing Arthur appears to have accomplished.'

'You touch the heart of it just there, Master Wistan. Slaughter children, you say. And yet Arthur charged us at all times to spare the innocents caught in the clatter of war. More, sir, he commanded us to rescue and give sanctuary when we could to all women, children and elderly, be they Briton or Saxon. On such actions were bonds of trust built, even as battles raged.'

'What you say rings true, and yet it still seems to me a curious wonder,' Wistan said. 'Master Axl, do you not feel it a remarkable thing, how Arthur has united this country?'

'Master Wistan, once again,' Beatrice exclaimed, 'who do you take my husband to be? He knows nothing, sir, of the wars!'

But suddenly no one was listening any more, for Edwin, who had drifted back to the road, was now shouting, and then came the beating of rapidly approaching hooves. Later when he thought back to it, it occurred to Axl that Wistan must indeed have become preoccupied with his curious speculations about the past, for the usually alert warrior had barely risen to his feet as the rider turned into the clearing, then slowing the horse with admirable control, came trotting towards the great oak.

Axl recognised immediately the tall, grey-haired soldier who had spoken courteously to Beatrice at the bridge. The man still wore a faint smile, but was approaching them with his sword drawn, though pointed downwards, the hilt resting on the edge of the saddle. He came to a halt where just a few more of the animal's strides would have brought him to the tree. 'Good day, Sir Gawain,' he said, bowing his head a little.

The old knight gazed up contemptuously from where he sat. 'What do you mean by this, sir, arriving here sword unsheathed?'

'Forgive me, Sir Gawain. I wish only to question these companions of yours.' He looked down at Wistan, who had again let his jaw drop slackly, and was giggling to himself. Without taking his eyes off the warrior, the soldier shouted: 'Boy, move that horse no closer!' For indeed, behind him, Edwin had been approaching with Wistan's mare. 'Hear me, lad! Let go the rein and come stand here before me beside your idiot brother. I'm waiting, lad.'

Edwin appeared to comprehend the soldier's wishes, if not his actual words, for he left the mare and came to join Wistan. As he did so, the soldier adjusted slightly the position of his horse. Axl, noticing this, understood immediately that the soldier was maintaining a particular angle and distance between himself and his charges that would give him the greatest advantage in the event of sudden conflict. Before, with Wistan standing where he was, the head and neck of the soldier's own horse would momentarily have obstructed his first swing of the sword, giving Wistan vital time either to unsettle the horse, or run to its blind side, where the sword's reach was diminished in scope and power by having to be brought across the body. But now the small adjusting of the horse had made it practically suicidal for an unarmed man, as Wistan was, to storm the rider. The soldier's new position seemed also to have taken expert account of Wistan's mare, loose some distance behind the soldier's back. Wistan was now unable to run for his horse without describing a wide curve to avoid the sword side of the rider, making it a near-certainty he would be run through from behind before reaching his destination.

Axl noted all this with a sense of admiration for the soldier's strategic skill, as well as dismay at its implications. There had been a time when Axl, too, had once nudged his horse forward, in another small but subtly vital manoeuvre, bringing himself in line with a fellow rider. What had he been doing that day? The two of them, he and the other rider, had been waiting on horse-back, staring out across a vast grey moor. Until that moment his companion's horse had been in front, for Axl remembered its tail flicking and swaying before him, and wondering how much of this action was due to the animal's reflexes, and how much to the fierce wind sweeping across the empty land.

Axl pushed these puzzling thoughts away as he struggled to his feet, then helped up his wife. Sir Gawain remained seated, apparently stuck to the foot of the oak, glowering at the new-comer. Then he said quietly to Axl: 'Sir, help me rise.'

It took both Axl and Beatrice, one on each arm, to bring the old knight to his feet, but when finally he straightened to his full height in his armour and pulled back his shoulders, he was an impressive sight. But Sir Gawain seemed content to stare moodily at the soldier, and eventually it was Axl who spoke.

'Why do you come upon us like this, sir, and we but simple wayfarers? Do you not remember how you quizzed us not an hour before by the waterfall?'

'I recall you well, uncle,' the grey-haired soldier said. 'Though when we last met a strange spell had fallen on us guarding the bridge that we forgot our very purpose being there. Only now, my post relieved and riding to our camp, it all suddenly returns to me. Then I thought of you, uncle, and your party slipping past, and turned my horse to hurry after you. Boy! Don't wander, I say! Remain beside your idiot brother!'

Edwin sulkily returned to Wistan's side and looked enquiringly at the warrior. The latter was still giggling quietly, a line of saliva spilling from one corner of his mouth. His eyes were roaming wildly, but Axl guessed the warrior was in fact taking careful measure of the distance to his own horse, and the proximity of his opponent, and in all probability coming to the same conclusions as Axl's.

'Sir Gawain,' Axl whispered. 'If there's to be trouble now, I beg you assist me to defend my good wife here.'

'I'll do so on my honour, sir. Rest assured of it.'

Axl nodded gratefully, but now the grey-haired soldier was dismounting. Again Axl found himself admiring the skilful way he did this, so that when finally he stood to face Wistan and the boy, he was once more at exactly the correct distance and angle to them; his sword, moreover, was carried so as not to exhaust his arm, while his horse shielded him from any unexpected assault from the rear.

'I'll tell you what slipped our mind when we last met, uncle. We'd just received word of a Saxon warrior left a nearby village bringing with him a wounded lad.' The soldier nodded at Edwin. 'A lad the age of that one there. Now, uncle, I don't know what you and the good woman here are to this matter. I seek only this Saxon and his lad. Speak frankly and no harm will visit you.'

'There's no warrior here, sir. And we've no quarrel with you, nor with Lord Brennus who I suppose to be your master.'

'Do you know what you speak of, uncle? Lend a mask to our enemies and you'll answer to us, whatever your years. Who are these you travel with, this mute and this lad?'

'As I said before, sir, they're given to us by debtors, in place of corn and tin. They'll work a year to pay their family's debt.'

'Sure you're not mistaken, uncle?'

'I know not whom you seek, sir, but it wouldn't be these poor Saxons. And while you spend your time with us, your enemies move freely elsewhere.'

The soldier gave this consideration – Axl's voice had carried unexpected authority – uncertainty entering his manner. 'Sir Gawain,' he asked. 'What do you know of these people?'

'They chanced on us as Horace and I rested here. I believe them to be simple creatures.'

The soldier once more scrutinised Wistan's features. 'A mute fool, is it?' He took two steps forward and raised the sword so the point was aimed at Wistan's throat. 'But he surely fears death like the rest of us.'

Axl saw that for the first time the soldier had made an error. He had come too close to his opponent, and although it would be a hideous risk, it was now conceivable for Wistan to move very suddenly and seize the arm holding the sword before it could strike. Wistan, however, went on giggling, then smiled foolishly at Edwin beside him. This latest action, however, seemed to arouse Sir Gawain's anger.

'They may be strangers to me only an hour ago, sir,' he boomed. 'But I'll not see them treated with rudeness.'

'This doesn't concern you, Sir Gawain. I would ask you to remain silent.'

'Do you dare speak to a knight of Arthur that way, sir?'

'Can it be possible,' the soldier said, completely ignoring Sir Gawain, 'this idiot here is a warrior disguised? With no weapon about him, it makes little difference. Mine's a blade sharp enough whichever he may be.'

'How dare he!' Sir Gawain muttered to himself.

The grey-haired soldier, perhaps suddenly realising his error, took two paces back till he was exactly where he had been before, and lowered the sword to waist height. 'Boy,' he said. 'Step forward to me.'

'He speaks only the Saxon tongue, sir, and a shy boy too,' Axl said.

'He needn't speak, uncle. Only raise his shirt and we'll know if he's the one left the village with the warrior. Boy, a step closer to me.'

As Edwin came nearer the soldier reached out with his free hand. A tussle ensued as Edwin tried to fight him off, but the shirt was soon dragged up the boy's torso, and Axl saw, a little way below the ribs, a swollen patch of skin encircled by tiny dots of dried blood. On either side of him, Beatrice and Gawain were now leaning forward to see better, but the soldier himself, reluctant to take his gaze off Wistan, did not glance at the wound for some time. When finally he did so, he was obliged to make a swift turn of his head, and at that very moment, Edwin produced a piercing, high-pitched noise – not a scream exactly, but something that reminded Axl of a forlorn fox. The soldier was for an instant distracted by it, and Edwin seized the chance to break from his grasp. Only then did Axl realise the noise was coming not from the boy, but from Wistan; and that in response, the warrior's mare, until then languidly munching the ground, had suddenly turned and was charging straight for them.

The soldier's own horse had made a panicked motion behind him, causing him further confusion, and by the time he had recovered, Wistan had gone clear of the sword's reach. The mare kept coming at daunting speed, and Wistan, feinting one way, then moving the other, produced another shrill call. The mare slowed to a canter, bringing herself between Wistan and his opponent, enabling the warrior, in an almost leisurely manner, to take up a position several strides from the oak. The mare turned again, moving smartly in pursuit of her master. Axl supposed Wistan's intention was to mount the animal as she came past, for the warrior was now waiting, both arms poised in the air. Axl even saw him reach towards the saddle just before the mare momentarily obscured him from view. But then the horse cantered on riderless towards the spot where so recently she had been enjoying the grass. Wistan had remained standing quite still, but now with a sword in his hand.

A small exclamation escaped Beatrice, and Axl, placing an arm around her, drew her closer. On his other side, Gawain made a grunting noise which seemed to signify his appreciation of Wistan's manoeuvre. The old knight had placed a foot up on one of the raised roots of the oak, and was watching with keen interest, a hand on his knee.

The grey-haired soldier's back was now turned to them: in this, of course, he had had little choice, for he had now to face Wistan. Axl was surprised to see that this soldier, so controlled and expert only a moment ago, had become quite disorientated. He was looking towards his horse – which had trotted some way away in panic – as though for reassurance, then raised his sword, the tip just above the level of his shoulder, gripping tightly with both hands. This posture, Axl knew, was premature, and would only exhaust the arm muscles. Wistan, in contrast, looked calm, almost nonchalant, just as he had done the previous night when they had first glimpsed him setting off out of the village. He came slowly towards the soldier, stopping a few steps before him, sword held low in just one hand.

'Sir Gawain,' the soldier said, a new note in his voice, 'I hear you move at my back. Do you stand with me against this foe?'

'I stand here to protect this good couple, sir. Otherwise, this dispute is not my concern, as you so lately reported. This warrior may be your foe, but he isn't yet mine.'

'This fellow's a Saxon warrior, Sir Gawain, and here to do us mischief. Help me face him, for though I'm keen to do my duty, if this is the man we seek he's a fearful fellow by all accounts.'

'What reason have I to take arms against a man simply for being a stranger? It's you, sir, came into this tranquil place with your rude manners.'

There was silence for a while. Then the soldier said to Wistan: 'Do you stay mute, sir? Or will you reveal yourself now we face one another!'

'I'm Wistan, sir, a warrior from the east visiting this country. It seems your Lord Brennus would have me hurt, though for what reason I know not since I travel in peace on an errand for my king. And it's my belief you mean to harm that innocent boy, and seeing this I must now frustrate you.'

'Sir Gawain,' the soldier cried, 'will you come to the aid of a fellow Briton, I ask you once again. If this is Wistan, it's said more than fifty sea raiders have fallen by his hand alone.'

'If fifty fierce raiders fell to him, what difference can one old and weary knight make to the outcome now, sir?'

'I beg you, do not jest, Sir Gawain. This is a wild fellow, and he'll strike at any moment. I see it in his eye. He's here to do us all mischief, I tell you.'

'Name the mischief I bring,' Wistan said, 'travelling peace-fully through your country, a single sword in my pack to defend against wild creatures and bandits. If you can name my crime, do so now, for I'd hear the charge before I strike you.'

'I'm ignorant of the nature of your mischief, sir, but have faith enough in Lord Brennus's desire to be free of you.'

'No charge to name, then, yet you hurry here to slay me.'

'Sir Gawain, I beg you help me! Fierce as he is, the two of us with careful strategy might overcome him.'

'Sir, let me remind you, I'm a knight of Arthur, no foot sol-dier of your Lord Brennus. I don't take up arms against strangers on rumour or for their foreign blood. And it seems to me you're unable to give good cause for taking against him.'

'You force me to speak then, sir, though these are confidences to which a man of my humble rank has no right, even if Lord Brennus himself let me hear them. This man is come to this country on a mission to slay the dragon Querig. This is what brings him here!'

'Slay Querig?' Sir Gawain sounded genuinely dumbfounded. He strode forward from the tree and stared at Wistan as if seeing him for the first time. 'Is this true, sir?'

'I've no wish to lie to a knight of Arthur, so let me declare it. Further to my duty reported earlier, I've been charged by my king to slay the she-dragon roams this country. But what objection could there be to such a task? A fierce dragon bringing danger to all alike. Tell me, soldier, why is it such a mission makes me your enemy?'

'Slay Querig?! You really mean to slay Querig?!' Sir Gawain was now shouting. 'But sir, this is a mission entrusted to *me*! Do you not know this? A mission entrusted to me by Arthur himself!'

'A dispute for some other time, Sir Gawain. Let me first attend to this soldier who would make an enemy of me and my friends when we would go by in peace.'

'Sir Gawain, if you'll not come to my aid, I fear this is my final hour! I implore you, sir, remember the affection Lord Brennus has for Arthur and his memory and take arms against this Saxon!'

'It is *my* duty to slay Querig, Master Wistan! Horace and I have laid careful plans to lure her out and we seek no assistance!'

'Lay down your sword, sir,' Wistan said to the soldier, 'and I may spare you yet. Otherwise end your life on this ground.'

The soldier hesitated, but then said: 'I see now I was foolish to suppose myself strong enough to take you alone, sir. I may be punished yet for my vanity. But I won't now lay down my sword like a coward.'

'By what right', Sir Gawain cried, 'does your king order you to come from another country and usurp the duties given to a knight of Arthur?'

'Forgive me, Sir Gawain, but it's many a year you've had to slay Querig, and small children have become grown men in the time. If I can do this country a service and rid it of this scourge, why be angry?'

'Why be angry, sir? You know not what you're about! You think it an easy matter to slay Querig? She's as wise as she's fierce! You'll only anger her with your foolishness, and this whole country will need suffer her wrath, where we've hardly heard a thing of her these past several years. It requires the most delicate handling, sir, or a calamity will befall the innocent right across this country! Why do you suppose Horace and I have so bided our time? One misstep will have grave consequences, sir!'

'Then help me, Sir Gawain,' the soldier shouted, now making no effort to hide his fear. 'Let's together put out this menace!'

Sir Gawain looked at the soldier with a puzzled air, as if he had forgotten for the moment who he was. Then he said in a calmer voice: 'I'll not aid you, sir. I'm no friend of your master, for I fear his dark motives. I fear too the harm you intend to these others here, who must be innocents in whatever intrigue enfolds us.'

'Sir Gawain, I hang here between life and death as a fly caught in a web. I make my last appeal to you, and though I don't understand the full part of this matter, I beg you consider why he comes to our country if not to do us mischief!'

'He gives good account of his errand here, sir, and though he angers me with his careless plans, it's hardly reason to join you in arms against him.'

'Fight now, soldier,' Wistan said, his tone almost conciliatory. 'Fight and be done with it.'

'Will it do harm, Master Wistan,' Beatrice said suddenly, 'to let this soldier surrender his sword and ride away? He spoke kindly to me before on the bridge and he's perhaps not a bad man.'

'If I do as you ask, Mistress Beatrice, he'll take news back of us and surely return before long with thirty or more soldiers.

There'll be little mercy shown then. And mark you, he means sinister harm to the boy.'

'Perhaps he would willingly swear an oath not to betray us.'

'Your kindness touches me, mistress,' the grey-haired soldier intervened, never taking his eyes off Wistan. 'But I'm no scoundrel and won't take rude advantage of it. What the Saxon says is true. Spare me and I'll do just as he says, for duty allows me no other course. Yet I thank you for your gentle words, and if these are to be my last moments, then I'll leave this world a little more peacefully for them.'

'What's more, sir,' Beatrice said, 'I've not forgotten your earlier request, concerning your mother and father. You made it then in jest, I know, and it's not likely we'll encounter them. But if ever we do so, they'll know of how you waited with longing to see them again.'

'I thank you once more, mistress. But this is no time for me to soften my heart with such thoughts. Fortune may favour me yet in this contest, no matter this man's reputation, and then you may regret you ever wished me kindness.'

'Most likely so,' Beatrice said and sighed. 'Then Master Wistan, you must do your best for us. I'll look away, for I take no pleasure in slaughter. And I bid you tell young Master Edwin do the same, for I'm sure he'll only heed if you command it.'

'Pardon me, mistress,' Wistan said, 'but I would the boy witness all that unfolds, just as I was often made to do at his age. I know he'll not flinch or retch to witness the ways of warriors.' He now spoke several sentences in Saxon, and Edwin, who had been standing by himself a short way away, walked over to the tree and stood beside Axl and Beatrice. His eyes, watchful, seemed never to blink.

Axl could hear the grey-haired soldier's breathing, more audible now because the man was releasing a low growl with each
breath. When he charged forward he did so with his sword high
above his head in what seemed an unsophisticated, even suicidal
attack; but just before he reached Wistan, he abruptly altered his
trajectory, and feinted to his left, his sword lowered to his hip. The
grey-haired soldier, Axl understood with a twinge of pity, knowing he stood little chance should the combat mature, had wagered
everything on this one desperate ploy. But Wistan had anticipated
it, or perhaps it was that his instincts were enough. The Saxon
side-stepped neatly, and drew his own sword across the oncoming
man in a single simple movement. The soldier let out a sound such
as a bucket makes when, dropped into a well, it first strikes the
water; he then fell forward onto the ground. Sir Gawain muttered
a prayer, and Beatrice asked: 'Is it done now, Axl?'

'It's done, princess.'

Edwin was staring at the fallen man, his expression barely
changed from before. Following the boy's gaze, Axl saw that a
serpent, disturbed in the grass by the soldier's fall, was now sliding
out from under the body. Though dark, the creature was mottled
with yellows and whites, and as it revealed more of itself, travelling swiftly across the ground, Axl caught the powerful odour
of a man's insides. He instinctively stepped to one side, moving
Beatrice with him, in case the creature should come searching for
their feet. Still it kept coming their way, parting in two around
a clump of thistle, as a stream might part around a rock, before
becoming one again and continuing ever closer.

'Come away, princess,' Axl said, leading her. 'It's done, and it's
as well. This man meant us harm, though the reason's still not
clear.'

'Let me enlighten you as far as I can, Master Axl,' Wistan said. He had been cleaning his sword on the ground, but now rose and came towards them. 'It's true our Saxon kin in this country live in good harmony with your people. But we've reports at home of Lord Brennus's ambitions to conquer this land for himself and make war on all Saxons now living on it.'

'I hear the same reports, sir,' Sir Gawain said. 'It was another reason I wouldn't side with this wretch now gutted like a trout. I fear this Lord Brennus is one who would undo the great peace won by Arthur.'

'We at home hear more, sir,' said Wistan. 'That Brennus entertains in his castle a dangerous guest. A Norseman said to possess the wisdom to tame dragons. It's my king's fear Lord Brennus means to capture Querig to fight in the ranks of his army. This she-dragon would make a fierce soldier indeed, and Brennus would then rightly harbour ambition. It's for this I'm sent to destroy the dragon before her savagery turns on all who oppose Lord Brennus. Sir Gawain, you look aghast, but I speak sincerely.'

'If I'm aghast, sir, it's because there's a sound ring to your words. When I was a young man, I once faced a dragon in an opposing army, and a fearful thing it was. My comrades, hungry for victory the moment before, froze for fear at the sight, and this a creature not half the equal of Querig in might or cunning. If Querig is made a servant of Lord Brennus, it will surely tempt new wars. Yet it's my hope she's too wild to be tamed by any man.' He paused, looked towards the fallen soldier and shook his head.

Wistan strode over to where Edwin was standing, and grasping the boy by the arm, began gently to lead him towards the corpse. Then for a little while the two of them stood side by side over the soldier, Wistan talking quietly, pointing occasionally, and looking into Edwin's face to check the response. At one stage, Axl saw Wistan's finger trace a smooth line through the air, as perhaps he explained to the boy the journey made by his blade. All the while, Edwin went on gazing blankly at the fallen man.

Sir Gawain, appearing now at Axl's side, said: 'It's a great sadness this tranquil spot, surely a gift from God to all weary travellers, is now polluted by blood. Let's bury this man quickly, before anyone else comes this way, and I'll take his horse to Lord Brennus's camp, together with news of how I came upon him attacked by bandits, and where his friends may find his grave. Meanwhile, sir' – he turned to address Wistan – 'I urge you return straight away east. Think no more of Querig, for you can be assured Horace and I, hearing all we have today, will redouble our efforts to slay her. Now come, friends, let's put this man in the earth that he may return to his maker peacefully.'

PART II

Chapter Six

For all his tiredness, Axl was finding sleep elusive. The monks had provided them with a room on the upper storey, and while it was a relief not to have to contend with the cold seeping up from the soil, he had never slept easily above ground. Even when sheltering in barns or stables, he had often climbed ladders to a restless night troubled by the cavernous space beneath him. Or perhaps his restlessness tonight had to do with the presence of the birds in the dark above. They were now largely silent, but every so often would come a small rustle, or a beating of wings, and he would feel the urge to fling his arms over Beatrice's sleeping form to protect her from the foul feathers drifting down through the air.

The birds had been there when they had first entered the chamber earlier in the day. And had he not felt, even then, something malevolent in the way these crows, blackbirds, woodpigeons looked down on them from the rafters? Or was it just that his memory had become coloured by subsequent events?

Or perhaps the sleeplessness was on account of the sounds, even now echoing across the monastery grounds, of Wistan chopping firewood. The noise had not prevented Beatrice from sinking easily into sleep, and on the other side of the room, beyond the dark shape he knew to be the table on which they had earlier eaten, Edwin had settled to a gentle snoring. But Wistan, as far as Axl knew, had not slept at all. The warrior had remained sitting over in the far corner, waiting for the last monk to leave the courtyard below, then gone out into the night. And now here he was again – and despite Father Jonus's warning – cutting more firewood.

The monks had taken some time to disperse after emerging from their meeting. Several times Axl had come close to sleep only to be brought to the surface again by voices below. Sometimes they were four or five, always lowered, often filled with anger or fear. There had been no voices now for some time, and yet as he drifted again towards slumber, Axl could not shake the feeling there were still monks below their window, not just a few, but dozens of robed figures, standing silently under the moonlight, listening to Wistan's blows resounding across the grounds.

Earlier, with the afternoon sun filling the chamber, Axl had looked out of the window to see what appeared to be the entire community – more than forty monks – waiting in clusters all around the courtyard. There was a furtive mood among them, as if they were keen their words were not overheard even by those in their own ranks, and Axl could see hostile glances exchanged. Their habits were all of the same brown cloth, sometimes missing a hood or a sleeve. They seemed anxious to go into the large stone building opposite, but there had been a delay and their impatience was palpable.

Axl had been gazing down on the courtyard for several moments when a noise made him lean further out of the window and look directly beneath him. He had seen then the outer wall of the building, its pale stone revealing yellow hues in the sun, and the staircase cut into it rising from the ground towards him. Midway up these stairs was a monk – Axl could see the top of his head – holding a tray laden with food and a jug of milk. The man was pausing to rebalance the tray, and Axl watched the manoeuvre with alarm, knowing how these steps were worn unevenly, and that with no rail on the outside, one had always to keep pressed to the wall to be sure not to plunge down onto the hard cobbles. On top of it all, the monk now ascending appeared to have a limp, yet he kept coming, slowly and steadily.

Axl went to the door to relieve the man of the tray, but the monk – Father Brian, as they were soon to learn he was called – insisted on carrying it to the table himself, saying: 'You are our guests, so let me serve you as such.'

Wistan and the boy had left by then, and perhaps the sound of their woodcutting was already ringing through the air. So it had been just he and Beatrice who had sat down, side by side, at the wooden table and devoured gratefully the bread, fruit and milk. As they did so, Father Brian had chatted happily, sometimes dreamily, about past visitors, the fish to be caught in nearby streams, a stray dog that had lived with them until its death the previous winter. Sometimes Father Brian, an elderly but sprightly man, got up from the table and shuffled about the room dragging about his bad leg, talking all the while, every now and then going to the window to check on his colleagues below.

Meanwhile, above their heads, the birds had been criss-crossing the underside of the roof, their feathers occasionally drifting down to blemish the surface of the milk. Axl had been tempted to chase off these birds, but had refrained in case the monks regarded them with affection. He was taken aback then when rapid footsteps came up the stairs outside, and a large monk with a dark beard and a flushed face burst into the room.

'Demons! Demons!' he shouted, glaring up at the rafters. 'I'll see them soak in blood!'

The newcomer was carrying a straw bag, and he now reached into it, brought out a stone and hurled it up at the birds. 'Demons! Foul demons, demons, demons!'

As the first stone ricocheted down to the ground, he threw a second and then a third. The stones were landing away from the table, but Beatrice had covered her head with both arms, and Axl, rising, began to move towards the bearded man. But Father Brian had reached him first, and clutching both the man's arms, said:

'Brother Irasmus, I beg you! Stop this and calm yourself!'

The birds by now were screeching and flying in all directions, and the bearded monk shouted over the commotion: 'I know them! I know them!'

'Calm yourself, brother!'

'Don't you stop me, father! They're agents of the devil!'

'They may yet be agents of God, Irasmus. We don't yet know.'

'I know them to be of the devil! Look at their eyes! How can they be of God and gaze at us with such eyes?'

'Irasmus, calm yourself. We have guests present.'

At these words, the bearded monk became aware of Axl and Beatrice. He stared angrily at them, then said to Father Brian: 'Why bring guests into the house at a time like this? Why do they come here?'

'They're just good people travelling by, brother, and we're happy to give them hospitality as is ever our custom.'

'Father Brian, you're a fool to tell strangers of our affairs! Look, they spy on us!'

'They spy on no one, nor do they have any interest in our problems, having plenty of their own, I don't doubt.'

Suddenly the bearded man drew out another stone and prepared to hurl it, but Father Brian managed to prevent him. 'Go back down, Irasmus, and let go this bag. Here, leave it with me. It won't do, carrying it everywhere the way you do.'

The bearded man shook off the older monk, and clutched his sack jealously to his chest. Father Brian, allowing Irasmus this small victory, ushered him to the doorway, and even as the latter turned to glare again at the roof, pushed him gently out onto the stairway.

'Go back down, Irasmus. They miss you down there. Go back down and take care you don't fall.'

When the man had finally gone, Father Brian came back into the room, waving his hand at the feathers floating in the air.

'My apologies to you both. He's a good man, but this way of life no longer suits him. Please be seated again and finish your meal in peace.'

'And yet, father,' Beatrice said, 'that fellow may be right when he says we intrude on you at an uneasy time. We've no desire to increase your burdens here, and if you'll only let us quickly consult Father Jonus, whose wisdom's well known, we'll be on our way. Is there word yet if we might see him?'

Father Brian shook his head. 'It's as I told you earlier, mistress. Jonus has been unwell, and the abbot's given strict orders no one will disturb him other than with permission given by the abbot himself. Knowing of your desire to meet with Jonus, and the pains you took to come here, I've been trying since your arrival to attract the abbot's ear. Yet as you see, you come at a busy time, and now there's a visitor of some importance arrived for the abbot, delaying our conference further. The abbot's even now gone back to his study to talk with the visitor while the rest of us wait for him.'

Beatrice had been standing at the window to watch the bearded monk's departure down the stone steps, and she now pointed, saying: 'Good father, isn't that the abbot returning now?'

Axl, coming to her side, saw a gaunt figure striding with authority into the centre of the courtyard. The monks, breaking from their conversations, were all moving towards him.

'Ah yes, there's the abbot returned. Now finish your meal in peace. And regarding Jonus, be patient, for I fear I'll not be able to bring you the abbot's decision till after this conference is over. Yet I'll not forget, I promise, and will petition well for you.'

It was surely the case that then, as now, the warrior's axe blows had been ringing across the courtyard. In fact, Axl could distinctly recall asking himself, as he watched the monks filing into the building opposite, if he was hearing one woodcutter or two; for a second blow would follow so close behind the first it was hard to tell if it was a real sound or an echo. Thinking about it now, lying in the dark, Axl was sure Edwin had been chopping alongside Wistan, matching the warrior blow for blow. In all likelihood the boy was already an expert woodcutter. Earlier that day, before they had come to this monastery, he had astonished them by digging so rapidly with two flat stones he had happened to find nearby.

Axl by then had ceased to dig, having been persuaded by the warrior to preserve his strength for the climb to the monastery. So he had stood beside the oozing body of the soldier, guarding it from the birds gathering in the branches. Wistan, Axl recalled, had been using the dead man's sword to dig the grave, remarking that he was reluctant to blunt his own on such a task. Sir Gawain, however, had said: 'This soldier died honourably, no matter the schemes of his master, and a knight's sword is put to good use giving him a grave.' Both men, though, had paused to watch in wonder the progress being made by Edwin with his rudimentary tools. Then, as they resumed their work, Wistan had said:

'I fear, Sir Gawain, Lord Brennus will not believe such a story.'

'He'll believe it well enough, sir,' Gawain had replied, continuing to dig. 'There's a coolness between us, but he has me for an honest fool without the wit to invent devious tales. I may tell them how the soldier spoke of bandits even as he bled to death in my arms. Some will think it a grave sin to tell such a lie, yet I know God will look mercifully on it, for isn't it to stop further bloodshed? I'll make Brennus believe me, sir. Even so, you remain in danger and have good reason to hurry home.'

'I'll do so without delay, Sir Gawain, as soon as my errand here's finished. If my mare's foot isn't soon healed, I may even trade her for another, for that's a long ride to the fens. Yet I'll be sorry for she's a rare horse.'

'A rare one indeed! My Horace, alas, no longer possesses such agility, yet he's come to me in many an hour of need, as your mare came to you just now. A rare horse, and one you'll be sad to lose. Even so, speed is crucial, so be on your way and never mind your errand. Horace and I will see to the she-dragon, so you've no cause to think further of her. In any case, now I've had time to dwell on it, I see Lord Brennus can never succeed in recruiting Querig into his army. She's the most wild and untameable of creatures and will as quickly spew fire on her own ranks as on Brennus's foes. The whole idea's outlandish, sir. Think no more of it and hurry home before your enemies corner you.' Then when Wistan continued to dig without responding, Sir Gawain asked: 'Do I have your word on it, Master Wistan?'

'On what, Sir Gawain?'

'That you'll think no more of the she-dragon and hurry home.'

'You seem keen to hear me say so.'

'I think not just of your safety, sir, but of those on whom Querig will turn should you arouse her. And what of these companions who travel with you?'

'It's true, the safety of these friends gives me concern. I'll go beside them as far as the monastery, for I can hardly leave them defenceless on these wild roads. Thereafter, it may be best we part.'

'So after the monastery, you'll make your way home.'

'I'll set off home when I'm ready, sir knight.'

The smell rising from the dead man's innards had obliged Axl to take a few steps away, and when he did so, he found he had a better view of Sir Gawain. The knight was now waist deep in the ground, and the perspiration had drenched his forehead, so perhaps that was why his expression had lost its customary benevolence. He was regarding Wistan with intense hostility, while the latter, oblivious, carried on digging.

Beatrice had been upset by the soldier's death. As the grave had grown deeper, she had walked slowly back to the great oak and seated herself again in its shade, her head bowed. Axl had wanted to go and sit with her, and but for the gathering crows, would have done so. Now, lying in the darkness, he too began to feel a sadness for the slain man. He remembered the soldier's courtesy towards them on the little bridge, and the gentle way he had spoken to Beatrice. Axl recalled too the precise way he had positioned his horse when first entering the clearing. Something in the way he had done so had tugged on his memory at the time, and now, in the night's stillness, Axl remembered the rise and fall of moorland, the brooding sky, and the flock of sheep coming through the heather.

He had been on horseback, and in front of him was mounted his companion, a man called Harvey, the smell of whose heavy body overpowered that of their horses. They had halted in the midst of the windswept wilderness because they had spotted movement in the distance, and once it was clear it signified no threat, Axl had stretched his arms – they had been riding a long time – and watched the tail of Harvey's horse swinging from side to side as though to prevent the flies settling on its rear. Although his companion's face was hidden from him at that moment, the shape of Harvey's back, indeed his whole posture, announced the malevolence aroused by the sight of the approaching party. Gazing past Harvey, Axl could now make out the dark dots that were the sheep's faces, and moving among them four men – one on a donkey, the others on foot. There appeared to be no dogs. The shepherds, Axl supposed, must long ago have spotted them – two riders clearly outlined against the sky – but if they had felt apprehension there was no sign of it in their slow, relentless trudge forwards. There was, in any case, just the one long path across the moor, and Axl supposed the shepherds could avoid them only by turning back.

As the group came nearer, he could see that all four men, though far from old, were sickly and thin. This observation brought a sinking to his heart, for he knew the men's condition would only further provoke his companion's savagery. Axl waited until the party was almost within hailing distance, then nudged forward his horse, positioning it carefully to the side of Harvey where he knew the shepherds, and most of the flock, were bound to pass. He made sure to keep his own horse a nose behind, to allow his companion the illusion of seniority. Yet Axl was now in a position that would shield the shepherds from any sudden assault Harvey might launch with his whip, or with the club hooked to his saddle. All the while, the manoeuvre would have suggested on the surface only camaraderie, and in any case, Harvey did not possess the subtlety of mind even to suspect its real purpose. Indeed, Axl recalled his companion nodding absent-mindedly as he drew up, before turning back to stare moodily across the moor.

Axl had been especially anxious on behalf of the approaching shepherds because of something that had occurred a few days earlier in a Saxon village. It had been a sunny morning, and on that occasion Axl had been as startled as any of the villagers. Without warning, Harvey had heeled his horse forward and started to rain down blows on the people waiting to draw water from the well. Had Harvey used his whip or his club on that occasion? Axl had tried to recall this detail that day on the moor. If Harvey chose to assault the passing shepherds with his whip, the reach would be greater and require less leverage of the arm; he might even dare to swing it over the head of Axl's horse. If, however, he chose his club, with Axl positioned as he now was, Harvey would be obliged to push his horse beyond Axl's and rotate partially before attacking. Such a manoeuvre would appear too deliberate for his companion: Harvey was the type that liked his savagery to look impulsive and effortless.

He could not remember now if his careful actions had saved the shepherds. He had a vague recollection of sheep drifting innocently past them, but his memory of the shepherds themselves had become confusingly bound up with that attack on the villagers by the well. What had brought the pair of them to that village that morning? Axl remembered the cries of outrage, children crying, the looks of hatred, and his own fury, not so much at Harvey himself, but at those who had handicapped him with such a companion. Their mission, if accomplished, would surely be an achievement unique and new, one so supreme God himself would judge it a moment when men came a step closer to him. Yet how could Axl hope to do anything tethered to such a brute?

The grey-haired soldier came back into his thoughts, and the little half-gesture he had made on the bridge. As his stocky colleague had shouted and pulled on Wistan's hair, the grey-haired man had started to raise his arm, his fingers almost in a pointing gesture, a reprimand all but escaping his lips. Then he had let his arm fall. Axl had understood exactly what the grey-haired man had experienced during those moments. The soldier had then spoken with particular gentleness to Beatrice, and Axl had been grateful to him. He recalled Beatrice's expression as she had stood before the bridge, changing from grave and guarded to the softly smiling one so dear to him. The picture now seized his heart, and at the same time made him fearful. A stranger – a potentially dangerous one at that – had but to say a few kindly words and there she was, ready to trust the world again. The thought troubled him and he felt the urge to run his hand gently over the shoulder now beside him. But had she not always been thus? Was it not part of what made her so precious to him? And had she not survived these many years with no great harm coming to her?

'It can't be rosemary, sir,' he remembered Beatrice saying to him, her voice tense with anxiety. He was crouching down, one knee pressed into the ground, for it was a fine day and the soil dry. Beatrice must have been standing behind him, for he could remember her shadow on the forest floor before him as he parted the undergrowth with his hands. 'It can't be rosemary, sir. Whoever saw rosemary with such yellow flowers on it?'

'Then I have its name wrong, maiden,' Axl had said. 'But I

know for certain it's one commonly seen, and not one to bring you mischief.'

'But are you really one who knows his plants, sir? My mother taught me everything grows wild in this country, yet what's before us now is strange to me.'

'Then it's likely something foreign to these parts lately arrived. Why distress yourself so, maiden?'

'I distress myself, sir, because it's likely this is a weed I'm brought up to fear.'

'Why fear a weed except that it's poisonous, and then all's needed is not to touch it. Yet there you were, reaching down with your hands, and now getting me to do the same!'

'Oh, it's not poisonous, sir! At least not in the way you mean. Yet my mother once described closely a plant and warned that to see it in the heather was bad luck for any young girl.'

'What sort of bad luck, maiden?'

'I'm not bold enough to tell you, sir.'

But even as she said this, the young woman – for that was what Beatrice was that day – had crouched down beside him so that their elbows touched for a brief moment, and smiled trustingly into his gaze.

'If it's such bad luck to see it,' Axl had said, 'what kindness is it to bring me from the road just to place my gaze on it?'

'Oh, it's not bad luck for *you*, sir! Only for unmarried girls. There's another plant entirely brings bad luck to men like yourself.'

'You'd better tell me what this other looks like, so I may dread it as you do this one.'

'You may enjoy mocking me, sir. Yet one day you'll take a tumble and find the weed next to your nose. You'll see then if it's a laughing matter or not.'

He could remember now the feel of the heather as he had passed his hand through it, the wind in the branches above, and the presence of the young woman beside him. Could that have been the first time they had conversed? Surely they had at least known one another by sight; surely it was inconceivable even Beatrice would have been so trusting of a total stranger.

The woodcutting noises, which had paused for a while, now started up again, and it occurred to Axl the warrior might remain outside the entire night. Wistan appeared calm and thoughtful, even in combat, yet it was possible the tensions of the day and previous night had mounted on his nerves, and he needed to work them off in this way. Even so, his behaviour was odd. Father Jonus had specifically warned against further woodcutting, yet here he was, back at it again and with night well fallen. Earlier, when they had first arrived, it had seemed a simple courtesy on the warrior's part. And at that point, as Axl had discovered, Wistan had had his own reasons for cutting wood.

'The woodshed is well positioned,' the warrior had explained. 'The boy and I were able to keep good watch on the comings and goings while we worked. Even better, when we delivered the wood where it was needed, we roamed at will to inspect the surroundings, even if a few doors stayed barred to us.'

The two of them had been talking up by the high monastery wall overlooking the surrounding forest. The monks had long gone into their meeting by then, and a hush had fallen over the grounds. Several moments before, with Beatrice dozing in the chamber, Axl had wandered out under the late afternoon sun, and climbed the worn stone steps to where Wistan was looking down on the dense foliage below.

'But why go to such trouble, Master Wistan?' Axl had asked.

'Can it be you're suspicious of these good monks here?'

The warrior, a hand raised to shield his eyes, said: 'When we were climbing that path earlier, I wanted nothing but to curl in a corner adrift in my dreams. Yet now we're here, I can't keep away the feeling this place holds dangers for us.'

'It must be weariness makes your suspicions keen, Master Wistan. What can trouble you here?'

'Nothing yet I can point to with conviction. But consider this. When I returned to the stables earlier to see all was well with the mare, I heard sounds coming from the stall behind. I mean, sir, this other stall was separated by a wall, but I could hear another horse beyond, though no horse was there when we first arrived and I led in the mare. Then when I walked to the other side, I found there the stable door shut and a great lock hanging on it only a key would release.'

'There may be many innocent explanations, Master Wistan. The horse may have been at pasture and lately brought in.'

'I spoke to a monk on that very point, and learnt they keep no horses here from a wish not to ease their burdens unduly. It would seem since our own arrival some other visitor has come, and one anxious to keep his presence hidden.'

'Now you mention it, Master Wistan, I recall Father Brian made mention of an important visitor arriving for the abbot, and their great conference being delayed on account of his coming. We know nothing of what goes on here, and in all likelihood, none of it touches us.'

Wistan nodded thoughtfully. 'Perhaps you're right, Master Axl. A little sleep would calm my suspicions. Even so, I sent the boy to wander further this place, supposing he'd be excused a natural curiosity more readily than a grown man. Not long ago he returned to report he'd heard a groaning from those quarters over there' – Wistan turned and pointed – 'as of a man in pain. Creeping indoors after this sound, Master Edwin saw marks of blood both old and fresh outside a closed chamber.'

'Curious certainly. Yet there'd be no mystery in a monk meeting some unfortunate accident, perhaps tripping on these very steps.'

'I concede, sir, I've no hard reason to suppose anything amiss here. Perhaps it's a warrior's instinct makes me wish my sword was in my belt and I was done pretending to be a farmboy. Or maybe my fears derive simply from what these walls whisper to me of days gone by.'

'What can you mean, sir?'

'Only that not long ago, this place was surely no monastery, but a hillfort, and one well made to fight off foes. You recall the exhausting road we climbed? How the path turned back and forth as though eager to drain our strength? Look down there now, sir, see the battlements running above those same paths. It's from there the defenders once showered their guests from above with arrows, rocks, boiling water. It would have been a feat merely to reach the gate.'

'I see it. It can't have been an easy climb.'

'Further, Master Axl, I'd wager this fort was once in Saxon hands, for I see about it many signs of my kin perhaps invisible to you. Look there' – Wistan pointed down to a cobbled yard below hemmed in by walls – 'I fancy just there stood a second gate, much stronger than the first, yet hidden to invaders climbing the road. They saw only the first and strained to storm it, but that gate would have been what we Saxons call a watergate, after those barriers that control a river's flow. Through this watergate would be let past, quite deliberately, a measured number of the enemy. Then the watergate would close on those following. Now those isolated between the two gates, in that space just there, would find themselves outnumbered, and once again, attacked from above. They would be slaughtered before the next group let through. You see how it worked, sir. This is today a place of peace and prayer, yet you needn't gaze so deep to find blood and terror.'

'You read it well, Master Wistan, and I shudder at what you show me.'

'I'd wager too there were Saxon families here, fled from far and wide seeking protection in this fort. Women, children, wounded, old, sick. See over there, the yard where the monks gathered earlier. All but the weakest would have come out and stood there, all the better to witness the invaders squeal like trapped mice between the two gates.'

'That I can't believe, sir. They would surely have hidden themselves below and prayed for deliverance.'

'Only the most cowardly of them. Most would have stood there in that yard, or even come up here where we now stand, happy to risk an arrow or spear to enjoy the agonies below.'

Axl shook his head. 'Surely the sort of people you speak of would take no pleasure in bloodshed, even of the enemy.'

'On the contrary, sir. I speak of people at the end of a brutal road, having seen their children and kin mutilated and ravished. They've reached this, their sanctuary, only after long torment, death chasing at their heels. And now comes an invading army of overwhelming size. The fort may hold several days, perhaps even a week or two. But they know in the end they will face their own slaughter. They know the infants they circle in their arms will before long be bloodied toys kicked about these cobbles.

They know because they've seen it already, from whence they fled. They've seen the enemy burn and cut, take turns to rape young girls even as they lie dying of their wounds. They know this is to come, and so must cherish the earlier days of the siege, when the enemy first pay the price for what they will later do. In other words, Master Axl, it's vengeance to be relished *in advance* by those not able to take it in its proper place. That's why I say, sir, my Saxon cousins would have stood here to cheer and clap, and the more cruel the death, the more merry they would have been.'

'I won't believe it, sir. How is it possible to hate so deeply for deeds not yet done? The good people who once took shelter here would have kept alive their hopes to the end, and surely watched all suffering, of friend and foe, with pity and horror.'

'You're much the senior in years, Master Axl, but in matters of blood, it may be I'm the elder and you the youth. I've seen dark hatred as bottomless as the sea on the faces of old women and tender children, and some days felt such hatred myself.'

'I won't have it, sir, and besides, we talk of a barbarous past hopefully gone for ever. Our argument need never be put to the test, thank God.'

The warrior looked strangely at Axl. He appeared about to say something, then to change his mind. Then he turned to survey the stone buildings behind them saying: 'Wandering these grounds earlier, my arms heavy with firewood, I spotted at every turn fascinating traces of that past. The fact is, sir, even with the second gate breached, this fort would have held many more traps for the enemy, some devilishly cunning. The monks here hardly know what they pass each day. But enough of this. While we share this quiet moment, let me ask your forgiveness, Master Axl, for the discomfort I caused you earlier. I refer to my questioning that good knight about you.'

'Think no more of it, sir. There's no offence, even if you did surprise me, and my wife also. You mistook me for another, an easy error.'

'I thank you for your understanding. I took you for one whose face I can never forget, even though I was a small boy when I saw it last.'

'In the west country then.'

'That's right, sir, in the time before I was taken. The man I speak of was no warrior, yet wore a sword and rode a fine stallion. He came often to our village, and to us boys who knew only farmers and boatmen, was a thing of wonder.'

'Yes. I see how he might be.'

'I recall we followed him all about the village, though always at a shy distance. Some days he'd move with urgency, talking with elders or calling a crowd to gather in the square. Other days he'd wander at leisure, talking to one and all as if to pass the day. He knew little of our tongue, but our village being on the river, the boats coming and going, many spoke his language, so he never lacked for companions. He'd sometimes turn to us with a smile, but we being young would scatter and hide.'

'And was it in this village you learnt our tongue so well?'

'No, that came later. When I was taken.'

'Taken, Master Wistan?'

'I was taken from that village by soldiers and trained from a tender age to be the warrior I am today. It was Britons took me, so I soon learnt to speak and fight in their manner. It's long ago and things take strange shapes in the mind. When I first saw you today in that village, perhaps a trick of the morning light, I felt

I was that boy again, shyly peeking at that great man with his flowing cloak, moving through our village like a lion amongst pigs and cows. I fancy it was a small corner of your smile, or something about your way of greeting a stranger, head bowed a little. Yet now I see I was mistaken, since you could not have been that man. No more of this. How is your good wife, sir? Not exhausted, I hope?'

'She's recovered her breath well, I thank you for asking, though I've told her to rest further just now. We're forced, in any case, to wait till the monks return from their meeting and the abbot gives permission to visit the wise physician Jonus.'

'A resolute lady, sir. I admired how she made her way here giving no complaint. Ah, here's the boy back again.'

'See how he holds his injury, Master Wistan. We must take him also to Father Jonus.'

Wistan seemed not to hear this. Leaving the wall, he went down the little steps to meet Edwin, and for a few moments the two conferred in low voices, heads close together. The boy's manner was animated, and the warrior listened with a frown, nodding occasionally. As Axl came down the steps to their level, Wistan said quietly:

'Master Edwin reports a curious discovery we may do well to see with our own eyes. Let's follow him, but walk as we've no clear purpose, in case that old monk there is left on purpose to spy on us.'

Indeed, a solitary monk was sweeping the courtyard and as they came closer, Axl noticed he was mouthing words silently to himself, lost in his world. He barely glanced their way as Edwin led them across the courtyard and into a gap between two buildings. They emerged where thin grass covered uneven sloping ground, and a row of withered trees, hardly taller than a man, marked a path leading away from the monastery. As they followed Edwin under a setting sky, Wistan said softly:

'I'm much taken by this boy. Master Axl, we may yet revise our plan to leave him at your son's village. It would suit me well to keep him by me a while longer.'

'I'm troubled to hear you say so, sir.'

'Why so? He hardly longs for a life feeding pigs and digging the cold soil.'

'Yet what will become of him at your side?'

'Once my mission's complete, I'll take him back to the fens.'

'And what will you have him do there, sir? Fight Norsemen all his days?'

'You frown, sir, but the boy has an unusual temperament. He'll make a fine warrior. But hush, let's see what he has for us.'

They had come to where three wooden shacks stood at the side of the lane, in such disrepair that each appeared to be held up by its neighbour. The wet ground was rutted with wheeltracks, and Edwin paused to point these out. Then he led them into the furthest of the three shacks.

There was no door, and much of the roof was open to the sky. As they came in, several birds flew off in furious commotion, and Axl saw, in the gloomy space vacated, a crudely made cart – perhaps the work of the monks themselves – its two wheels sunk into the mud. What arrested the attention was a large cage mounted on its carriage, and coming closer, Axl noticed that though the cage was itself iron, a thick wooden pillar ran down its spine, fixing it firmly to the boards underneath. This same post was festooned with chains and manacles, and at head height, what appeared to be a blackened iron mask, though with no holes for the eyes, and only a small one for the mouth. The cart, and the area all around it, was covered with feathers and droppings. Edwin pulled open the cage door and proceeded to move it back and forth on its squeaking hinge. He was again speaking excited words, to which Wistan, throwing searching glances around the shed, returned the occasional nod.

'It's curious,' Axl said, 'these monks should have need of such an object as this. No doubt to aid some pious ritual.'

The warrior started to move around the cart, stepping carefully to avoid the stagnant puddles. 'I saw something like this once before,' he said. 'You may suppose this device intended to expose the man within it to the cruelty of the elements. Yet look, see how these bars stand far enough apart to allow my shoulder to pass through. And here, look, how these feathers stick to the iron in hardened blood. A man fastened here is offered thus to the mountain birds. Caught in these cuffs, he has no way to fight off the hungry beaks. This iron mask, though it may look frightful, is in fact a thing of mercy, for with it the eyes at least aren't feasted on.'

'There may yet be some more gentle purpose,' Axl said, but Edwin had started to talk again, and Wistan turned and looked out of the shed.

'The boy says he followed these tracks out to a spot nearby on the cliff's edge,' the warrior said, eventually. 'He says the ground's well rutted there, showing where this wagon has often stayed. In other words, the signs all support my guess, and I can see too this cart's been wheeled out just lately.'

'I don't know what it means, Master Wistan, but I admit I now begin to share your uneasiness. This object sends a chill through me and makes me want to return to my wife's side.'

'It's as well we do, sir. Let's stay no longer.'

But as they came out of the shack, Edwin, who again was leading, stopped abruptly. Looking past him into the evening gloom, Axl could see a robed figure in the tall grass a short distance from them.

'I'd say it's the monk lately sweeping the yard,' the warrior said to Axl.

'Does he see us?'

'I'd say he sees us and knows we see him. Yet he stands there still as a tree. Well, let's go to him.'

The monk was standing at a spot to the side of their path, the grass up to his knee. As they approached the man remained quite still, though the wind pulled at his robe and long white hair. He was thin, almost emaciated, and his protruding eyes stared at them without expression.

'You observe us, sir,' Wistan said, stopping, 'and you know what we've just discovered. So perhaps you'd tell us the purpose to which you monks put that device.'

Saying nothing, the monk pointed towards the monastery.

'It may be he's vowed to silence,' Axl said. 'Or else as mute as you lately pretended, Master Wistan.'

The monk came out of the grass and onto the path. His strange eyes fixed each of them in turn, then he pointed again towards the monastery and set off. They followed him, just a short distance behind, the monk continually glancing back at them over his shoulder.

The monastery buildings were now dark shapes against the setting sky. As they drew closer, the monk paused, moved his forefinger over his lips, then continued at a more cautious pace. He seemed anxious they remain unseen, and to avoid the central courtyard. He took them down narrow passageways behind buildings where the earth was pitted or sloped severely. Once, as they went with heads bowed along a wall, there came from the very windows above sounds from the monks' conference. One voice was shouting over a hubbub, then a second voice – perhaps that of the abbot – called for order. But there was no time to loiter, and soon they were gathered at an archway through which could be seen the main courtyard. The monk now indicated with urgent signs that they were to proceed as quickly and quietly as possible.

As it was they were not obliged to cross the courtyard, where torches were now burning, but only to skirt one corner under the shadows of a colonnade. When the monk halted again, Axl whispered to him:

'Good sir, since your intention must be to take us somewhere, I'd ask you to let me go fetch my wife, for I'm uneasy leaving her alone.'

The monk, who had turned immediately to fix Axl in a stare, shook his head and pointed into the semi-dark. Only then did Axl spot Beatrice standing in a doorway further down the cloister. Relieved, he gave a wave, and as the party moved towards her, there came from behind them a surge of angry voices from the monks' meeting.

'How is it with you, princess?' he asked, reaching to take her outstretched hands.

'Peacefully taking my rest, Axl, when this silent monk appeared before me, the way I took him for a phantom. But he's keen to lead us somewhere and we'd best follow.'

The monk repeated his gesture for silence, then beckoning, pushed past Beatrice across the threshold where she had been waiting.

The corridors now became as tunnel-like as those of their war-ren at home, and the lamps flickering in the little alcoves hardly dispelled the darkness. Axl, with Beatrice holding his arm, kept a hand held out before him. For a moment they were back in the open air, crossing a muddy yard between ploughed allot-ments, then into another low stone building. Here the corridor was wider and lit by larger flames, and the monk seemed finally to relax. Recovering his breath, he looked them over once more, then signalling for them to wait, vanished under an arch. After a little time, the monk appeared again and ushered them forward. As he did so, a frail voice from within said: 'Come in, guests. A poor chamber this to receive you, but you're welcome.'

* * *

As he waited for sleep to come to him, Axl recalled once again how the four of them, together with the silent monk, had squeezed into the tiny cell. A candle was burning next to the bed, and he had felt Beatrice recoil as she caught sight of the figure lying in it. Then she had taken a breath and moved further into the room. There was hardly space for them all, but they had before long arranged themselves around the bed, the warrior and the boy in the corner furthest away. Axl's back was pressed against the chilly stone wall, but Beatrice, standing just in front and leaning into him as if for reassurance, was almost up to the sickbed. There was a faint smell of vomit and urine. The silent monk, meanwhile, was fussing about the man in the bed, helping to raise him to a sitting position.

Their host was white-haired and advanced in years. His frame was large, and until recently must have been vigorous, but now the simple act of sitting up appeared to cause multiple agonies. A coarse blanket fell from around him as he raised himself, revealing a nightshirt patched with bloodstains. But what had caused Beatrice to shrink back was the man's neck and face, starkly illuminated by the bedside candle. A swollen mound under one side of the chin, a deep purple fading to a yellow, obliged the head to be held at a slight angle. The peak of the mound was split and caked with pus and old blood. On the face itself, a gouge ran from just below the cheek bone down to the jaw, exposing a section of the man's inner mouth and gum. It must have cost him greatly to smile, but once he was settled in his new position, the monk did just this.

'Welcome, welcome. I'm Jonus, whom I know you came a long way to see. My dear guests, don't look at me with such pity. These wounds are no longer new, and hardly bring the pain they once did.'

'We see now, Father Jonus,' Beatrice said, 'why your good abbot's so reluctant to have strangers impose on you. We'd have waited for his permission, but this kind monk led us to you.'

'Ninian here is my most trusted friend, and even if he's vowed to silence, we understand one another perfectly. He's watched each of you since your arrival and brought me frequent reports. I thought it time we met, even if the abbot knows nothing of it.'

'But what can have caused you such injuries, father?' Beatrice asked. 'And you a man famed for kindness and wisdom.'

'Let's leave the topic, mistress, for my feeble strength won't allow us to speak for long. I know two of you here, yourself and this brave boy, seek my advice. Let me see the boy first, who I understand carries a wound. Come closer into the light, dear lad.'

The monk's voice, though soft, possessed a natural command,

and Edwin started to move towards him. But immediately Wistan reached forward and gripped the boy by the arm. Perhaps it was an effect of the candle flame, or the warrior's trembling shadow cast on the wall behind him, but it seemed to Axl that for an instant Wistan's eyes were fixed on the injured monk with peculiar intensity, even hatred. The warrior drew the boy back to the wall, then took a step forward himself as though to shield his charge.

'What's wrong, shepherd?' asked Father Jonus. 'Do you fear poison from my wounds will travel to your brother? Then my hand needn't touch him. Let him step closer and my eyes alone will test his injury.'

'The boy's wound is clean,' Wistan said. 'It's just this good woman now seeks your help.'

'Master Wistan,' Beatrice said, 'how can you say such a thing? You must know well how a wound clean one moment turns fevered the next. The boy must seek this wise monk's guidance.'

Wistan seemed not to hear Beatrice, and continued to stare at the monk. Father Jonus, in turn, regarded the warrior as though he were a thing of great fascination. After a while, Father Jonus said:

'You stand with remarkable boldness for a humble shepherd.'

'It must be the habit of my trade. A shepherd must stand long hours watchful of wolves gathering in the night.'

'No doubt that's so. I imagine too how a shepherd must judge quickly, hearing a sound in the dark, if it heralds danger or the approach of a friend. Much must rest on the ability to make such decisions quickly and well.'

'Only a foolish shepherd hears a snapping twig or spots a shape in the dark and assumes a companion come to relieve him. We're a cautious breed, and what's more, sir, I've just now seen with my own eyes the device in your barn.'

'Ah. I thought you'd come upon it sooner or later. What do you make of your discovery, shepherd?'

'It angers me.'

'Angers you?' Father Jonus rasped this with some force, as though himself suddenly angered. 'Why does it anger you?'

'Tell me if I'm wrong, sir. My surmise is that the custom here has been for the monks to take turns in that cage exposing their bodies to the wild birds, hoping this way to atone for crimes once committed in this country and long unpunished. Even these ugly wounds I see here before me have been gained in this way, and for all I know a sense of piety eases your suffering. Yet let me say I feel no pity to see your gashes. How can you describe as penance, sir, the drawing of a veil over the foulest deeds? Is your Christian god one to be bribed so easily with self-inflicted pain and a few prayers? Does he care so little for justice left undone?'

'Our god is a god of mercy, shepherd, whom you, a pagan, may find hard to comprehend. It's no foolishness to seek forgiveness from such a god, however great the crime. Our god's mercy is boundless.'

'What use is a god with boundless mercy, sir? You mock me as a pagan, yet the gods of my ancestors pronounce clearly their ways and punish severely when we break their laws. Your Christian god of mercy gives men licence to pursue their greed, their lust for land and blood, knowing a few prayers and a little penance will bring forgiveness and blessing.'

'It's true, shepherd, that here in this monastery, there are those who still believe such things. But let me assure you, Ninian and I have long let go such delusions, and neither are we alone.

We know our god's mercy is not to be abused, yet many of my brother monks, the abbot included, will not yet accept this. They still believe that cage, and our constant prayers, will be enough. Yet these dark crows and ravens are a sign of God's anger. They never came before. Even last winter, though the wind made the strongest of us weep, the birds were but mischievous children, their beaks bringing only small sufferings. A shake of the chains or a shout was enough to keep them at bay. But now a new breed comes to find us, larger, bolder and with fury in their eyes. They tear at us in calm anger, no matter how we struggle or cry out. We've lost three dear friends these past months, and many more of us carry deep wounds. These surely are signs.'

Wistan's manner had been softening, but he had kept himself firmly in front of the boy. 'Are you saying', he asked, 'I have friends here in this monastery?'

'In this room, shepherd, yes. Elsewhere, we remain divided and even now they argue in great passion about how we are to continue. The abbot will insist we carry on as always. Others of our view will say it's time to stop. That no forgiveness awaits us at the end of this path. That we must uncover what's been hidden and face the past. But those voices, I fear, remain few and will not carry the day. Shepherd, will you trust me now to see this boy's wound?'

For a moment Wistan remained still. Then he moved aside, signalling to Edwin to step forward. Immediately the silent monk helped Father Jonus to a more upright position – both monks had become suddenly quite animated – then grasping the candleholder from the bedside, tugged Edwin closer, impatiently raising the boy's shirt for Father Jonus to see. Then, for what seemed a long time, both monks went on looking at the boy's wound – Ninian moving the light one way then the other

– as though it were a pool within which a miniature world was contained. Eventually the monks exchanged what seemed to Axl looks of triumph, but the very next moment Father Jonus fell shaking back onto his pillows, with an expression closer to resignation or else sadness. As Ninian hastily put down the candle to attend to him, Edwin slipped back into the shadows to stand beside Wistan.

'Father Jonus,' Beatrice said, 'now you've seen the boy's wound, tell us if it's clean and will heal on its own.'

Father Jonus's eyes were closed, and he was still breathing heavily, but he said quite calmly: 'I believe it will heal if he takes good care. Father Ninian will prepare an ointment for him before he leaves this place.'

'Father,' Beatrice went on, 'your present conversation with Master Wistan isn't entirely within my understanding. Yet it interests me greatly.'

'Is that so, mistress?' Father Jonus, still recovering his breath, opened his eyes and looked at her.

'Last night in a village below,' Beatrice said, 'I spoke with a woman wise with medicines. She had much to tell about my sickness, but when I asked her about this mist, the same that makes us forget the last hour as readily as a morning many years past, she confessed she had no idea what or whose work it was. Yet she said if there was one wise enough to know, it would be you, Father Jonus, up here in this monastery. So my husband and I made our way here, even though it's a harder road to our son's village where we're impatiently awaited. It was my hope you'd tell us something of this mist and how Axl and I might be free of it. It may be I'm a foolish woman, but it seemed to me just now, for all the talk of shepherds, you and Master Wistan were speaking of this same mist, and much bothered by what's been lost of our past. So let me ask this of you, and Master Wistan too. Do the both of you know what causes this mist to fall over us?'

Father Jonus and Wistan exchanged looks. Then Wistan said quietly:

'It's the dragon Querig, Mistress Beatrice, that roams these peaks. She's the cause of the mist you speak of. Yet these monks here protect her, and have done so for years. I'd wager even now, if they're wise to my identity, they'll have sent for men to destroy me.'

'Father Jonus, can this be true?' Beatrice asked. 'The mist is the work of this she-dragon?'

The monk, who for an instant had seemed far away, turned to Beatrice. 'The shepherd tells the truth, mistress. It's Querig's breath which fills this land and robs us of memories.'

'Axl, do you hear that? The she-dragon's the cause of the mist! If Master Wistan, or anyone else, even that old knight met on the road, can slay the creature, our memories will be restored to us! Axl, why so quiet?'

Indeed, Axl had been lost in thought, and although he had heard his wife's words, and noticed her excitement, it was all he could do simply to reach out a hand to her. Before he could find any words, Father Jonus said to Wistan:

'Shepherd, if you know your danger, why do you dally here? Why not take this boy and be on your way?'

'The boy needs rest, as I do.'

'But you don't rest, shepherd. You cut firewood and wander like a hungry wolf.'

'When we arrived your log pile was low. And the nights are cold in these mountains.'

'There's something else puzzles me, shepherd. Why does Lord Brennus hunt you as he does? For many days now, his soldiers have searched the country for you. Even last year, when another man came from the east to hunt Querig, Brennus believed it might be you and sent men out to search for you. They came up here asking for you. Shepherd, who are you to Brennus?'

'We knew one another as young lads, even before the age of this boy here.'

'You've come to this country on an errand, shepherd. Why jeopardise it to settle old scores? I say to you, take this boy and be on your way, even before the monks come out of their meeting.'

'If Lord Brennus does me the courtesy to come here after me this night, I'm obliged then to stand and face him.'

'Master Wistan,' Beatrice said, 'I don't know what's between you and Lord Brennus. But if it's your mission to slay the great dragon Querig, I beg you, don't be distracted from it. There'll be time to settle scores later.'

'The mistress is right, shepherd. I fear I know too the purpose of all this woodcutting. Listen to what we say, sir. This boy gives you a unique chance the like of which may not come your way again. Take him and be on your way.'

Wistan looked thoughtfully at Father Jonus, then bowed his head politely. 'I'm happy to have met you, father. And I apologise if earlier I addressed you discourteously. But now let me and this boy take our leave of you. I know Mistress Beatrice still wishes for advice, and she's a brave and good woman. I beg you preserve some strength to attend to her. Now I'll thank you for your counsel, and bid you farewell.'

Lying in the darkness, still hopeful sleep would overtake him, Axl tried to remember why he had been so oddly silent for much of his time in Father Jonus's cell. There had been some reason, and even when Beatrice, triumphant to discover the origin of the mist, had turned to him and exclaimed, he had been able only to reach out his hand to her, still not speaking. He had been in the throes of some powerful and strange emotion, one that had all but put him in a dream, though every word being spoken around him still reached his ears with perfect clarity. He had felt as one standing in a boat on a wintry river, looking out into dense fog, knowing it would at any moment part to reveal vivid glimpses of the land ahead. And he had been caught in a kind of terror, yet at the same time had felt a curiosity – or something stronger and darker – and he had told himself firmly, 'Whatever it may be, let me see it, let me see it.'

Had he actually spoken these words out loud? Perhaps he had done so, and just at the instant Beatrice had turned to him in excitement, exclaiming, 'Axl, do you hear that? The she-dragon's the cause of the mist!'

He could not remember clearly what had happened once Wistan and the boy had departed Father Jonus's chamber. The silent monk, Ninian, must have left with them, probably to provide the ointment for the boy's wound, or simply to lead them back unobserved. In any case, he and Beatrice had been left alone with Father Jonus, and the latter, despite his wounds and his exhaustion, had examined his wife thoroughly. The monk had not asked her to remove any clothing – Axl had been relieved – and though here too his recollection was hazy, an image came to him of Jonus pressing an ear to Beatrice's side, eyes closed in concentration as though some faint message might be heard coming from within. Axl remembered too the monk, with blinking eyes, putting to Beatrice a series of questions. Did she feel sick after drinking water? Did she ever feel pain at the back of her neck? There were other questions Axl could now no longer remember, but Beatrice had replied in the negative to one after the next, and the more she did so, the more pleased Axl had become. Only once, when Jonus asked if she had noticed blood in her urine, and she replied that yes, she sometimes had, did Axl feel unease. But the monk had nodded, as though this was normal and to be expected, and gone straight on to the next question. How then had this examination ended? He remembered Father Jonus smiling and saying, 'So you can go to your son with nothing to fear,' and Axl himself saying, 'You see, princess, I always knew it was nothing.' Then the monk had eased himself carefully back down in his bed and lain there, recovering his breath. In Ninian's absence, Axl had hurried to fill the monk's drinking cup from the jug, and as he had placed it to the sick man's mouth, had seen tiny droplets of blood slide from the lower lip and spread in the water. Then Father Jonus had looked up at Beatrice and said:

'Mistress, you seem happy to know the truth about this thing you call the mist.'

'Happy indeed, father, for now there's a way forward for us.'

'Take care, for it's a secret guarded jealously by some, though it's maybe for the best it remains so no longer.'

'It's not for me to care if it's a secret or not, father, but I'm glad Axl and I know it and can now act on it.'

'Yet are you so certain, good mistress, you wish to be free of this mist? Is it not better some things remain hidden from our minds?'

'It may be so for some, father, but not for us. Axl and I wish to have again the happy moments we shared together. To be robbed of them is as if a thief came in the night and took what's most precious from us.'

'Yet the mist covers all memories, the bad as well as the good. Isn't that so, mistress?'

'We'll have the bad ones come back too, even if they make us weep or shake with anger. For isn't it the life we've shared?'

'You've no fear, then, of bad memories, mistress?'

'What's to fear, father? What Axl and I feel today in our hearts for each other tells us the path taken here can hold no danger for us, no matter that the mist hides it now. It's like a tale with a happy end, when even a child knows not to fear the twists and turns before. Axl and I would remember our life together, whatever its shape, for it's been a thing dear to us.'

A bird must have flown across the ceiling above him. The sound had startled him, and then Axl realised that for a moment or two he had actually been asleep. He realised too there were no more woodcutting noises, and the grounds were silent. Had the warrior returned to their chamber? Axl had heard nothing, and there were no signs, beyond the dark shape of the table, of anyone else asleep on Edwin's side of the room. What had Father Jonus said after examining Beatrice and concluding with his questions? Yes, she had said, she had noticed blood in her urine, but he had smiled and asked something else. You see, princess, Axl had said, I always told you it was nothing. And Father Jonus had smiled, despite his wounds and his exhaustion, and said, you can go to your son with nothing to fear. But these had never been the questions Beatrice had feared. Beatrice, he knew, feared the boatman's questions, harder to answer than Father Jonus's, and that was why she had been so pleased to learn the cause of the mist. Axl, do you hear that? She had been triumphant. Axl, do you hear that? she had said, her face radiant.

Chapter Seven

A hand had been shaking him, but by the time Axl sat up the figure was already on the other side of the room, bending over Edwin and whispering, 'Quickly, boy, quickly! And not a sound!' Beatrice was awake beside him, and Axl rose unsteadily to his feet, the cold air startling him, then reached down to grasp his wife's outstretched hands.

It was still the depths of night, but voices were calling outside and surely torches had been lit in the courtyard below, for there were now illuminated patches on the wall facing the window. The monk who had awoken them was dragging the boy, still half asleep, over to their side, and Axl recognised Father Brian's limping gait before his face emerged from the dark.

'I'll try and save you, friends,' Father Brian said, his voice still a whisper, 'but you must be quick and do as I say. There are soldiers arrived, twenty, even thirty, with a will to hunt you down. They already have the older Saxon brother trapped, but he's a lively one and keeps them occupied, giving you a chance of escape. Be still, boy, stay with me!' Edwin was moving to the window, but Father Brian had reached out and clasped his arm. 'I mean to lead you to safety, but we must first leave this chamber unseen. Soldiers cross the square below, but their eyes are on the tower where the Saxon still holds out. With God's help they won't notice us go down the steps outside, and then the worst will be behind us. But cause no sound to make their gazes turn, and take care not to trip on the steps. I'll descend first, then signal your moment to follow. No, mistress, you must leave your bundle here. Let it be enough to keep your lives!'

They crouched near the door and listened to Father Brian's footsteps descend with agonising slowness. Eventually, when Axl peered cautiously through the doorway, he saw torches moving at the far end of the courtyard; but before he could discern clearly what was going on, his attention was drawn by Father Brian, standing directly below and signalling frantically.

The staircase, running diagonally down the side of the wall, was mostly in shadow except for one patch, quite near the ground, lit up brightly by the nearly full moon.

'Follow close behind me, princess,' Axl said. 'Don't look across the yard, but keep your eyes on where your foot may find the next step, or it'll be a hard fall and only enemies to come to our aid. Tell the boy what I've just said, and let's have this behind us.'

Despite his own instructions, Axl could not help glancing across the courtyard as he went down. On the far side, soldiers had gathered around a cylindrical stone tower overlooking the building in which the monks had earlier had their meeting. Blazing torches were being waved, and there appeared to be disorder in their ranks. When Axl was halfway down the steps, two soldiers broke away and came running across the square, and he was sure they would be spotted. But the men vanished into a doorway, and before long Axl was gratefully ushering both Beatrice and Edwin into the shadows of the cloisters where Father Brian was waiting.

They followed the monk along narrow corridors, some of which may have been the same as those taken earlier with the silent Father Ninian. Often they moved through complete darkness, following the rhythmic hiss of their guide's dragged foot. Then they came into a chamber whose ceiling had partly fallen away. Moonlight was pouring in, revealing piles of wooden boxes and broken furniture. Axl could smell mould and stagnant water.

'Take heart, friends,' Father Brian said, no longer whispering. He had gone into a corner and was moving objects aside. 'You're nearly safe.'

'Father,' Axl said, 'we're grateful to you for this rescue, but please tell us what's occurred.'

Father Brian continued clearing the corner, and did not look up as he said: 'A mystery to us, sir. They came this night without invitation, pouring through the gates and through our home as if it were their own. They demanded the two young Saxons lately arrived here, and though they made no mention of you or your wife, I wouldn't trust them to treat you gently. This boy here, they would clearly wish to murder, as they do even now his brother. You must save yourselves and there'll be time later to ponder the soldiers' ways.'

'Master Wistan was a stranger to us only this morning,' Beatrice said, 'yet we're uneasy making our escape while a terrible fate threatens him.'

'The soldiers may yet come on our heels, mistress, for we left no barred doors behind us. And if that fellow bravely buys your escape, even with his own life, you must grasp it gratefully. Under this trap-door is a tunnel dug in ancient times. It will take you underground into the forest, where you'll emerge far from your pursuers. Now help me raise it, sir, for it's too heavy for my hands alone.'

Even for the two of them, it took some effort to raise the door till it stood up at a steep angle before them, revealing a square of deeper blackness.

'Let the boy go down first,' the monk said, 'for it's years since any of us used this passage and who knows if the steps haven't crumbled. He's nimble-footed and could take a fall better.'

But Edwin was saying something to Beatrice, and she now said: 'Master Edwin would go to Master Wistan's aid.'

'Tell him, princess, we might help Wistan yet by making our escape through this tunnel. Tell the boy what you must, but persuade him to come quickly.'

As Beatrice spoke to him, a change seemed to come over the boy. He kept staring at the hole in the floor, and his eyes, caught in the moonlight, seemed to Axl at that moment to have something strange about them, as though he were steadily coming under a spell. Then even as Beatrice was speaking, Edwin walked towards the trap-door and without looking back at them, stepped into the blackness and vanished. As his footsteps grew fainter, Axl took Beatrice's hand and said:

'Let's go too, princess. Stay close to me.'

The steps leading underground were shallow – flat stones sunk into earth – and felt solid enough. They could see something of the way ahead by the light from the open trap-door above them, but just as Axl turned to speak to Father Brian, the door closed with what seemed a thunderous crash.

They all three stopped and for a while remained quite still. The air did not feel as stale as Axl had expected; in fact he thought he could feel a faint breeze. Somewhere in front of them, Edwin started to speak, and Beatrice answered him in a whisper. Then she said softly:

'The boy asks why Father Brian closed the door on us as he did. I told him he was most likely anxious to hide the tunnel from the soldiers maybe even now entering the room. All the same, Axl, it struck me a little queer too. And isn't that him now, surely, moving objects over the door? If we find the way ahead obstructed by earth or water, the father himself saying it's years since anyone came this way, how will we return and open that door, the way it's so heavy and now with objects above it?'

'Queer right enough. But there's no doubting there's soldiers in the monastery, for didn't we see them ourselves just now? I don't see what choice we have but to go on and pray this tunnel brings us safely to the forest. Tell the boy to keep moving forward, but slowly and always a hand to this mossy wall, for I fear this passage will only grow darker.'

Yet as they went forward they found there was a feeble light, so that at times they could even make out each other's outlines. There were sudden puddles that surprised their feet, and more than once during this phase of their journey, Axl thought he heard a noise up ahead, but since neither Edwin nor Beatrice reacted he put it down to his overwrought imagination. But then Edwin suddenly halted, almost causing Axl to collide into him. He felt Beatrice behind him squeeze his hand, and for a moment they stood there very still in the dark. Then Beatrice moved even closer to him, and her breath felt warm on his neck as she said in the softest of whispers: 'Do you hear it, Axl?'

'Hear what, princess?'

Edwin's hand touched him warningly, and they were silent again. Eventually Beatrice said in his ear: 'There's something here with us, Axl.'

'Perhaps a bat, princess. Or a rat.'

'No, Axl. I hear it now. It's a man's breathing.'

Axl listened again. Then there came a sharp noise, a striking sound repeating three times, four times, just beyond where they were standing. There were bright flashes, then a tiny flame which grew momentarily to reveal the shape of a seated man, then all was darkness again.

'Fear not, friends,' a voice said. 'It's only Gawain, Arthur's knight. And as soon as this tinder lights we'll see each other better.'

There were more noises of flints, then eventually a candle flamed and began to burn steadily.

Sir Gawain was sitting on a dark mound. It evidently did not make an ideal seat for he was at an odd angle, like a giant doll about to topple. The candle in his hand illuminated his face and upper torso with wobbling shadows, and he was breathing heavily. As before, he was in tunic and armour; his sword, unsheathed, had been thrust at an angle into the ground near the foot of the mound. He stared at them balefully, moving the candle from one face to the next.

'So you're all here,' he said finally. 'I'm relieved.'

'You surprise us, Sir Gawain,' Axl said. 'What do you mean by hiding yourself here?'

'I've been down here a while and walking before you, friends. Yet with this sword and armour, and my great height which forces me to stumble and go with bowed head, I can't walk quickly and now you discover me.'

'You hardly explain yourself, sir. Why do you walk before us?'

'To defend you, sir! The melancholy truth is the monks have deceived you. There's a beast dwells down here and they mean you to perish by it. Happily, not every monk thinks alike. Ninian, the silent one, brought me down here unseen and I'll guide you to safety yet.'

'Your news overwhelms us, Sir Gawain,' said Axl. 'But first

tell us of this beast you speak of. What is its nature and does it threaten us even as we stand here?'

'Assume it does, sir. The monks wouldn't have sent you down here if they didn't mean you to meet the beast. It's always their way. As men of Christ, it's beyond them to use a sword or even poison. So they send down here those they wish dead, and in a day or two they'll have forgotten they ever did so. Oh yes, that's their way, especially the abbot's. By Sunday he may even have convinced himself he saved you from those soldiers. And the work of whatever prowls this tunnel, should it cross his mind, he'll disown, or even call God's will. Well, let's see what God wills tonight now a knight of Arthur walks before you!'

'You're saying, Sir Gawain,' Beatrice asked, 'the monks wish us dead?'

'They certainly wish this boy dead, mistress. I tried to make them see it wasn't necessary, even made a solemn promise to take him far away from this country, but no, they don't listen to me! They won't risk this boy loose, even with Master Wistan captured or killed, for who's to say there won't come some other fellow one day to find this boy. I'll take him far away, I said, but they fear what may happen and wish him dead. You and your good husband they might have spared but that you'd inevitably be witnesses to their deeds. Had I seen all this in advance, would I have travelled here to this monastery? Who knows? It seemed my duty then, did it not? But their plans for the boy, and for an innocent Christian couple, I could not allow it! Luckily not all the monks think alike, you know, and Ninian, the silent one, led me down here unwatched. It was my intention to go before you much further, but this armour and my stumbling height – how many times over the years have I cursed this height! What advantage does it bring a man to be so tall? For every high-dangling pear I reached there's been an arrow threatened me would have flown over a smaller man!'

'Sir Gawain,' Axl said, 'what kind of beast is it, this one you say dwells down here?'

'I never saw it, sir, only know those the monks send this way perish by it.'

'Is it one can be killed by an ordinary sword held by a mortal man?'

'What do you say, sir? I'm a mortal man, I don't deny it, but I'm a knight well trained and nurtured for long years of my youth by the great Arthur, who taught me to face all manner of challenge with gladness, even when fear seeps to the marrow, for if we're mortal let us at least shine handsomely in God's eyes while we walk this earth! Like all who stood with Arthur, sir, I've faced beelzebubs and monsters as well as the darkest intents of men, and always upheld my great king's example even in the midst of ferocious conflict. What is it you suggest, sir? How dare you? Were you there? *I* was there, sir, and saw all with these same eyes that fix you now! But what of it, what of it, friends, this is a discussion for some other time. Forgive me, we have other matters to attend to, of course we have. What is it you asked, sir? Ah yes, this beast, yes, I understand it's monstrous fierce but no demon or spirit and this sword is good enough to slay it.'

'But Sir Gawain,' Beatrice said, 'do you really propose we walk further down this tunnel knowing what we now do?'

'What choice have we, mistress? If I'm not mistaken, the way back to the monastery is locked to us, and yet that same door may open any time to pour forth soldiers into this tunnel. There's nothing for it but to go on, and but for this one beast in our way, we may soon find ourselves in the forest far from your pursuers, for Ninian assures me this is a true tunnel and well maintained. So let's be on our way before this candle burns down, it's the only one I have.'

'Do we trust him, Axl?' Beatrice asked, making no effort to prevent Sir Gawain hearing. 'My mind's giddy now and loath to believe our kind Father Brian's betrayed us. Yet what this knight says has the ring of truth to it.'

'Let's follow him, princess. Sir Gawain, we thank you for your trouble. Please lead us now to safety, and let's hope this beast's dozing or gone prowling the night.'

'I fear we have no such luck. But come, friends, we'll go with courage.' The old knight rose slowly to his feet, then held out the candle at arm's length. 'Master Axl, perhaps you'll carry for us this flame, for I'll need both my hands to keep my sword at the ready.'

They went on into the tunnel, Sir Gawain leading, Axl following with the flame, Beatrice holding his arm from behind, and Edwin now at the rear. There was no option but to go in single file, the passage remaining narrow, and the ceiling of dangling moss and sinewy roots grew lower and lower until even Beatrice had to stoop. Axl did his best to hold the candle high, but the breeze in the tunnel was now stronger, and he was often obliged to lower it and cover the flame with his other hand. Sir Gawain though never complained, and his shape going before them, sword raised over his shoulder, seemed never to vary. Then Beatrice let out an exclamation and tugged Axl's arm.

'What is it, princess?'

'Oh, Axl, stop! My foot touched something then, but your candle moved too quickly.'

'What of it, princess? We have to move on.'

'Axl, I thought it a child! My foot touched it and I saw it before your light passed. Oh, I believe it's a small child long dead!'

'There, princess, don't distress yourself. Where was it you saw it?'

'Come, come, friends,' Sir Gawain said from the dark. 'Many things in this place are best left unseen.'

Beatrice seemed not to hear the knight. 'It was over here, Axl. Bring the flame this way. Down there, Axl, shine it down there, though I dread to see its poor face again!'

Despite his counsel, Sir Gawain had doubled back, and Edwin too was now at Beatrice's side. Axl crouched forward and moved the candle here and there, revealing damp earth, tree roots and stones. Then the flame illuminated a large bat lying on its back as though peacefully asleep, wings stretched right out. Its fur looked wet and sticky. The pig-like face was hairless, and little puddles had formed in the cavities of the outspread wings. The creature might indeed have been sleeping but for what was on the front of its torso. As Axl brought the flame even closer, they all stared at the circular hole extending from just below the bat's breast down to its belly, taking in parts of the ribcage to either side. The wound was peculiarly clean, as though someone had taken a bite from a crisp apple.

'What could have done work like this?' Axl asked.

He must have moved the candle too swiftly, for at that moment the flame guttered and went out.

'Don't worry, friends,' Sir Gawain said. 'I'll find my tinder again.'

'Didn't I tell you, Axl?' Beatrice sounded close to tears. 'I knew it was a baby the moment my foot touched it.'

'What are you saying, princess? It's not a baby. What are you saying?'

'What could have happened to the poor child? And what of its parents?'

'Princess, it's simply a bat, the like of which often haunts dark places.'

'Oh Axl, it was a baby, I'm sure of it!'

'I'm sorry this flame's out, princess, or I'd show you again. A bat it is, nothing more, yet myself I'd look again at what it lies on. Sir Gawain, did you notice the creature's bed?'

'I don't know what you mean, sir.'

'It seemed to me the creature lay on a bed of bones, for I thought I saw a skull or two that could only have belonged to men.'

'What do you suggest, sir?' Sir Gawain's voice became carelessly loud. 'What skulls? I saw no skulls, sir! Only a bat fallen on misfortune!'

Beatrice was now sobbing quietly, and Axl straightened to embrace her.

'It was no child, princess,' he said more gently. 'Don't upset yourself.'

'Such a lonely death. Where were its parents, Axl?'

'What are you suggesting, sir? Skulls? I saw no skulls! And what if there are a few old bones here? What of it, is that anything extraordinary? Aren't we underground? But I saw no bed of bones, I don't know what you suggest, Master Axl. Were you there, sir? Did you stand beside the great Arthur? I'm proud to say I did, sir, and he was a commander as merciful as he was gallant. Yes, indeed, it was I who came to the abbot to warn of Master Wistan's identity and intentions, what choice had I? Was I to guess how dark the hearts of holy men could turn? Your suggestions are unwarranted, sir! An insult to all who ever stood alongside the great Arthur! There are no beds of bones here! And am I not here now to save you?'

'Sir Gawain, your voice booms too much and who knows where the soldiers are this moment.'

'What could I do, sir, knowing what I did? Yes, I rode here and spoke to the abbot, yet how was I to know the darkness of that man's heart? And the better men, poor Jonus, his liver pecked and his days not long, while that abbot lives on with barely a scratch from those birds . . .'

Sir Gawain broke off, interrupted by a noise from further down the tunnel. It was hard to determine how distant or near it had been, but the sound was unmistakably the cry of a beast; it had resembled the howl of a wolf, though there had also been something of the deeper roar of a bear. The cry had not been prolonged, but it made Axl clasp Beatrice to him, and Sir Gawain snatched his sword from out of the ground. Then, for several moments, they remained standing in silence, listening for the sound to return. But nothing further came, and suddenly Sir Gawain began to laugh, quietly and breathlessly. As his laughter went on, Beatrice said into Axl's ear: 'Let's leave this place, husband. I wish no more reminding of this lonely grave.'

Sir Gawain stopped laughing and said: 'Perhaps we heard then the beast, but we have no choice but to go on. So, friends, let's finish our quarrel. We'll light the candle again before long, but let's go a little way now without it in case it hastens the beast our way. See, here's a pale light and enough to walk by. Come, friends, no more of this quarrel. My sword's ready and let's continue.'

The tunnel became more tortuous, and they moved with greater caution, fearing what each turn would reveal. But they encountered nothing, nor heard the cry again. Then the tunnel descended steeply for a good distance before coming out into a large underground chamber.

They all paused to recover their breaths and look around at their new surroundings. After the long walk with the earth brushing their heads, it was a relief to see the ceiling not only so high above them, but composed of more solid material. Once Sir Gawain had lit the candle again, Axl realised they were in some sort of mausoleum, surrounded by walls bearing traces of murals and Roman letters. Before them a pair of substantial pillars formed a gateway into a further chamber of comparable proportions, and falling across this threshold was an intense pool of moonlight. Its source was not obvious: perhaps somewhere behind the high arch crossing the two pillars there was an opening which at that moment, by sheer chance, was aligned to receive the moon. The light illuminated much of the moss and fungus on the pillars, as well as a section of the next chamber, whose floor appeared to be covered in rubble, but which Axl soon realised was comprised of a vast layer of bones. Only then did it occur to him that under his feet were more broken skeletons, and that this strange floor extended for the entirety of both chambers.

'This must be some ancient burial place,' he said aloud. 'Yet there are so many buried here.'

'A burial place,' Sir Gawain muttered. 'Yes, a burial place.' He had been moving slowly around the chamber, sword in one hand, candle in the other. Now he went towards the arch, but stopped short of the second chamber, as if suddenly daunted by the brilliant moonlight. He thrust his sword into the ground, and Axl watched his silhouette leaning on his weapon, moving the candle up and down with a weary air.

'We need not quarrel, Master Axl. Here are the skulls of men, I won't deny it. There an arm, there a leg, but just bones now. An old burial ground. And so it may be. I dare say, sir, our whole country is this way. A fine green valley. A pleasant copse in the springtime. Dig its soil, and not far beneath the daisies and buttercups come the dead. And I don't talk, sir, only of those who received Christian burial. Beneath our soil lie the remains of old slaughter. Horace and I, we've grown weary of it. Weary and we no longer young.'

'Sir Gawain,' Axl said, 'we have but one sword between us. I ask you not to grow melancholic, nor forget the beast is near.'

'I don't forget the beast, sir. I merely consider this gateway before us. Look up there, you see it?' Sir Gawain was holding up the candle to reveal along the lower edge of the arch what appeared to be a row of spearheads pointing down to the ground.

'A portcullis,' Axl said.

'Exactly, sir. This gate isn't so ancient. Younger than either of us, I'd wager. Someone has raised it for us, wishing us to pass through. See there, the ropes that hold it. And there, the pulleys. Someone comes here often to make this gate rise and fall, and perhaps feed the beast.' Sir Gawain stepped towards one of the pillars, his feet crunching over bones. 'If I cut this rope, the gate will surely come down, it will bar our way out. Yet if the beast's beyond, we'll be shielded from it. Is that the Saxon boy I hear or some pixie stolen in here?'

Indeed Edwin, back in the shadows, had started to sing; faintly at first so that Axl had thought the boy was simply soothing his nerves, but then his voice had become steadily more conspicuous. His song seemed to be a slow lullaby, and he was rendering it with his face to the wall, his body rocking gently.

'The boy behaves as one bewitched,' Sir Gawain said. 'Never mind him, we must now decide, Master Axl. Do we walk on? Or do we cut this rope to give us at least a moment shielded from what lies beyond?'

'I say we cut the rope, sir. We can surely raise the gate again when we wish. Let's first discover what we face while the gate's down.'

'Wise counsel, sir. I'll do as you say.'

Handing Axl the candle, Sir Gawain took a further step forward, raised his sword and swung at the pillar. There was the sound of metal striking stone, and the lower section of the gate shook, but remained suspended. Sir Gawain sighed with a hint of embarrassment. Then he repositioned himself, raised the sword again, and struck once more.

This time there was a snapping sound, and the gate crashed down raising a cloud of dust in the moonlight. The noise felt immense – Edwin abruptly stopped his singing – and Axl stared through the iron grid now fallen before them to see what it would summon. But there was no sign of the beast, and after a moment they all let go their breaths.

For all that they were now effectively trapped, the lowering of the portcullis brought a sense of relief, and they all four began to wander around the mausoleum. Sir Gawain, who had sheathed his sword, went up to the bars and touched them gingerly.

'Good iron,' he said. 'It'll do its work.'

Beatrice, who had been quiet for some time, came up to Axl and pressed her head against his chest. As he put an arm around her, he realised her cheek was wet with tears.

'Come, princess,' he said, 'take heart. We'll be out in the night air before long.'

'All these skulls, Axl. So many! Can this beast really have killed so many?'

She had spoken softly, but Sir Gawain turned to them. 'What do you suggest, mistress? That *I* committed this slaughter?' He said this tiredly, with none of the anger he had shown earlier in the tunnel, but there was a peculiar intensity in his voice. 'So many skulls, you say. Yet are we not underground? What is it you suggest? Can just one knight of Arthur have killed so many?' He turned back to the gate and ran a finger along one of the bars. 'Once, years ago, in a dream, I watched myself killing the enemy. It was in my sleep and long ago. The enemy, in their hundreds, perhaps as many as this. I fought and I fought. Just a foolish dream, but still I recall it.' He sighed, then looked at Beatrice. 'I hardly know how to answer you, mistress. I acted as I thought would please God. How was I to guess how dark had grown the hearts of these wretched monks? Horace and I came to this monastery while the sun was up, not long after you yourself arrived, for I supposed then I had need to speak urgently with the abbot. Then I discovered what he plotted against you, and I feigned complacence. I bade him farewell, and they all believed me gone, but I left Horace in the forest and returned up here on foot hidden by the night. Not all the monks think alike, thank God. I knew the good Jonus would receive me. And learning from him the abbot's schemes, I had Ninian bring me unseen down to this place to await you. Curse it, the boy starts again!'

Sure enough, Edwin was singing once more, not as loudly as before, but now in a curious posture. He had bent forward, a fist to each temple, and was moving slowly about in the shadows like someone in a dance enacting the part of an animal.

'The recent events surely overwhelm him,' Axl said. 'It's a

wonder he's shown the fortitude he has, and we must attend to him well once we're away from here. But Sir Gawain, tell us now, why do the monks seek to murder such an innocent lad?'

'No matter how I argued, sir, the abbot would have the boy destroyed. So I left Horace in the forest and retraced my steps . . .'

'Sir Gawain, please explain. Has this to do with his ogre's wound? Yet these are men of Christian learning.'

'That's no ogre's bite the boy carries. It's a dragon gave him that wound. I saw it right away when yesterday that soldier raised his shirt. Who knows how he met with a dragon, but a dragon's bite it is, and now the desire will be rising in his blood to seek congress with a she-dragon. And in turn, any she-dragon near enough to scent him will come seeking him. This is why Master Wistan is so fond of his protégé, sir. He believes Master Edwin will lead him to Querig. And for this same reason, the monks and these soldiers would have him dead. Look, the boy grows ever wilder!'

'What are all these skulls, sir?' Beatrice suddenly asked the knight. 'Why so many? Can they all have belonged to babies? Some are surely small enough to fit in your palm.'

'Princess, don't distress yourself. This is a burial place, nothing more.'

'What is it you suggest, mistress? The skulls of babes? I've fought men, beelzebubs, dragons. But a slaughterer of infants? How dare you, mistress!'

Suddenly Edwin, still singing, pushed past them, and going up to the portcullis pressed himself against the bars.

'Get back, boy,' Sir Gawain said, grasping his shoulders. 'There's danger here, and that's enough of your songs!'

Edwin gripped the bars with both hands, and for a moment he and the old knight tussled. Then they both broke off and stepped back from the gate. Beatrice, at Axl's breast, let out a small gasp, but at that instant Axl's view was obscured by Edwin and Sir Gawain. Then the beast came into the pool of moonlight, and he saw it more clearly.

'God protect us,' Beatrice said. 'Here's a creature escaped from the Great Plain itself, and the air grows colder.'

'Don't worry, princess. It can't breach those bars.'

Sir Gawain, who had immediately drawn his sword again, began to laugh quietly. 'Not nearly as bad as I feared,' he said, then laughed a little more.

'Surely bad enough, sir,' Axl said. 'It looks well able to devour each of us in turn.'

They might have been gazing at a large skinned animal: an opaque membrane, like the lining of a sheep's stomach, was stretched tightly over the sinews and joints. Swathed as it was now in moonshadow, the beast appeared roughly the size and shape of a bull, but its head was distinctly wolf-like and of a darker hue – though even here the impression was of blackening by flames rather than of naturally dark fur or flesh. The jaws were massive, the eyes reptilian.

Sir Gawain was still laughing to himself. 'Coming down that gloomy tunnel my wild imaginings had readied me for worse. Once, sir, on the marshes at Dumum, I faced wolves with the heads of hideous hags! And at Mount Culwich, double-headed ogres that spewed blood at you even as they roared their battle-cry! Here's little more than an angry dog.'

'Yet it bars our way to freedom, Sir Gawain.'

'It does that for sure. So we may stare at it for an hour until the soldiers come down the tunnel behind us. Or we may lift this gate and fight it.'

'I'm inclined to think it a foe darker than a fierce dog, Sir Gawain. I ask you not to grow complacent.'

'I'm an old man, sir, and it's many a year since I swung this blade in anger. Yet I'm still a knight well trained, and if this be a beast of this earth, I'll get the better of it.'

'See, Axl,' Beatrice said, 'how its eyes follow Master Edwin.'

Edwin, now strangely calm, had been walking experimentally, first left, then to the right, always staring back at the beast whose gaze never left him.

'The dog hungers for the boy,' Sir Gawain said thoughtfully. 'It may be there's dragon spawn within this monster.'

'Whatever its nature,' Axl said, 'it awaits our next move with strange patience.'

'Then let me propose this, friends,' said Sir Gawain. 'I'm loath to use this Saxon boy like a young goat tied to trap a wolf. Yet he seems a brave lad, and in no less danger wandering here weaponless. Let him take the candle and go stand there at the back of the chamber. Then if you, Master Axl, can somehow raise this gate again, perhaps even with your good wife's help, the beast will be free to come through. My fancy is it will make straight for the boy. Knowing the path of its charge, I'll stand here and cut it down as it passes. Do you approve the scheme, sir?'

'It's a desperate one. Yet I too fear the soldiers will soon discover this tunnel. So let's try it, sir, and even with my wife and I hanging together on the rope, we'll do our best to raise this gate. Princess, explain to Master Edwin our plan and let's see if he'll enter into it.'

But Edwin seemed to have grasped Sir Gawain's strategy without a word being said to him. Taking the candle from the knight, the boy measured out ten good strides over the bones till he was back in the shadows. When he turned again, the candle below his face barely trembled, and revealed blazing eyes fixed on the creature beyond the bars.

'Quick then, princess,' Axl said. 'Climb on my back and try to reach the rope's end. See where it dangles there.'

At first they nearly toppled over. Then they used the pillar itself to support them, and after a little more groping, he heard her say: 'I hold it, Axl. Release me and it'll surely come down with me. Catch me so I don't fall all at once.'

'Sir Gawain,' Axl called softly. 'Are you ready, sir?'

'We're ready.'

'If the beast passes you, then surely it's the end of this brave boy.'

'I know it, sir. And it will not pass.'

'Let me down slowly, Axl. If I'm still in the air holding the rope, reach up and tug me down.'

Axl released Beatrice and for an instant she hung suspended in the air, her body weight insufficient to raise the gate. Then Axl managed to grip another portion of the rope close to her two hands, and they tugged together. At first nothing happened, then something yielded, and the gate rose with a shudder. Axl continued tugging, and unable to see the effect, called out: 'Is it high yet, sir?'

There was a pause before Sir Gawain's voice came back. 'The dog stares our way and nothing now between us.'

Twisting, Axl looked around the pillar in time to see the beast leap forward. The old knight's face, caught in moonlight, looked aghast as he swung his sword, but too late, and the creature was past him and moving unerringly towards Edwin.

The boy's eyes grew large, but he did not drop the candle.

Instead he moved aside, almost as if out of politeness, to let the beast pass. And to Axl's surprise, the creature did just that, running on into the blackness of the tunnel out of which not long ago they had all emerged.

'I'll hold it up yet,' Axl shouted. 'Cross the threshold and save yourselves!'

But neither Beatrice beside him, nor Sir Gawain, who had lowered his sword, seemed to hear. Even Edwin appeared to have lost interest in the terrible creature that had just sped past him and would surely return any moment. The boy, candle held before him, came over to where the old knight was standing, and together they stared down at the ground.

'Let the gate fall, Master Axl,' Sir Gawain said without looking up. 'We'll raise it again soon enough.'

The old knight and the boy, Axl realised, were regarding with fascination something moving on the ground before them. He let the gate fall, and as he did so, Beatrice said:

'A fearsome thing, Axl, and I've no need to see it. But go and look if you will and tell me what you see.'

'Didn't the beast run into the tunnel, princess?'

'Some of it did, and I heard its footsteps cease. Now, Axl, go and see the part of it lies at the knight's feet.'

As Axl came towards them, Sir Gawain and Edwin both started as though shaken from a trance. Then they moved aside and Axl saw the beast's head in the moonlight.

'The jaws will not cease,' Sir Gawain said in a perturbed tone. 'I've a mind to take my sword to it again, yet fear that would be a desecration to bring more evil upon us. Yet I wish it would cease moving.'

Indeed it was hard to believe the severed head was not a living thing. It lay on its side, the one visible eye gleaming like a sea creature. The jaws moved rhythmically with a strange energy, so that the tongue, flopping amidst the teeth, appeared to stir with life.

'We're beholden to you, Sir Gawain,' Axl said.

'A mere dog, sir, and I'd happily face worse. Yet this Saxon boy shows rare courage, and I'm glad to have done him some service. But now we must hurry on, and with caution too, for who knows what occurs above us, or even if a second beast awaits beyond that chamber.'

They now discovered a crank behind one of the pillars, and fastening the rope end to it, soon raised the gate without difficulty. Leaving the beast's head where it had fallen, they passed under the portcullis, Sir Gawain once more leading, sword poised, and Edwin at the rear.

The second chamber of the mausoleum showed clear signs of having served as the beast's lair: amidst the ancient bones were fresher carcasses of sheep and deer, as well as other dark, foul-smelling shapes they could not identify. Then they were once more walking stooped and short of breath along a winding passage. They encountered no more beasts, and eventually they heard birdsong. A patch of light appeared in the distance, and then they came out into the forest, the early dawn all around them.

In a kind of daze, Axl came upon a cluster of roots rising between two large trees, and taking Beatrice's hand, helped her sit down on it. At first Beatrice was too short of breath to speak, but after a moment she looked up, saying:

'There's room here beside me, husband. If we're safe for now, let's sit together and watch the stars fade. I'm thankful we're both well and that evil tunnel's behind us.' Then she said: 'Where's Master Edwin, Axl? I don't see him.'

Looking about him in the half-light, Axl spotted Sir Gawain's figure nearby, silhouetted against the dawn, head bowed, a hand on a tree trunk to steady him while he regained his breath. But there was no sign of the boy.

'Just now he was behind us,' Axl said. 'I even heard him exclaim as we came into the fresh air.'

'I watched him hasten on, sir,' Sir Gawain said without turning, his breath still laboured. 'Not being elderly as the rest of us, he's no need to lean on oaks panting and gasping. I suppose he hurries back to the monastery to rescue Master Wistan.'

'Didn't you think to delay him, sir? Surely he hurries to grave danger, and Master Wistan by now killed or captured.'

'What would you have me do, sir? I did all I could. Hid myself in that airless place. Overcame the beast though it had devoured many brave men before us. Then at the end of it all, the boy runs back to the monastery! Am I to give chase with this heavy armour and sword? I'm all done in, sir. All done in. What's my duty now? I must pause and think it over. What would Arthur have me do?'

'Are we to understand, Sir Gawain,' Beatrice asked, 'that it was you in the first place came to tell the abbot of Master Wistan's real identity as a Saxon warrior from the east?'

'Why go through it again, mistress? Did I not lead you to safety? So many skulls we trod upon before coming out to this sweet dawn! So many. No need to look down, one hears their cackle with each tread. How many dead, sir? A hundred? A thousand? Did you count, Master Axl? Or were you not there, sir?' He was still a silhouette beside a tree, his words sometimes hard to catch now the birds had begun their early chorus.

'Whatever the history of this night,' Axl said, 'we owe you much thanks, Sir Gawain. Clearly your courage and skill remain undiminished. Yet I too have a question to put to you.'

'Spare me, sir, enough. How can I chase a nimble youth up these wooded slopes? I'm drained, sir, and perhaps not just of breath.'

'Sir Gawain, were we not comrades once long ago?'

'Spare me, sir. I did my duty tonight. Is that not enough? Now I must go find my poor Horace, tied to a branch so he wouldn't wander, yet what if a wolf or bear comes upon him?'

'The mist hangs heavily across my past,' Axl said. 'Yet lately I find myself reminded of some task, and one of gravity, with which I was once entrusted. Was it a law, a great law to bring all men closer to God? Your presence, and your talk of Arthur, stirs long-faded thoughts, Sir Gawain.'

'My poor Horace, sir, so dislikes the forest at night. The hooting owl or the screech of a fox is enough to frighten him, no matter he'll face a shower of arrows without flinching. I'll go to him now, and let me urge you good people not to rest here too late. Forget the young Saxons, the pair of them. Think now of your own cherished son waiting for you at his village. Best go on your way quickly, I say, now you're without your blankets and provisions. The river's near and a fast tide on it flowing east. A friendly word with a bargeman may secure you a ride downstream. But don't dally here, for who knows when soldiers will come this way? God protect you, friends.'

With a rustle and a few thumps, Sir Gawain's form disappeared into the dark foliage. After a moment, Beatrice said:

'We didn't bid him farewell, Axl, and I feel poorly for it. Yet that was a strange leave he took of us and a sudden one.'

'I thought so too, princess. But perhaps he gives us wise counsel. We should hurry on to our son and never mind our recent

companions. I feel concern for poor Master Edwin, yet if he'll
hasten back to the monastery, what can we do for him?'

'Let's rest just a moment longer, Axl. Soon we'll be on our way,
the two of us, and we'd do well to seek a barge to speed our journey. Our son must be wondering what keeps us.'

Chapter Eight

The young monk was a thin, sickly-looking Pict who spoke Edwin's language well. No doubt he had been delighted to have in his company someone nearer his own age, and for the first part of the journey down through the dawn mists, he had talked with relish. But since entering the trees, the young monk had fallen silent and Edwin now wondered if he had in some way offended his guide. More likely the monk was simply anxious not to attract the attention of whatever lurked in these woods; amidst the pleasant birdsong, there had been some strange hissings and murmurs. When Edwin had asked once again, more from a wish to break the silence than for reassurance, 'So my brother's wounds seemed not to be mortal?' the reply had been almost curt.

'Father Jonus says not. There's none wiser.'

Wistan, then, could not be so badly hurt. Indeed, he must have managed this same journey down the hill not long ago, and while it was still dark. Had he had to lean heavily on the arm of his guide? Or had he managed to go mounted on his mare, perhaps with a monk holding steady the bridle?

'Show this boy down to the cooper's cottage. And take care no one sees you leave the monastery.' Such, according to the young monk, had been Father Jonus's instruction to him. So Edwin would soon be reunited with the warrior, but what sort of welcome could he expect? He had let Wistan down at the first challenge. Instead of hurrying to his side at the first sign of battle, Edwin had run off into the long tunnel. But his mother had not been down there, and only when the tunnel's end had finally appeared, distant and moon-like in the blackness, had he felt lifting from him the heavy clouds of dream and realised with horror what had occurred.

At least he had done his utmost once he had emerged into the chilly morning air. He had run almost the whole way back up to the monastery, slowing only for the steepest slopes. Sometimes, pushing through the woods, he had felt himself lost, but then the trees had thinned and the monastery had appeared against the pale sky. So he had gone on climbing and arrived at the big gate, breathless and with his legs aching.

The small door beside the main gate was unlocked, and he had managed to collect himself sufficiently to enter the grounds with stealthy care. He had been aware of smoke for the latter part of his climb, but now it tickled his chest, making it hard not to cough loudly. He knew then for sure it was too late to move the hay wagon, and felt a great emptiness opening within him. But he had pushed the feeling aside for another moment, and pressed on into the grounds.

For some time he came across neither monk nor soldier. But as he moved along the high wall, ducking his head so as not to be spotted from some far-off window, he had seen below the soldiers' horses crowded together in the small yard inside the main gate. Bound on all sides by high walls, the animals, still saddled, were circling nervously, even though there was scarcely space to do so without colliding. Then as he came towards the monks' quarters, where another of his age might well have rushed on to the central courtyard, he had had the presence of mind to recall the geography of the grounds and proceed by a roundabout route, utilising what he remembered of the back ways. Even on reaching his destination, he had placed himself behind a stone pillar and peered round cautiously.

The central courtyard was barely recognisable. Three robed figures were sweeping wearily, and as he watched, a fourth arrived with a pail and tossed water across the cobbles, setting to flight several lurking crows. The ground was strewn in places with straw and with sand, and his eyes were drawn to the several shapes covered over with sackcloth, which he supposed to be corpses. The old stone tower, where he knew Wistan had held out, loomed over the scene, but this too had changed: it was charred and blackened in many places, especially around its arched entryway and each of its narrow windows. To Edwin's eyes the tower as a whole appeared to have shrunk. He had been craning his neck around the pillar to ascertain if the pools surrounding the covered shapes were of blood or of water, when the bony hands had grasped his shoulders from behind.

He had twisted around to find Father Ninian, the silent monk, staring into his eyes. Edwin had not cried out, but had said, in a low voice, pointing towards the bodies: 'Master Wistan, my Saxon brother. Does he lie there?'

The silent monk appeared to understand, and shook his head emphatically. But even as he raised a finger to his lips in the familiar manner, he had stared warningly into Edwin's face. Then, glancing furtively around him, Ninian had tugged Edwin away from the courtyard.

'Can we be certain, warrior,' he had asked Wistan the day before, 'the soldiers will really come? Who'll tell them we're here? Surely these monks believe us but simple shepherds.'

'Who knows, boy. Perhaps we'll be left in peace. But there's one I fancy may betray our presence here, and even now the good Brennus may be issuing his orders. Test it well, young comrade. Britons have a way of dividing a bale from within with wooden slats. We need it pure hay all the way down.'

He and Wistan had been in the barn behind the old tower. Having for the moment done with woodcutting, the warrior had been seized by the urge to load the rickety wagon high with the hay stored at the back of the shed. As they had set about this task, Edwin had been required at regular intervals to clamber up onto the bales and prod into them with a stick. The warrior, observing carefully from the ground, would sometimes make him go over a section again, or order him to thrust a leg as far down as possible into a particular spot.

'These holy men are just the sort to get absent-minded,' Wistan had said by way of explanation. 'They may have left a spade or pitchfork in the hay. If so, it would be a service to retrieve it for them, tools being scarce up here.'

Although at that point the warrior had given no hint as to the purpose of the hay, Edwin had known straight away it had to do with the confrontation ahead, and that was why, as the bales had piled up, he had asked his question about the soldiers.

'Who'll betray us, warrior? The monks don't suspect us. They're so concerned with their holy quarrels, they hardly glance our way.'

'Maybe so, boy. But test there too. Just there.'

'Can it be, warrior, it's the old couple will betray us? Surely they're too foolish and honest.'

'They may be Britons, but I don't fear their treachery. Yet you'd be wrong to suppose them foolish, boy. Master Axl, for one, is a deep fellow.'

'Warrior, why do we travel with them? They slow us at every turn.'

'They slow us, right enough, and we'll part ways soon. Yet this morning as we set off, I felt eager for Master Axl's company. And I may wish for more of it yet. As I say, he's a deep one. He and I may have a little more to discuss. But just now let's concentrate on what faces us here. We must load this wagon in a sure and steady way. We need pure hay. No wood or iron there. See how I depend on you, boy.'

But Edwin had let him down. How could he have gone on sleeping for so long? It had been a mistake to lie down at all. He should simply have sat upright in the corner, napping a few winks the way he had seen Wistan do, ready at the first noise to start to his feet. Instead, like an infant, he had accepted from the old woman a cup of milk, and fallen into a deep sleep in his corner of the chamber.

Had his real mother called him in his dreams? Perhaps that was why he had remained asleep for so long. And why, when he had been shaken awake by the crippled monk, instead of rushing to the warrior's side, he had followed after the others down into the long, strange tunnel, for all the world as if he were still in the depths of dreaming.

It had been his mother's voice without doubt, the same voice that had called to him in the barn. 'Find the strength for me, Edwin. Find the strength and come rescue me. Come rescue me. Come rescue me.' There had been an urgency there he had not heard the previous morning. And there had been more: as he had stood at that open trap-door, staring down at the steps leading into the darkness, he had felt something pull at him with such force he had become giddy, almost sick.

The young monk was holding back blackthorn with a stick, waiting for Edwin to go ahead of him. Now at last he spoke, though in a hushed voice.

'A short cut. We'll soon see the roof of the cooper's cottage.'

As they came out of the woods to where the land swept down into the receding mist, Edwin could still hear movement and hissing in the nearby bracken. And he thought of the sunny evening towards the end of summer, when he had talked with the girl.

He had not at first seen the pond that day, for it had been small and well hidden by rushes. A cloud of brightly coloured insects had flown up before him, an event normally to draw his attention, but on this occasion he had been too preoccupied by the noise coming from the water's edge. An animal in a trap? There it was again, behind the birdsong and the wind. The noise followed a pattern: an intense burst of rustling, as of a struggle, then silence. Then soon, more rustling. Approaching cautiously, he had heard laboured breathing. Then the girl had been before him.

She was lying on her back in the rough grass, her torso twisted to one side. She was a few years older than him – fifteen or sixteen – and her eyes were fixed on him without fear. It took a while to realise her odd posture had to do with her hands being tied under her body. The flattened grass around her marked the area where, by pushing with her legs, she had been sliding about in her struggles. Her cloth smock, tied at the waist, was discoloured – perhaps soaked – all along one side, and both her legs, unusually dark-skinned, bore fresh scratches from the thistles.

It occurred to him she was an apparition or a sprite, but when she spoke her voice had no echo to it.

'What do you want? Why have you come?'

Recovering himself, Edwin said: 'If you like, I could help you.'

'These knots aren't difficult. They just tied me more tightly than usual.'

Only now did he notice her face and neck were covered in perspiration. Even as she spoke, her hands, under her back, were busily struggling.

'Are you hurt?' he asked.

'Not hurt. But a beetle landed on my knee just now. It clung on and bit me. There'll be a swelling now. I can see you're still too much of a child to help me. It doesn't matter, I'll manage myself.'

Her gaze remained fixed on him, even as her face tightened and she twisted and raised her torso a little way off the ground. He watched, transfixed, expecting at any moment to see the hands come out from under her. But she sagged down defeated and lay in the grass, breathing hard and staring angrily at him.

'I could help,' Edwin said. 'I'm good with knots.'

'You're just a child.'

'I'm not. I'm nearly twelve.'

'They'll come back soon. If they find you've untied me, they'll beat you.'

'Are they grown-ups?'

'They think they are, but they're just boys. Older than you though and there's three of them. They'd like nothing better than to beat you. They'll force your head into that muddy water until you pass out. I've watched them do it before.'

'Are they from the village?'

'The village?' She looked at him with contempt. '*Your* village? We pass village after village every day. What do we care about your village? They may come back soon, then you'll be in trouble.'

'I'm not afraid. I could free you if you like.'

'I always free myself.' She twisted again.

'Why did they tie you?'

'Why? I suppose so they could watch. Watch me try to get free. But they're gone now, to steal food.' Then she said: 'I thought you villagers worked all day. Why does your mother let you wander?'

'I'm allowed because I finished three corners by myself already today.' Then he added: 'My real mother's not in the village any more.'

'Where's she gone?'

'I don't know. She was taken. I live with my aunt now.'

'When I was a child like you,' she said, 'I lived in a village. Now I travel.'

'Who do you travel with?'

'Oh . . . with them. We pass this way quite often. I remember them tying me and leaving me here once before, this very spot, last spring.'

'I'll release you,' he said suddenly. 'And if they come back, I won't be frightened of them.'

Yet something still held him back. He had expected her eyes to shift away, or her body at least to accommodate the prospect of his approach. But she had gone on staring at him, while under her arched back her hands continued their struggle. Only when she let out a long sigh did he realise she had been holding her breath for some time.

'I can usually do it,' she said. 'If you weren't here, I'd have done it by now.'

'Do they tie you to stop you running away?'

'Run away? Where would I run away? I travel with them.' Then she said: 'Why did you come to me? Why don't you go help your mother instead?'

'My mother?' He was genuinely surprised. 'Why should my mother want me to help her?'

'You said she was taken, didn't you?'

'Yes, but that was long ago. She's happy now.'

'How can she be happy? Don't you think she wants someone to come and help her?'

'She's just travelling. She wouldn't want me to . . .'

'She didn't want you to come before because you were a child. But you're nearly a man now.' She fell silent, arching her back as she made another concerted effort. Then she sagged back down again. 'Sometimes,' she said, 'if they come back and I haven't got myself free, they don't untie me. They watch and don't say a word until I manage by myself and my hands come loose. Until then they sit there watching and watching, their devil's horns growing between their legs. I'd mind it less if they spoke. But they stare and stare and don't say anything.' Then she said: 'When I saw you, I thought you'd do the same. I thought you'd sit and stare and not say a thing.'

'Shall I untie you? I'm not afraid of them, and I'm good with knots.'

'You're only a child.' Suddenly tears appeared. It happened so quickly, and because her face showed no other sign of emotion, Edwin thought at first he was watching perspiration. But then he realised they were tears, and because her face was half-upturned, the tears rolled oddly, past the bridge of her nose and down the opposite cheek. All the while she held her gaze on him. The tears confused him, making him stop in his tracks.

'Come on then,' she said, and for the first time moved onto her side, letting her gaze fall away towards the bulrushes in the water.

Edwin hurried forward, like a thief spying an opportunity, and crouching in the grass began to tug at the knots. The twine was thin and coarse, cutting cruelly into her wrists; the palms, in contrast, spread open one across the other, were small and tender. At first the knots did not yield, but he forced himself to be calm and studied carefully the path the coils took. Then when he tried again, the knot gave under his touch. Now he went about his work more confidently, glancing from time to time at the soft palms, waiting like a pair of docile creatures.

After he pulled the twine from her, she turned and sat facing him at what suddenly felt an uncomfortably close distance. She did not, he noticed, smell of stale excrement the way most people did: her odour was like that of a fire made from damp wood.

'If they come,' she said quietly, 'they'll drag you through the reeds then half-drown you. You'd better go. Go back to your village.' She reached out a hand experimentally, as though unsure if even now it was under her control, and pushed his chest. 'Go. Hurry.'

'I'm not afraid of them.'

'You're not afraid. But they'll still do all these things to you. You helped me, but you have to go away now. Go, hurry.'

When he returned just before sunset, the grass was still flattened where she had lain, but there was no other trace left of her. All the same, the spot felt almost uncannily tranquil, and he had sat down in the grass for some moments, watching the bulrushes waving in the wind.

He never told anyone about the girl – not his aunt, who would quickly have concluded she was a demon, nor any of the other boys. But in the weeks that followed, a vivid image of her had often returned to him unbidden; sometimes at night, within his dreams; often in broad daylight, as he was digging the ground or helping to mend a roof, and then the devil's horn would grow between his legs. Eventually the horn would go away, leaving him with a feeling of shame, and then the girl's words would return to him: 'Why did you come to me? Why don't you go help your mother instead?'

But how could he go to his mother? The girl herself had said he was 'only a child'. Then again, as she had pointed out, he would soon be a man. Whenever he recalled those words, he would feel his shame anew, and yet he had been able to see no way forward.

But that had all changed the moment Wistan had thrown open the barn door, forcing in the dazzling light, and declared that it was he, Edwin, who had been chosen for the mission. And now here they were, Edwin and the warrior, travelling across the country, and surely it would not be long till they came upon her. Then the men travelling with her would tremble.

But had it really been her voice that had led him away? Had it not been sheer terror of the soldiers? Such questions drifted into his mind as he followed the young monk down a barely trodden path beside a descending stream. Was he sure he had not simply panicked when he had been awoken and seen from the window the soldiers running about the old tower? But now, when he considered it all carefully, he was certain he had felt no fear. And earlier, during the day, when the warrior had led him into that same tower and they had talked, Edwin had felt only an impatience to stand at Wistan's side in the face of the oncoming enemy.

Wistan had been preoccupied with the old tower from the time they had first arrived at the monastery. Edwin could remember him continually glancing up at it while they had been cutting logs in the woodshed. And when they had pushed the barrow around the grounds to deliver the firewood, they had twice made diversions just to go past it. So it had come as no surprise, once the monks had disappeared into their meeting and the courtyard was empty, that the warrior should lean the axe on the woodpile and say: 'Come a moment, young comrade, and we'll examine more closely this tall and ancient friend who stares down at us. It seems to me he watches where we go, and takes offence we've yet to pay him a visit.'

As they had entered under the low arch into the chilly dimness of the tower's interior, the warrior had said to him: 'Take care. You think you're inside, but look to your feet.'

Glancing down, Edwin had seen in front of him a kind of moat which followed the circular wall all the way to form a ring. It was too wide for a man to leap, and the simple bridge of two planks was the only way to reach the central floor of trodden earth. As he stepped onto the planks, gazing down into the darkness below, he heard the warrior say behind him:

'Notice there's no water there, young comrade. And even if you fell right in, I'd say you'd find it no deeper than your own height. Curious, don't you think? Why a moat on the *inside*? Why a moat at all for a small tower like this? What good can it do?' Wistan came over the planks himself and tested with his heel the central floor. 'Perhaps,' he went on, 'the ancients built this tower to slaughter animals. Perhaps once this was their killing floor. What they didn't wish to keep of an animal, they simply pushed over the side into the moat. What do you think, boy?'

'That's possible, warrior,' Edwin said. 'Yet it would have been no easy thing to lead a beast across narrow planks like that.'

'Perhaps in olden times there was a better bridge here,' Wistan said. 'Sturdy enough to bear an ox or a bull. Once the beast had been led over, and it guessed its fate, or when the first blow failed to make it sink to its knees, this arrangement ensured it could not easily flee. Imagine the animal twisting, trying to charge, yet finding the moat wherever it turned. And the one small bridge so hard to locate in a frenzy. It's no foolish notion, that this was once such a place of slaughter. Tell me, boy, what do you find when you look up?'

Edwin, seeing the circle of sky high above, said: 'It's open at the top, warrior. Like a chimney.'

'You say something interesting there. Let's hear it again.'

'It's like a chimney, warrior.'

'What do you make of it?'

'If the ancients used this place for their slaughter, warrior, they'd have been able to build a fire just where we now stand. They could have jointed the animal, roasted the meat, the smoke escaping up to the sky.'

'It's likely, boy, just as you say. I wonder if these Christian monks have any inkling of what went on here once? These gentlemen, I fancy, come inside this tower for its quiet and seclusion. See how thick is this circling wall. Hardly a sound comes through it, though the crows were shrieking as we entered. And the way the light comes from on high. It must remind them of their god's grace. What do you say, boy?'

'The gentlemen might come in here and pray, right enough, warrior. Though this ground's too soiled to kneel on.'

'Perhaps they pray standing, guessing little how this was once a place of slaughter and burning. What else do you see looking up, boy?'

'Nothing, sir.'

'Nothing?'

'Only the steps, warrior.'

'Ah, the steps. Tell me about the steps.'

'They first rise over the moat, then circle and circle, bending with the roundness of the wall. They rise till they reach the sky at the top.'

'That's well observed. Now listen carefully.' Wistan stepped closer and lowered his voice. 'This place, not just this old tower, but this entire place, all of what men today call this monastery, I'd wager was once a hillfort built by our Saxon forefathers in times of war. So it contains many cunning traps to welcome invading Britons.' The warrior moved away and slowly paced the perimeter of the floor, staring down into the moat. Eventually he looked up again and said: 'Imagine this place a fort, boy. The siege broken after many days, the enemy pouring in. Fighting in every yard, on every wall. Now picture this. Two of our Saxon cousins, out there in the yard, hold back a large body of Britons. They fight bravely, but the enemy's too great in number and our heroes must retreat. Let's suppose they retreat here, into this very tower. They skip across the little bridge and turn to face their foes at this very spot. The Britons grow confident. They have our cousins cornered. They press in with their swords and axes, hurry over the bridge towards our heroes. Our brave kin bring down the first of them, but soon must retreat further. Look there, boy. They retreat up those winding stairs along the wall. Still more Britons cross the moat until this space where we stand is filled. Yet the Britons' greater numbers can't yet be turned to advantage. For our brave cousins fight two abreast on the stairs, and the invaders can but meet them two against two. Our heroes are skilled, and though they retreat higher and higher, the invaders cannot overwhelm them. As Britons fall, those following take their place, then fall in their turn. But surely our cousins grow weary. Higher and higher they retreat, the invaders pursue them stair by stair. But what's this? What's this, Edwin? Do our kin finally lose their nerve? They turn and run the remaining circles of steps, only now and then striking behind them. This is surely the end. The Britons are triumphant. Those watching from down here smile like hungry men before a banquet. But look carefully, boy. What do you see? What do you see as our Saxon cousins near that halo of sky above?' Grasping Edwin's shoulders, Wistan repositioned him, pointing up to the opening. 'Speak, boy. What do you see?'

'Our cousins spring a trap, sir. They retreat upwards only to draw in the Britons as ants to a honey pot.'

'Well said, lad! And how's the trap made?'

Edwin considered for a moment, then said: 'Just before the stairway reaches its highest point, warrior, I can see what looks from here to be an alcove. Or is it a doorway?'

'Good. And what do you suppose hides there?'

'Can it be a dozen of our greatest warriors? Then together with our two cousins, they can fight their way down again till they cut into the ranks of the Britons here below.'

'Think again, boy.'

'A fierce bear, then, warrior. Or a lion.'

'When did you last meet a lion, boy?'

'Fire, warrior. There's fire behind that alcove.'

'Well said, boy. We can't know for sure what happened so long ago. Yet I'd wager that's what waited up there. In that little alcove, hardly glimpsed from down here, was a torch, or maybe two or three, blazing behind that wall. Tell me the rest, boy.'

'Our cousins throw the torches down.'

'What, onto the heads of the enemy?'

'No, warrior. Down into the moat.'

'The moat? Filled with water?'

'No, warrior. The moat's filled with firewood. Just like the fire-wood we've sweated to cut.'

'Just so, boy. And we'll cut more yet before the moon's high. And we'll find ourselves plenty of dry hay too. A chimney, you said, boy. You're right. It's a chimney we stand in now. Our fore-fathers built it for just such a purpose. Why else a tower here, when a man looking from the top has no better view than one at the wall outside? But imagine, boy, a torch dropping into this so-called moat. Then another. When we circled this place earlier, I saw at its back, close to the ground, openings in the stone. That means a strong wind from the east, such as we have tonight, will fan the flames ever higher. And how are the Britons to escape the inferno? A solid wall around them, only a single narrow bridge to freedom, and the moat itself ablaze. But let's leave this place, boy. It may be this ancient tower grows displeased we should guess so many of his secrets.'

Wistan turned towards the planks, but Edwin was still gazing up to the top of the tower.

'But warrior,' he said. 'Our two brave cousins. Must they burn in the flames with their foes?'

'If they did, wouldn't it be a glorious bargain? Yet perhaps it needn't come to that. Perhaps our two cousins, even as the scald-ing heat rises, race to the rim of the opening and leap from the top. Would they do that, boy? Even though they lack wings?'

'They have no wings,' Edwin said, 'but their comrades may have brought a wagon behind the tower. A wagon loaded deep with hay.'

'It's possible, boy. Who knows what went on here in ancient days? Now let's finish with our dreaming and cut a little more wood. For surely these good monks face many chilly nights yet before the summer comes.'

In a battle, there was no time for elaborate exchanges of information. A swift look, a wave of a hand, a barked word over the noise: that was all true warriors needed to convey their wishes to one another. It had been in such a spirit Wistan had made his thoughts clear that afternoon in the tower, and Edwin had let him down utterly.

But had the warrior expected too much? Even old Steffa had only talked of Edwin's great promise, what he would become *once he had been taught the warrior's ways*. Wistan had yet to finish training him, so how was Edwin to respond with such understanding? And now, it seems, the warrior was wounded, but surely this could not be Edwin's fault alone.

The young monk had paused by the edge of the stream to unfasten his shoes. 'This is where we ford,' he said. 'The bridge is much further down and the land there's too open. We may be seen from even the next hilltop.' Then pointing to Edwin's shoes, he said: 'Those look skilfully crafted. Did you make them yourself?'

'Master Baldwin made them for me. The most skilled shoe-maker in the village, even though he has fits every full moon.'

'Off with them. A soaking's sure to wreck them. Can you see the stepping stones? Lower your head more, and try to gaze beneath the water's surface. There, you see them? That's our pathway. Keep them in your sight and you'll stay dry.'

Again, the young monk's tone had something curt about it. Could it be that since they had set off he had had time to piece together in his mind Edwin's role in what had occurred? At the start of their journey, the young monk had not only been warmer in manner, he had hardly been able to stop talking.

They had met in the chilly corridor outside Father Jonus's cell, where Edwin had been waiting while several voices, lowered but passionate, argued from within. The dread of what he might soon be told had mounted, and Edwin had been relieved when instead of being summoned inside, he had seen the young monk emerge, a cheerful smile on his face.

'I've been chosen to be your guide,' he had said triumphantly, in Edwin's language. 'Father Jonus says we're to go at once and slip out unseen. Be brave, young cousin, you'll be at your brother's side before long.'

The young monk had an odd way of walking, clutching himself tightly like someone intensely cold, both arms lost within his robe, so that Edwin, following him down the mountain path, had wondered at first if he was one of those born with missing limbs. But as soon as the monastery was safely behind them, the young monk had fallen in step beside him, and producing a thin, long arm had placed it supportively around Edwin's shoulders.

'It was foolish of you to come back as you did, and after you'd made good your escape. Father Jonus was angry to hear of it. But here you are, safely away again, and with luck no one's the wiser about your return. But what an affair this is! Is your brother always so quarrelsome? Or is it one of the soldiers made some fierce insult to him in passing? Perhaps once you reach his bedside, young cousin, you'll ask him how it all began, for none of us can make head or tail of it. If it was he who insulted the soldiers, then it must have been something strong indeed, for they as one forgot whatever purpose brought them to see the abbot, and turning into wild men, set about trying to extract payment for his boldness. I myself woke at the sounds of the shouting, even though my own chamber's far from the courtyard. I ran there in alarm, only to stand helpless alongside my fellow monks, watching in horror all that unfolded. Your brother, they soon told me, had run into the ancient tower to escape the wrath of the soldiers, and though they rushed in after him with a mind to tear him limb from limb, it seems he began to fight them as best he knew. And a surprising match he seemed to be, even though they were thirty or more and he just one Saxon shepherd. We watched expecting any moment to see his bloody remains brought out, and instead it's soldier after soldier running from that tower in panic, or staggering out carrying wounded comrades. We could hardly believe our eyes! We were praying for the quarrel soon to end, for whatever the original insult, such violence's surely uncalled for. Yet it went on and on, and then, young cousin, the dreadful accident occurred. Who knows it wasn't God himself, frowning on so black a quarrel within his holy buildings, pointed a finger and struck them with fire? More likely it was one of the soldiers running back and forth with torches tripped and made his great error. The horror of it! Suddenly the tower was ablaze! And who'd think an old damp tower could offer so much kindling? Yet blaze it did and Lord Brennus's men together with your brother caught within. They'd have done better forgetting their quarrel at once and running out as fast as they could, but I fancy they thought instead to fight the flames, and saw only too late the fires engulfing them. An accident of true ghastliness, and the few who came out did so just to die twisting horribly on the ground. Yet miracle of miracles, young cousin, your brother it turns out escaped! Father Ninian found him wandering the darkness of the grounds, dazed and wounded, but still alive, even as the rest of us watched the blazing tower and prayed for the trapped men inside. Your brother lives, but Father Jonus, who himself treated his wounds, has counselled the few of us who know this news to keep it a solemn secret, even from the abbot himself. For he fears if the news gets further, Lord Brennus will send out more soldiers seeking vengeance, not caring that most died by accident and not by your brother's hand. You'd do well not to whisper a word of it to anyone, at least not until you're both far from this country. Father Jonus was angry you should risk yourself returning to the monastery, yet he's contented he can the more easily reunite you with your brother. "They must travel together out of this country," he said. The best of men is Father Jonus, and still our wisest, even after what the birds have done to him. I dare say your brother owes him and Father Ninian his life.'

But that had been earlier. Now the young monk had become distant, and his arms were once again tucked firmly within his robe. As Edwin followed him across the stream, trying his best to see the rocks beneath the swiftly running water, the thought came to him that he should make a clean breast of it to the warrior; tell him about his mother and how she had called to him. If he explained it all from the start, honestly and frankly, it was possible Wistan would understand and give him another chance.

A shoe in each hand, Edwin sprang lightly towards the next rock, faintly cheered by this possibility.

PART III

Gawain's First Reverie

Those dark widows. For what purpose did God place them on this mountain path before me? Does he wish to test my humility? Is it not enough he watches me save that gentle couple, the wounded boy also, slay a devil dog, sleep barely an hour on dew-soaked leaves before rising to learn my tasks are yet far from done, that Horace and I must set off again, not down to some sheltering village, but up another steep path beneath a grey sky? Yet he placed those widows there in my way, no doubt about it, and I did well to address them courteously. Even as they sank to foolish insults and throwing clumps of earth at Horace's hindquarters – as though Horace could be panicked into an unseemly gallop! – I gave them not so much as a backward glance, speaking instead into Horace's ear, reminding him we must bear all such trials well, for a far greater one awaited us up in those distant peaks where storm clouds now gathered. Besides, those weathered women with their flapping rags were once innocent maidens, some possessing beauty and grace, or at least the freshness that will often serve as well in a man's eye. Was she not that way, the one I sometimes remember when there stretches before me as much land, empty and companionless, as I could ride on a dreary autumn's day? No beauty was she, yet delightful enough for me. I only glimpsed her once, when I was young, and did I even speak to her then? Yet she returns sometimes in my mind's eye, and I believe she has visited me in my sleep, for I often awake with a mysterious contentment even as my dreams fade from me.

I felt the lingering joys of just such a feeling as Horace woke me this morning, stamping the soft forest ground where I had lain down after the night's exertions. He knows full well I no longer have the old stamina, that after such a night it is no easy thing for me to sleep but a short hour before setting off once more. Yet seeing the sun already high over the shady roof of the forest, he would not let me sleep on. He stamped his feet until I rose, chainmail complaining. I curse this armour more and more. Has it really saved me from much? A small wound or two at best. It is the sword, not the armour, I have to thank for this abiding health. I rose and observed the leaves around me. Why so many fallen and the summer not yet old? Do these trees ail, even as they shelter us? A shaft of sun breaking through the high foliage fell across Horace's muzzle, and I watched him shake his nose from side to side, as though that beam were a fly sent to torment him. He had no pleasant night either, listening to noises of the forest all about him, wondering to what dangers his knight had gone. Displeased though I was that he aroused me so soon, when I stepped towards him, it was only to hold his neck gently in both my arms, and for a brief moment rest my head in his mane. A hard master he has, I know that. I push him on when I know him to be weary, curse him when he has done no wrong. And all this metal as much burden for him as for me. How much further will we ride together? I patted him gently, saying, 'We'll find a friendly village soon, and you'll have a better breakfast than the one you just had.'

I spoke this way believing the problem of Master Wistan settled. But we were hardly down the path, not yet out of the woods, when we came across the bedraggled monk, his shoes broken, hurrying before us to Lord Brennus's camp, and what does he tell us but that Master Wistan has escaped the monastery, leaving his pursuers of the night dead, many no more than charred bones. What a fellow! Strange how my heart fills with joy to hear the news, even though it brings back a heavy task I thought behind us. So Horace and I put aside our thoughts of hay and roast meat and good company, and now we climb uphill once more. Thankfully, at least, we travel further from that cursed monastery. In my heart, it is true, I am relieved Master Wistan did not perish at the hands of those monks and the wretched Brennus. But what a fellow! The blood he sheds each day would make the Severn overflow! He was wounded, the bedraggled monk thought, but who can rely on one such as Master Wistan to lie down and die easily? How foolish I was to let the boy Edwin run off that way, and now who will wager against the two of them finding each other? So foolish, yet I was weary then, and besides, little imagined Master Wistan could escape. What a fellow! Had he been a man of our day, Saxon though he is, he would have won Arthur's admiration. Even the best of us would have feared to meet him as a foe. Yet yesterday, when I saw him meet Brennus's soldier in combat, I might have seen a small weakness on his left side. Or was it his clever ploy of the moment? If I watch him fight once more, I will know better. A skilful warrior all the same, and it would take a knight of Arthur to suspect it, but I thought it so, as I watched the fight. I said to myself, look there, a small lapse on the left side. One a canny opponent might just exploit. Yet which of us would not have respected him?

Yet these dark widows, why do they cross our path? Is our day not busy enough? Our patience not yet sufficiently taxed? We'll stop at the next crest, I was saying to Horace as we came up the slope. We'll stop and rest even though black clouds gather and we most likely face a storm. And if there be no trees I'll still sit down right there on the scrubbed heather and we shall rest all the same. Yet when the road finally levelled, what do we see but great birds perched on their rocks, and they rise as one, not to fly into the darkening sky, but towards us. Then I saw they were no birds, but old women in flapping cloaks, assembling on the path before us.

Why choose such a barren spot to gather? Not a cairn, nor a dry well to mark it. No thin tree nor shrub to comfort a wayfarer from sun or rain. Just these chalky rocks from which they rose, sunk into the earth on either side of the road. Let's be sure, I said to Horace, let's be sure my old eyes don't let me down and these are not bandits come to set upon us. But there was no need to draw the sword – its blade still stinks of that devil dog's slime, no matter I thrust it deep in the ground before I slept – for they were old women sure enough, though we might have made good use of a shield or two against them. Ladies, let us remember them as ladies, Horace, now we are finally beyond them, for are they not to be pitied? We will not call them hags, even if their manners tempt us to. Let us remember that once, some among them at least possessed grace and beauty.

'Here he comes,' cried one, 'the impostor knight!' Others took up the cry as I came closer, and we might have trotted through their ranks, but I am not one to shy from adversity. So I brought Horace to a halt right in their midst, though gazing towards the next peak as if studying the gathering clouds. Only when their rags flapped around me, and I could feel the blast of their shouts, did I gaze down from the saddle at them. Were there fifteen?

Twenty? Hands reached to touch Horace's flanks, and I whispered to calm him. Then I straightened and said, 'Ladies, if we are to talk, you must cease this noise!' To which they quietened, but their looks stayed angry, and I said then, 'What do you want of me, ladies? Why come upon me this way?' To which one woman calls up, 'We know you for the foolish knight too timid to complete the task given him.' And another, 'If you'd done long ago what God asked of you, would we be wandering the land in woe this way?' And yet another, 'He dreads his duty! See it on his face. He dreads his duty!'

I contained my anger and asked them to explain themselves. Whereupon one a little more civil than the rest stepped forward. 'Forgive us, knight. It's long days we've wandered under these skies and to see you in person come riding boldly our way, we cannot but make you hear our laments.'

'Mistress,' I said to her, 'I may look burdened by years. But I remain a knight of the great Arthur. If you'll tell me your troubles, I'll gladly help you as I can.'

To my dismay the women – the civil one included – all broke into a sarcastic laugh, and then a voice said: 'Had you done your duty long ago and slain the she-dragon, we'd not be wandering distressed this way.'

This shook me, and I cried out, 'What do you know of it? What do you know of Querig?' but saw in time the need for restraint. And so I spoke calmly: 'Explain it, ladies, what compels you to walk the roads this way?' To which a parched voice behind said, 'If you ask why I wander, knight, I'll happily tell you. When the boatman put to me his questions, my beloved already in the boat and reaching out to help me in, I found my most treasured memories robbed from me. I didn't know then but know now,

Querig's breath was the thief robbed me, the very creature you were to have slain long ago.'

'How can you know this, mistress?' I demanded, no longer able to hide my consternation. For how can it be such vagabonds know a secret so well guarded? To which the civil one then smiles strangely and says, 'We're widows, knight. There's little can be hidden from us now.'

Only then do I feel Horace give a tremble, and I hear myself ask, 'What are you, ladies? Are you living or dead?' To which the women once more break into laughter, a jeering sound to it that makes Horace shift a hoof uneasily. I pat him gently while I say, 'Ladies, why do you laugh? Was that so foolish a question?' And the raspy voice behind says, 'See how fearful he is! Now he fears us as readily as he does the dragon!'

'What nonsense is this, lady?' I shout more forcefully, as Horace takes a step back against my wishes, and I have to tug to steady him. 'I fear no dragon, and fierce though Querig is, I've faced far greater evils in my time. If I've been slow to slay her, it's only because she hides herself with great cunning in those high rocks. You rebuke me, madam, but what do we hear of Querig now? A time was she thought nothing of raiding a village or more each month, yet boys have grown into men since we last heard of the like. She knows I close in, so she dares not show herself beyond these hills.'

Even as I spoke, one woman opened her raggy cloak and a clump of mud struck Horace's neck. Intolerable, I told Horace, we must go on. What can these old crones know of our mission? I nudged him to move forward but he was strangely frozen, and I had to dig in my spur to make him push forward. Thankfully the dark figures parted before us and I was gazing again at the distant peaks. My heart sank at the thought of those desolate high grounds. Even the company of these unholy hags, I thought, might be preferable to those bleak winds. But as though to disabuse me of such sentiments, the women started up their chant behind me, and I felt more mud flung our way. But what do they chant? Do they dare cry 'coward'? I had a mind to turn and show my wrath, yet remembered myself in time. Coward, coward. What do they know? Were they there? Were they there that day long ago we rode out to face Querig? Would they have called me coward then, or any of us five? And even after that great mission – from which only three returned – did I not then, ladies, with hardly a rest, hurry to the valley's edge to make good my promise to the young maid?

Edra, she later told me was her name. She was no beauty, and dressed in the simplest weeds, but like that other I sometimes dream of, she had a bloom tugged my heart. I saw her on the roadside carrying her hoe in both her arms. Only lately become a woman, she was small and slight, and the sight of such innocence, wandering unprotected so near the horrors from which I just came made it impossible for me to ride by, even if I went to such a mission as I did.

'Turn back, maiden,' I called down from the stallion, this being before the days of Horace, when even I was young. 'What great foolishness makes you go that way? Don't you know a battle rages down in this valley?'

'I know it well, sir,' she says, and no fear meeting my eye. 'It's a long journey I've made to come this far, and soon I'll be down the valley and join the battle.'

'Has some sprite bewitched you, maiden? I came from the valley floor just now where seasoned warriors spew out their stomachs from dread. I'd not have you hear even a distant echo of it. And why that hoe so large for you?'

'There's a Saxon lord I know is down in the valley now, and I pray with all my heart he isn't fallen and God will protect him well. For I will have him die at my hands only, after what he did to my dear mother and sisters, and I carry this hoe to do the work. It breaks the ground of a winter's morning, so it will do well enough on this Saxon's bones.'

I was obliged then to dismount and hold her by the arm even as she tried to pull away. If she still lives today – Edra, she later told me was her name – she would now be near your age, ladies. It may even be she was among you just now, how would I know? No great beauty, but like that other, her innocence spoke to me. 'Let me go, sir!' she cries, to which I say, 'You'll not go down into that valley. The sight from the edge alone will make you swoon.' 'I'm no weakling, sir,' she cries. 'Let me go!' And there we stand on the roadside like two quarrelling children, and I can calm her only by saying:

'Maiden, I see nothing will dissuade you. But think how remote the chances of your finding alone the vengeance you crave. Yet with my help your chances will improve manyfold. So be patient and sit a while out of this sun. Look there, sit beneath that elder tree, and wait for my return. I go to join four comrades on a mission which though grave with danger, won't keep me long. Should I perish you'll see me come this way again tied across the saddle of this same horse, and you'll know I can no longer keep my promise. Otherwise I swear I'll return and we'll together go down to make your dream of vengeance true. Be patient, maiden, and if your cause is just, as I believe it to be, God will see this lord doesn't fall before we reach him.'

Were these the words of a coward, ladies, uttered that very day, even as I rode out to face Querig? And once we were done with our task, and I saw I had been spared – though two of us five had not – I hastened back, weary as I was, to that valley's edge and the elder tree where the maid still waited, her hoe in her arms. She sprang to her feet, and the sight of her again tugged my heart. Yet when I tried once more to sway her from her intent, for I dreaded to see her enter that valley, she said angrily, 'Are you false, sir? Will you not keep your promise to me?' So I placed her on the saddle – she held the rein even as she clasped the hoe to her bosom – and I led on foot both horse and maiden down the valley slopes. Did she blanch as we first heard the din? Or when on the outskirts of the battle we met desperate Saxons, their pursuers on their heels? Did she wilt when exhausted warriors groped across our path trailing wounds along the ground? Small tears appeared and I saw her hoe tremble, but she did not turn away. For her eyes had their task, searching that bloody field left and right, far and near. Then I mounted the horse myself, and carrying her before me as if she were some gentle lamb, we rode together into the thick. Did I look timid then, thrashing with my sword, covering her with my shield, turning the horse this way and that until finally the battle tossed us both into the mud? But she was quickly on her feet, and recovering her hoe, began to tread a path through the mashed and quartered heaps. Our ears filled with the strange cries, but she seemed not to hear, the way a good Christian maid refuses the lewd shouts of the coarse men she passes. I was young then and nimble of foot, so ran about her with my sword, cutting down any who would do her harm, sheltering her with my shield from the arrows that regularly fell among us. Then she saw at last the one she sought, yet it was as if we were adrift on choppy waves and though an isle seems near, the tides somehow keep it beyond reach. It was that way for us that day. I fought and battered and kept her safe, yet it seemed an eternity till we stood before him, and even then three men specially to guard him. I passed my shield to the maid, saying, 'Shelter well, for your prize is almost yours,' and though I faced three, and I saw they were warriors of skill, I defeated them one by one till I faced the Saxon lord she so hated. His knees were thick with the gore he waded through, but I saw this was no warrior, and I brought him down till he lay breathing on the earth, his legs no more use to him, staring his hatred up at the sky. So she came then and stood above him, the shield tossed aside, and the look in her eyes chilled my blood over all else to be seen across that ghastly field. Then she brought the hoe down not with a swing, but a small prod, then another, the way she is searching for crops in the soil, until I am made to cry, 'Finish it, maiden, or I'll do it myself!' to which she says, 'Leave me now, sir. I thank you for your service, but now it's done.' 'Only half done, maiden,' I cry, 'till I see you safe from this valley,' but she no longer listens and goes on with her foul work. I would have quarrelled further, but it was then he appeared from the crowd. I mean Master Axl, as I now know him, a younger man that day to be sure, but a wise countenance even then, and when I saw him it was as if the noise of battle receded to a hush around us.

'Why stand so exposed, sir?' I say to him. 'And your sword still in its sheath? Take up a fallen shield at least and cover yourself.'

But he keeps a faraway look, as if he stands in a meadow of daisies on a fragrant morning. 'If God chooses to direct an arrow this way,' he says, 'I'll not impede it. Sir Gawain, I'm pleased to see you well. Are you lately arrived, or have you been here from its start?'

This as if we meet at some summer fair, and I am obliged to cry again, 'Cover yourself, sir! The field remains thick with the foe.' And when he continues to survey the scenery, I say, remembering his question to me: 'I was here at the battle's start, but Arthur then chose me as one of five to ride to a mission of great import. I'm only now returned from it.'

At last I draw his attention. 'A mission of great import? And did it go well?'

'Sadly, two comrades lost, but we accomplished it to Master Merlin's satisfaction.'

'Master Merlin,' he says. 'A sage he may be, but that old man makes me shudder.' Then he glances about once more, saying, 'I'm sorry to hear of your lost friends. Many more will be missed before the day closes.'

'Yet the victory's surely ours,' I say. 'These cursed Saxons. Why fight on this way with only Death to thank them for it?'

'I believe they do so for sheer anger and hatred of us,' he says. 'For it must be by now word has reached their ears of what's been done to their innocents left in their villages. I'm myself just come from them, so why would the news not reach also the Saxon ranks?'

'What news do you speak of, Master Axl?'

'News of their women, children and elderly, left unprotected after our solemn agreement not to harm them, now all slaughtered by our hands, even the smallest babes. If this were lately done to us, would our hatred exhaust itself? Would we not also fight to the last as they do, each fresh wound given a balm?'

'Why dwell on this matter, Master Axl? Our victory today's secure and will be a famous one.'

'Why do I dwell on it? Sir, these are the very villages I

befriended in Arthur's name. In one village they called me the Knight of Peace, and today I watched a mere dozen of our men ride through it with no hint of mercy, the only ones to oppose them boys not yet grown to our shoulders.'

'I'm saddened to hear this news. But I press you again, sir, pick up a shield at least.'

'I came upon village by village the same, and our own men boasting of what they did.'

'Don't blame yourself, sir, nor my uncle. The great law you once brokered was a thing truly wondrous while it held. How many innocents, Briton or Saxon, were spared over the years for it? That it didn't hold forever is none of your doing.'

'Yet they believed in our bargain till this day. It was I won their trust where first there was only fear and hatred. Today our deeds make me a liar and a butcher, and I take no joy in Arthur's victory.'

'What will you do with such wild words, sir? If it's treachery you contemplate, let's face one another with no more delay!'

'Your uncle's safe from me, sir. Yet how do you rejoice, Sir Gawain, in a victory won at this price?'

'Master Axl, what was done in these Saxon towns today my uncle would have commanded only with a heavy heart, knowing of no other way for peace to prevail. Think, sir. Those small Saxon boys you lament would soon have become warriors burning to avenge their fathers fallen today. The small girls soon bearing more in their wombs, and this circle of slaughter would never be broken. Look how deep runs the lust for vengeance! Look even now, at that fair maid, one I escorted here myself, watch her there still at her work! Yet with today's great victory a rare chance comes. We may once and for all sever this evil circle, and a great king must act boldly on it. May this be a famous day, Master Axl, from which our land can be in peace for years to come.'

'I fail to understand you, sir. Though today we slaughter a sea of Saxons, be they warriors or babes, there are yet many more across the land. They come from the east, they land by ship on our coasts, they build new villages by the day. This circle of hate is hardly broken, sir, but forged instead in iron by what's done today. I'll go now to your uncle and report what I've seen. I would see from his face if he believes God will smile on such deeds.'

A slaughterer of babes. Is that what we were that day? And what of that one I escorted, what became of her? Was she among you just now, ladies? Why gather about me this way as I ride to my duty? Let an old man go in peace. A slaughterer of babes. Yet I was not there, and even had I been, what good for me to argue with a great king, and he my uncle too? I was but a young knight then, and besides, is he not proved right each year that passes? Did you not all grow old in a time of peace? So leave us to go our way without insults at our back. The Law of the Innocents, a mighty law indeed, one to bring men closer to God – so Arthur himself always said, or was it Master Axl called it that? We called him Axelum or Axelus then, but now he goes by Axl, and has a fine wife. Why taunt me, ladies? Is it my fault you grieve? My time will come before long, and I will not turn back to roam this land as you do. I shall greet the boatman contentedly, enter his rocking boat, the waters lapping all about, and I may sleep a while, the sound of his oar in my ears. And I will move from slumber to half-waking, and see the sun sunk low over the water, and the shore moved further still, and nod myself back into dreams till the boatman's voice stirs me gently once more. And were he to ask questions, as some say he will, I would answer honestly, for what have I left to hide? I had no wife, though at times I longed for one. Yet I was a good knight who performed his duty to the end. Let me say so, and he will see I do not lie. I will not mind him. The gentle sunset, his shadow falling over me as he moves from one side of his vessel to the other. But this will wait. Today Horace and I must climb below this grey sky, up the barren slope towards the next peak, for our work is unfinished and Querig awaits us.

Chapter Ten

He had never intended to deceive the warrior. It was as if the deception itself had come quietly over the fields to envelop the two of them.

The cooper's hut appeared to be built inside a deep ditch, its thatch roof so close to the earth that Edwin, lowering his head to pass under it, felt he was climbing into a hole. So he had been prepared for the darkness, but the stifling warmth – and the thick woodsmoke – took him aback, and he announced his arrival with a fit of coughing.

'I'm pleased to see you safe, young comrade.'

Wistan's voice came out of the darkness beyond the smouldering fire, then Edwin discerned the warrior's form on a turf bed.

'Are you badly hurt, warrior?'

As Wistan sat up, slowly moving into the glow, Edwin saw his face, neck and shoulders were covered in perspiration. Yet the hands that reached to the fire were trembling as if from cold.

'The wounds are trivial. But they brought with them this fever. It was worse earlier, and I've little memory of coming here. The good monks say they tied me to the mare's back, and I fancy I was muttering all the while as when playing the slack-jawed fool in the forest. What of you, comrade? You bear no wounds, I trust, beyond the one you carried before.'

'I'm perfectly well, warrior, yet stand before you in shame. I'm a poor comrade to you, sleeping while you fought. Curse me and banish me from your sight, for it'll be a thing well earned.'

'Not so fast, Master Edwin. If you failed me last night, I'll soon tell you a way to make up your debt to me.'

The warrior carefully brought both feet to the earth floor, reached down and tossed a log onto the flames. Edwin saw then how his left arm was bound tightly in sacking, and that one side of his face had a spreading bruise that partially closed one eye.

'True,' Wistan said, 'when I first looked down from the top of that burning tower and the wagon we so carefully prepared wasn't there, I'd a mind to curse you. A long fall to stony ground and hot smoke already around me. Listening to the agonies of my enemies below, I asked, do I mingle with them even as we become ash together? Or better be smashed alone under the night sky? Yet before I could find an answer, the wagon arrived after all, tugged by my own mare, a monk pulling her bridle. I hardly asked if this monk was friend or foe, but leapt from that chimney mouth, and our earlier work was well enough done, comrade, for though I plunged through the hay as if it were water, I met nothing to pierce me. I awoke on a table, gentle monks loyal to Father Jonus attending me all around as if I was their supper. The fever must already have taken hold by then, whether from these wounds or from the great heat, for they say they had to muffle my ravings till they brought me down here out of harm's way. But if the gods favour us, the fever will pass soon and we'll set off to finish our errand.'

'Warrior, I still stand here in shame. Even after I awoke and saw the soldiers around the tower, I let some sprite possess me, and fled the monastery behind those elderly Britons. I'd beg you to curse me now or beat me, but I heard you say there was some way I might make up to you for last night's disgrace. Tell me the way, warrior, and I'll fall on whatever task you give me with impatience.'

Even as he said this, his mother's voice had called, resounding around the little hovel so Edwin was hardly sure he had spoken these words aloud. But he must have done, for he heard Wistan say:

'Do you suppose I chose you for your courage alone, young comrade? You've remarkable spirit right enough, and if we survive this errand, I'll see you learn the skills to make you a true warrior. But just now you're rough-hewn, not yet a blade. I chose you above others, Master Edwin, because I saw you had the hunter's gift to match your warrior spirit. A rare thing indeed to have both.'

'How can that be, warrior? I know nothing of hunting.'

'A wolf cub, drinking its mother's milk, can pick up the scent of a prey in the wild. I believe it a gift of nature. Once this fever leaves me, we'll go further into these hills and I'll wager you'll find the sky itself whispering to you which path to take till we stand before the she-dragon's very lair.'

'Warrior, I fear you misplace your faith where it will find no shelter. No kin of mine ever boasted of such skills, and no one suspected me of them. Even Steffa, who saw my warrior's soul, never mentioned such skills as these.'

'Then leave it to me alone to believe in them, young comrade. I'll never say you made any such boast. As soon as this fever leaves me, we'll set off towards those eastern hills, where all talk has it Querig has her lair, and I'll follow in your footsteps at each fork.'

It was then the deception had begun. He had never planned it, nor welcomed it when, like a pixie stepping out from its dark corner, it had entered their presence. His mother had continued to call. 'Find the strength for me, Edwin. You're almost grown.

Find the strength and come rescue me.' And it was as much the wish to appease her as his eagerness to redeem himself in the warrior's eyes that had made him say:

'It's curious, warrior. Now you speak of it, I feel already this she-dragon's pull. More a taste in the wind than a scent. We should go without delay, for who knows how long I'll feel it.'

Even as he said this, the scenes were rapidly filling his mind: how he would enter their camp, startling them as they sat silently in their semi-circle to watch his mother trying to free herself. They would be full-grown men by now; most likely bearded and heavy-bellied, no longer the lithe young men who had come swaggering into their village that day. Burly, coarse men, and as they reached for their axes, they would see the warrior following behind Edwin and fear would enter their eyes.

But how could he deceive the warrior – his teacher and the man he admired above all others? And here was Wistan nodding with satisfaction, saying: 'I knew it as soon as I saw you, Master Edwin. Even as I released you from those ogres by the river.' He would enter their camp. He would free his mother. The burly men would be killed, or perhaps be allowed to flee into the mountain fog. And then what? Edwin would have to explain why, even as they were hurrying to complete an urgent errand, he had chosen to deceive the warrior.

Partly to distract himself from such thoughts – for he now sensed it was too late for a retreat – he said: 'Warrior, there's a question I have of you. Though you may think it impertinent.'

Wistan was receding back into the darkness, reclining once more onto his bed. Now all Edwin could see of him was one bare knee moving slowly from side to side.

'Ask it, young comrade.'

'I'm wondering, warrior. Is there some special feud between you and Lord Brennus makes you stay and fight his soldiers when we might have fled the monastery and be half a day closer to Querig? It must be some mighty reason to make you put aside even your errand.'

The silence that followed was so long Edwin thought the warrior had passed out in the stifling air. But then there was the knee still moving slowly, and when the voice eventually came out of the darkness, the slight tremor of the fever seemed to have evaporated.

'I've no excuse, young comrade. I can only confess my folly, and that after the good father's warning not to forget my duty! See how weak is the resolve of your master. Yet I'm a warrior before all else, and it's no easy thing to flee a battle I know I can win. You're right, we could even now be standing at the she-dragon's den, calling her to come greet us. But Brennus I knew it to be, even a hope he'd come in person, and it was more than I could do not to stay and welcome them.'

'Then I'm right, warrior. There's some feud between you and Lord Brennus.'

'No feud worth the name. We knew each other as boys, as young as you are now. This was in a country further west of here, in a well-guarded fort where we boys, twenty or more, were trained morning till night to become warriors in the Britons' ranks. I grew to feel great affection for my companions of those days, for they were splendid fellows and we lived like brothers. All except Brennus, that is, for being the lord's son, he loathed to mix with us. Yet he often trained with us, and though his skills were feeble, whenever one of us faced him with a wooden sword, or at wrestling in the sandpit, we had to let him win. Anything short of glorious victory for the lord's son would result in punishments for us all. Can you imagine it, young comrade? To be proud young boys, as we were, and have such an inferior opponent appear to conquer us day after day? Worse, Brennus delighted in heaping humiliations on his opponents even as we feigned defeat. It pleased him to stand on our necks, or to kick us as we lay for him on the ground. Imagine how this felt to us, comrade!'

'I see it well, warrior.'

'But today I've reason to be grateful to Lord Brennus, for he saved me from a pitiable fate. I've told you already, Master Edwin, I'd begun to love my companions in that fort as my own brothers, even though they were Britons and I a Saxon.'

'But is that so shameful, warrior, if you were brought up beside them facing harsh tasks together?'

'Of course it's shameful, boy. I feel shame even now remembering the affection I had for them. But it was Brennus showed me my error. Perhaps because even then my skills stood out, he delighted to choose me as his sparring opponent, and reserved his greatest humiliations for me. And he was not slow to notice I was a Saxon boy, and before long, turned each of my companions against me on that account. Even those once closest to me joined against me, spitting in my food, or hiding my clothes as we hurried to our training on a harsh winter's morning, fearful of our teachers' wrath. It was a great lesson Brennus taught me then, and when I understood how I shamed myself loving Britons as my brothers, I made up my mind to leave that fort, even with no friend or kin beyond those walls.'

Wistan ceased speaking for a moment while his breath came heavily from beyond the fire.

'So did you take your revenge on Lord Brennus, warrior, before you left that place?'

'Judge for me if I did or not, comrade, for I'm undecided on the question. The custom in that fort was for us apprentices, after our day's training, to be allowed an hour after supper to idle away together. We'd build a fire in the yard and sit around it talking and jesting the way boys will. Brennus never joined us, of course, for he had his privileged quarters, but on that evening, for whatever reason, I saw him walk past. I moved away from the rest then, my companions suspecting nothing. Now that fort, like any other, had many hidden passages, all of which I knew well, so that before long I was in an unwatched corner where the battlements cast black shadows over the ground. Brennus came strolling my way, alone, and when I moved from the gloom he stopped and looked at me with terror. For he saw at once this could be no chance encounter, and further, that his usual powers were suspended. It was curious, Master Edwin, to see this swaggering lord turned so swiftly to an infant ready to make water before me for fear. I was sorely tempted to say to him, "Good sir, I see your sword on your hip. Knowing how much more skilfully you wield it, you'll have no fear drawing it against mine." Yet I said no such thing, for had I hurt him in that dark corner, what of my dreams of a life beyond those walls? I said nothing, but remained before him in silence, letting the moment grow long between us, for I wished it to be one never forgotten. And though he cowered back and would have cried for help had not some remnant of pride told him to do so would ensure his abiding humiliation, we neither of us spoke to the other. Then in time I left him, and so you see, Master Edwin, nothing and yet everything had passed between us. I knew then I'd do well to leave that very night, and since these were no longer times of war, the watch wasn't strict. I slipped quietly past the guards, saying no farewells, and was soon a boy under the moonlight, my dear companions left behind, my own kin long slaughtered, nothing but my courage and lately learned skills to carry on my journey.'

'Warrior, does Brennus hunt you even today fearing your vengeance from those days?'

'Who knows what demons whisper in that fool's ear? A great lord now, in this country and the next, yet he lives in dread of any Saxon traveller from the east passing through his lands. Has he fed the fear of that night again and again that it now sits in his belly a giant worm? Or is it the she-dragon's breath makes him forget whatever cause he once had to fear me, yet the dread grows all the more monstrous for being unnamed? Only last year a Saxon warrior from the fens, one I knew well, was killed as he travelled in peace through this very country. Yet I remain indebted to Lord Brennus for the lesson he taught me, for without it I might even now be counting Britons as my brother warriors. What troubles you, young comrade? You shift from foot to foot as if my fever possesses you also.'

So he had failed to hide his restlessness, but surely Wistan could not suspect his deception. Was it possible the warrior too could hear his mother's voice? She had been calling all the while the warrior had been speaking. 'Will you not find the strength for me, Edwin? Are you too young after all? Will you not come to me, Edwin? Did you not promise me that day you would?'

'I'm sorry, warrior. It's my hunter's instinct makes me impatient, for I fear to lose the scent, and the morning sun already rising outside.'

'We'll be gone as soon as I'm able to climb onto that mare's back. But leave me a little longer, comrade, for how else can we face such an opponent as this dragon when I'm too fevered to lift a sword?'

Chapter Eleven

He longed for a patch of sun to warm Beatrice. But though the opposite bank was often bathed in morning light, their side of the river remained shaded and cold. Axl could feel her leaning on him as they walked, and her shivering had grown steadily worse. He had been about to suggest another rest when at last they spotted the roof behind the willows, jutting out into the water.

It took some time to negotiate the muddy slope down to the boathouse, and when they stepped under its low arch, the near-darkness and the proximity of the lapping water seemed only to make Beatrice shiver more. They moved further inside, over damp wooden boards, and saw beyond the roof's overhang tall grass, rushes, and an expanse of the river. Then a man's figure rose from the shadows to their left, saying: 'Who might you be, friends?'

'God be with you, sir,' Axl said. 'We're sorry if we brought you from your sleep. We're just two weary travellers wishing to go downriver to our son's village.'

A broad, bearded man of middle years, clad in layers of animal skins, emerged into the light and scrutinised them. Eventually he asked, not unkindly:

'Is the lady there unwell?'

'She's only tired, sir, but unable to walk the remaining way. We hoped you might spare a barge or small boat to carry us. We depend on your kindness, for some misfortune lately took the bundles we carried, and with them the tin to recompense you. I can see, sir, you have but one boat now in the water. I can at least promise you safe passage for any cargo you'd entrust should you allow us to use it.'

The boatkeeper looked out at the boat rocking gently under the roof, then back at Axl. 'It'll be a while yet, friend, till this boat goes downstream, for I'm waiting for my companion to return with barley to fill it. But I see you're both weary and lately suffered some misfortune. So let me make this suggestion. Look there, friends. You see those baskets.'

'Baskets, sir?'

'They may look flimsy, but float well and will bear your weight, though you'll have to go one in each. We're accustomed to filling them with full sacks of corn, or even at times a slaughtered pig, and tethered behind a boat they'll travel even a rough river without jeopardy. And today, as you see, the water's steady, so you'll travel without worry.'

'You're kind, sir. But have you no basket large enough for the two of us?'

'You must go one to each basket, friends, or else fear drowning. But I'll gladly tether two together so you'll go almost as good as one. When you see the lower boathouse on this same side, your journey will be over, and I'll ask you to leave the baskets there well tied.'

'Axl,' Beatrice whispered, 'let's not separate. Let's go together on foot, slow though it may be.'

'Walking's beyond us now, princess. We both need warmth and food, and this river will carry us swiftly to our son's welcome.'

'Please, Axl. I don't want us to separate.'

'But this good man says he'll truss our two baskets together, and it'll be as good as we're arm in arm.' Then turning to the boatkeeper, he said: 'I'm grateful to you, sir. We'll do as you suggest. Please tie the baskets tightly, so there's no chance a swift tide will move us apart.'

'The danger isn't the river's speed, friend, but its slowness. It's easy to get caught in the weeds near the bank and move no further. Yet I'll lend you a strong staff to push with, so you'll have little to fear.'

As the boatkeeper went to the edge of his jetty and began to busy himself with rope, Beatrice whispered:

'Axl, please let's not be parted.'

'We're not to be parted, princess. Look how he makes his knots to keep us together.'

'The tide may part us, Axl, never mind what this man tells us.'

'We'll be fine, princess, and soon at our son's village.'

Then the boatkeeper was calling them, and they stepped carefully down the little stones to where he was steadying with a long pole two baskets bobbing in the water. 'They're well lined with hide,' he said. 'You'll hardly feel the river's cold.'

Though he found it painful to crouch, Axl kept both hands on Beatrice until she had safely lowered herself into the first basket.

'Don't try and rise, princess, or you'll endanger the vessel.'

'Won't you get in yourself, Axl?'

'I'm getting in right beside you. Look, this good man's fastened us tight together.'

'Don't leave me here alone, Axl.'

But even as she said this, she appeared reassured, and lay down in the basket like a child going to sleep.

'Good sir,' Axl said. 'See how my wife trembles from the cold.

Is there something you might lend to cover her?'

The boatkeeper too was looking at Beatrice, who had now curled up on her side and closed her eyes. Suddenly he removed one of the furs he was wearing, and bending forward, laid it on top of her. She seemed not to notice – her eyes remained closed – so it was Axl who thanked him.

'Welcome, friend. Leave everything at the lower boathouse for me.' The man pushed them into the tide with his pole. 'Sit low and keep the staff handy for the weeds.'

It was bitingly cold on the river. Broken ice drifted here and there in sheets, but their baskets moved past them with ease, sometimes bumping gently one against the other. The baskets were shaped almost like boats, with a bow and stern, but had a tendency to rotate, so that at times Axl found himself gazing back up the river to the boathouse still visible on the bank.

The dawn was pouring through the waving grass beside them, and as the boatkeeper had promised, the river moved at an easy pace. Even so, Axl found himself glancing continuously over at Beatrice's basket, which appeared to be filled entirely by the animal skin, with only a small portion of her hair visible to betray her presence. Once he called out: 'We'll be there in no time, princess,' and when there was no response, reached over to tug her basket closer.

'Princess, are you sleeping?'

'Axl, are you still there?'

'Of course I'm still here.'

'Axl. I thought maybe you'd left me again.'

'Why would I leave you, princess? And the man's tied our vessels so carefully together.'

'I don't know if it's a thing dreamt or remembered. But I saw myself just then, standing in our chamber in the dead of night. It was long ago and I had tight around me that cloak of badger hides you made once as a tender gift to me. I was standing like that, and in our former chamber too, not the one we have now, for the wall had branches of beech crossing left to right, and I was watching a caterpillar crawling slowly along it, and asking why a caterpillar wouldn't be asleep so late at night.'

'Never mind caterpillars, what were you doing yourself awake and staring at a wall in the pit of the night?'

'I think I was standing that way because you'd gone and left me, Axl. Maybe this fur the man's put over me reminds me of that one then, for I was holding it to myself while I stood there, the one you'd made for me from badger skins, which later we lost in that fire. I was watching the caterpillar and asking why it didn't sleep and if a creature like that even knew night from day. Yet I believe the reason was that you'd gone away, Axl.'

'A wild dream, princess, and maybe a fever coming too. But we'll be beside a warm fire before long.'

'Are you still there, Axl?'

'Of course I'm here, and the boathouse long out of sight now.'

'You'd left me that night, Axl. And our precious son too. He'd left a day or two before, saying he'd no wish to be at home when you returned. So it was just me alone, in our former chamber, the dead of night. But we had a candle in those days, and I was able to see that caterpillar.'

'That's a strange dream you speak of, princess, no doubt brought on by your fever and this cold. I wish the sun would rise with less patience.'

'You're right, Axl. It's cold here, even under this rug.'

'I'd warm you in my arms but the river won't allow it.'

'Axl. Can it be our own son left us in anger one day and we closed our door to him, telling him never to return?'

'Princess, I see something before us in the water, maybe a boat stuck in the reeds.'

'You're drifting further away, Axl. I can hardly hear you.'

'I'm here beside you, princess.'

He had been sitting low in his basket, his legs spread before him, but now shifted carefully into a crouching posture, holding the rim to either side.

'I see it better now. A small rowing boat, stuck in the reeds where the bank turns ahead. It's in our path and we'll have to take care or we'll be stuck the same way.'

'Axl, don't go away from me.'

'I'm here beside you, princess. But let me take this staff and keep us clear of the rushes.'

The baskets were moving ever more slowly now, pulling inwards towards the sludge-like water where the bank made its turn. Thrusting the staff into the water, Axl found he could touch the bottom easily, but when he tried to push off back into the tide, the river floor sucked at the stick, allowing him no purchase. He could see too, in the morning light breaking over the long-grassed fields, how weeds had woven thickly around both baskets, as though to bind them further to this stagnant spot. The boat was almost before them, and as they drifted lethargically towards it, Axl held out the staff to touch against its stern and brought them to a halt.

'Is it the other boathouse, husband?'

'Not yet.' Axl glanced over to that part of the river still gliding downstream. 'I'm sorry, princess. We're caught in the reeds. But here's a rowing boat before us, and if it's worthy, we'll use it ourselves to complete the journey.' Pushing the staff once more into the water, Axl manoeuvred them slowly to a position alongside the vessel.

From their low vantage point, the boat loomed large, and Axl could see in fine detail the damaged, coarsened wood, and the underside of the gunwale, where a row of tiny icicles hung like candlewax. Planting the staff in the water, he now rose carefully to his full height within his basket and peered into the boat.

The bow end was bathed in an orange light and it took him a moment to see that the pile of rags heaped there on the boards was in fact an elderly woman. The unusual nature of her garment – a patchwork of numerous small dark rags – and the sooty grime smeared over her face had momentarily deceived him. Moreover, she was seated in a peculiar posture, her head tilted heavily to one side, so that it was almost touching the boat's floor. Something about the old woman's clothes tugged at his memory, but now she opened her eyes and stared at him.

'Help me, stranger,' she said quietly, not altering her posture.

'Are you sick, mistress?'

'My arm won't obey me, or I'd by now be up and taken the oar. Help me, stranger.'

'Who do you speak to, Axl?' Beatrice's voice came from behind him. 'Take care it's not some demon.'

'It's just a poor woman of our years or more, injured in her boat.'

'Don't forget me, Axl.'

'Forget you? Why would I ever forget you, princess?'

'This mist makes us forget so much. Why should it not make us forget each other?'

'Such a thing can't ever happen, princess. Now I must help this poor woman, and perhaps with luck we'll all three use her boat to journey downstream.'

'Stranger, I hear what you say. You'll be most welcome to share my boat. But help me now for I'm fallen and hurt.'

'Axl, don't leave me here. Don't forget me.'

'I'm just stepping onto this boat beside us, princess. I must attend to this poor stranger.'

The cold had stiffened his limbs, and he almost lost his balance as he climbed into the larger vessel. But he steadied himself, then looked around him.

The boat seemed simple and sturdy, with no obvious signs of leakage. There was cargo piled near the stern, but Axl paid this little attention, for the woman was saying something again. The morning sun was still fully upon her, and he could see how her gaze was fixed with some intensity on his feet – so much so that he could not help looking down at them himself. Noticing nothing remarkable, he continued towards her, stepping carefully over the boat's bracing.

'Stranger. I see you're not young, but you've strength left. Show them a fierce face. A fierce face to make them flee.'

'Come, mistress. Are you able to sit up?' He had said this for he was troubled by her strange posture – her loose grey hair was hanging down and touching the damp boards. 'Here, I'll help you. Try to sit higher.'

As he leant forward and touched her, a rusted knife she had been holding fell from her grasp onto the boards. In the same instant, some small creature scampered out from her rags and away into the shadows.

'Do the rats bother you, mistress?'

'They're over there, stranger. Show them a fierce face, I say.'

It now occurred to him she had not been staring at his feet, but beyond him, to something at the back of the boat. He turned, but the low sun dazzled him and he could not discern clearly whatever was moving there.

'Are they rats, mistress?'

'They fear you, stranger. They feared me too for a little while, but they sapped me little by little as they will. Had you not come they'd be covering me even now.'

'Wait a moment, mistress.'

He stepped towards the stern, a hand raised against the low sun, and gazed down at the objects piled in the shadows. He could make out tangled nets, a soaked-through blanket left in a heap, a long-handled tool, like a hoe, lying across it. And there was a wooden, lidless box – the sort fishermen used to keep fresh the dying fish they had caught. But when he peered into it, he saw not fish but skinned rabbits – a considerable number of them, pressed so closely one against the other their tiny limbs appeared to be locked together. Then, as he watched, the whole mass of sinews, elbows and ankles began to shift. Axl took a step back even as he saw an eye open, and then another. A sound made him turn, and he saw at the other end of the boat, still bathed in orange light, the old woman slumped against the bow with pixies – too many to count – swarming over her. At first glance she looked contented, as if being smothered in affection, while the small, scrawny creatures ran through her rags and over her face and shoulders. And now there came more and more out of the river, climbing over the rim of the boat.

Axl reached down for the long-handled tool before him, but he too had become enveloped by a sense of tranquillity, and he found himself extracting the pole from the tangled netting in a strangely leisurely manner. He knew more and more creatures were rising from the water – how many might have boarded now? Thirty? Sixty? – and their collective voices seemed to him to resemble the sound of children playing in the distance. He had the presence of mind to raise the long tool – a hoe, surely, for was that not a rusted blade on the end rising into the sky, or yet another creature clinging to it? – and bring it crashing down onto the tiny knuckles and knees mounting the side of the boat. Then a second swing, this time towards the box with the skinned rabbits from which more pixies were running out. But then he had never been much of a swordsman, his skill being for diplomacy and, when required, intrigue, though who could claim he had ever betrayed the trust his skills had won? On the contrary, it was he who had been betrayed, but he could still wield a weapon in some fashion, and now he would bring it down this way and that, for had he not to defend Beatrice from these swarming creatures? But here they came, more and more – were they still coming from that box, or from the shallow waters? Were they even now gathering around Beatrice asleep in her basket? The last blow of the hoe had had some effect, for several creatures had fallen back into the water, and then another blow had sent two, even three, flying through the air, and the old woman was a stranger, what obligation did he have to her before his own wife? But there she was, the strange woman, hardly visible now beneath the writhing creatures, and Axl crossed the length of the boat, hoe raised, and made another arc in the air to sweep off as many as possible without injury to the stranger. Yet how they clung on! And now they even dared to speak to him – or was that the old woman herself from beneath them?

'Leave her, stranger. Leave her to us. Leave her, stranger.'

Axl swung the hoe again, and it moved as though the air were thick water, but found its mark, scattering several creatures even as more arrived.

'Leave her to us, stranger,' the old woman said again, and only this time did it occur to him, with a stab of fear that seemed bottomless, that the speaker was talking not of the dying stranger before him but of Beatrice. And turning to his wife's basket in the reeds, he saw the waters around it alive with limbs and shoulders. His own basket was nearly capsizing from the pull of the creatures trying to climb in, preserved only by the ballast of those already inside. But they were boarding his basket only to gain access to its neighbour. He could see other creatures massing over the animal skin covering Beatrice, and uttering a cry, he climbed the side of the boat and let himself fall into the water. It was deeper than he had anticipated, coming above his waist, but the shock of it took his breath only for an instant, before he let out a warrior's bellow that came to him as if from a distant memory, and he lurched towards the baskets, the hoe held high above him. There was tugging at his clothes, and the water felt honey-like, but when he brought the hoe down onto his own basket, even though his weapon travelled with frustrating slowness through the air, once it landed more creatures than he could have suspected tumbled out into the water. The next swing caused even greater destruction – he must this time have swung with the blade outwards, for was that not bloodied flesh he saw flying up into the sunlight? And yet Beatrice remained an age away, floating complacently even as the creatures rose about her, and now they came from the land too, pouring through the grass on the riverbank. Creatures were now even hanging from his hoe and he let it fall into the water, suddenly wishing only to be at Beatrice's side.

He waded through the weeds, the broken bulrushes, the mud tugging at his feet, but Beatrice remained further away than ever. Then came the stranger's voice again, and even though now, down in the water, he could no longer see her, Axl could picture the old woman with startling clarity in his mind's eye, slumped on the floor of her boat in the morning sun, the pixies moving freely over her as she uttered the words he could hear:

'Leave her, stranger. Leave her to us.'

'Curse you,' Axl muttered under his breath, as he pushed himself forward. 'I'll never, never give her up.'

'A wise man like you, stranger. You've known a long time now there's no cure to save her. How will you bear it, what now lies in wait for her? Do you long for that day you watch your dearest love twist in agony and with nothing to offer but kind words for her ear? Give her to us and we'll ease her suffering, as we've done for all these others before her.'

'Curse you! I'll not give her to you!'

'Give her to us and we'll see she suffers no pain. We'll wash her in the river's waters, the years will fall from her, and she'll be as in a pleasant dream. Why keep her, sir? What can you give her but the agony of an animal in slaughter?'

'I'll be rid of you. Get off. Get off her.'

Locking his hands together to make a club, he swung one way then the other, clearing a path in the water as he waded on, till at last he was before Beatrice, still fast asleep in her basket. The pixies were swarming over the animal skin that covered her, and he began to pull them off one by one, hurling them away.

'Why will you not give her to us? This is no kindness you show her.'

He pushed the basket through the water until the ground rose

up and the basket was sitting on wet mud amidst grass and bulrushes. He leant forward then and gathered his wife in his arms,
lifting her out. Thankfully she came back to wakefulness enough
to cling to his neck, and they made faltering steps together, first
onto the bank, then further, into the fields. Only when the land
felt hard and dry beneath them did Axl lower her, and they sat in
the grass together, he recovering his breath, she becoming steadily more awake.

'Axl, what is this place we've come to?'

'Princess, how are you feeling now? We must get away from
this spot. I'll carry you on my back.'

'Axl, you're soaked through! Did you fall in the river?'

'This is an evil spot, princess, and we must leave quickly. I'll
gladly carry you on my back, the way I used to do when we were
young and foolish and enjoying a warm spring's day.'

'Must we leave the river behind us? Sir Gawain's right surely
that it will carry us all the more swiftly where we'll go. The land
here looks as high in the mountains as we ever were before.'

'We've no choice, princess. We must get far from here. Come,
I'll have you on my back. Come, princess, reach for my shoulders.'

Chapter Twelve

He could hear the warrior's voice below him, appealing to him to climb more slowly, but Edwin ignored it. Wistan was too slow, and in general appeared not to appreciate the urgency of their situation. When they were still not halfway up the cliff, he had asked Edwin: 'Can that be a hawk just flew past us, young comrade?' What did it matter what it was? His fever had made the warrior soft, both in mind and body.

Only a little further to climb, then he at least would be over the edge and standing on firm ground. He could then run – how he longed to run! – but to where? Their destination had, for the moment, drifted beyond his recall. What was more, there had been something important to tell the warrior: he had been deceiving Wistan about something, and now it was almost time to confess. When they had started their climb, leaving the exhausted mare tied to a shrub beside the mountain path, he had resolved to make a clean breast of it once they reached the top. Yet now he was almost there, his mind held nothing but confused wisps.

He clambered over the last rocks and pulled himself up over the precipice. The land before him was bare and wind-scarred, rising gradually towards the pale peaks on the horizon. Nearby were patches of heather and mountain grass, but nothing taller than a man's ankle. Yet strangely, there in the mid-distance, was what appeared to be a wood, its lush trees standing calmly against the battling wind. Had some god, on a whim, picked up in his fingers a section of rich forest and set it down in this inhospitable terrain?

Though out of breath from the climb, Edwin pushed himself forward into a run. For those trees, surely, were where he had to be, and once there he would remember everything. Wistan's voice was shouting again somewhere behind him – the warrior must finally have arrived at the top – but Edwin, not glancing back, ran all the faster. He would leave his confession until those trees. Within their shelter, he would be able to remember more clearly, and they could talk without the wind's howl.

The ground came up to meet him and knocked the breath from him. It happened so unexpectedly he was obliged to lie there a moment, quite dazed, and when he tried to spring back to his feet something soft but forceful kept him down. He realised then that Wistan's knee was on his back, and that his hands were being tied behind him.

'You asked before why we must carry rope with us,' Wistan said. 'Now you see how useful it can be.'

Edwin began to remember their exchange down on the path below. Eager to start the climb, he had been annoyed by the way the warrior was carefully transferring items from his saddle into two sacks for them to carry.

'We must hurry, warrior! Why do we need all these things?'

'Here, carry this, comrade. The she-dragon's foe enough without us growing weak with cold and hunger to aid her.'

'But the scent will be lost! And what need do we have of rope?'

'We may need it yet, young comrade, and we won't find it growing on branches up there.'

Now the rope had been wound around his waist as well as his

wrists, so that when finally he rose to his feet, he could move forward only against the pull of his leash.

'Warrior, are you no longer my friend and teacher?'

'I'm still that and your protector too. From here you must go with less haste.'

He found he did not mind the rope. The gait it obliged him to adopt was like that of a mule, and he was reminded of a time not long ago when he had had to impersonate just such a beast, going round and round a wagon. Was he the same mule now, stubbornly pushing his way up the slope even as the rope pulled him back?

He pulled and pulled, occasionally managing several steps at a run before the rope jerked him to a halt. A voice was in his ears – a familiar voice – half-singing, half-chanting a children's rhyme, one he knew well from when he was younger. It was comforting and disturbing in equal measure and he found if he chanted along while tugging on the rope, the voice lost something of its unsettling edge. So he chanted, at first under his breath, then with less inhibition into the wind: 'Who knocked over the cup of ale? Who cut off the dragon's tail? Who left the snake inside the pail? 'Twas your Cousin Adny.' There were further lines he did not remember, but he was surprised to find that he had but to chant along with the voice and the words would come out correctly.

The trees were near now and the warrior tugged him back again.

'Slowly, young comrade. We need more than courage to enter this strange grove. Look there. Pine trees at this height's no mystery, but aren't those oaks and elms beside them?'

'No matter what trees grow here, warrior, or what birds fly these skies! We have little time left and must hurry!'

They entered the wood and the ground changed beneath them: there was soft moss, nettles, even ferns. The leaves above them were dense enough to form a ceiling, so that for a while they wandered in a grey half-light. Yet this was no forest, for soon they could see before them a clearing with its circle of open sky above it. The thought came to Edwin that if this was indeed the work of a god, the intention must have been to conceal with these trees whatever lay ahead. He pulled angrily at the rope, saying:

'Why dally, warrior? Can it be you're afraid?'

'Look at this place, young comrade. Your hunter's instincts have served us well. This must be the dragon's lair before us now.'

'I'm the hunter of us two, warrior, and I tell you that clearing holds no dragon. We must hurry past it and beyond, for we've further to go!'

'Your wound, young comrade. Let me see if it remains clean.'

'Never mind my wound! I tell you the scent will be lost! Let go the rope, warrior. I'll run on even if you will not!'

This time Wistan released him, and Edwin pushed past thistles and tangled roots. Several times he lost his balance, for trussed as he was he had no hand to put out to steady himself. But he reached the clearing without injury, and stopped at its edge to take in the sight before him.

At the centre of the clearing was a pond. It was frozen over, so a man – were he brave or foolish enough – might cross it in twenty or so strides. The smoothness of the ice's surface was interrupted only near the far side, where the hollowed-out trunk of a dead tree burst up through it. Along the bank, not far from the ruined tree, a large ogre was crouching down on its knees and elbows at the water's very edge, its head completely submerged. Perhaps the creature had been drinking – or searching for something beneath the surface – and had been overtaken by the sudden freeze. To a careless observer, the ogre might have been a headless corpse, decapitated as it crawled to quench its thirst.

The patch of sky above the pond cast a strange light down on the ogre, and Edwin stared at it for a while, almost expecting it to return to life, bringing up a ghastly and flushed face. Then, with a start, he realised there was a second creature in an identical posture on the far right-hand edge of the pond. And there! – yet a third, not far before him, on the near bank, half-concealed by the ferns.

Ogres usually aroused only revulsion in him, but these creatures, and the eerie melancholy of their postures, made Edwin feel a tug of pity. What had brought them to such a fate? He began to move toward them, but the rope was taut again, and he heard Wistan say close behind him:

'Do you still deny this is a dragon's lair, comrade?'

'Not here, warrior. We must go further.'

'Yet this spot whispers to me. Even if not her lair, isn't this a place she comes to drink and bathe?'

'I say it's cursed, warrior, and no place to do battle with her. We'll have only ill luck here. Look at those poor ogres. And they almost as large as the fiends you killed the other night.'

'What do you speak of, boy?'

'Don't you see them? Look, there! And there!'

'Master Edwin, you've become exhausted, as I feared. Let's rest a while. Even if this is a gloomy spot, it gives us respite from the wind.'

'How can you talk of rest, warrior? And isn't that how those poor creatures met their fate, loitering in this bewitched place too long? Heed their warning, warrior!'

'The only warning I heed tells me to make you rest before you drive your own heart to burst.'

He felt himself tugged, and his back struck against the bark of a tree. Then the warrior was trudging around him, circling rope about his chest and shoulders till he could hardly move.

'This good tree means you no harm, young comrade.' The warrior placed a gentle hand on his shoulder. 'Why waste strength this way to uproot it? Calm yourself and rest, I say, while I study more closely this place.'

He watched Wistan picking his way through the nettles down to the pond. Reaching the water's edge, the warrior spent several moments walking slowly back and forth, staring closely at the ground, sometimes crouching down to examine whatever caught his eye. Then he straightened, and for a long time seemed to fall into a reverie, gazing over at the trees on the far side of the pond. For Edwin, the warrior was now a near-silhouette against the frozen water. Why did he not even glance towards the ogres?

Wistan made a movement and suddenly the sword was in his hand, the arm poised and unmoving in the air. Then the weapon was returned to its scabbard and the warrior, turning from the water, came walking back towards him.

'We're hardly the first visitors here,' he said. 'Even this past hour, some party's come this way, and it's no she-dragon. Master Edwin, I'm glad to see you calmer.'

'Warrior, I've a confession to make. One that may make you slay me even as I stand trussed to this tree.'

'Speak, boy, and don't fear me.'

'Warrior, you claimed for me the hunter's gift, and even as you spoke of it I felt a strong pull, so let you believe I had Querig in my nostrils. But I was always deceiving you.'

Wistan came closer till he was standing right before him.

'Go on, comrade.'

'I can't go on, warrior.'

'You've more to fear from your silence than my anger. Speak.'

'I can't, warrior. When we began to climb, I knew just what to tell you. Yet now . . . I'm uncertain what it is I've kept hidden from you.'

'It's the she-dragon's breath, nothing more. It's had little sway over you before, but now overpowers you. A sure sign we're close to her.'

'I fear it's this cursed pool bewitches me, warrior, and maybe bewitches you too, making you content to dally this way and hardly glancing at those drowned ogres. Yet I know there's a confession I have to make and only wish I could find it.'

'Show me the way to the she-dragon's lair and I'll forgive whatever small lies you've told me.'

'But that's just it, warrior. We rode the mare till her heart nearly burst, then climbed this steep mountainside, yet I'm not leading you at all to the she-dragon.'

Wistan had come so close Edwin could feel the warrior's breath.

'Where could it be then, Master Edwin, you lead me?'

'It's my mother, warrior, I remember it now. My aunt's not my mother. My real mother was taken, and even though I was a small boy then, I was watching. And I promised her I'd one day bring her back. Now I'm nearly grown, and have you beside me, even those men would tremble to face us. I deceived you, warrior, but understand my feelings and help me now we're so near her.'

'Your mother. You say she's near us now?'

'Yes, warrior. But not here. Not this cursed place.'

'What do you remember of the men who took her?'

'They looked fierce, warrior, and well used to killing. Not a man in the village dared come out to face them that day.'

'Saxons or Britons?'

'They were Britons, warrior. Three men, and Steffa said they must not long before have been soldiers, for he recognised their soldiers' ways. I wasn't yet five years old, or else I'd have fought for her.'

'My own mother was taken, young comrade, so I understand your thoughts well. And I too was a child and weak when she was taken. These were times of war, and in my foolishness, seeing how the men slaughtered and hanged so many, I rejoiced to see the way they smiled at her, believing they meant to treat her with gentleness and favour. Perhaps it was this way for you too, Master Edwin, when you were young and still to know of men's ways.'

'My mother was taken in peaceful times, warrior, so no great harm has met her. She's been travelling country to country, and it may not be such a bad life. Yet she longs to return to me, and it's true, the men who travel with her are sometimes cruel. Warrior, accept this confession, punish me later, but help me now face her captors, for it's long years she's waited for me.'

Wistan stared at him strangely. He seemed on the brink of saying something, but then shook his head and walked a few steps away from the tree, almost like one ashamed. Edwin had never seen the warrior wear such an air, and watched him with surprise.

'I'll readily forgive you this deception, Master Edwin,' Wistan said eventually, turning back to face him. 'And any other small lies you may have told. And soon I'll release you from this tree and we'll go to face whatever foe you may lead us to. But in return I ask you to make a promise.'

'Tell me, warrior.'

'Should I fall and you survive, promise me this. That you'll carry in your heart a hatred of Britons.'

'What do you mean, warrior? Which Britons?'

'All Britons, young comrade. Even those who show you kindness.'

'I don't understand, warrior. Must I hate a Briton who shares with me his bread? Or saves me from a foe as lately did the good Sir Gawain?'

'There are Britons who tempt our respect, even our love, I know this only too well. But there are now greater things press on us than what each may feel for another. It was Britons under Arthur slaughtered our kind. It was Britons took your mother and mine. We've a duty to hate every man, woman and child of their blood. So promise me this. Should I fall before I pass to you my skills, promise me you'll tend well this hatred in your heart. And should it ever flicker or threaten to die, shield it with care till the flame takes hold again. Will you promise me this, Master Edwin?'

'Very well, warrior, I promise it. But now I hear my mother calling, and surely we've stayed in this gloomy place too long.'

'Let's go to her then. But be prepared in case we come too late for her rescue.'

'What can you mean, warrior? How can that ever be, for I hear her call even now.'

'Then let's hasten to her call. Just know one thing, young comrade. When the hour's too late for rescue, it's still early enough for revenge. So let me hear your promise again. Promise me you'll hate the Briton till the day you fall from your wounds or the heaviness of your years.'

'I gladly promise it again, warrior. But release me from this tree, for I now feel clearly which way we must go.'

Chapter Thirteen

The goat, Axl could see, was well at home on this mountain terrain. It was eating happily the stubbly grass and heather, not caring about the wind, or that its left legs were poised so much lower than the right. The animal had a fierce tug – as Axl had discovered all too well during their ascent – and it had not been easy to find a way of safely tethering it while he and Beatrice took their rest. But he had spotted a dead tree root protruding from the slope, and had carefully bound the rope to it.

The goat was clearly visible from where they now sat. The two large rocks, leaning one towards the other like an old married couple, had been visible from some way down, but Axl had hoped to come across a shelter from the wind long before they reached them. Yet the bare hillside had offered nothing, and they had had to persevere up the little path, the goat tugging as impulsively as the fierce gusts. But when at last they reached the twin rocks, it was as if God had crafted for them this sanctuary, for while they could still hear the blasts around them, they felt only faint stirrings in the air. Even so, they sat close against one another, as if in imitation of the stones above them.

'Here's all this country still below us, Axl. Didn't that river carry us down at all?'

'We were halted before we could get far, princess.'

'And now we climb uphill again.'

'Right enough, princess. I fear that young girl hid from us the true hardship of this task.'

'No doubt about it, Axl, she made it sound an easy stroll. But who'll blame her? Still a child and more cares than one her age should bear. Axl, look there. Down in that valley, do you see them?'

A hand raised to the glare, Axl tried to discern what his wife was indicating, but eventually shook his head. 'My eyes aren't as good as yours, princess. I see valley after valley where the mountains descend, but nothing remarkable.'

'There, Axl, follow my finger. Aren't those soldiers walking in a line?'

'I see them now, right enough. But surely they're not moving.'

'They're moving, Axl, and might be soldiers, the way they go in a long line.'

'To my poor eyes, princess, they seem not to move at all. And even if they're soldiers, they're surely too far to bother us. It's those storm clouds to the west concern me more, for they'll bring mischief swifter than any soldiers in the distance.'

'You're right, husband, and I wonder how much further it is we're to go. That young girl wasn't honest, insisting it was but a simple stroll. Yet can we blame her? Her parents absent and her younger brothers to worry over. She must have been desperate to have us do her bidding.'

'I can see them more clearly, princess, now the sun peeks from behind the clouds. They're not soldiers or men at all, but a row of birds.'

'What foolishness, Axl. If they're birds, how would we see them from here at all?'

'They're closer than you imagine, princess. Dark birds sat in a line, the way they do in the mountains.'

'Then why is it one doesn't fly into the air as we watch them?'

'One may fly up yet, princess. And I for one won't blame that young lass, for isn't she in a black plight? And where would we have been without her help, soaked and shivering as we were when we first saw her? Besides, princess, as I remember it, it wasn't the girl alone keen to have this goat go up to the giant's cairn. Is it even an hour gone by you were as anxious?'

'I'm still as anxious for it, Axl. For wouldn't it be a fine thing if Querig were slain and this mist no more? It's just when I see that goat chewing the earth that way, it's hard to believe a foolish creature like that could ever do away with a great she-dragon.'

The goat had been eating with equal appetite earlier that morning when they had first come upon the little stone cottage. The cottage had been easy to miss, hidden within a pocket of shadow at the foot of a looming cliff, and even when Beatrice had pointed it out to him, Axl had mistaken it for the entrance to a settlement not unlike their own, dug deep into the mountainside. Only as they had come closer had he realised it was an isolated structure, the walls and roof alike built from shards of dark grey rock. Water was falling from high above in a fine thread just in front of the cliffside, to collect in a pool not far from the cottage and trickle away where the land dipped out of view. A little way before the cottage, just now brightly illuminated by the morning sun, was a small fenced paddock, the sole occupant of which was the goat. As usual the animal had been eating busily, but broke off to stare in astonishment at Axl and Beatrice.

The children though had remained unaware of their approach. The girl and her two younger brothers were standing at the edge of a ditch, their backs to their visitors, preoccupied with something beneath their feet. Once, one of the small boys crouched down to throw something into the ditch, provoking the girl to pull him back by the arm.

'What can they be doing, Axl?' Beatrice said. 'Mischief by the look of it, and the youngest of them still small enough to tumble in without meaning to.'

When they had gone past the goat and the children still were unaware of them, Axl called out as gently as he could: 'God be with you,' causing all three to spin round in alarm.

Their guilty countenances supported Beatrice's notion that they had been up to no good, but the girl – a head taller than the two boys – recovered quickly and smiled.

'Elders! You're welcome! We prayed to God only last night to send you and here you've come to us! Welcome, welcome!'

She came splashing over the marshy grass towards them, her brothers close behind.

'You mistake us, child,' Axl said. 'We're just two lost travellers, cold and weary, our clothes wet from the river where we were attacked only lately by savage pixies. Would you call your mother or father to allow us warmth and the chance to dry ourselves beside a fire?'

'We're not mistaken, sir! We prayed to the God Jesus last night and now you've come! Please, elders, go inside our house, where a fire's still burning.'

'But where are your parents, child?' Beatrice asked. 'Weary as we are, we'd not intrude, and so wait for the lady or master of the house to call us through the door.'

'It's just us three now, mistress, so you can call me lady of the house! Please go inside and warm yourselves. You'll find food in the sack hanging from the beam, and there's wood beside the fire to add. Go inside, elders, and we'll not disturb your rest for a while yet, for we must see to the goat.'

'We accept your kindness gratefully, child,' Axl said. 'But tell us if the nearest village is far from here.'

A shadow crossed the girl's face, and she exchanged looks with her brothers, now lined up beside her. Then she smiled again and said: 'We're very high in the mountains here, sir. It's far to any village, so we'd ask you to stay here with us, and the warm fire and food we offer. You must be very weary, and I see how this wind makes you both shiver. So please, no more talk of going away. Go inside and rest, elders, for we've waited for you so long!'

'What is it so interests you in that ditch there?' Beatrice asked suddenly.

'Oh, it's nothing, mistress! Nothing at all! But here you're standing in this wind and your clothes wet! Won't you accept our hospitality, and rest yourselves beside our fire? See how even now its smoke rises from the roof!'

* * *

'There!' Axl took his weight from the rock and pointed. 'A bird flown to the sky. Didn't I tell you, princess, those are birds standing in a line? Do you see it climbing in the sky?'

Beatrice, who had risen to her feet a few moments before, now took a step beyond the sanctuary of their rocks, and Axl saw the wind immediately pull at her clothes.

'A bird, right enough,' she said. 'But it didn't rise from those figures yonder. It could be you still don't see what I point to, Axl. I mean there, on the further ridge, those dark shapes almost against the sky.'

'I see them well enough, princess. But come back out of the wind.'

'Soldiers or not, they move slowly on. The bird was never one of them.'

'Come out of the wind, princess, and sit down. We must gather strength the best we can. Who knows how much further we must pull this goat?'

Beatrice came back to their shelter, holding close to herself the cloak borrowed from the children. 'Axl,' she said, as she seated herself again beside him, 'do you really believe it? That before the great knights and warriors, it's a weary old couple like us, forbidden a candle in our own village, who may slay the she-dragon? And with this ill-tempered goat to aid us?'

'Who knows it'll be so, princess. Maybe it's all just a young girl's wishing and nothing more. But we were grateful for her hospitality, and so we shouldn't mind doing as she asks. And who knows she isn't right, and Querig will be slain this way.'

'Axl, tell me. If the she-dragon's really slain, and the mist starts to clear. Axl, do you ever fear what will then be revealed to us?'

'Didn't you say it yourself, princess? Our life together's like a tale with a happy end, no matter what turns it took on the way.'

'I said so before, Axl. Yet now it may even be we'll slay Querig with our own hands, there's a part of me fears the mist's fading. Can it be so with you, Axl?'

'Perhaps it is, princess. Perhaps it's always been so. But I fear most what you spoke of earlier. I mean as we rested beside the fire.'

'What was it I said then, Axl?'

'You don't remember, princess?'

'Did we have some foolish quarrel? I've no memory of it now, except that I was near my wit's end from cold and want of rest.'

'If you've no memory of it, princess, then let it stay forgotten.'

'But I've felt something, Axl, ever since we left those children. It's as if you're holding yourself away from me as we walk, and not just on account of that tugging goat. Can it be we quarrelled earlier, though I've no memory of it?'

'I'd no intention to hold myself away from you, princess. Forgive me. If it's not the goat pulling this way and that, then it must be I'm still thinking of some foolishness that was said between us. Trust me, it's best forgotten.'

* * *

He had got the fire blazing again in the centre of the floor, and all else inside the small cottage had fallen into shadow. Axl had been drying his clothes, holding each garment up to the flames, while Beatrice slept peacefully nearby in a nest of rugs. But then quite suddenly, she had sat up and looked around her.

'Is the fire too hot for you, princess?'

For a moment she continued to look bewildered, then wearily lowered herself back down onto the rugs. Her eyes though remained open and Axl was about to repeat his question when she had said quietly:

'I was thinking of a night long ago, husband. When you were gone, leaving me in a lonely bed, wondering to myself if you'd ever come back to me.'

'Princess, though we escaped those pixies on the river, I fear some spell still lingers on you to give you such dreams.'

'No dream, husband. Just a memory or two returning. The night as dark as any, and there I was, alone in our bed, knowing all the while you were gone to another younger and fairer.'

'Won't you believe me, princess? This is the work of those pixies still working mischief between us.'

'You may be right, Axl. And if they were true memories, they're of long ago. Even so . . .' She became silent, so that Axl thought she had dozed off again. But then she said: 'Even so, husband, they're remembrances to make me shrink from you. When we've finished resting here, and we're on our path again, let me walk a little way in front and you behind. Let's go on our way like that, husband, for I'll not welcome your step beside me now.'

He said nothing to this at first. Then he lowered the garment away from the fire and turned to look at her. Her eyes were closed again, yet he was sure she had not fallen asleep. When Axl finally found his voice, it had come out as no more than a whisper.

'It would be the saddest thing to me, princess. To walk separately from you, when the ground will let us go as we always did.'

Beatrice gave no indication of having heard, and within moments her breathing had grown long and even. He had then put on his newly warmed clothes and lain down on a blanket not far from his wife, but without touching her. An overwhelming tiredness swept over him, and yet he saw again the pixies swarming in the water before him, and the hoe he had swung through the air landing in their midst, and he remembered the noise as of children playing in the distance, and how he had fought, almost like a warrior with fury in his voice. And now she had said what she had. A picture came into his mind, clear and vivid, of himself and Beatrice on a mountain road, large grey skies above them, she walking several steps before him, and a great melancholy welled up within him. There they went, an elderly couple, heads bowed, five, six paces apart.

He awoke to find the fire smouldering, and Beatrice on her feet, peering out through one of the small gaps in the stone that constituted the windows of an abode such as this. Thoughts of their last exchange returned to him, but Beatrice turned, her features caught in a triangle of sunlight, and said in a cheerful voice:

'I thought to wake you before, Axl, seeing the morning grow outside. But then I kept thinking of the soaking you got in the river and that you needed more than a brief nod or two.'

Only when he did not reply did she ask: 'What is it, Axl? Why look at me like that?'

'I'm just gazing at you in relief and happiness, princess.'

'I'm feeling much better, Axl. Rest was all I needed.'

'I see that now. Then let's soon be on our way, for as you say, the morning's grown while we slept.'

'I've been watching these children, Axl. Even now they stand by that same ditch as when we first came upon them. They've something down there draws them and it's some mischief, I'll wager, for they often glance back the way they think some adult will discover and scold them. Where can their people be, Axl?'

'It's not our concern, and besides, they seem well enough fed and clothed. Let's say our farewells and be gone.'

'Axl, can it be you and I were quarrelling earlier? I feel something came between us.'

'Nothing we can't put aside, princess. Though we may speak of it before the day's finished, who knows? But let's be on our way before hunger and cold overtake us again.'

When they emerged into the chilly sunshine, Axl saw patches of ice on the grass, a large sky and mountains fading into the distance. The goat was eating over in its enclosure, a muddy upturned bucket near its feet.

The three children were still beside the ditch, looking down into it, their backs to the cottage, and appeared to be quarrelling. The girl was the first to realise Axl and Beatrice were approaching, and even as she spun around her face broke into a bright smile.

'Dear elders!' She started to come quickly away from the ditch, pulling her brothers with her. 'I hope you found our home comfortable, humble though it is!'

'We did, child, and we're most grateful to you. Now we're well rested and ready to be on our way. But what's become of your people that they leave you alone?'

The girl exchanged glances with her brothers, who had taken up positions on either side of her. Then she said, a little hesitantly: 'We manage by ourselves, sir,' and put an arm around each of the boys.

'And what is it down in that ditch draws you so?' Beatrice asked.

'It's just our goat, mistress. It was once our best goat, but it died.'

'How did your goat come to die, child?' Axl asked gently. 'The other there looks well enough.'

The children exchanged more glances, and a decision seemed to pass among them.

'Go look if you will, sir,' the girl said, and letting go of her brothers, she stepped to one side.

Beatrice fell in step beside him as he went towards the ditch. Before they were halfway there, Axl stopped and said in a whisper: 'Let me go alone first, princess.'

'Do you think I never saw a dead goat before, Axl?'

'Even so, princess. Wait here a moment.'

The ditch was as deep as a man's height. The sun, now shining almost directly into it, should have made it easier to discern what was before him, but instead created confusing shadows, and where there was puddle and ice, a myriad of dazzling surfaces. The goat appeared to have been of monstrous proportions, and now lay in several dismembered pieces. Over there, a hind leg; there the neck and head – the latter wearing a serene expression. It took a little longer to identify the soft upturned belly of the animal, because pressed into it was a giant hand emerging from the dark mud. Only then did he see that much of what initially he had taken to be of the dead goat belonged to a second creature entangled with it. That mound there was a shoulder; that a stiffened knee. Then he saw movement and realised the thing in the ditch was still alive.

'What do you see, Axl?'

'Don't come forward, princess. It's no sight to raise your spirits. Some poor ogre, I'd suppose, dying a slow death, and maybe these children have foolishly thrown it a goat, thinking it might recover itself with eating.'

Even as he spoke, a large hairless head revolved slowly in the slime, a gaping eye moving with it. Then the mud sucked greedily and the head vanished.

'We didn't feed the ogre, sir,' the girl's voice said behind him. 'We know never to feed an ogre, but to bar ourselves inside at their coming. And so we did with this one, sir, and we watched from our window while he pulled down our fence and took our best goat. Then he sat down just there, sir, where you are now, his legs dangling over like he's an infant, and happily eating the goat raw, the way ogres will. We knew not to unbar the door, and the sun getting lower, and the ogre still eating our goat, but we could see he's getting weaker, sir. Then at last he stands up, holding what's left of the goat, then he falls down, first to his knees, then onto his side. Next thing he rolls into the ditch, goat and all, and it's two days he's been down there and still not dead.'

'Let's come away, child,' Axl said. 'This is no sight for you or your brothers. But what is it made this poor ogre so sick? Can it be your goat was diseased?'

'Not diseased, sir, poisoned! We'd been feeding it more than a full week just the way Bronwen taught us. Six times each day with the leaves.'

'Why did you do such a thing, child?'

'Why, sir, to make the goat poisonous for the she-dragon. This poor ogre wasn't to know that and so he poisoned himself. But it's not our fault, sir, because he shouldn't have been marauding the way he was!'

'A moment, child,' Axl said. 'Are you saying you fed the goat deliberately to fill it with poison?'

'Poison for the she-dragon, sir, but Bronwen said it wouldn't harm any of us. So how could we know the poison might harm an ogre? We weren't to blame, sir, and meant no wickedness!'

'No one will ever blame you, child. Yet tell me, why were you wishing to prepare poison for Querig, for I take it this is the she-dragon you talk of?'

'Oh, sir! We said our prayers morning and night and often in the day too. And when you came this morning, we knew God had sent you. So please say you'll help us, for we're just poor children forgotten by our parents! Will you take that goat there, the only one left to us now, and go with it up that path to the giant's cairn? It's an easy walk, sir, less than half a day there and back, and I'd do it myself but can't leave these young ones alone. We've fed this goat just the way we did the one eaten by the ogre, and this with three more days' leaves in it. If only you'd take it to the giant's cairn and leave it tethered there for the she-dragon, sir, and it's but an easy stroll. Please say you'll do it, elders, for we're fearing nothing else will bring our dear mother and father back to us.'

'At last you speak of them,' Beatrice said. 'What's to be done to bring your parents back to you?'

'Didn't we just tell you, mistress? If you'd only take the goat up to the giant's cairn, where it's well known food's regularly left for the she-dragon. Then who knows, she'll perish the same way that poor ogre has, and he was a strong-looking one before his meal! We'd always been afraid before of Bronwen because of her wise arts, but when she saw we were here alone, forgotten by our own parents, she took pity on us. So please help us, elders, for who knows when anyone else will come this way? We're afraid to show ourselves to soldiers or strange men who pass, but you're the ones we prayed for to the God Jesus.'

'But what is it young children like you can know of this world,' asked Axl, 'that you believe a poisonous goat will bring your parents back to you?'

'It's what Bronwen told us, sir, and though she's a terrible old woman, she never lies. She said it's the she-dragon lives over us here made our parents forget us. And even though we often make our mother angry with our mischief, Bronwen says the day she remembers us again, she'll hurry back and hold us one by one like this.' The girl suddenly clutched an invisible child to her breast, her eyes closing, and rocked gently for a moment. Then opening her eyes again, she went on: 'But for now the she-dragon's cast some spell to make our parents forget us, so they'll not come home.

Bronwen says the she-dragon's a curse not just to us but to everyone and the sooner she perishes the better. So we worked hard, sir, feeding both goats exactly as she said, six times each day. Please do as we ask, or we won't ever see our mother and father again. All we ask is you tether the goat at the giant's cairn then go your way.'

Beatrice started to speak, but Axl said over her quickly: 'I'm sorry, child. We wish we could help you, but to climb higher into these hills is now beyond us. We're elderly, and as you see, weary from days of hard travel. We've no choice but to hurry on our way before further misfortune takes us.'

'But, sir, it was God himself sent you to us! And it's but a short stroll, and not even a steep path from here.'

'Dear child,' Axl said, 'our hearts go out to you, and we'll raise help at the next village. But we're too weak to do what you ask, and surely others will pass this way soon, happy to take the goat for you. It's beyond us old ones, but we'll pray for your parents' return and that God will keep you safe always.'

'Don't go, elders! It wasn't our fault the ogre was poisoned.'

Taking his wife's arm, Axl led her away from the children. He did not look back until they had passed the goat's pen, and then he saw the children still standing there, three abreast, watching silently, the towering cliffs behind them. Axl waved encouragingly, but something like shame – and perhaps the trace of some distant memory, a memory of another such departure – made him increase his pace.

But before they had gone far – the marshy ground had started to descend and the valleys to open before them – Beatrice tugged his arm to slow them.

'I didn't wish to talk across you before those children, husband,' she said. 'But is it really beyond us to do as they ask?'

'They're in no immediate peril, princess, and we have our own worries. How goes your pain now?'

'My pain's no worse. Axl, look how those children stand as we left them, watching as we grow ever smaller in their sight. Can't we at least pause beside this stone and talk further on it? Let's not hasten away carelessly.'

'Don't look back to them, princess, for you only taunt their hopes. We'll not go back to their goat, but down into this valley, a fire and what food kind strangers may give us.'

'But think on what it is they ask, Axl.' Beatrice had now brought them to a halt. 'Will a chance like this ever come our way again? Think on it! We stumble to this spot so near Querig's lair. And these children offer a poisonous goat by which even the two of us, old and weak though we are, might bring down the she-dragon! Think on it, Axl! If Querig falls, the mist will fast begin to clear. Who's to say those children aren't right and God himself didn't bring us this way?'

Axl remained silent for a moment, fighting the urge to look back towards the stone cottage. 'There's no telling that goat will bring any harm at all to Querig,' he said eventually. 'A hapless ogre's one thing. This she-dragon's a creature to scatter an army. And can it be wise for two elderly fools like us to wander so near her lair?'

'We're not to face her, Axl, only to tether the goat and flee. It may be days before Querig comes to the spot, and we'll by then be safe at our son's village. Axl, don't we want returned to us our memories of this long life lived together? Or will we become like strangers met one night in a shelter? Come, husband, say we'll turn back and do as those children bid us.'

* * *

So here they were, climbing still higher, the winds growing stronger. For the moment, the twin rocks provided good shelter, but they could not stay like this for ever. Axl wondered yet again if he had been foolish to give in.

'Princess,' he said eventually. 'Suppose we really do this thing. Suppose God allows us to succeed, and we bring down the she-dragon. I'd like you then to promise me something.'

She was sitting close beside him now, though her eyes were still on the distance and the line of tiny figures.

'What is it you ask, Axl?'

'It's simply this, princess. Should Querig really die and the mist begin to clear. Should memories return, and among them of times I disappointed you. Or yet of dark deeds I may once have done to make you look at me and see no longer the man you do now. Promise me this at least. Promise, princess, you'll not forget what you feel in your heart for me at this moment. For what good's a memory's returning from the mist if it's only to push away another? Will you promise me, princess? Promise to keep what you feel for me this moment always in your heart, no matter what you see once the mist's gone.'

'I'll promise it, Axl, and no hardship to do so.'

'Words can't tell how it comforts me to hear you say it, princess.'

'A queer mood you're in, Axl. But who knows how much further it is till the giant's cairn? Let's not spend any more time sitting between these great stones. Those children were anxious when we left, and they'll be awaiting our return.'

Gawain's Second Reverie

This cursed wind. Is this a storm before us? Horace will mind neither wind nor rain, only that a stranger sits astride him now and not his old master. 'Just a weary woman,' I tell him, 'with greater need of the saddle than me. So carry her in good grace.' Yet why is she here at all? Does Master Axl not see how frail she grows? Has he lost his mind to bring her to these unforgiving heights? But she presses on as determined as he, and nothing I say will turn them back. So I stagger here on foot, a hand on Horace's bridle, heaving this rusty coat. 'Did we not always serve ladies with courtesy?' I murmur to Horace. 'Would we ride on, leaving this good couple tugging at their goat?'

I saw them first as small figures far below and took them for those others. 'See down there, Horace,' I said then. 'Already they've found each other. Already they come, and as though that fellow took no wounds at all from Brennus.'

And Horace looked my way thoughtfully, as though to ask, 'Then, Gawain, will this be the last time we climb this bleak slope together?' And I gave no reply but to stroke gently his neck, though I thought to myself, 'That warrior's young and a terrible fellow. Yet I may have the beating of him, who's to say? I saw something even as he brought down Brennus's man. Another would not see it, yet I did. A small opening on the left for a canny foe.'

But what would Arthur have me do now? His shadow still falls across the land and engulfs me. Would he have me crouch like a beast awaiting its prey? Yet where to hide on these bare slopes? Will the wind alone conceal a man? Or should I perch on some precipice and hurl down a boulder at them? Hardly the way for a knight of Arthur. I would rather show myself openly, greet him, try once more a little diplomacy. 'Turn back, sir. You endanger not just yourself and your innocent companion, but all the good folk of this country. Leave Querig to one who knows her ways. You see me even now on my way to slay her.' But such pleas were ignored before. Why would he hear me now he is come so close, and the bitten boy to guide him to her very door? Was I a fool to rescue that boy? Yet the abbot appals me so, and I know God will thank me for what I did.

'They come as surely as they have a chart,' I said to Horace. 'So where shall we wait? Where shall we face them?'

The copse. I remembered it then. Strange how the trees grow so lush there, when the wind sweeps all around so bare. The copse will provide covering for a knight and his horse. I will not pounce like a bandit, yet why show myself a good hour before the encounter?

So I put a little spur on Horace, though it hardly makes an impression on him now, and we crossed the high edge of the land, neither rising nor falling, battered all the way by the wind. We were both thankful to reach those trees, even if they grow so strangely one wonders if Merlin himself cast a spell here. What a fellow was Master Merlin! I thought once he had placed a spell on Death himself, yet even Merlin has taken his path now. Is it heaven or hell he makes his home? Master Axl may believe Merlin a servant of the devil, yet his powers were often enough spent in ways to make God smile. And let it not be said he was without courage. Many times he showed himself to the falling arrows and wild axes alongside us. These may well be Merlin's woods, and made for this very purpose: that I may some day shelter here to await the one who would undo our great work of that day. Two of us five fell to the she-dragon, yet Master Merlin stood beside us, moving calmly within the sweep of Querig's tail, for how else could his work be done?

The woods were hushed and peaceful when Horace and I reached them. Even a bird or two singing in the trees, and if the branches stirred wildly, down below was as a calm spring's day where at last an old man's thoughts may drift from one ear to the other without tossing in a tempest! It must be several years now since Horace and I were last in these woods. Weeds have grown monstrous here, a nettle rightly the spread of a small child's palm stands large enough to wrap around a man twice over. I left Horace at a gentle spot to chew on what he could, and wandered a while beneath the sheltering leaves. Why should I not rest here, leaning on this good oak? And when in time they come to this place, as they surely will, he and I will face each other as fellow warriors.

I pushed through the giant nettles – is it for this I have worn this creaking metal? To defend my shins from these feathery stings? – until I reached the clearing and the pond, the grey sky above it peeping through. Around its rim, three great trees, yet each one cracked at the waist and fallen forward into the water. Surely they stood proudly when we were last here. Did lightning strike them? Or did they in weary old age long for the pond's succour, always so near where they grew, yet beyond reach? They drink all they wish now, and mountain birds nest in their broken spines.

Will it be at such a spot I meet the Saxon? If he defeats me I may have life left to crawl to the water. I would not tumble in, even if the ice would admit me, for it would be no pleasure to grow bloated beneath this armour, and what chance Horace, missing his master, will come tip-toeing through the gnarled roots and drag out my remains? Yet I've seen comrades in battle yearn for water as they lie with their wounds, and watched yet others crawl to the edge of a river or lake, even though they double their agonies to do so. Is there some great secret known only to dying men? My old comrade, Master Buel, longed for water that day, as he lay on the red clay of that mountain. There's water here left in my gourd, I told him, but no, he demands a lake or river. But we're far from any such thing, I say. 'Curse you, Gawain,' he cries. 'My last wish, will you not grant it, and we comrades through many bold battles?' 'But this she-dragon's all but parted you in two,' I tell him. 'If I must carry you to water, I'll have to go under this summer sun, a separate part of you under each arm before we reach any such place.' But he says to me, 'My heart will welcome death only when you lay me down beside water, Gawain, where I hear its gentle lapping as my eyes close.' He demands this, and cares not whether our errand is well done, or if his life is given at a good price. Only when I reach down to raise him does he ask: 'Who else survives?' And I tell him Master Millus is fallen, yet three of us still stand, and Master Merlin too. And still he asks not if the errand is well finished, but talks of lakes and rivers, and now even of the sea, and it is all I can do to remember this is my old comrade, and a brave one, chosen like me by Arthur for this great task, even as a battle rages down in the valley. Does he forget his duty? I lift him, and he cries out to the heavens, and only then understands the cost even of a few small steps, and there we are, atop a red mountain in the summer heat, an hour's journey even on horseback to the river. And as I lower him he talks now only of the sea. His eyes blind now, when I sprinkle water on his face from my gourd, he thanks me the way I suppose in his mind's eye he stands upon a shore. 'Was it sword or axe finished me?' he asks, and I say, 'What do you talk of, comrade? It's the she-dragon's tail met you, but our task's done and you depart with pride and honour.' 'The she-dragon,' he says. 'What's become of the she-dragon?' 'All but one of the spears rest in her flank,' I say, 'and now she sleeps.' Yet he forgets the errand again, and talks of the sea, and of a boat he knew as a small boy when his father took him far from the shore on a kind evening.

When my own time comes, will I too long for the sea? I think I will be content enough with the soil. And I will not demand the exact spot, but let it be within this country Horace and I have spent the years roaming contentedly. Those dark widows of earlier would cackle to hear me, and hasten to remind me with what I may share my plot of earth. 'Foolish knight! You above all need choose your resting place well, or find yourself a neighbour to the very ones you slaughtered!' Did they not make some such jest even as they threw mud at Horace's rump? How dare they! Were they there? Can it be this woman now rides in my saddle would say as much if she could hear my thoughts? She talked of slaughtered babes down in that foul-aired tunnel, even as I delivered her from the monks' black plans. How dare she? And now she sits in my saddle, astride my dear battlehorse, and who knows how many more journeys are left to Horace and me?

For a while we thought this might be our last, but I had mistaken this good couple for those others, and a while longer we travel in peace. Yet even as I lead Horace by the bridle, I must glance back, for surely they are coming, even if we go well ahead. Master Axl walks beside me, his goat forbidding him a steady step. Does he guess why I look back so often? 'Sir Gawain, were we not comrades once?' I heard him ask it early this morning as we came out of the tunnel, and I told him to find a boat to go downstream. Yet here he is, still in the mountains, his good wife beside him. I will not meet his eye. Age cloaks us both, as the grass and weeds cloak the fields where we once fought and slaughtered. What is it you seek, sir? What is this goat you bring?

'Turn back, friends,' I said when they came upon me in the woods. 'This is no walk for elderly travellers like you. And look how the good mistress holds her side. Between here and the giant's cairn there's still a mile or more, and the only shelter small rocks behind which one must curl with bowed head. Turn back while you still have strength, and I'll see this goat's left at the cairn and tethered well.' But they both eyed me suspiciously, and Master Axl would not let go the goat. The branches rustled above, and his wife seated on the roots of an oak, gazing to the pond and the cracked trees stooping to water, and I said softly: 'This is no journey for your good wife, sir. Why did you not do as I advised and take the river down out of these hills?' 'We must take this goat where we promised,' says Master Axl. 'A promise made to a child.' And does he look at me strangely as he says so, or do I dream it? 'Horace and I will take the goat,' I say. 'Will you not trust us with the errand? I hardly believe this goat will much trouble Querig even if devoured whole, yet she may be a little slowed and lend me an advantage. So give me the creature and turn back down the mountain before one or the other of you fall in your own footsteps.'

They moved then into the trees away from me, and I could hear the shape of their lowered voices, but no words. Then Master Axl comes to me and says: 'A moment more for my wife to rest, then we will carry on, sir, to the giant's cairn.' I see it is useless to argue more, and I also eager to continue on our way, for who knows how far behind is Master Wistan and his bitten boy?

PART IV

Chapter Fifteen

Some of you will have fine monuments by which the living may remember the evil done to you. Some of you will have only crude wooden crosses or painted rocks, while yet others of you must remain hidden in the shadows of history. You are in any case part of an ancient procession, and so it is always possible the giant's cairn was erected to mark the site of some such tragedy long ago when young innocents were slaughtered in war. This aside, it is not easy to think of reasons for its standing. One can see why on lower ground our ancestors might have wished to commemorate a victory or a king. But why stack heavy stones to above a man's height in so high and remote a place as this?

It was a question, I am sure, equally to baffle Axl as he came wearily up the mountain slope. When the young girl had first mentioned the giant's cairn, he had pictured something atop a large mound. Yet this cairn had simply appeared before them on the incline, no feature around it to explain its presence. The goat, nonetheless, seemed immediately to sense its significance, struggling frantically as soon as the cairn had become visible as a dark finger against the sky. 'It knows its fate,' Sir Gawain had remarked, guiding his horse up with Beatrice in the saddle.

But now the goat had forgotten its earlier dread and was chewing the mountain grass contentedly.

'Can it be Querig's mist works its mischief on goats and men alike?'

It was Beatrice who asked this as she held with both hands the animal's rope. Axl had for the moment relinquished the creature while he hammered into the ground with a stone the wooden stake around which the rope had been wound.

'Who knows, princess. But if God cares at all for goats, he'll bring the she-dragon here before long, or it'll be a lonely wait for this poor animal.'

'If the goat dies first, Axl, do you suppose she'll still sup on meat not living and fresh?'

'Who knows how a she-dragon likes her meat? But there's grass here to keep this goat a while, princess, even if it's of a mean sort.'

'Look there, Axl. I thought the knight would help us, weary as we both are. But he's forgotten his usual manners.'

Indeed Sir Gawain had become oddly reticent since their arrival at the cairn. 'This is the place you seek,' he had said in an almost sulky voice, before wandering off. And now he stood with his back to them, staring at the clouds.

'Sir Gawain,' Axl called out, pausing from his work. 'Will you not assist holding this goat? My poor wife grows tired from it.'

The old knight did not react, and Axl, assuming he had not heard, was about to repeat his request, when Gawain turned suddenly, and with such a look of solemnity, they both stared at him.

'I see them below,' the old knight said. 'And nothing now to turn them.'

'Who is it you see, sir?' Axl asked. Then when the knight remained silent, 'Are they soldiers? We watched earlier some long column on the horizon, but thought they moved away from us.'

'I speak of your recent companions, sir. The same with whom you travelled yesterday when we met. They emerge from the wood below, and who'll stop them now? For a moment, I raised a hope I merely looked on two black widows strayed from that infernal procession. But it was the cloudy sky playing its tricks, and it's them, no mistake.'

'So Master Wistan escaped the monastery after all,' Axl said.

'That he did, sir. And now he comes, and on his rope not a goat, but the Saxon boy to guide him.'

At last Sir Gawain seemed to notice Beatrice struggling with the animal and came hurriedly from the cliff edge to seize the rope. But Beatrice did not let go, and for a moment it was as if she and the knight were tussling for control of the goat. In time they stood steadily, both holding the rope, the old knight a step or two in front of Beatrice.

'And have our friends in turn seen us here, Sir Gawain?' Axl asked, returning to his task.

'I'll wager that warrior has keen eyes, and sees us even now against the sky, figures in a tug contest, the goat our opponent!' He laughed to himself, but a melancholy lingered in his voice. 'Yes,' he said finally. 'I fancy he sees us well enough.'

'Then he joins forces with us,' Beatrice said, 'to bring down the she-dragon.'

Sir Gawain looked from one to the other of them uneasily. Then he said: 'Master Axl, do you still persist in believing it?'

'Believing what, Sir Gawain?'

'That we gather here in this forsaken spot as comrades?'

'Make your meaning clearer, sir knight.'

Gawain led the goat to where Axl was kneeling, oblivious of Beatrice following behind, still clutching her end of the rope.

'Master Axl, didn't our ways part years ago? Mine remained with Arthur, while yours . . .' He seemed now to become aware of Beatrice behind him, and turning, bowed politely. 'Dear lady, I beg you let go this rope and rest. I'll not let the animal escape. Sit down beside the cairn there. It will shelter at least some part of you from this wind.'

'Thank you, Sir Gawain,' Beatrice said. 'Then I'll trust you with this creature, and it's a precious one to us.'

She began to make her way towards the cairn, and something about the way she did so, her shoulders hunched against the wind, caused a fragment of recollection to stir on the edges of Axl's mind. The emotion it provoked, even before he could hold it down, surprised and shocked him, for mingled with the overwhelming desire to go to her now and shelter her, were distinct shadows of anger and bitterness. She had talked of a long night spent alone, tormented by his absence, but could it be he too had known such a night, or even several, of similar anguish? Then, as Beatrice stopped before the cairn and bowed her head to the stones as if in apology, he felt both memory and anger growing firmer, and a fear made him turn away from her. Only then did he notice Sir Gawain also gazing over at Beatrice, a look of tenderness in his eyes, seemingly lost in his thoughts. But the knight soon collected himself, and coming closer to Axl, leant right down as though to remove any small chance of Beatrice overhearing.

'Who's to say your path wasn't the more godly?' he said. 'To leave behind all great talk of war and peace. Leave behind that fine law to bring men closer to God. To leave behind Arthur once and for all and devote yourself to . . .' He glanced over again at Beatrice, who had remained on her feet, her forehead almost touching the piled stones in her effort to escape the wind. 'To a good wife, sir.

I've watched how she goes beside you as a kind shadow. Should I have done the same? Yet God guided us down separate paths. I had a duty. Ha! And do I fear him now? Never, sir, never. I accuse you of nothing. That great law you brokered torn down in blood! Yet it held well for a time. Torn down in blood! Who blames us for it now? Do I fear youth? Is it youth alone can defeat an opponent? Let him come, let him come. Remember it, sir! I saw you that very day and you talked of cries in your ears of children and babes. I heard the same, sir, yet were they not like the cries from the surgeon's tent when a man's life is spared even as the cure brings agonies? Yet I admit it. There are days I long for a kind shadow to follow me. Even now I turn in hope to see one. Doesn't every animal, every bird in the sky crave a tender companion? There were one or two I'd willingly have given my years. Why should I fear him now? I've fought fanged Norsemen with reindeer snouts, and they no masks! Here, sir, tie your goat now. How much deeper will you drive that stake? Is it a goat you tether or a lion?'

Handing Axl the rope, Gawain went striding off, not stopping till he stood where the land's edge appeared to meet the sky. Axl, one knee pressed into the grass, tied the rope tightly around the notch in the wood, then looked once more over to his wife. She was standing at the cairn much as before, and though something in her posture again tugged at him, he was relieved to find in himself no trace of the earlier bitterness. Instead he felt almost overcome by an urge to defend her, not just from the harsh wind, but from something else large and dark even then gathering around them. He rose and hurried to her.

'The goat's well secured, princess,' he said. 'Just as soon as you're ready, let's be off down this slope. For haven't we completed the errand promised to those children and to ourselves?'

'Oh Axl, I don't want to go back to those woods.'

'What are you saying, princess?'

'Axl, you never went to the pond's edge, you were so busy talking to this knight. You never looked into that chilly water.'

'These winds have tired you, princess.'

'I saw their faces staring up as if resting in their beds.'

'Who, princess?'

'The babes, and only a short way beneath the water's surface. I thought first they were smiling, and some waving, but when I went nearer I saw how they lay unmoving.'

'Just another dream came to you while you rested against that tree. I remember seeing you asleep there and took comfort from it at the time, even as I talked with the old knight.'

'I truly saw them, Axl. Among the green weed. Let's not go back to that wood, for I'm sure some evil lingers there.'

Sir Gawain, gazing down at the view, had raised his arm in the air, and now without turning, shouted through the wind: 'They'll soon be upon us! They come up the slope eagerly.'

'Let's go to him, princess, but keep the cloak around you. I was foolish to bring you this far, but we'll soon find shelter again. Yet let's see what troubles the good knight.'

The goat was pulling at its rope as they passed, but the stake showed no sign of shifting. Axl had been keen to see how near the approaching figures were, but now the old knight came walking towards them, and they all three halted not far from where the animal was tethered.

'Sir Gawain,' Axl said, 'my wife grows weak and must return to shelter and food. May we carry her down on your horse as we brought her up?'

'What's this you ask? Too much, sir! Did I not tell you when we met in Merlin's wood to climb this hill no further? It was you both insisted on coming here.'

'Perhaps we were foolish, sir, but we had a purpose, and if we must turn back without you, you must promise not to free this goat cost us so dearly to bring here.'

'Free the goat? What do I care for your goat, sir? The Saxon warrior will soon be upon us, and what a fellow he is! Go, look if you doubt it! What do I care for your goat? Master Axl, I see you before me now and I'm reminded of that night. The wind as fierce then as this one. And you, cursing Arthur to his face while the rest of us stood with heads bowed! For who wanted the task of striking you down? Each of us hiding from the king's eye, for fear he'd command with one glance to run you through, unarmed though you were. But see, sir, Arthur was a great king, and here's more proof of it! You cursed him before his finest knights, yet he replied gently to you. You recall this, sir?'

'I recall nothing of it, Sir Gawain. Your she-dragon's breath keeps it all from me.'

'My eyes lowered like the rest, expecting your head to roll past my feet even as I gazed down at them! Yet Arthur spoke to you with gentleness! You don't recall even a part of it? The wind that night almost as strong as this one, our tent ready to fly into the dark sky. Yet Arthur meets curses with gentle words. He thanked you for your service. For your friendship. And he bade us all think of you with honour. I myself whispered farewell to you, sir, as you took your fury into the storm. You didn't hear me, for it was said under my breath, but a sincere farewell all the same, and I wasn't alone. We all shared something of your anger, sir, even if you did wrong to curse Arthur, and on the very day of his great victory! You say now Querig's breath keeps this from your mind, or is it the years alone, or even this wind enough to make the wisest monk a fool?'

'I don't care for any of these memories, Sir Gawain. Today I seek others from another stormy night my wife speaks of.'

'A sincere farewell I bade you, sir, and let me confess it, when you cursed Arthur a small part of me spoke through you. For that was a great treaty you brokered, and well held for years. Didn't all men, Christian and pagan, sleep more easily for it, even on the eve of battle? To fight knowing our innocents safe in our villages? And yet, sir, the wars didn't finish. Where once we fought for land and God, we now fought to avenge fallen comrades, themselves slaughtered in vengeance. Where could it end? Babes growing to men knowing only days of war. And your great law already suffering violation . . .'

'The law was well held on both sides until that day, Sir Gawain,' Axl said. 'It was an unholy thing to break it.'

'Ah, now you recall it!'

'My memory's of God himself betrayed, sir. And I'm not sorry if the mist robs me further of it.'

'For a time I wished the same of the mist, Master Axl. Yet soon I understood the hand of a truly great king. For the wars stopped at last, wasn't that so, sir? Hasn't peace been our companion since that day?'

'Remind me no more, Sir Gawain. I don't thank you for it. Let me see instead the life I led with my dear wife, shivering here beside me. Will you not lend us your horse, sir? At least down to the woods where we met. We'll leave him safely there to await you.'

'Oh Axl, I'll not return to those woods! Why insist we leave this place now and go down there? Can it be, husband, you still fear the mist's fading, never mind the promise I made you?'

'My horse, sir? You imply I've no more use of my Horace? You go too far, sir! I don't fear him, even if he's youth on his side!'

'I imply nothing, Sir Gawain, only ask for the assistance of your excellent horse to carry my wife down to shelter . . .'

'My horse, sir? Do you insist his eyes be masked or watch his master's fall? He's a battlehorse, sir! Not some pony frolics in buttercups! A battlehorse, sir, and well ready to see me fall or triumph as God wills!'

'If my wife must travel on my own back, sir knight, so be it. Yet I thought you might spare your horse at least the distance down to the wood . . .'

'I'll remain here, Axl, never mind this cruel wind, and if Master Wistan's nearly upon us, we'll stay and see if it's him or the she-dragon survives this day. Or is it you'd rather not see the mist fade after all, husband?'

'I've seen it before many times, sir! An eager young one brought down by a wise old head. Many times!'

'Sir, let me implore you again to remember your gentlemanly ways. This wind drains my wife of strength.'

'Is it not enough, husband, I swore you an oath, and only this morning, I'd not let go what I feel in my heart for you today, no matter what the mist's fading reveals?'

'Will you not understand the acts of a great king, sir? We can only watch and wonder. A great king, like God himself, must perform deeds mortals flinch from! Do you think there were none that caught my eye? A tender flower or two passed on the way I didn't long to press to my bosom? Is this metal coat to be my only bedfellow? Who calls me a coward, sir? Or a slaugh-terer of babes? Where were you that day? Were you with us? My helmet! I left it in those woods! But what need of it now?

The armour too I'd take off but I fear you all laughing to see the skinned fox beneath!'

For a moment, all three of them were shouting over each other, the howl of the wind a fourth voice against theirs, but now Axl became aware that both Gawain and his wife had fallen silent and were staring past his shoulder. Turning, he saw the warrior and the Saxon boy standing at the cliff's edge, almost on the very spot where before Sir Gawain had been gazing broodingly out at the view. The sky had thickened, so that to Axl it was as if the newcomers had been carried here on the clouds. Now both of them, in near-silhouette, appeared peculiarly transfixed: the warrior holding firm his rein in both hands like a charioteer; the boy leaning forward at an angle, both arms outstretched as though for balance. There was a new sound in the wind, and then Axl heard Sir Gawain say: 'Ah! the boy sings again! Can you not make him cease, sir?'

Wistan gave a laugh, and the two figures lost their rigidity and came towards them, the boy pulling in front.

'My apologies,' the warrior said. 'Yet it's all I can do to stop him leaping rock to rock till he breaks himself.'

'What can be the matter with the boy, Axl?' Beatrice said, close to his ear, and he was grateful to hear the gentle intimacy returned to her voice. 'He was just this way before that dog appeared.'

'Must he sing so untunefully?' Sir Gawain addressed Wistan again. 'I'd box his ears but fear he'd not even feel me!'

The warrior, still approaching, laughed again, then glanced cheerfully at Axl and Beatrice. 'My friends, this is a surprise. I fancied you'd be in your son's village by now. What brings you instead to this lonely spot?'

'The same business as yours, Master Wistan. We crave the end to this she-dragon who robs us of treasured memories. You see, sir, we've brought with us a poisoned goat to do our work.'

Wistan regarded the animal and shook his head. 'This must be a mighty and cunning creature we face, friends. I fear your goat may not trouble her beyond a belch or two.'

'It taxed us greatly bringing it here, Master Wistan,' Beatrice said, 'even if we were helped by this good knight met again on the way up. But seeing you here, I'm cheered, for it must be our hopes no longer rest solely with our animal.'

But now Edwin's singing was making it hard for them to hear one another, and the boy was tugging more than ever, the object of his attention quite evidently a spot at the crest of the next slope. Wistan gave the rope a sharp pull, then said:

'Master Edwin appears anxious to reach those rocks up there. Sir Gawain, what lies in them? I see stones piled one upon another, as though to hide a pit or lair.'

'Why ask me, sir?' said Sir Gawain. 'Ask your young companion and he may even stop his songs!'

'I hold him by a leash, sir, but can no more control him than a crazed goblin.'

'Master Wistan,' Axl said, 'we share a duty to keep this boy from harm. We must watch him carefully in this high place.'

'Well said, sir. I'll tether him, if I may, to the same post as your goat.'

The warrior led Edwin to where Axl had hammered in the stake, and crouching down began securing the boy's rope to it. Indeed it seemed to Axl that Wistan lavished unusual care on this task, testing repeatedly each knot he made, as well as the soundness of Axl's handiwork. Meanwhile the boy himself remained oblivious. He calmed somewhat, but his gaze stayed fixed on the rocks at the top of the slope, and he continued to tug with quiet insistence. His singing, though far less shrill, had gained a dogged quality that reminded Axl of the way exhausted soldiers sing to keep marching. For its part, the goat had moved as far away as its own rope would allow, but was nonetheless gawping in fascination.

As for Sir Gawain, he had been watching Wistan's every movement with care, and – so it seemed to Axl – a kind of sly cunning had come into his eyes. As the Saxon warrior had become absorbed in his task, the knight had moved stealthily closer, drawn out his sword, and planting it into the soil, leant his weight on it, forearms resting on the broad hilt. In this stance, Gawain was now watching Wistan, and it struck Axl he might be memorising details concerning the warrior's person: his height, his reach, the strength in the calves, the strapped left arm.

His work completed to his satisfaction, Wistan rose and turned to face Sir Gawain. For a small moment there was a strange uneasiness in the looks they exchanged, then Wistan smiled warmly.

'Now here's a custom divides Britons from Saxons,' he said, pointing. 'See there, sir. Your sword's drawn and you use it to rest your weight, as if it's cousin to a chair or footstool. To any Saxon warrior, even one taught by Britons as I was, it seems a strange custom.'

'Grow to my creaky years, sir, you'll see if it seems so strange! In days of peace like these, I fancy a good sword's only too glad of the work, even if just to relieve its owner's bones. What's odd about it, sir?'

'But observe, Sir Gawain, how it presses into the earth. Now to us Saxons, a sword's edge is a thing of never-sleeping worry. We fear to show a blade even the air lest it lose a tiny part of its edge.'

'Is that so? A sharp edge's of importance, Master Wistan, I'll not dispute. But isn't there too much made of it? Good footwork, sound strategy, calm courage. And that little wildness makes a warrior hard to predict. These are what determine a contest, sir. And the knowledge God wills one's victory. So let an old man rest his shoulders. Besides, aren't there times a sword left in the sheath's drawn too late? I've stood this way on many a battlefield to gather breath, comforted my blade's already out and ready, and it won't be rubbing its eyes and asking me if it's afternoon or morn even as I try to put it to good use.'

'Then it must be we Saxons keep our swords more heartlessly. For we demand they not sleep at all, even as they rest in the dark of their scabbards. Take my own here, sir. It knows my manner well. It doesn't expect to take the air without soon touching flesh and bone.'

'A difference in custom then, sir. It reminds me of a Saxon I once knew, a fine fellow, and he and I gathering kindling on a cold night. I would be busying my sword to hack from a dead tree, yet there he is beside me, employing his bare hands and sometimes a blunt stone. "Have you forgotten your blade, friend?" I asked him. "Why go at it like a sharp-clawed bear?" But he wouldn't hear me. At the time I thought him crazed, yet now you enlighten me. Even with my years, there are still lessons to learn!'

They both laughed briefly, then Wistan said:

'There may be more than custom on my side, Sir Gawain. I was always taught that even as my blade travels through one opponent, I must in my thought prepare the cut that will follow. Now if my edge isn't sharp, sir, and the blade's passage slowed even a tiny instant, snagged in bone or dawdling through the tangles of a man's insides, I'll surely be late for the next cut, and on such may hang victory or defeat.'

'You're right, sir. I believe it's old age and these long years of peace make me careless. I'll follow your example from here, yet just now my knees sag from the climb, and I beg you allow me this small relief.'

'Of course, sir, take your comfort. Merely a thought struck me seeing you rest that way.'

Suddenly Edwin stopped singing and began to shout. He was making the same statement over and over, and Axl, turning to Beatrice beside him, asked quietly: 'What is it he says, princess?'

'He talks of some bandits' camp lies up there. He bids us all follow him to it.'

Wistan and Gawain were both staring at the boy with something like embarrassment. For another moment, Edwin continued to shout and pull, then fell silent, slumping down onto the ground, and appeared on the verge of tears. No one spoke for what seemed a long time, the wind howling between them.

'Sir Gawain,' Axl said finally. 'We look now to you, sir. Let's keep no more disguises between us. You're the she-dragon's protector, are you not?'

'I am, sir.' Gawain gazed at each of them in turn, Edwin included, with an air of defiance. 'Her protector, and lately her only friend. The monks kept her fed for years, leaving tethered animals at this spot, as you do. But now they quarrel among themselves, and Querig senses their treachery. Yet she knows I stay loyal.'

'Then Sir Gawain,' Wistan said, 'will you care to tell us if we stand near the she-dragon now?'

'She's near, sir. You've done well to arrive here, even if you had good fortune stumbling on that boy for a guide.'

Edwin, who was back on his feet, began to sing once more, albeit in a low chant-like manner.

'Master Edwin here may prove of greater fortune yet,' said the warrior. 'For I've a hunch he's a pupil to quickly surpass his poor master and one day do great things for his kin. Perhaps even as your Arthur did for his.'

'What, sir? This boy now singing and tugging like a half-wit?'

'Sir Gawain,' Beatrice interrupted, 'tell a weary old woman if you will. How is it a fine knight like you, and a nephew to the great Arthur, turns out this she-dragon's protector?'

'Perhaps Master Wistan here's keen to explain it, mistress.'

'On the contrary, I'm as eager as Mistress Beatrice to hear your account of it. Yet all in good time. First, we must settle one question. Will I cut loose Master Edwin to see where he runs? Or will you, Sir Gawain, lead the way to Querig's lair?'

Sir Gawain stared emptily at the struggling boy, then sighed. 'Leave him where he is,' he said heavily. 'I'll lead the way.' He straightened to his full height, pulled the sword from the ground and carefully returned it to its scabbard.

'I thank you, sir,' Wistan said. 'I'm grateful we spare the boy the danger. Yet I may now guess the way without a guide. We must go to those rocks atop this next slope, must we not?'

Sir Gawain sighed again, glanced at Axl as though for help, then shook his head sadly. 'Quite right, sir,' he said. 'Those rocks circle a pit, and no small one. A pit as deep as a quarry, and you'll find Querig asleep there. If you really mean to fight her, Master Wistan, you'll have to climb down into it. Now I ask you, sir, do you really mean to do such a wild thing?'

'I've come this long way to do so, sir.'

'Master Wistan,' Beatrice said, 'if you'll excuse an old woman's intrusion. You laughed just now at our goat, but this is a great battle you face. If this knight will not help you, at least allow us to take our goat up this last slope and prod it down into this pit. If you must fight a she-dragon single-handed, let it be one slowed by poison.'

'Thank you, mistress, your concern's well received. Yet while I may take advantage of her slumber, poison's a weapon I don't care to employ. Besides, I lack the patience now to wait another half day or more to discover if the she-dragon will sicken from her supper.'

'Then let's have it over with,' Sir Gawain said. 'Come, sir, I'll lead the way.' Then to Axl and Beatrice: 'Wait down here, friends, and hide from the wind beside the cairn. You'll not wait long.'

'But Sir Gawain,' Beatrice said, 'my husband and I've stretched our strength to come this far. We'd walk with you this last slope if there's a way to do so without danger.'

Sir Gawain once again shook his head helplessly. 'Then let's all go together, friends. I dare say no harm will befall you, and I'll be easier myself for your presence. Come, friends, let's go to Querig's lair, and keep your voices low lest she stir from her sleep.'

* * *

As they ascended the next path, the wind grew less harsh, even though they felt more than ever to be touching the sky. The knight and the warrior were striding steadily before them, for all the world like two old companions taking the air together, and before long a distance had opened between them and the elderly couple.

'This is foolishness, princess,' Axl said as they walked. 'What business do we have following these gentlemen? And who knows what dangers lie ahead? Let's turn back and wait beside the boy.'

But Beatrice's step remained determined. 'I'll have us go on,' she said. 'Here, Axl, take my hand and help me keep my courage. For I'm thinking now I'm the one to fear most the mist's clearing, not you. I stood beside those stones just now and it came to me there were dark things I did to you once, husband. Feel how this hand trembles in yours to think they may be returned to us! What will you say to me then? Will you turn away and leave me on this bleak hill? There's a part of me would see this brave warrior fall even as he walks before us now, yet I'll not have us hide. No, I'll not, Axl, and aren't you the same? Let's see freely the path we've come together, whether it's in dark or mellow sun. And if this warrior must really face the she-dragon in her own pit, let's do what we can to keep up his spirits. It may be a shout of warning in the right place, or one to rouse him from a fierce blow will make the difference.'

Axl had let her talk on, listening with only half his mind as he walked, because he had become aware once more of something at the far edge of his memory: a stormy night, a bitter hurt, a loneliness opening before him like unfathomed waters. Could it really have been he, not Beatrice, standing alone in their chamber, unable to sleep, a small candle lit before him?

'What became of our son, princess?' he asked suddenly, and felt her hand tighten on his. 'Does he really wait for us in his village? Or will we search this country for a year and still not find him?'

'It's a thought came to me too, but I was afraid to think it aloud. But hush now, Axl, or we'll be heard.'

Indeed Sir Gawain and Wistan had halted on the path ahead to wait for them, and appeared to be in genial conversation. As he came up to them, Axl could hear Sir Gawain saying with a small chuckle:

'I'll confess, Master Wistan, my hope's that even now Querig's breath will rob you of the memory of why you walk beside me. I await eagerly your asking where it is I lead you! Yet I see from both your eye and step you forget little.'

Wistan smiled. 'I believe, sir, it's this very gift to withstand strange spells won me this errand from my king. For in the fens, we've never known a creature quite like this Querig, yet have known others with wonderful powers, and it was noticed how little I was swayed, even as my comrades swooned and wandered in dreams. I fancy this was my king's only reason to choose me, for almost all my comrades at home are better warriors than this one walks beside you now.'

'Impossible to believe, Master Wistan! Both report and observation tell of your extraordinary qualities.'

'You overestimate me, sir. Yesterday, needing to bring down that soldier under your gaze, I was all too aware how a man of your skill might view my small accomplishments. Sufficient to defeat a frightened guardsman, but far short of your approval, I fear.'

'What nonsense, sir! You're a splendid fellow, and no more of it! Now, friends' – Gawain turned his gaze to include Axl and Beatrice – 'it's not so far now. Let's be moving on while she still sleeps.'

They continued in silence. This time Axl and Beatrice did not fall behind, for a sense of solemnity seemed to descend on Gawain and Wistan, making them proceed in front at an almost ceremonial pace. In any case, the ground had become less demanding, levelling to something like a plateau. The rocks they had discussed from below now loomed before them, and Axl could see, as they came ever nearer, how they were arranged in a rough semi-circle around the top of a mound to the side of their path. He could see too how a row of smaller stones rose in a kind of stairway up the side of the mound, leading right up to the rim of what could only be a pit of significant depth. The grass all around where they had now arrived seemed to have been blackened or burnt, lending the surroundings – already without tree or shrub – an atmosphere of decay. Gawain, bringing the party to a halt near where the crude stairway began, turned to face Wistan with some deliberation.

'Will you not consider a last time, sir, leaving this dangerous plan? Why not return now to your orphan tied to his stick? There's his voice in the wind even now.'

The warrior glanced back the way they had come, then looked again at Sir Gawain. 'You know it, sir. I cannot turn back. Show me this dragon.'

The old knight nodded thoughtfully, as though Wistan had just made some casual but fascinating observation.

'Very well, friends,' he said. 'Then keep your voices low, for what purpose should we wake her?'

Sir Gawain led the way up the side of the mound and on reaching the rocks signalled for them to wait. He then peered over carefully, and after a moment, beckoned to them, saying in a low voice: 'Come stand along here, friends, and you'll see her well enough.'

Axl helped his wife onto a ledge beside him, then leant over one of the rocks. The pit below was broader and shallower than he had expected – more like a drained pond than something actually dug into the ground. The greater part of it was now in pale sunlight, and seemed to consist entirely of grey rock and gravel

– the blackened grass finishing abruptly at the rim – so that the only living thing visible, aside from the dragon herself, was a solitary hawthorn bush sprouting incongruously through the stone near the centre of the pit's belly.

As for the dragon, it was hardly clear at first she was alive. Her posture – prone, head twisted to one side, limbs outspread – might easily have resulted from her corpse being hurled into the pit from a height. In fact it took a moment to ascertain this was a dragon at all: she was so emaciated she looked more some worm-like reptile accustomed to water that had mistakenly come aground and was in the process of dehydrating. Her skin, which should have appeared oiled and of a colour not unlike bronze, was instead a yellowing white, reminiscent of the underside of certain fish. The remnants of her wings were sagging folds of skin that a careless glance might have taken for dead leaves accumulated to either side of her. The head being turned against the grey pebbles, Axl could see only the one eye, which was hooded in the manner of a turtle's, and which opened and closed lethargically according to some internal rhythm. This movement, and the faintest rise and fall along the creature's backbone, were the only indicators that Querig was still alive.

'Can this really be her, Axl?' Beatrice said quietly. 'This poor creature no more than a fleshy thread?'

'Yet look there, mistress,' Gawain's voice said behind them. 'So long as she's breath left, she does her duty.'

'Is she sick or perhaps already poisoned?' asked Axl.

'She simply grows old, sir, as we all must do. But she still breathes, and so Merlin's work lingers.'

'Now a little of this comes back to me,' Axl said. 'I remember Merlin's work here and dark it was too.'

'Dark, sir?' said Gawain. 'Why dark? It was the only way. Even before that battle was properly won, I rode out with four good comrades to tame this same creature, in those days both mighty and angry, so Merlin could place this great spell on her breath. A dark man he may have been, but in this he did God's will, not only Arthur's. Without this she-dragon's breath, would peace ever have come? Look how we live now, sir! Old foes as cousins, village by village. Master Wistan, you fall silent before this sight. I ask again. Will you not leave this poor creature to live out her life? Her breath isn't what it was, yet holds the magic even now. Think, sir, once that breath should cease, what might be awoken across this land even after these years! Yes, we slaughtered plenty, I admit it, caring not who was strong and who weak. God may not have smiled at us, but we cleansed the land of war. Leave this place, sir, I beg you. We may pray to different gods, yet surely yours will bless this dragon as does mine.'

Wistan turned away from the pit to look at the old knight.

'What kind of god is it, sir, wishes wrongs to go forgotten and unpunished?'

'You ask it well, Master Wistan, and I know my god looks uneasily on our deeds of that day. Yet it's long past and the bones lie sheltered beneath a pleasant green carpet. The young know nothing of them. I beg you leave this place, and let Querig do her work a while longer. Another season or two, that's the most she'll last. Yet even that may be long enough for old wounds to heal for ever, and an eternal peace to hold among us. Look how she clings to life, sir! Be merciful and leave this place. Leave this country to rest in forgetfulness.'

'Foolishness, sir. How can old wounds heal while maggots linger so richly? Or a peace hold for ever built on slaughter and a magician's trickery? I see how devoutly you wish it, for your old horrors to crumble as dust. Yet they await in the soil as white bones for men to uncover. Sir Gawain, my answer's unchanged. I must go down into this pit.'

Sir Gawain nodded gravely. 'I understand, sir.'

'Then I must ask you in turn, sir knight. Will you leave this place to me and return now to your fine old stallion awaits you below?'

'You know I cannot, Master Wistan.'

'It's as I thought. Well then.'

Wistan came past Axl and Beatrice, and down the rough-hewn steps. When he was once more at the foot of the mound, he looked around him and said, in a quite new voice: 'Sir Gawain, this earth looks curious here. Can it be the she-dragon, in her more vigorous days, blasted it this way? Or does lightning strike here often to burn the ground before new grasses return?'

Gawain, who had followed him down the mound, also came off the steps, and for a moment the two of them strolled about randomly like companions pondering at which spot to pitch their tent.

'It's something always puzzled me too, Master Wistan,' Gawain was saying. 'For even when younger, she remained above, and I don't suppose it's Querig made this blasted ground. Perhaps it was always thus, even when we first brought her here and lowered her into her lair.' Gawain tapped his heel experimentally on the soil. 'A good floor, sir, nevertheless.'

'Indeed.' Wistan, his back to Gawain, was also testing the ground with his foot.

'Though perhaps a little short in width?' remarked the knight. 'See how that edge rolls over the cliffside. A man who fell here would rest on friendly earth, sure enough, yet his blood may run swiftly through these burnt grasses and over the side. I don't speak for you, sir, but I'll not fancy my insides dripping over the cliff like a gull's white droppings!'

They both laughed, then Wistan said:

'A needless worry, sir. See how the ground lifts slightly before the cliff there. As for the opposite edge, it's too far the other way and plenty of thirsty soil first.'

'That's well observed. Well, then, it's no bad spot!' Sir Gawain looked up at Axl and Beatrice, who were still up on the ledge, though now with their backs to the pit. 'Master Axl,' he called cheerfully, 'you were always the great one for diplomacy. Do you care to use your fine eloquence now to let us leave this place as friends?'

'I'm sorry, Sir Gawain. You've shown us much kindness and we thank you for it. Yet we're now here to see the end of Querig, and if you'll defend her, there's nothing I or my wife can say on your side. Our will's with Master Wistan in this matter.'

'I see it, sir. Then let me ask at least this of you. I don't fear this fellow before me. Yet if I should be the one to fall, will you take my good Horace back down this mountain? He'll welcome a pair of good Britons on his back. You may think he grumbles, but you'll not be too much for him. Take my dear Horace far away from here and when you've no more use of him, find him a fine green meadow where he may eat to his heart's content and think of old days. Will you do this for me, friends?'

'We'll do it gladly, sir, and your horse will be the saving of us too, for it's a harsh journey down these hills.'

'On that point, sir.' Gawain had now come right to the foot of the mound. 'I urged you once before to use the river, and do so again. Let Horace take you down these slopes, but once you meet the river, search for a boat to take you east. There's tin and coins in the saddle to buy your passage.'

'We thank you, sir. Your generosity moves us.'

'But Sir Gawain,' Beatrice said. 'If your horse takes the two of us, then how's your fallen body to be carried from this mountain? In your kindness you neglect your own corpse. And we'd be sorry to bury you in so lonely a spot as this.'

For an instant, the old knight's features became solemn, almost sorrowful. Then they creased into a smile, and he said: 'Now, mistress. Let's not discuss burial plans while I still expect to emerge victorious! In any case, this mountain's no less lonely a spot to me now than any other, and I'd fear the sights my ghost must witness on lower ground should this contest go another way. So no more talk of corpses, madam! Master Wistan, have you anything to ask of these friends should fortune not go your way?'

'Like you, sir, I prefer not to think of defeat. Yet only a mighty fool will believe you anything other than a formidable foe, no matter your years. So I too will burden this good couple with a request. If I'm no more, please see to it Master Edwin reaches a kind village, and let him know I considered him the worthiest of apprentices.'

'We'll do so, sir,' Axl said. 'We'll seek the best for him, even though the wound he carries makes his future a dark one.'

'That's well said. Now I'm reminded I must do even more to survive this meeting. Well, Sir Gawain, shall we go to it?'

'Yet one more request,' said the old knight, 'and this one to you, Master Wistan. I raise the matter with embarrassment, for it touches what we discussed with pleasure a moment ago. I mean, sir, the question of drawing the sword. With my heavy years, I find it takes a foolishly long time to pull this old weapon out of its sheath. If you and I faced each other, swords undrawn, my fear is I'd provide you with feeble entertainment, knowing how fast you draw. Why, sir, I might still be hobbling about, muttering small curses and tugging at this iron with one grip then another even as you take the air, wondering if to cut off my head or else sing an ode while waiting! Yet if we were to agree to draw our swords in our own time . . . Why this embarrasses me greatly, sir!'

'Not another word on it, Sir Gawain. I never think well of a warrior who leans on the speedy draw of a blade to take advantage of his opponent. So let's meet with swords ready drawn, just as you suggest.'

'I thank you, sir. And in return, though I see your arm strapped, I vow not to seek any special advantage of it.'

'I'm grateful, sir, though this injury's a trivial one.'

'Well then, sir. With your permission.'

The old knight drew his sword – indeed it seemed to take some time – and placed the point into the ground, just as he had done earlier at the giant's cairn. But instead of leaning on it, he stood there regarding his weapon up and down with a mixture of weariness and affection. Then he took the sword in both hands and raised it – and Gawain's posture took on an unmistakable grandeur.

'I'll turn away now, Axl,' Beatrice said. 'Tell me when it's finished, and let it not be long or unclean.'

At first both men held their swords pointing downwards, so as not to exhaust their arms. From his vantage point, Axl could see their positions clearly: at most five strides apart, Wistan's body angled slightly to the left away from his opponent's. They held these positions for a time, then Wistan moved three slow steps to his right, so that to all appearances, his outside shoulder was no longer protected by his sword. But to take advantage, Gawain would have had to close the gap very rapidly, and Axl was hardly surprised when the knight, gazing accusingly at the warrior, himself moved to the right with deliberate strides. Wistan meanwhile changed the grip of both his hands on his sword, and Axl could not be sure Gawain had noticed the change – Wistan's body possibly obscuring the knight's view. But now Gawain too was changing his hold, letting the sword's weight fall from the right arm to the left. Then the two men became fixed in their new positions, and to an innocent spectator, they may have looked, in relation to one another, practically unchanged from before. Yet Axl could sense that these new positions had a different significance. It had been a long time since he had had to consider combat in such detail, and there remained a frustrating sense that he was failing to see half of what was unfolding before him. But he knew somehow the contest had reached a critical point; that things could not be held like this for long without one or the other combatant being forced to commit himself.

Even so, he was taken aback by the suddenness with which Gawain and Wistan met. It was as if they had responded to a signal: the space between them vanished, and the two were suddenly locked in tense embrace. It happened so quickly it appeared to Axl the men had abandoned their swords and were now holding one another in a complicated and mutual armlock. As they did so, they rotated a little, like dancers, and Axl could then see that their two blades, perhaps because of the huge impact of their coming together, had become melded as one. Both men, mortified by this turn of events, were now doing their best to prise the weapons apart. But this was no easy task, and the old knight's features were contorted with the effort. Wistan's face, for the moment, was not visible, but Axl could see the warrior's neck and shoulders shaking as he too did all he could to reverse the calamity. But their efforts were in vain: with each moment, the two swords seemed to fasten more thoroughly, and surely there was nothing for it but to abandon the weapons and start the contest afresh. Neither man, though, appeared willing to give up, even as the effort threatened to drain them of their strength. Then something gave and the blades came apart. As they did so, some dark grain – perhaps the substance that had caused the blades to fasten together in the first place – flew up into the air between them. Gawain, with a look of astonished relief, reeled halfway round and sank to one knee. Wistan, for his part, had been carried by the momentum into turning a near circle, and had come to a halt pointing his now liberated sword towards the clouds beyond the cliff, his back fully turned to the knight.

'God protect him,' Beatrice said beside him, and Axl realised she had been watching all the while. When he looked down again, Gawain had lowered his other knee to the ground. Then the tall figure of the knight fell slowly, twistingly, onto the dark grass. There he struggled a moment, like a man in his sleep trying to make himself more comfortable, and when his face was turned to the sky, even though his legs were still folded untidily beneath him, Gawain seemed content. As Wistan approached with a concerned stride, the old knight appeared to say something, but Axl was too far to hear. The warrior remained standing over his opponent for some time, his sword held forgotten at his side, and Axl could see dark drops falling from the tip of the blade onto the soil.

Beatrice pressed herself against him. 'He was the she-dragon's defender,' she said, 'yet showed us kindness. Who knows where we'd be now without him, Axl, and I'm sorry to see him fallen.'

He pressed Beatrice close to him. Then releasing her, he climbed down a little way to where he could see better Gawain's body lying on the earth. Wistan had been correct: the blood had flowed only to where the ground rose in a kind of lip at the cliff's edge, and was pooling there with no danger of spilling over. The sight caused a melancholy to sweep over him, but also – though it was a distant and vague one – the feeling that some great anger within him had at long last been answered.

'Bravo, sir,' Axl called down. 'Now there's nothing stands between you and the she-dragon.'

Wistan, who had all the while been staring down at the fallen knight, now came slowly, somewhat giddily, to the foot of the mound, and when he looked up appeared to be in something of a dream.

'I learned long ago', he said, 'not to fear Death as I fought. Yet I thought I heard his soft tread behind me as I faced this knight. Long in years, yet he was close to getting the better of me.'

The warrior seemed then to notice the sword still in his hand, and made as though to thrust it into the soft earth at the foot of the mound. But at the last moment he stopped himself, the blade almost at the soil, and straightening, said: 'Why clean this sword yet? Why not let this knight's blood mingle with the she-dragon's?'

He came up the side of the mound, his gait still somewhat like a drunkard's. Brushing past them, he leant over a rock and gazed down into the pit, his shoulders moving with each breath.

'Master Wistan,' Beatrice said gently. 'We're now impatient to see you slay Querig. But will you bury the poor knight after? My husband here's weary and must save his strength for what remains of our journey.'

'He was a kin of the hated Arthur,' Wistan said, turning to her, 'yet I'll not leave him to the crows. Rest assured, mistress, I'll see to him, and may even lay him down in this pit, beside the creature he so long defended.'

'Then hurry, sir,' Beatrice said, 'and finish the task. For though she's feeble, we'll not be easy till we know she's slain.'

But Wistan seemed no longer to hear her, for he was now gazing at Axl with a faraway expression.

'Are you well, sir?' Axl asked eventually.

'Master Axl,' the warrior said, 'we may not meet again. So let me ask one last time. Could you be that gentle Briton from my boyhood who once moved like a wise prince through our village, making men dream of ways to keep innocents beyond the reach of war? If you have a remembrance of it, I ask you to confide in me before we part.'

'If I was that man, sir, I see him today only through the haze of this creature's breath, and he looks a fool and a dreamer, yet one who meant well, and suffered to see solemn oaths undone in cruel slaughter. There were others spread the treaty through the Saxon villages, but if my face stirs something in you, why suppose it was another's?'

'I thought it when we first met, sir, but couldn't be sure. I thank you for your frankness.'

'Then speak frankly to me in turn, for it's a thing shifts within me since our meeting yesterday, and perhaps, in truth, for far longer. This man you remember, Master Wistan. Is he one of whom you would seek vengeance?'

'What are you saying, husband?' Beatrice pushed forward, placing herself between Axl and the warrior. 'What quarrel can there be between you and this warrior? If there is one, he'll need strike me first.'

'Master Wistan talks of a skin I shed before we two ever met, princess. One I hoped had long crumbled on a forgotten path.' Then to Wistan: 'What do you say, sir? Your sword still drips. If it's vengeance you crave, it's a thing easily found, though I beg you protect my dear wife who trembles for me.'

'That man was one I once adored from afar, and it's true there were times later I wished him cruelly punished for his part in the betrayal. Yet I see today he may have acted with no cunning, wishing well for his own kin and ours alike. If I met him again, sir, I'd bid him go in peace, even though I know peace now can't hold for long. But excuse me, friends, and let me go down and end my errand.'

Down in the pit, neither the dragon's position nor posture had changed: if her senses were warning her of the proximity of strangers – and of one in particular making his way down the steep side of the pit – Querig gave no indication of it. Or could it be the rise and fall of her spine had become a little more pronounced? And was there a new urgency in the hooded eye as it opened and shut? Axl could not be sure. But as he continued to gaze down at the creature, the idea came to him that the hawthorn bush – the only other thing alive in the pit – had become a source of great comfort to her, and that even now, in her mind's eye, she was reaching for it. Axl realised the idea was fanciful, yet the more he watched, the more credible it seemed. For how was it a solitary bush was growing in a place like this? Could it not be that Merlin himself had allowed it to grow here, so that the dragon would have a companion?

Wistan was continuing his descent, his sword still unsheathed. His gaze rarely strayed from the spot where the creature lay, as if he half expected her to rise suddenly, transformed into a formidable demon. At one stage he slipped, and dug his sword into the ground to avoid sliding some way down on his backside. This episode sent stones and gravel cascading down the slope, but Querig still gave no response.

Then Wistan was safely on the ground. He wiped his forehead, glanced up at Axl and Beatrice, then moved towards the dragon, stopping several strides away. He then raised his sword and began to scrutinise the blade, apparently taken aback to discover it streaked with blood. For several moments, Wistan remained like this, not moving, so that Axl wondered if the strange mood that had overtaken the warrior since his victory had momentarily made him forget his reason for entering the pit.

But then with something of the unexpectedness that had characterised his contest with the old knight, Wistan suddenly moved forward. He did not run, but walked briskly, stepping over the dragon's body without breaking stride, and hurried on as though anxious to reach the other side of the pit. But his sword had described a swift, low arc in passing, and Axl saw the dragon's head spin into the air and roll a little way before coming to rest on the stony ground. It did not remain there long, however, for it was soon engulfed by the rich tide that first parted around it, then buoyed it up till it swam glidingly across the floor of the pit. It came to a stop at the hawthorn, where it lodged, the throat up to the sky. The sight brought back to Axl the head of the monster dog Gawain had severed in the tunnel, and again a melancholy threatened to sweep over him. He made himself look away from the dragon, and watch instead the figure of Wistan, who had not stopped walking. The warrior was now circling back, avoiding the ever-spreading pool, and then with his sword still unsheathed, began the climb out of the pit.

'It's done, Axl,' Beatrice said.

'It is, princess. Yet there's still a question I wish to ask this warrior.'

* * *

Wistan took a surprisingly long time to climb out of the pit. When at last he appeared before them again, he looked overwhelmed and not in the least triumphant. Without a word, he sat down on the blackened ground right on the rim of the pit, and at last thrust his sword deep into the earth. Then he gazed emptily, not into the pit, but beyond, at the clouds and the pale hills in the distance.

After a moment, Beatrice went over to him and touched his arm gently. 'We thank you for this deed, Master Wistan,' she said. 'And there'll be many more across the land would thank you if they were here. Why look so despondent?'

'Despondent? No matter, I'll regain my spirit soon, mistress. Yet just at this moment . . .' Wistan turned away from Beatrice and once more gazed at the clouds. Then he said: 'Perhaps I've been too long among you Britons. Despised the cowardly among you, admired and loved the best of you, and all from a tender age. And now I sit here, shaking not from weariness, but at the very thought of what my own hands have done. I must soon steel my heart or be a frail warrior for my king in what's to come.'

'What is this you speak of, sir?' Beatrice asked. 'What further task awaits you now?'

'It's justice and vengeance await, mistress. And they'll soon hurry this way, for both are much delayed. Yet now the hour's almost upon us, I find my heart trembles like a maid's. It can only be I've been too long among you.'

'I didn't fail to notice, sir,' Axl said, 'your earlier remark to me.

You said you'd wish me to go in peace, yet that peace couldn't hold much longer. I wondered then what you meant by it, even as you descended into this pit. Will you explain yourself to us now?'

'I see you begin to understand, Master Axl. My king sent me to destroy this she-dragon not simply to build a monument to kin slain long ago. You begin to see, sir, this dragon died to make ready the way for the coming conquest.'

'Conquest, sir?' Axl moved closer to him. 'How can this be, Master Wistan? Are your Saxon armies so swelled by your cousins from overseas? Or is it that your warriors are so fierce you talk of conquest in lands well held in peace?'

'It's true our armies are yet meagre in numbers, even in the fenlands. Yet look across this whole land. In every valley, beside every river, you'll now find Saxon communities, and each with strong men and growing boys. It's from these we'll swell our ranks even as we come sweeping westward.'

'Surely you speak in the confusion of your victory, Master Wistan,' Beatrice said. 'How can this be? You see yourself how in these parts it's your kin and mine mingle village by village. Who among them would turn on neighbours loved since childhood?'

'Yet see your husband's face, mistress. He begins to understand why I sit here as before a light too fierce for my gaze.'

'Right enough, princess, the warrior's words make me tremble. You and I longed for Querig's end, thinking only of our own dear memories. Yet who knows what old hatreds will loosen across the land now? We must hope God yet finds a way to preserve the bonds between our peoples, yet custom and suspicion have always divided us. Who knows what will come when quick-tongued men make ancient grievances rhyme with fresh desire for land and conquest?'

'How right to fear it, sir,' Wistan said. 'The giant, once well buried, now stirs. When soon he rises, as surely he will, the friendly bonds between us will prove as knots young girls make with the stems of small flowers. Men will burn their neighbours' houses by night. Hang children from trees at dawn. The rivers will stink with corpses bloated from their days of voyaging. And even as they move on, our armies will grow larger, swollen by anger and thirst for vengeance. For you Britons, it'll be as a ball of fire rolls towards you. You'll flee or perish. And country by country, this will become a new land, a Saxon land, with no more trace of your people's time here than a flock or two of sheep wandering the hills untended.'

'Can he be right, Axl? Surely he speaks in a fever?'

'He may yet be mistaken, princess, but this is no fever. The she-dragon's no more, and Arthur's shadow will fade with her.' Then to Wistan, he said: 'I'm comforted at least, sir, to find you take no delight in these horrors you paint.'

'I'd take delight if I could, Master Axl, for it'll be vengeance justly served. Yet I'm enfeebled by my years among you, and try as I will, a part of me turns from the flames of hatred. It's a weakness shames me, yet I'll soon offer in my place one trained by my own hand, one with a will far cleaner than mine.'

'You speak of Master Edwin, sir?'

'I do, and I dare say he'll be growing quickly more calm now the dragon's slain and her pull gone from him. That boy has a true warrior's spirit given only to a few. The rest he'll learn fast enough, and I'll train his heart well to admit no soft sentiments as have invaded mine. He'll show no mercy in our work ahead.'

'Master Wistan,' Beatrice said, 'I still don't know if you speak only in a mad fever. But my husband and I grow weak, and must return to lower ground and shelter. Will you remember your promise to bury well the gentle knight?'

'I promise to do so, mistress, though I fear even now the birds find him. Good friends, forewarned as you are, you've time enough to escape. Take the knight's horse and ride fast from these parts. Seek your son's village if you must, but linger there no more than a day or two, for who knows how soon the flames will be lit before our coming armies. If your son will not hear your warnings, leave him and flee as far west as you can. You may yet keep ahead of the slaughter. Go now and find the knight's horse. And should you find Master Edwin much calmed, his strange fever passed, cut him free and bid him come up here to me. A fierce future now opens before him, and it's my wish he sees this place, the fallen knight and the broken she-dragon, all before his next steps. Besides, I recall how well he digs a grave with a stray stone or two! Now hurry away, gentle friends, and farewell.'

Chapter Sixteen

For some time now the goat had been trampling the grass very near Edwin's head. Why did the animal have to come so close? They might be tied to the same post, but surely there was territory enough for each of them.

He might have got up and chased the goat away, but Edwin felt too tired. The exhaustion had swept over him a little earlier, and with such intensity that he had fallen forward onto the ground, the mountain grass pressing against his cheek. He had reached the edges of sleep, but then had been startled back to wakefulness by the sudden conviction that his mother had gone. He had not moved, and had kept his eyes closed, but he had muttered aloud into the ground: 'Mother. We're coming. Only a little longer now.'

There had been no answer, and he had felt a great emptiness opening within him. Since then, drifting between sleep and waking, he had several more times called to her, to be answered only by silence. And now the goat was chewing the grass next to his ear.

'Forgive me, mother,' he said softly into the earth. 'They tied me. I couldn't get free.'

There were voices above him. Only then did it occur to him the footsteps around him were not those of the goat. Someone was untying his hands, and the rope was pulling away from under

him. A gentle hand raised his head, and he opened his eyes to see
the old woman – Mistress Beatrice – peering down at him. He
realised he was no longer tied, and rose to his feet.

One of his knees ached badly, but when a gust of wind rocked
him, he was able to keep his balance. He looked about him: there
was the grey sky, the rising land, the rocks up on the crest of the
next hill. Not long ago, those rocks had meant everything to him,
but now she was gone, of that there was no doubt. And he remembered something the warrior had said: that when it was too late
for rescue, it was still early enough for revenge. If that were true,
those who had taken his mother would pay a terrible price.

There was no sign of Wistan. It was just the old couple here,
but Edwin felt comforted by their presence. They were standing before him, gazing at him with concern, and the sight of the
kindly Mistress Beatrice made him feel suddenly close to tears.
But Edwin realised she was saying something – something about
Wistan – and made an effort to listen.

Her Saxon was hard to understand, and the wind seemed to
carry her words away. In the end he cut across her to ask: 'Is
Master Wistan fallen?'

She fell silent, but did not reply. Only when he repeated himself, in a voice that rose above the wind, did Mistress Beatrice
shake her head emphatically and say:

'Don't you hear me, Master Edwin? I tell you Master Wistan is
well and awaits you at the top of that path.'

The news filled him with relief, and he broke into a run, but
then a giddiness quickly overtook him, obliging him to stop
before he had even reached the path. He steadied himself, then
glancing back, saw the old couple had taken a few steps in his
direction. Edwin noticed now how frail they seemed. There they

were standing together in the wind, each leaning against the other, looking far older than when he had first met them. Did they have strength left to descend the mountainside? But now they were gazing at him with an odd expression, and behind them, the goat too had ceased its restless activity to stare at him. A strange thought went through Edwin's mind, that he was at that moment covered head to toe in blood, and this was why he had become the object of such scrutiny. But when he glanced down, though his clothes were marked with mud and grass, he saw nothing unusual.

The old man suddenly called out something. It was in the Britons' tongue and Edwin could not understand. Was it a warning? A request? Then Mistress Beatrice's voice came through the wind.

'Master Edwin! We both beg this of you. In the days to come, remember us. Remember us and this friendship when you were still a boy.'

As he heard this, something else came back to Edwin: a promise made to the warrior; a duty to hate all Britons. But surely Wistan had not meant to include this gentle couple. And now here was Master Axl, raising a hand uncertainly into the air. Was it in farewell or an attempt to detain him?

Edwin turned away, and this time when he ran, even with the wind pushing from one side, his body did not fail him. His mother was gone, most likely gone beyond all retrieving, but the warrior was well and waiting for him. He continued to run, even as the path grew steeper and the ache in his knee grew worse.

Chapter Seventeen

They came riding through the rainstorm as I sheltered under the pines. No weather for a pair so long in years and the sagging horse no less weary. Does the old man fear for the animal's heart with one more step? Why else halt in the mud with twenty paces still to the nearest tree? Yet the horse stands with patience under the downpour as the old man lifts her down. Could they perform the task more slowly were they painted figures in a picture? 'Come, friends,' I call to them. 'Hurry and take shelter.'

Neither hears me. Perhaps it's the hiss of the rain or is it their age seals their ears? I call again, and now the old man looks about him and sees me at last. Finally she slides down into his arms, and though she's but a thin sparrow, I see he's barely strength left to hold her. So I leave my shelter, and the old man turns in alarm to see me splash across the grass. But he accepts my assistance, for wasn't he about to sink to the earth, his good wife's arms still circling his neck? I take her from him and hurry back to the trees, she no burden to me at all. I hear the old man panting at my heels. Perhaps he fears for his wife in the arms of a stranger. So I set her down with care, to show I mean them only friendship. I place her head against the soft bark, and well sheltered above, even if a drop or two still falls around her.

The old man crouches beside her, speaking words of encouragement, and I move away, not wishing to intrude on their intimacy. I stand again at my old spot where the trees meet the open ground, and watch the rain sweep across the moorland. Who can blame me sheltering from rain like this? I will easily make up time on my journey, and be all the better for the weeks of unbroken toil to come. I hear them talk at my back, yet what am I to do? Step into the rain to be beyond their murmurings?

'It's just the fever talking, princess.'

'No, no, Axl,' she says. 'It comes back to me, something more. How did we ever forget? Our son lives on an island. An island seen from a sheltered cove, and surely near us now.'

'How can that be, princess?'

'Don't you hear it, Axl? I hear it even now. Isn't that the sea near us?'

'Just the rain, princess. Or maybe a river.'

'We forgot it, Axl, with the mist over us, but now it starts to clear. There's an island near, and our son waits there. Axl, don't you hear the sea?'

'Just your fever, princess. We'll find shelter soon and you'll be fine again.'

'Ask this stranger, Axl. He knows this country better than us. Ask if there's not a cove nearby.'

'He's just a kind man came to our aid, princess. Why should he have any special wisdom of such things?'

'Ask him, Axl. What harm can it do?'

Do I remain silent? What am I to do? I turn and say, 'The good lady's right, sir.' The old man starts, and there's fear in his eyes. A part of me wishes to fall silent again; to turn away and watch the old horse standing steadfast in the rain. Yet now I've spoken I must go on. I point beyond the spot where they huddle.

'A path there, between those trees, leads down to a cove such as the one the lady speaks of. For the most part covered in shingle, though when the tide's low, as it will be now, the pebbles give way to sand. And as you say, good lady. There's an island a little way out to sea.'

They watch me in silence, she with a weary happiness, he with mounting fear. Will they not say anything? Do they expect me to tell more?

'I've watched the sky,' I say. 'This rain will clear shortly and the evening will be a fine one. So if you wish me to row you over to the island, I'd be pleased to do so.'

'Didn't I tell you, Axl!'

'Are you then a boatman, sir?' the old man asks solemnly. 'And can it be we met somewhere before?'

'I'm a boatman, sure enough,' I tell him. 'It's more than I can remember if we met before, for I'm obliged to ferry so many and for long hours each day.'

The old man looks more fearful than ever, holds his wife close as he crouches beside her. Judging it best to change the topic, I say:

'Your horse still stands in the rain. Even though he's untethered and nothing to stop him seeking the nearby trees.'

'He's an old battlehorse, sir.' The old man, happy to leave talk of the cove, speaks with quick eagerness. 'He keeps his discipline, even though his master's no more. We must see to him in time, the way we lately promised his brave owner. But just now I worry for my dear wife. Do you know where we may find shelter, sir, and a fire to warm her?'

I cannot lie and I have my duty. 'As it happens,' I reply, 'there's a small shelter found on this very cove. It's one I stitched myself, a simple roof of twigs and rags. I left a fire smouldering beside it this last hour and it'll not be beyond reviving.'

He hesitates, searching my face carefully. The old woman's eyes are now closed and her head rests on his shoulder. He says, 'Boatman, my wife spoke just now in a fever. We've no need of islands. Better we shelter beneath these friendly trees till the rain's gone, then we'll journey on our way.'

'Axl, what are you saying?' the woman says, opening her eyes. 'Hasn't our son waited long enough? Let this good boatman lead us to the cove.'

The old man hesitates still, but feels his wife shiver in his arms, and his eyes look to me with desperate entreaty.

'If you wish,' I say, 'I'll carry the good lady and make the way to the cove easier.'

'I'll carry her myself, sir,' he says, like one defeated yet defiant. 'If she's not able to go by her own feet, then she'll go in my arms.'

What to say to this, the husband now almost as weak as the wife?

'The cove's not far,' I say gently. 'But the way down's steep, with pits and twisted roots. Please allow me to carry her, sir. It's the safest thing. You'll walk close beside us where the way allows. Come, when the rain eases, we'll hurry down, for see how the good lady trembles for cold.'

The rain stopped before long and I carried her down the hill-path, the old man stumbling behind, and when we came out to the beach, the dark clouds were swept to one side of the sky as if by an impatient hand. The reddish hues of evening all across the shore, a foggy sun falling towards the sea, and my boat rocking out in the waves. With another show of gentleness, I laid her down under the rude cover of dried skins and branches, placing her head against a cushion of mossy rock. He comes fussing about her even before I can step away.

'See there,' I say, and crouch beside the slumbering fire. 'There's the island.'

Only a small turn of the head gives the woman a view of the sea, and she lets out a soft cry. He must turn on the hard pebbles, and stares bewildered here and there at the waves.

'There, friend,' I say. 'Look there. Midway between the shore and the horizon.'

'My eyes aren't so good,' he says. 'But yes, I believe I see it now. Are those the tops of trees? Or jagged rocks?'

'They'll be trees, friend, for it's a gentle place.' I say this all the while breaking twigs and attending the fire. They both look out to the island and I kneel down, the pebbles harsh against my bones, to blow at the embers. This man and woman, did they not come of their own will? Let them decide their own paths, I say to myself.

'Do you feel the warmth now, princess?' he cries. 'You'll soon be yourself again.'

'I see the island, Axl,' she says, and how can I but intrude upon this intimacy? 'That's where our son awaits. So strange how we ever forgot such a thing.'

He mumbles a reply and I see he grows troubled again. 'Surely, princess,' he says, 'we're not yet decided. Do we really want to cross to such a place? Besides, we've no way to pay for our passage, for we left the tin and coins with the horse.'

Am I to remain silent? 'That's no matter, friends,' I say. 'I'll gladly take what's owed later from the saddle. That steed won't wander far.' Some may call this cunning, but I spoke from simple charity, knowing well I would never come upon the horse again. They talked on in gentle voices, and I kept my back to them, attending to the fire. For do I wish to intrude on them? Yet she lifts her voice, and one more steady than before.

'Boatman,' she says. 'There's a tale I once heard, perhaps as a small child. Of an island full of gentle woods and streams, yet also a place of strange qualities. Many cross to it, yet for each who dwells there, it's as if he walks the island alone, his neighbours unseen and unheard. Can this be true of the island now before us, sir?'

I go on breaking twigs and placing them carefully about the flame. 'Good lady, I know of several islands to fit such a description. Who knows if this one is among them?'

An evasive answer, and one to give her boldness. 'I also heard, boatman,' she says, 'there are times when these strange conditions cease to prevail. Of special dispensations granted certain travellers. Did I hear right, sir?'

'Dear lady,' I say, 'I'm just a humble boatman. It's not for me to talk of such matters. But since there's no one else here, let me offer this. I've heard it said there may be certain times, perhaps during a storm such as the one just passed, or on a summer's night when the moon's full, an islander may get a sense of others moving beside him in the wind. This may be what you once heard, good lady.'

'No, boatman,' she says, 'it was something more. I heard it said a man and woman, after a lifetime shared, and with a bond of love unusually strong, may travel to the island with no need to roam it apart. I heard they may enjoy the pleasures of one another's company, as they did through all the years before. Could this be a true thing I heard, boatman?'

'I'll say it again, good lady. I'm just a boatman, charged with ferrying over those who wish to cross the water. I can speak only of what I observe in my daily toil.'

'Yet there's no one here now but you to guide us, boatman. So

I ask this of you, sir. If you now ferry my husband and me, can it be we'll not be parted, but free to walk the island arm in arm the way we go now?'

'Very well, good lady. I'll speak to you frankly. You and your husband are a pair as we boatmen rarely set eyes upon. I saw your unusual devotion to each other even as you came riding through the rain. So there's no question but that you'll be permitted to dwell on the island together. Be assured on that point.'

'What you say fills me with happiness, boatman,' she says, and appears to sag in relief. Then she says, 'And who knows? During a storm, or on a calm moonlit night, Axl and I may glimpse our son close by. Even speak with him a word or two.'

The fire now burning steadily I rise to my feet. 'See there,' I say, pointing out to sea. 'The boat stirs in the shallows. But I keep my oar hidden in a nearby cave, dipped in a rockpool where tiny fish circle. Friends, I'll go now to fetch it, and while I'm gone, you may talk here between you, unhindered by my presence. Let's have you come to your decision once and for all if this is a voyage you wish to make. Now I'll leave you a moment.'

But she will not release me so easily. 'One word more before you go, boatman,' she says. 'Tell us if when you return, before you'll consent to ferry us, you intend to question us each in turn. For I heard this was the way among boatmen, to discover those rare ones fit to walk the island unseparated.'

They both gaze at me, the evening light upon their faces, and I see his filled with suspicion. I meet her eyes, not his.

'Good lady,' I say, 'I'm grateful for this reminder. In my haste I may easily have neglected what I'm bound by custom to do. It's as you say, yet in this case only for the sake of tradition. For as I said, I saw from the first how you were a pair tied by an extraordinary devotion. Now excuse me, friends, for my time grows short. Have your decision for my return.'

So I left them then, and walked across the evening shore till the waves grew loud and the pebbles turned underfoot to wet sand. Whenever I looked back at them, I saw the same sight, if each time a little smaller: the grey old man, crouched in solemn conference before his woman. Of her I could see little, for the rock she leant on hid all but the rise and fall of her hand as she spoke. A devoted couple, but I had my duty, and I went on to the cave and the oar.

When I came back to them, the oar upon my shoulder, I could see their decision in their eyes even before he said, 'We ask you to take us to the island, boatman.'

'Then let's hasten to the boat, for I'm already much delayed,' I say, and move away as though to hurry towards the waves. But then I turn back, saying, 'Ah, but wait. We must first go through this foolish ritual. Then, friends, let me propose this. Good sir, if you'd rise now and walk a little way from us. Once you're out of hearing, I'll speak briefly with your gentle wife. She needn't stir from where she sits. Then in time I'll come to you wherever you stand on this beach. We'll soon be done and return here to fetch this good lady to the boat.'

He stares at me, a part of him now longing to trust me. He says at last, 'Very well, boatman, I'll wander a moment about this shore.' Then to his woman, 'We'll be parted but an instant, princess.'

'There's no concern, Axl,' she says. 'I'm much restored, and safe under this kind man's protection.'

Away he goes, walking slowly to the east of the cove and the great shadow of the cliff. The birds scatter before him, but return quickly to peck as before at their seaweed and rock. He limps slightly, and his back bent like one close to defeat, yet I see still some small fire within him.

The woman sits before me looking up with a soft smile. What am I to ask?

'Don't fear my questions, good lady,' I say. I would wish now for a long wall nearby, to which to turn my face even as I speak to her, but there's only the evening breeze, and the low sun on my face. I crouch before her, as I saw her husband do, pulling my robe up to my knees.

'I don't fear your questions, boatman,' she says quietly. 'For I know what I feel in my heart for him. Ask me what you will. My answers will be honest, yet prove only one thing.'

I ask a question or two, the usual questions, for have I not done this often enough? Then every now and then, to encourage her and to show I attend, I ask another. But there's hardly the need, for she speaks freely. She talks on, her eyes sometimes closing, her voice always clear and steady. And I listen with care, as is my duty, even as my gaze goes across the cove, to the figure of the tired old man pacing anxiously among the small rocks.

Then remembering the work awaiting me elsewhere, I break into her recollections, saying, 'I thank you, good lady. Let me now hurry to your good husband.'

Surely he begins to trust me now, for why else wander so far from his wife? He hears my footsteps and turns as from a dream. The evening glow upon him, and I see his face no longer filled with suspicion, but a deep sorrow, and small tears in his eyes.

'How goes it, sir?' he asks quietly.

'A pleasure to listen to your good lady,' I reply, matching my voice to his soft tones, though the wind grows unruly. 'But now, friend, let's be brief, so we can be on our way.'

'Ask what you will, sir.'

'I have no searching question, friend. But your good wife just now recalled a day the two of you carried eggs back from a market. She said she held them in a basket before her, and you walked beside her, peering into the basket all the way for fear her steps would injure the eggs. She recalled the time with happiness.'

'I think I do too, boatman,' he says, and looks at me with a smile. 'I was anxious for the eggs because she'd stumbled on a previous errand, breaking one or two. A small walk, but we were well contented that day.'

'It's as she remembers it,' I say. 'Well then, let's waste no more time, for this talk was only to satisfy custom. Let's go fetch the good lady and carry her to the boat.'

And I begin to lead the way back to the shelter and his wife, but now he goes at a dreary pace, slowing me with him.

'Don't be afraid of those waves, friend,' I say, thinking here's the source of his worry. 'The estuary's well protected and no harm can come between here and the island.'

'I'll readily trust your judgement, boatman.'

'Friend, as it happens,' I say, for why not fill this slow journey with a little more talk? 'There was a question I might have asked just now had we more time. Since we walk together this way, would you mind my telling you what it was?'

'Not at all, boatman.'

'I was simply going to ask, was there some remembrance from your years together still brought you particular pain? That's all it was.'

'Do we still speak as part of the questioning, sir?'

'Oh no,' I say. 'That's over and finished. I asked the same of your good wife earlier, so it was merely to satisfy my own curiosity.

Remain silent on it, friend, I take no offence. Look there.' I point to a rock we are passing. 'Those aren't mere barnacles. With more time, I'd show how to prise them from the rockside to make a handy supper. I've often toasted them over a fire.'

'Boatman,' he says gravely, and his steps slow further still. 'I'll answer your question if you wish. I can't be certain how she answered, for there's much held in silence even between those like us. What's more, until this day, a she-dragon's breath polluted the air, robbing memories both happy and dark. But the dragon's slain and already many things grow clearer in my mind. You ask for a memory brings particular pain. What else can I say, boatman, than it's of our son, almost grown when we last saw him, but who left us before a beard was on his face. It was after some quarrel and only to a nearby village, and I thought it a matter of days before he returned.'

'Your wife spoke of the same, friend,' I tell him. 'And she said she's to blame for his leaving.'

'If she convicts herself for the first part of it, there's plenty to lay at my door for the next. For it's true there was a small moment she was unfaithful to me. It may be, boatman, I did something to drive her to the arms of another. Or was it what I failed to say or do? It's all distant now, like a bird flown by and become a speck in the sky. But our son was witness to its bitterness, and at an age too old to be fooled with soft words, yet too young to know the many strange ways of our hearts. He left vowing never to return, and was still away from us when she and I were happily reunited.'

'This part your wife told me. And how soon after came news of your good son taken by the plague swept the country. My own parents were lost in that same plague, friend, and I remember it well. But why blame yourself for it? A plague sent by God or the devil, but what fault lies with you for it?'

'I forbade her to go to his grave, boatman. A cruel thing. She wished us to go together to where he rested, but I wouldn't have it. Now many years have passed and it's only a few days ago we set off to find it, and by then the she-dragon's mist had robbed us of any clear knowledge of what we sought.'

'Ah, so that's it,' I say. 'That part your wife was shy to reveal. So it was you stopped her visiting his grave.'

'A cruel thing I did, sir. And a darker betrayal than the small infidelity cuckolded me a month or two.'

'What did you hope to gain, sir, preventing not just your wife but even yourself grieving at your son's resting place?'

'Gain? There was nothing to gain, boatman. It was just foolishness and pride. And whatever else lurks in the depths of a man's heart. Perhaps it was a craving to punish, sir. I spoke and acted forgiveness, yet kept locked through long years some small chamber in my heart that yearned for vengeance. A petty and black thing I did her, and my son also.'

'I thank you for confiding this, friend,' I say to him. 'And perhaps it's as well. For though this talk intrudes in no part on my duty, and we speak now as two companions passing the day, I confess there was before a small unease in my mind, a feeling I'd yet to hear all there was. Now I'll be able to row you with a carefree contentment. But tell me, friend, what is it made you break your resolve of so many years and come out at last on this journey? Was it something said? Or a change of heart as unknowable as the tide and sky before us?'

'I've wondered myself, boatman. And I think now it's no single thing changed my heart, but it was gradually won back by the years shared between us. That may be all it was, boatman. A wound that healed slowly, but heal it did. For there was a morning not long ago, the dawn brought with it the first signs of this spring, and I watched my wife still asleep though the sun already lit our chamber. And I knew the last of the darkness had left me. So we came on this journey, sir, and now my wife recalls our son crossing before us to this island, so his burial place must be within its woods or perhaps on its gentle shores. Boatman, I've spoken honestly to you, and I hope it doesn't cast your earlier judgement of us in doubt. For I suppose there's some would hear my words and think our love flawed and broken. But God will know the slow tread of an old couple's love for each other, and understand how black shadows make part of its whole.'

'Don't worry, friend. What you told me merely echoes what I saw when you and your wife first came through the rain on that weary steed. Well, sir, no more talk, for who knows if another storm will come our way. Let's hurry to her and carry her to the boat.'

She sits asleep at the rock with a look of contentment, the fire smoking beside her.

'I'll carry her myself this time, boatman,' he says. 'I feel my strength restored to me.'

Can I allow this? It will make my task no easier. 'These pebbles make hard walking, friend,' I say. 'What will be the cost of your stumbling as you carry her? I'm well used to the work, for she'll not be the first to need carrying to a boat. You can walk beside us, talking to her as you wish. Let it be like when she carried those eggs and you went anxiously beside her.'

The fear returns to his face. Yet he replies quietly, 'Very well, boatman. Let's do as you say.'

He walks at my side, muttering encouragement to her. Do I
stride too swiftly? For now he lags behind, and as I carry her
into the sea I feel his hand grasp desperately at my back. Yet this
is no place to loiter, for my feet must discover the quay where it
hides beneath the chilly water's surface. I step onto the stones, the
lapping waves grow shallow again, and I enter the boat, hardly
tilting though I carry her in my arms. My rugs near the stern wet
from the rain. I kick away the soaked early layers and lay her
down gently. I leave her sitting up, her head just beneath the gunwale, and search the chest for dry blankets against the sea wind.

I feel him climb into the boat even as I wrap her and the floor
rocks with his tread. 'Friend,' I say, 'you see the waters grow more
restless. And this is but a small vessel. I daren't carry more than
one passenger at a time.'

I see the fire in him well enough now, for it blazes through his
eyes. 'I thought it well understood, boatman,' he says, 'my wife
and I would cross to the island unseparated. Didn't you say so
repeatedly, and this the purpose of your questions?'

'Please don't misunderstand, friend,' I say. 'I speak only of the
practical matter of crossing this water. It's beyond question the
two of you will dwell on the island together, going arm in arm
as you've always done. And if your son's burial place is found in
some shaded spot, you may think of placing wild flowers about
it, such as you'll find growing around the island. There'll be bell
heather, even marigold in the woodland. Yet for this crossing
today, I ask you to wait a while longer back on the shore. I'll see
to it the good lady's comfortable on the opposite one, for I know a
spot close to the boat's landing where three ancient rocks face one
another like old companions. I'll leave her there well sheltered,
yet with a view of the waves, and hasten back to fetch you. But

leave us for now and wait on the shore a moment longer.'

The red glow of the sunset on him, or is it still the fire in his gaze? 'I'll not step off this boat, sir, while my wife sits within it. Row us over together as you promised. Or must I row myself?'

'I hold the oar, sir, and it remains my duty to pronounce how many may ride in this vessel. Can it be, despite our recent friendship, you suspect some foul trickery? Do you fear I'll not return for you?'

'I accuse you of nothing, sir. Yet many rumours abound of boatmen and their ways. I mean no offence, but beg you take us both now, and no more dallying.'

'Boatman,' comes her voice, and I turn in time to see her hand reach at the empty air as though to find me there, though her eyes remain closed. 'Boatman. Leave us a small moment. Let my husband and I speak alone a while.'

Dare I leave the boat to them? Yet surely she now speaks for me. The oar firm in my hands, I step past him over the boards and into the water. The sea rises to my knee soaking the hem of my robe. The vessel's well tied and I have the oar. What mischief can come of it? Still I dare not wade far, and though I look to the shore and remain still as a rock, I find I again intrude on their intimacy. I hear them over the quiet lapping waves.

'Has he left us, Axl?'

'He stands in the water, princess. He was reluctant to leave his boat and I'd say he'll not give us long.'

'Axl, this is no time to quarrel with the boatman. We've had great fortune coming upon him today. A boatman who looks so favourably on us.'

'Yet we've often heard of their sly tricks, isn't that so, princess?'

'I trust him, Axl. He'll keep his word.'

'How can you be so sure, princess?'

'I know it, Axl. He's a good man and won't let us down. Do as he says and wait for him back on the land. He'll come for you soon enough. Let's do it this way, Axl, or I fear we'll lose the great dispensation offered us. We're promised our time together on the island, as only a few can be, even among those entwined a life-time. Why risk such a prize for a few moments of waiting? Don't quarrel with him, or who knows next time we'll face some brute of a man? Axl, please make your peace with him. Even now I fear he grows angry and will change his mind. Axl, are you still there?'

'I'm still before you, princess. Can it really be we're talking of going our ways separately?'

'It's only for a moment or two, husband. What does he do now?'

'Still stands there unmoving, showing only his tall back and shining head to us. Princess, do you really believe we can trust this man?'

'I do, Axl.'

'Your talk with him just now. Did it go happily?'

'It went happily, husband. Wasn't it the same for you?'

'I suppose it was, princess.'

The sunset on the cove. Silence at my back. Dare I turn to them yet?

'Tell me, princess,' I hear him say. 'Are you glad of the mist's fading?'

'It may bring horrors to this land. Yet for us it fades just in time.'

'I was wondering, princess. Could it be our love would never have grown so strong down the years had the mist not robbed us the way it did? Perhaps it allowed old wounds to heal.'

'What does it matter now, Axl? Mend your friendship with the boatman, and let him ferry us over. If it's one of us he'll row, then the other, why quarrel with him? Axl, what do you say?'

'Very well, princess. I'll do as you say.'

'So leave me now and return to the shore.'

'I'll do so, princess.'

'Then why do you still linger, husband? Do you think boatmen never grow impatient?'

'Very well, princess. But let me just hold you once more.'

Do they embrace now, even though I left her swaddled like a babe? Even though he must kneel and make a strange shape on the boat's hard floor? I suppose they do, and for as long as the silence remains, I dare not turn. The oar in my arms, does it cast a shadow in this swaying water? How much longer? At last their voices return.

'We'll talk more on the island, princess,' he says.

'We'll do that, Axl. And with the mist gone, we'll have plenty to talk of. Does the boatman still stand in the water?'

'He does, princess. I'll go now and make my peace with him.'

'Farewell then, Axl.'

'Farewell, my one true love.'

I hear him coming through the water. Does he intend a word for me? He spoke of mending our friendship. Yet when I turn he does not look my way, only to the land and the low sun on the cove. And neither do I search for his eye. He wades on past me, not glancing back. Wait for me on the shore, friend, I say quietly, but he does not hear and he wades on.

KAZUO ISHIGURO's seven previous books have won him wide renown and many honours around the world. His work has been translated into over forty languages. *The Remains of the Day* and *Never Let Me Go* have each sold in excess of 2,000,000 copies worldwide, and both were adapted into highly acclaimed films.